GARBER'S
TALES
FROM
THE
QUARTER

BY
LAWRENCE GARBER

Peter Martin Associates Limited

For

Martin Stone

All characters portrayed are mythical.
Any resemblance to persons alive, dead
or missing is unintentional.

PR
6057
.A6 / 64276
1969

Library of Congress Catalogue Card Number : 68-24256

Peter Martin Associates Limited 17 Inkerman Street Toronto 5

CONTENTS

"Not to be talked of was his only fear. A curious notion struck him . . . Suddenly inspired, he invented the water closet."

Lytton Strachey,
on Sir John Harington
(Portraits in Miniature)

I

A Few Friendships We Can Do Without

One

There are some women who are terribly narcissistic :
they keep kissing their own shadows and getting their lips
dirty. During the short time I strayed through Auteuil, I
knew a Czech girl called Catherine Cz; she was trim and
well-groomed and had a smile that barely split her mouth.
In fact, her smile was entirely financial; she could sum up
your assets without much trouble and the total would ring
on her face as if it were a kind of sibylline cash register.
I liked her, but not much.

Catherine Cz lived in an eight-room apartment in a
tiny street running south from the Boulevard Exelmans;
four of the rooms were closed up because she couldn't use
them and she had three bathrooms down one short hallway.
Each one had its own peculiar use; her need of them was
almost religious and they were — as she was — scented for
utility. Bathroom A contained a tub, ribbed in its hollow
like a swan's flank. There Catherine Cz bathed three times
daily; the faucet had a pale blue shower attachment and
there was an ominous box of pink kleenex where the soap
catch was. Bathroom B was tinier; it contained a huge mirror
above a larger sink and a great wicker basket for dirty
underwear — if that were possible. Here Catherine Cz
washed her hair morning and night; she was said to spend
half her week with soap suds running down her neck.
Bathroom C, and we are here at the very heart of her
matter, contained within its concave darkness a toilet; here
was no light. Beneath the toilet, resting comfortably within
the elbow of a pink pipe, lay a colorless box of kotex. The
rumour about this was twofold : a) that she used it three
times a year, b) that she used it always, rain or shine.
Neither was true.

Now like everyone we know, Catherine Cz had a dream. It was not a very practical dream, but everything Catherine Cz did about it was very practical indeed. The three bathrooms, the eight rooms proper, the Auteuil address, all had their little part to play; it was a grand web spun at great expense to catch spiders bigger than herself. For what Catherine Cz wanted was to marry rich; but not only to marry rich because that is easy; she wanted to marry well, and very well. Catherine Cz, with her nicely groomed legs picked and oiled to a high polish, her hair and body softened, warmed and gilded into the finest mint, wanted badly to marry into French aristocracy. "As if I didn't have more culture and sense than any three Frenchwomen," (at this point, armed with razor and cream and standing half-nude in a maze of mirrors) "Garber, if you could see them meeting every day on the bloody Capucines with their movie magazines, such dumb little bitches and all doing so well."

She had several prospects on the line : a dancer, two brokerage houses, an ambitious clerk and a sportsman who took her to Longchamps for the races every Sunday in the season. The dancer was Edouard and one of the brokerage houses was André, a bit of a fop with great purple hankies always curled up like flowers in his jacket. I didn't like André and neither did she, which was incidental. His eyes were too small and he had jagged, nicely kept teeth, a complexion smooth and vaguely orange, and fingers so beautiful that he was constantly distracted. She had never slept with him and that worried her a bit; frankly, I suspected the worst — but he had a nice car and a quiet manner and was no trouble at all. Edouard was a bit better; a tall goodlooking Frenchman for whom dancing was a kind of divertissement while he waited for the bulk of his inheritance. She liked to be seen with him everywhere and they went to the theatre, the country, the Bois, the galleries, the fashion shows, the cocktail parties. He was rather suave, with all sorts of *politesse,* cold green eyes and a thick, bony face. She felt rich, clean and luxurious with him, and he was screwing her pretty good.

They went to the sex shows together. He didn't care much about them (he had had a formal training) but he liked to watch her watching them. She had a habit (deliberate and precisely timed) of twitching her shoulders at the best possible moment, and he found that reasonably pleasurable and exciting. But all in all there was nothing much wrong with him, and she was as presentable as any woman he knew at the time. Through him, she met some other people who kindly offered to help her through life; someone in the House of Dior let her wear gowns to the best places on weekends, and she could borrow jewellery from the shops in the Rue de la Paix whenever she went to the right parties. New Jimmy's was their restaurant and after that L'Alsace aux Halles (upstairs) and then a tiny place called L'Armor (downstairs) in the Rue Hautefeuille. They were very gay.

Catherine Cz and Edouard weren't friends, they were lovers. Their times consisted of sex and small talk; her habit of touching him in public — a finger on the lapel, a tongue at the ear, a shoe rubbing his ankle — was their only substantial link. It wasn't that their tastes were different, their tastes were only private and kept from each other like dark, guarded secrets.

I met Catherine Cz through people at a café (now defunct), the Royal St. Germain. She seemed much taller sitting at the table watching things happen, but when she stood her mouth seemed smaller and the lips thin. We seemed at once to accept each other's pretenses, and that is no superficial bond. But I didn't like Edouard, of course. He spoke a broken, incorrect English, but he spoke it condescendingly, like a man fingering fish. One evening I was feeling lonely and in need of talk; I had wanted to walk through Père-Lachaise cemetery in the dark but the gates were locked for the night and so I called Catherine Cz on the phone instead. It was a strange business. Her voice through the wires had a flat, deadly sound. After some bickering over identity, the disenchanting explanation that no, I was not with Lloyds of London, and then a smooth, even-keeled bit of repartee, she invited me over for drinks.

I took a Métro from my own deprived world to her apartment and soon became a regular habit; she even let me use Bathroom A.

I never got to know her; our conversations together, for all their slickness and mock confidences, were always terse and full of care. Her English was deliberately sharp and abbreviated and her tiny eyes tried to buy the truth from you cheaply. Very soon, I began to stay nights. The Métros in that part of Paris stop sometime after midnight and there were evenings when we would talk till early in the morning, trading safe stories about the-things-we-could-have-been-if-we-had-been-better-at-the-things-we-did-now. Catherine Cz was lonely in this way; but it was the loneliness of the beast of prey, more the patience of waiting quietly for the kill. So I spent some of my nights in Auteuil; but I never slept with her. I usually lay on the couch in the front room until morning, finally smelling of the clean, perfumed air and sneezing out the talcum from the hallway. Whenever she spent time at Édouard's or took a trip to the sea, I'd move in for a few days and sleep in her bed. Her body had a faint vanilla smell to it and her sheets were never cold. Watching someone live their life from such a distance is somewhat like watching a laboratory experiment and a woman who is not loved by you is nothing but the sum of her habits. So for me, Catherine Cz could have no shame. This brilliant whoring for her daily bread made her seem no more than operable, a superb function; but there were many other sides to the lie. Certainly, she had a ruthlessness that put her body to sinister uses : she would purge herself with laxatives before an important dinner, was said to have a superb cunning in bed, and had learned long ago to take her pleasures without emotion. Yet, regardless of all this, she came to need Edouard the way a leopard needs its jungle; it was a funny kind of panic.

Her best prospects were actually with André : he was her supper man, sometimes a little theatre, but mostly meals, and he kept her from starving. All her money went for the apartment and the white Fiat she always parked in front of the entrance, and there was little left for necessities. André was short, but she was shorter; he was dark — white shirts looked particularly good on him — and she was white as chalk and blonde into the bargain, with lips as pink and eyes as blue as the colours of a carnival. To win him there were certain aspects of herself, certain resourceful illusions, that had to be stressed : she must appear to him as righteous but full of life, a *bon vivant* but of his thinking, one who offered him, but secretly, a special gaiety and recklessness. Except that he was uninteresting, an unattractive plum to pick, and she would betray him needlessly as if exercising a right. That was perhaps her basic weakness; she would have married the effete, cautious André had he steeled himself to ask for her, yet she was contemptuous of the choice at hand. There was no suppressing the contempt and she worked it off in secret ways. André did speak of deep affections, but he was rather stilted in his emotions and a bit retreating when it came to the more private outrages of the body. God, how she could pick holes in him at will, and what a labour it was for her to restrain her malice. She never did press him, however; she came to feel (unjustly) that his family would prove too difficult to surmount. Edouard, she came to reason, was the easier, the more bizarre, the more pliable. That was the ultimate cost of feeling; it destroyed her perspective and in the end lost her the fine edge she had built at so much sacrifice.

I'll add this. I made love to Catherine Cz once and not in her fine bed but on a couch during a phone call from André. I suppose I was her dildo and she was indulging her unpredictable vanity, but it was an intriguing experience and her sexual discipline was astonishing. She was completely dressed, down to her expensive shoes borrowed from a shop in the Rue Tronchet, and André was calling to say that he would be a quarter of an hour late *ma petite,* and while he spoke of his mother's illness and her need for him during her constant pains, Catherine Cz insisted I take her as she reclined half-seated, as dog takes dog, one leg heaved up in the air like a bitch spaniel.

For all her fine ways and slick contacts and nice smells, the truth was that Catherine Cz was a make for the French boys, a good easy lay, and they knew it and passed her around clannishly like the address to a good little restaurant. This was sad, and she was in the trap she had built, with no way of knowing anything except her own fabricated truths and coming across hopefully for the big money. It is difficult to find pity for one so calculating, yet she was pitiful and what seemed like vanity and sureness before took on distortions horrifying to watch. Edouard was a bit satanic into the bargain, and there were rumours that he had been selling her phone number to his old school friends as a mild joke. Someone had it on fair authority, too, that she had been taken by four cousins at an estate near Deauville one Christmas weekend; it was certain at least that somebody was having an awfully good time. Edouard himself — in a practiced mediocrity — began to treat her badly towards the end; she took it because there was no alternative to the one plan and no way of maneuvering a position so committed.

Then she became *enceinte,* but she couldn't believe it. The one and only time she ever called me was one chilly evening in February. It took me almost three minutes to run down all the stairs to the concierge's phone and by the time I got there she was hysterical with impatience; when betrayals come full circle, watch out. I took the Métro to her apartment and she had drinks ready for me when I arrived — at last the sudden, honoured guest. There was no question about her condition. "I'm always regular as clockwork," she said sharply, and produced a tiny notebook with the dates of her period marked down neatly month after month, "so you see I'm four weeks gone, there's no doubt about it." It was a long evening, that evening, and just sitting there and listening to her I knew that I was paying at last for the white Fiat, the Auteuil address, the eight rooms and the three bathrooms and the smell of perfume from the hallway. She started soberly enough, then gradually it all swelled to hysteria and finally it levelled off to a mean, even kind of pride that refused to accept the uglier corners of failure.

"Look," she said, "Edouard has been sleeping with women
for fourteen years and he's never made anyone pregnant
before." However, the French have a hard sense of humour,
and for Edouard it was merely the proper punch line.

Two

Some women have great beauty and are forever a mystery
to their peers and elders; others are irregular in form but
hold something back of great fascination — perhaps a
commitment to the kinds of life you intend for them in your
wildest dreams; or perhaps one sees only the outward marks
of their own inability to cope with the next ten minutes.
Marie-Babette was like neither. For she was unable to see
anything for the first time; all that was sadly impossible.
So what of Marie-Babette ? In Auteuil, as resident governess
to friends of her family, she was an uncurious object, someone who was around and accessible. Yet you neither cared
for, nor ignored her; both were too much like trouble, for
she was least of all a *woman* despite her looks and good
moves down a street. Which is unfair, because there were
those who found her tremendously attractive and desirable;
but you get that kind in every crowd.

Let me reveal her in another way. Marie-Babette was
one of the few women one stole money from on principle.
I stole her money, not because I needed it or because it
gave me a peculiar satisfaction, but in the way one once
stole marbles in a schoolyard or beat up the fat kid. I took
that money and bought a bag of apples with it and they
were tasteless — but that was Marie-Babette all over.

Try it this way. She had a ballerina's legs, strong in the
calf and ankle and tapering off into thin thighs and flat
belly; her eyes were like dead little squirts of green and her
nose was flat like the French nose; to top it off, her hair

was dark, a deep, unmysterious black. Marie-Babette looked exactly the same to me dressed and undressed; she pulled down her pants and there she was, just as you might have imagined her a hundred yards off, sporting a groin as impersonal as a Kresge's brush. Sitting in a Métro and crossing her legs high made no difference to anybody, and that's what I mean; her sense of absence was infectious. A man might feel himself impotent after failing to be moved by her varying poses in a chair.

Maybe this will persuade you. A lot of people made love to her in the beginning, particularly alcoholics and bad writers. I made love to her myself. She once told me — as a discriminating rule of thumb — how people who drank and people who were failures ultimately drove her to lonely farms where they proceeded to rape her against her will. "I won't say 'against my will' absolutely because we are all fundamentally sexual in time and space," she inevitably explained it to me (adding her own submission as the hooker to the experience), so that even the idea of raping her had at best the aura of an impulsive sham.

If that doesn't do it, try this one. She could unsex anything, given the proper chance. The apparatus for making love has its own unique fascination — the French tickler with the snake's tongue at its tip or tiny thorns down its shaft, the bidet in the corner, the diaphram in the purse, the pill dial on the mantle, the mustard on the shelf — it's all part of the unspoken mystique. Not for her it wasn't. Everything had to be analyzed and checked and in the end it was like making love to a slide rule; "My salvation is in *knowing,*" she used to sniff happily, yet I doubt that she had a knowledgeable day in her life. Certainly, she couldn't make love to save herself, and what can you *know* before that, Marie-Babette ?

From out of her life, I will pick for you a few random but pointed examples. When she went to her doctor to replace a diaphram gone faulty, she became frightened that perhaps this one would prove defective too and withhold from her the finer holds of love. "You won't be alarmed if I tell you something, Larry; I asked him to mount me on the table and test its grip." Notice the word "mount" here, as if she were a filly or a virgin; she was the undoubted master of the passive mood.

Concluding evidence. She was always stunned by the matriculations of her body and as a young girl erotic poetry had opened her pores and puzzled her instincts. She once read a poem in which an older man bewailed the struggle of remaining hard in a slow woman; she couldn't understand this mathematic, so to find out she did the only sensible thing : she gave her virginity to a middle-aged drunk. There was no blood and no pain, but there was nothing else either; it was just like sneezing. When it was over, she didn't understand the experience, but she understood the poem.

A basic indictment. As a governess instructing children (boy and girl, aged five and eight) she gave to her charges the benefit of her special craving and obsession in the form of certain inquiries which involved general disrobing. "In the Carlylean sense," she defined it, "we unmask ourselves." Games were indicated, "anatomical forays," she called them, and the children teemed and rustled through her body like mice in a nest. In all fairness though, she kept personal enjoyment at a minimum. "We do make a choice," she liked to say, "between *Turn Of The Screw* and *Mary Poppins :* to exorcise the evil or to disguise it as fable. Larry, I have sacrificed myself to the sexual revolution." Some sacrifice.

There is the uncanny story of the man who waited for her two years in a little sixty-cent-a-day room in Venice. He was slowly going out of his mind and had already memorized all the colours and cracks around him; the sound of his clock replaced the beat of his heart, he liked to say, and towards the end of the second year he became just as mechanical, little hand, big hand. Marie-Babette used to write him little aerogrammes from all over Europe where she was travelling as governess. Her letters were cool and unaffectionate, theses about time and space and the smell of museums; they didn't excite him at all, but they made him long for her terribly and his days and nights were built around the sexual promise of the mail rack in the hallway. After two long years filled with deprivation and hope, she finally came to him one evening from Amsterdam. He was waiting for her at the station in a gray, musty overcoat, and she walked towards him in bright red, looking clean and warm beneath. He couldn't leave her alone, and whenever he watched her he found himself watching his room, for she was all its sounds and the marks on the wall. They drove home in a taxi launch and he told her secret things and held her hand and showed her his bank book. They settled in that sinking, candy kingdom. Of course, she wasn't anything he really wanted; she was selfish, deceitful, pretentious, inept and, strangely enough, unbeautiful. He threw her out within a week — much to his own relief — and finally wrote a book to extract the poison; it took another two years in the same room and was very bad indeed, but it did him a world of good. Today he is a kind man. The point is that Marie-Babette's only strength was in appearing to others as something she was not and could never be. She was nothing more than an illusion culled from a poem and she scanned easily. "Are you human," I once put it, "or just a demonstrator's model?" She never entered a room, she always entered *stage left,* and the grand hysteria of her arms and legs and body proper was only stage business. She always tried to upstage life as if it were some devious minor character, and that was her first problem; her second was that she always got found out.

A more personal account of her might help. Once, I brought her to my room to bring her off as I saw fit, a difficult enough business even at the best of times. On the bed, she suddenly remembered in the foreglow of desire that she had forgotten not only to insert her diaphram, but to bring it at all. According to the calendar, which was scotch-taped to her compact, she was happily safe; but no, would I wait while she went home for it to Auteuil. "Darling, I want to be *sure,* oh can't you see?" Sure. Down the unlit corridor she stumbled, out onto the small bridge seven stories above the street, poising herself heroically near the staircase before descent. She took a taxi home and back, it was a matter of an hour or so, and when at last I took her it was vaguely like taking a coke machine that would not fail to give you the wrong change.

You see what I mean? "Yum yum," she said one morning, sitting up in bed in the pose of a sated pussy cat as I walked in with a vegetable baguette full of white cheese, tomatoes and lettuce green. She rolled her eyes and ticked her toes, but somehow beneath the mirage of her coy stare you saw the dead centre twitching away like a stillborn tooth, dominant, public and immutable.

A last parting shot. Because she could outthink sex, it never did her any real good; she wanted it because everyone was supposed to want it and she knew all the mock sounds in bed and was known as the loudest lay in Auteuil and even in parts of Trocadéro. She had even gone to the trouble of inventing a few key and excitable phrases, sensibly obscene, to replace the orgasm that was so seldom hers to have; often, she had someone else's. In the end, she began to masturbate — not out of self-love or even pleasure, but in order to add still another dramatic corner to her soul. "Some nights I *do have* to masturbate, its all very spatial so I shouldn't worry and Larry I think its helping me as a woman; now tell me, am I as good as Catherine Cz? I happen to know she's about two steps away from being a lesbian anyway."

Marie-Babette finally married somebody who was cancerous, a squat, sheepish etymologist who once described himself as a "bandage," though that was the last of his worries. Their marriage was to be something like a graduate experiment and together they were to form a lasting thesis. She went away with him, fondling the idea of his death like a martyr come to the cross at last. In bed she would be pure again, and in her own inadequate way give him her meagre blessings as he "mounted" her with his rotting guts. She thought for certain, did poor Marie-Babette, that hers was a life of great drama, that each desperate experience added to her emotional stockpile; yet they will only further contract that puny, dislikeable soul, isn't that right Marie-Babette?

Three

One of the redemptive features of promiscuity is that it is often self-consuming. The happy exemplum I have in mind was rooted in Toronto some years before Auteuil, a blind spot except for the fact that the girl in question, Cara Spume, was married in that city to a slow, fat Finn already well-aged, extremely rich and of no use at all. Wherein, of course, lay an irony so pure as to be almost of the text book variety.

Cara in college had been everyone's idea of carnal bright-ness, the well-washed, shrewd, amoral woman; never to be trusted, of course, but that was hardly necessary. She possessed in those days the sensual appeal of a Beardsley print and the kind of existential good time one usually acquired by reading the index of psychosexual studies. She seemed completely taken in by our show of rebellion; or, more properly, she really didn't care to know. Her indif-ference was part of the glamour then, and the calibre of her donation to the cause became legend. She broke in some good boys, and took apart a few others with the same blind simplicity; she had a horrible kind of pleasantness and never cracked and was amused by everything. At the age of twenty she had seen everything once.

Physical descriptions did her no justice (we all tried). To say that she had a small head and a slightly twisted nose, legs awfully thin and certainly bowed, a scrawny indefinable neck and no breasts at all, was to ignore her real, completed style. She loved *faire l'amour* and understood it and was way ahead of our time in the games she played. Her whole system was geared to trigger; when it did, the style made sense. No one was more beautiful in heat, or more taken with one's given mood. She was hungry but unspoilt, and used up people in the nicest ways.

But she really had no breasts. She had the chest of a twelve-year-old boy with slightly distended nipples and if there was anything truly complex about her it came in the form of something absent. She was sensitive about it in a very forbidding way : only she was free to make the comment, and it came by way of a litany which sometimes served as stimulant. Even breast cancer might have soothed that obsession. Anyway, for years she applied creams.

When schooldays were over and all the good underground parties had drifted to London and Paris, Cara Spume graduated to a better crowd. It lived in luxury apartments and had unlisted numbers and was very inbred; so she married into it as best she could and acquired a private phone, a modest penthouse, a pink sports car and a man of forty who spent his afternoons buying properties. But he spent his evenings being polite and distant and hardly there, and his bedroom etiquette consisted of sheepish, fingering gestures. So Cara Spume saved her marriage and took some lovers.

In a year she had exhausted her circle, and not long after that her style began to change. She bought an Arabian carpet crosshatched with eternal spirals, and made love on it according to pattern. Then she threw exploratory parties in special rented cellars. Then she deliberately began to mistake people over the phone and divulge secrets. Then she went silent for several months and never ventured anywhere and had food sent up. Her husband, meantime, oblivious to everything, kept up his little nocturnal efforts.

It was not enough, not even bitchiness, finally. She decided on divorce and a nice settlement. Her husband was taken by surprise and actually had the good sense to cry, but is was too late and soon lawyers' meetings took the place of cappuccino in her life. She was learning the value of self-pity and sentiment and emotional blocks, so she did not come away from it all completely empty or inadequate and she still had that great shift in bed. She sold her share of the furniture and invested her monthly checks and came to Paris, of all places, for a year.

She lived in a suite of rooms on the Boulevard Murat near St. Cloud and the fountains. She seldom came into the city proper. I was still living in a small storage room on the right bank so it was only by chance that one day I saw her in the Paris-Athènes near Brentano's. The Paris-Athènes was one of those moderately expensive cafés a few blocks from the Opéra and she seemed rather settled and natural there that chilly March afternoon. She was inside behind the window and her hair wasn't long anymore. It had been cut very short, was almost duck-tailed in fact; the nape of her neck had been recently shaven. She wore a very chic woolen suit, a white silk scarf that fell from the shoulder as she sipped her drink, and contemporary French shoes. I thought I would walk on past because I had not shaven in some days and was merely taking my afternoon stroll down the Avenue to the Louvre and through the Louvre to the river. But she kept looking up as people passed and spotted me a good three seconds before I turned my head. Of course it is always nice to meet old friends in Paris that time of year.

I was pretty much aware of how badly we both looked then. For various reasons, we had a sickly green pallor in common. But of course we talked of Toronto and college and of the few friends who were hopefully worse off than ourselves. It turned out to be quite a pleasant afternoon really, and she paid for the drinks and even bought me a pastry. I was receiving mail at the time from several sources in Toronto and knew a great deal about her already. I asked her when her ex-husband was coming over; I had received the news several days before, buried in a letter of at least a dozen items.

"Is he?" she said.

She rose without breaking her pleasant smile and went for the telephone.

"Yes," she said on returning, "the wire came yesterday evening."

Now we both knew what *that* meant, but — until I thought it over later — I really didn't care *where* she had spent the night or *who* had been in her suite evening and morning to receive the wire. The slip was obviously simple reflex, wasted motion; I certainly wasn't worth the desired effect.

Anyway, she had to go. We walked up to the Capucines and along it several blocks to where I lived. Prostitutes of some beauty and expense lined the street and, as she came out of the long shadows toward the broad Boulevard again, they made startling sounds and grabbed at her elbow. Her legs moved like warped pistons, increasingly slower as the women beckoned, but finally she made the turn and disappeared in the general direction of the Madeleine Métro station. The vision of her awful temptation haunted me for several minutes and on a careless impulse I ran along the Rue Mathurins and back up the Rue Vignon and just caught a final glimpse of her (tight-lipped) descending the Métro steps.

People are much simpler than we give them credit for. By the time I was in touch with her again, her ex-husband was in Paris for a month, living at the Hôtel Voltaire. I was at my neighbourhood café this time and she was passing by and she came in somewhat flushed. But we had a pleasant talk and finally went up to my room which was a few doors away. She found the conditions under which I was forced to live fascinating. So I attacked her. I discovered that she already smelled of sex — it was the first thing I had noticed in the closeness of my room — and, like the shark who smells blood, I made the simple response. She seemed to have a good dirty time of it and gave way to all sorts of appetites; the apparent squalor of my room added considerably to her enthusiasm. But although she still had that perfectly level smile, something new had been added, something defensive. Yet it was all fairly amusing for her and she still had most of the afternoon free.

"I just wish I had breasts," she pouted pleasantly. "I'd squeeze and squeeze."

"It wouldn't be you," I said.

Then she did a curious thing. I was already dressed and combing my hair before a rather misty mirror when she came up alongside me, still naked, wrapped her legs about my trousers, and rubbed her groin against my flank. It left quite a stain.

After which — she finally having dressed — we left my room and took a taxi to the Quai Voltaire. Her ex-husband was sitting outside the Café Voltaire, but not alone. Cara had invited some of her Paris friends and they had found him on the terrace and were busily talking around him as he sat there like some soft, oblivious Buddha; his head was slightly drooped as if dozing.

"Ello Carew," he said, immediately rising as we approached them through the traffic. The others kept seated, very handsome people all of them. When he had made this gesture, he fell back into the chair again and began to watch everyone with a kind of fading amusement; soon his eyes were closed and his head drooped over.

So the others talked. One of the men at the table was so incredibly good looking that it was impossible to take him seriously. The others were mostly women and they were more or less a variation on his style. We chatted for some time about particular people whom only Cara knew. Every once in a while her ex-husband would be startled out of his trance by a burst of wicked laughter; he would immediately create for us a look of tremendous understanding, but as we watched it would melt down again and the strange, drugged look would creep back like a social cancer.

In response to one particular outburst he half-jumped out of his mysterious nap and looked about him with a sharp, furtive little smile. Cara had frivolously brought the conversation round to the stain on my trousers. He looked at it awhile, the vague implication just out of his reach, until the whole thing receded into some convenient darkness and he was breathing deeply once more with the rind of his chin resting on his chest.

"It is a *nasty* stain," someone said.

"Eats *right through* cloth they say," someone said.

"It does have a *familiar* smell," someone said.

They carried on in this fashion awhile and then decided to go. We had all risen and were still laughing and just as we began to walk away, Cara's ex-husband snapped upright like a rubber raft filling with air. His shirt was unbuttoned at the belt and part of his belly protruded like an enormous muscle.

"Eny wewn intrewst ewn hoorsebeck rewding?" he called. But by that time we had all vanished up a side street.

Cara Spume made several trips from Auteuil into the city

early that spring and she was often around; in fact, I saw her at least twice a week in my district. She never deliberately paid me a call, but whenever I spotted her she made very little fuss about coming up to my room. There were times when she seemed downright relieved. It was apparently no trouble at all.

That was the Cara of the old days, but the closer you got the more you saw the change. She grew moods now and her ploys were more various; there was nothing motivated anymore about her sudden lapses in style, and there was a horrible new transparency to her smile, like finally being able to see ant tunnels under glass. We spent hours discussing breasts — hers and those of mutual friends — and we were never off that topic more than ten minutes an afternoon. She wore trick rubber cups and was planning an operation that summer; in the meantime, she kept playing with the flesh around her nipples, trying to loosen it. What was so different in her style now — aside from the exaggeration of old complaints — was that she had somehow developed *intellectual* problems, like an extra toe. That clean, bright indifference which had given her shrewdness and cunning and had been half her inventory, was burning itself out. She had begun the practice of Yoga, apparently to settle her body down while she read up on mysticism. She really didn't take any of it in, of course (her ultimate ambition being to force her intestines out her anal tract) but pretense poisons just like understanding, and the wish-to-seem-to-know drained something away and ruined her functions. Her system still triggered with incredible ease in Paris, but that was the vestige of a final skill. Yoga kept it to a minimum. I had friends myself in Auteuil, but I never saw her in that part of the city. Apparently, she lived a fairly private existence in her own territory.

Well, one never knows what really happens to people. Cara was seeing her ex-husband off and on that month and he was going through the odd process of wooing her at expensive restaurants and sending over roses every morning. She let him take her to Deauville for a weekend and when he became a bit surer of himself, he began to wear ascots and to show a bit of decisiveness over train schedules.

Her pretty friends went everywhere with them and apparently lived in her suite. It was obvious that she had become awfully dependent on their choric function in her life; they revolved about her conversations like the spindles of a wheel and were always thinking of ingenious things to do. To cure her of one mood, a seduction was planned in which one of the very attractive women in her train of people was to arouse her ex-husband by certain nefarious methods. There were bets — Cara, brightening, made book — and some question as to whether it could be done. The details remained a mystery to all but a few of the group. But for a week it was the standard allusion. The ex-husband disappeared for several days in the wake of the conspiracy and re-emerged more sheepish and sleepier than ever. He never again spoke in their company.

A great deal more happened of which I only caught glimpses. The day after her ex-husband had returned to Toronto, though, I saw Cara coming out of a hotel on my street with one of the *poules*. We talked around it successfully. She came up to my room and we fornicated solemnly for a while, but even her smile was missing this time. "You know, I really don't like it all that much," she said timidly, and two days later I came down with an unmentionable blister on my lip.

What does one say ? I called her on the phone.

"You filthy, titless little poove," I said.

"Hello ?"

"You have no breasts, you fucking freak."

"What ? Who is this ?"

"Whore. Slut."

"Oh please."

"You're known by the hairs on your filthy cunt, you diseased cretin."

"Oh God, for god sake."

"You heard me."

I don't flatter myself that the call had any beneficial effect on her life. She did become quite ill, however, and

went into the American hospital for "exploratory" surgery.
After that she seemed to struggle through her few remaining
pleasures. I made a similar call the week she was released,
and saw her once more, alone, at a film.

"Cara, how are you?"

"Terrible," she said.

"Come on up to my place."

"No."

"Come on. Why not?"

"I don't anymore."

So she went back to Toronto and remarried the Finn.
Not every tale, of course, ends badly.

Four

Little Dollie had a villa in Auteuil and before that she
had a husband. The villa was better than the husband
because she could roam in it whenever she wanted and only
had to take a bath once a month, while the husband was
somewhere else and couldn't tell her a thing. The husband
had been overbearing and dominant and practical and had
known the right things to do. When he was gone, she could
only speak of him in the nastiest terms; the one sure way
to hurt her was to tell her that her husband was having a
wonderful time.

Little Dollie was short and dumpy. She knew it and wore
short and dumpy dresses; her nose, which seemed to hold
her face together, looked like so much dried blood on the
end of a sausage and her lips were always dry and cracked
and thick. She was not what you would call stunning, but
she had many compensating virtues; first of all, she had a
heart of gold, which made it difficult for her to breath.
There wasn't any sacrifice she wasn't willing to make, and
she was so selfless in so many ways and so subtracted from

her pleasures that she seemed almost invisible with goodness; it was an imposing fortress.

Her stubby fingers and rich, strained smile became a fashion and soon a club was formed in Auteuil called the "We Love Little Dollie" Club that met officially Sunday nights. Its hungry members consisted of artists, writers, cripples, actors, fugitives and all-round family people, all of whom Little Dollie fed out of a great cauldron of lobster stew or banana mix. The writers took her typewriter, the artists slept on her carpets, and the all-round family people just left their babies. She served those who only knelt in wait. And if you refused to be served, she could always find some way to make you seem helpless. The ultimate caution was this : if you didn't need her, she couldn't use you.

However, Little Dollie really didn't like people at all; she only liked the idea of people, the vision of herself as Mother Earth to the multitudes, raised up (on a hassock) to bless the air and the little voices. When multitudes were around she just put up with them as best she could. Groups of people were her favourite device, but people singly or in tiny groups were unattractive to her sense of giving. Alone, one by one, people were indefinite and frightening (she once gave a Negro a shiny thing); but at her Sunday Nights she could handle the family of man that clogged her hallway and used her toilets, for they were only objects to be fed and wiped. In a huge crowd, with so many needy faces, there were no eyes to make her dizzy.

Away from her Sunday Nights, she was troublesome. During the week, she ventured often from the villa to visit the impoverished and the homesick and the unloved; she carried around a large straw purse full of chocolate and shiny new francs, and if you weren't in when she called, you would be the last to get served that Sunday. In her religious voyage through the city, the thing she looked for most, and which warmed her heart immeasurably, was unhappiness. Any kind. Unhappiness in marriage of course was the quality that most endeared you to her, with sexual unhappiness

running a close second; but for the long run she took anything she could get.

"Are you happy ?"

"Yes."

"I mean really happy."

"Yes."

"Is your husband good to you ?"

"Yes."

"Are you . . . all right together ?"

"Yes."

"Oh."

Physical disease did not please her greatly, unless it was
only an upset stomach or a migraine headache (preferably
habitual) because there were hospitals to look after these,
and she lost half the need that way. Despair was a good
one; it was like a lingering cough in the soul and she could
treat it endlessly and never run out of it. If you had despair,
you could establish a nice relationship with her and always
be sure of eating and using a nice toilet with soft toilet paper.
But if you were just plain mean and sadistic, that was one
of the top diseases. To be pricked by the point of an insult,
to be spitted and impaled by a master craftsman, that was
heroism at its Easter best. Little Dollie liked to glorify her
own innocence as if she were a lamb waiting in ambush for
the next slaughter. She was always the first to insist on
sacrifice.

Her first one was her most impressive. It involved a
French artist, Willi Verbre. His whole world was sustained
by a lack of food, and he looked as if the idea of evil had
been reinterpreted as a mobile, The Word Made Tin, for he
moved like a series of metallic nodes. Not that Verbre was
really decadent : he caught colds too easily for that; but he
lived a decentralized kind of life and as long as all things
came towards his left profile, he was happier than not.

When they first met, Little Dollie was immersed in her
Marriage Period and doing quite nicely. She and her husband
(who had made a small fortune orchestrating flute solos)
were living in a large flat near Montmartre and their functional evening was Thursday Night. Every Thursday night

the flat would be filled to the brim with outcasts and castoffs, the most easily defined being Verbre, slight to the point of consumption, teeth like old candy, with attitudes shocking, repulsive and beautifully pronounced. Little Dollie was shocked indeed, and repulsed too, but she was attracted at once by the immensity of the project. Since Little Dollie loved generally all forms of animal life, Verbre (nobody's fool) became an instant animal, reeking — he made it plain — of things vile and unspoken. Certainly, Little Dollie was no match for the sufferings he offered.

The husband laughed this off, of course; he was too busy not to trust others. And to prove how certain he was of Little Dollie's fidelity, he permitted Verbre to entertain her in cafés. Meanwhile, he pursued his interest in psychology which involved meeting new people all the time. This was a necessity since his analyses took only four days and he could work through whole groups at a sitting. His aptitude for understanding was enormous.

So Verbre, given the chance, took Little Dollie to his rooms in the Rue Amsterdam and showed her his life's work. It had one dominating theme : atrocity. Verbre had served with the French army in Algeria and with singular devotion he had documented his experiences in oils and pastels, water colours and charcoal. The work was lovely, highly finished, deeply felt. There was the great purple oil painting of the Moroccan hook torture as glimpsed through a Moorish keyhole, a smaller oil depicting, in dominant reds, the agony of French electrodes; in water colours, a rape scene pastoral : the hue of the sky a vivid orange, the haze of grass turquoise and azure gray. And many others he deemed fit to record for his own salvation and those of his loved ones; which Little Dollie became through no fault of his own. It was just one of those things.

A word of description concerning Little Dollie's esthetic sense; all her judgments were in the mind of the behoover. She felt a bond with all creators except God; she felt necessary to them as an objective means by which they could understand the greatness of their vision, for all work to her was equidistant to the Good. No artist in her eyes was bad, each had the gift of creation; if a man could draw a circle, he became at once worthy of her patronage and forgiveness.

So she forgave Verbre his surly ways; she accepted his sense of atrocity without question, abided by his perspective day and night, and learned to slaver at the mouth when called for. In return, Verbre allowed her into a reasonable fascimile of his own private hell. She went for the bait so quickly he hardly had time to plan her downfall.

The result of this distraction was that the Thursday Nights deteriorated into two camps. Her husband still maintained a faithful following of parasites, for he had analyzed them and sent them word tests; but when he left Paris for points east, his betrayed disciples were not permitted into the new shelter of the Sunday Nights : where the triumphant gathered.

There Verbre prevailed. His sense of contempt was contagious, and Little Dollie was an easy carrier of impressions. She was so impressed with him, in fact, that she began to affect what she trusted, hoped and believed was an evil eye. This consisted of deflating the lids and various complicated blinks. It only enhanced her graciousness; and it gave her character. She also began to indulge in a clumsy sort of sarcasm which consisted of stressing every second consonant preceding the truth. But, despite these tiny acts of idolatry, the affair was short-lived. Verbre did not find her awfully attractive, and good meals seemed a poor reason for confinement; anyway, he had flagellant work elsewhere. So he left her, and left her with such an immaculate sense of suffering that it did everyone some good. If you learned to cater to the ebb and flow of her sorrow, there was no real end to her generosity. The word got around. Verbre sent many of his friends to her for solace and refreshment, and happy she was to serve them in her fashion. She saved two cunning Frenchmen from starving, arranged facilities for a little old *clochard* who kept urinating in her villa garden like a burst hydrant, and provided sanctuary for an American who was fleeing the U.S. draft, letters of greeting in hot pursuit. As always, she clothed, bathed and fed, she pampered, wiped and indulged. Sometimes Verbre himself dropped in, perhaps to devastate her wittingly. She understood.

"I love him. Don't you love him?" she sighed week after week in litany. "He is good. He is honest. Oh, see Verbre, pretty Verbre. He is nice."

Once I was without a place to stay. Or, to put it more properly, the squalor of my surroundings was becoming impossible and I needed about two weeks of grace to put me back in the Spartan mood. Little Dollie heard of this at once through the grapevine, and within hours of my breakdown she had cornered me in a café and was insisting that I move in with her until I had recouped my losses.

"You are a writer. I like writers. They are so sensitive. See the sensitive writer. He is writing. What are you writing, sensitive writer? He is moody too."

I moved in.

Life with Little Dollie was worse than the most pagan kinds of torture; it was a life filled with goodness and mercy, a life of care and patience, with Little Dollie always nearby to wipe up my slop or scrub my underwear.

The first night, Little Dollie insisted I take the bed "You are tired. You have been writing. Tired writer." So she lay on the floor in a sleeping bag, groaning with cold the whole night. It was probably her finest hour but I wasn't noticing it; so the next night, after the last of the day's guests had been given their supplies and let free, she began to eye the bed warmly like an unfeathered bird. All right, I said, I'll take the sleeping bag; no no, she whimpered, for I had sucked her into making a choice, You're a writer, writer needs his strength, etc. It was true that I did need my strength, but only to watch out that she didn't give me an enema when I wasn't looking. At the time, "purge" was her favourite word. I took the bed.

About three in the morning, a strong wind came up from the river and loosened the window catch; I could see Little Dollie's short dumpy form waddle to the balcony and I watched her fumble awhile in the face of the chill. She groaned every few moments, and more than twice she turned and looked at me. I refused to notice; if she wants the bed, I thought, she'll have to ask for it like a man. I didn't exactly doze off, but I was startled to feel a pudgy finger prodding my shoulder about four in the morning. "Larry, I am so cold. It is very cold. Can I sleep on the edge of my bed, I'm sorry." She curled up in a bare sheet at my feet; the chill didn't let up and with concessions here and there, cajolements, offers, withdrawals, sacrifices, she was soon sleeping beside me, her cold fat bristly feet yanked under my legs like frogs beneath a rock.

All that next day, the evening went unmentioned. But that night there was no sleeping bag on the floor and Little Dollie was already in the bed when I came to the villa. "Don't be angry," said Little Dollie as I undressed quietly in the dark. "It is so very cold. See, I can't stand the cold. Okay?" I was not angry, I was just tired and slipped into bed without touching her once and went off to sleep. The next day I stayed in the villa all afternoon, one of those innumerable strays wandering about the grounds, and then towards supper time took a walk through the Bois. I came back about eight in the evening for supper and then read on the terrace till midnight. As I climbed into bed this time, my leg accidentally slid against her behind as she lay hunched towards the wall; she groaned ever so slightly, but she seemed to take the insult well and I lay in the dark feeling dangerous.

The next afternoon, Little Dollie went into Paris proper for groceries, and to make her charitable rounds among the unhappy, the despairing and the poor; at least they *were* on Wednesdays, or God help them. While she was out, I wandered around the villa and found a little fifty centime notebook on a window sill filled with childlike printing, almost exercises in making capital letters. "AH," they began on the last written page, "TO SLEEP BESIDE SOMEONE AND BE AFRAID TO TOUCH TO NIGHT AFTER NIGHT BE AFRAID TO SPEAK WHAT AN AGONY IF HE WOULD JUST HOLD ME BECAUSE IT IS COLD OUT JUST HOLD ME IN THE DARK BUT HOW PAINFUL JUST TO LIE THERE ALONE WITH SOMEONE BESIDE YOU SUCH DESPAIR SUFFERING WITHOUT PURGE . . ." (The three dots are hers.) I was so angry I almost threw up breakfast. So now I was her latest entry, the new episode put to use. I cringed at the idiotic simplicity of her moves, changed my clothes, packed a lunch, and picnicked in the Bois with a vengeance.

That night I went to bed early with no supper. Little Dollie came home by cab about twelve, made quite a few noises preparing some hot chocolate, and finally went into the bathroom where after some little while the toilet flushed. I had kept my eyes closed with my back to the open door and I had no way of knowing for certain if she had been watching me. But she came out of the bathroom and tripped on the rug coming through the front room; the noise startled me and I jerked my head around without thinking and there she was on her knees gathering up her clothes. There was the sound of a tiny, heartfelt whimper in her throat, a wailing, a keen; I was so enraged I knocked my forehead against the wall. And the moment she hit the bed I knew that she was naked. I had caught a true glimpse of her in that other instant but I hadn't believed it (she usually wore pajamas), it was too much, that fat little body with the thick thighs and the inchy little breasts. Not only that, she smelled — something you didn't notice during the day. But under the sheets, a thin odor like that of vaseline began to warm the bed. She knew I wasn't asleep; she lay on her back looking sadly at the ceiling, knees up, hand curled like a pink flower on her belly. She shifted strangely.

"Little Dollie," I whispered, stark still against the wall, "I meant to tell you what an incredibly wonderful relationship we have, you and I. Here we are, always in the same bed, and we can do it without any problems. You're more and less of a woman for it, by God. So it's very nice goodnight dear."

Little Dollie brought her knees in closer to her stomach and suddenly she ranged on the bed like an anchorite impaled.

"Less than a woman?" she said, "why?"

"Well you know Little Dollie like one of the boys."

"I hate that," said Little Dollie, "I'm not one of the boys, I'm me."

"Right, that's right Little Dollie, okay goodnight sweetheart," and I reached out to pat her on the head. But I
struck her leg instead, round and frizzled like a wild coconut.
Her knees were almost touching her chin. She put out her
hand and touched the tanned part of my neck and said
goodnight, was I comfortable ? then there was the sound of
the sheet wheezing and the prod of her fingers ticking my
groin.

"Little Dollie," I groaned, "I respect your husband very
much he's my friend funny huh ?"

"He stinks," said Little Dollie.

"Its a funny kind of loyalty that makes friends," I said,
"keeps a man honest no matter what."

"Peh," said Little Dollie.

The whole thing began to happen. She climbed astride
my caught torso, hoisting her buttocks wildly, puffing like
some asthmatic monster. Her knees locked me into place;
her wet little maw began to gnaw and settle.

Gobble.

"No please."

Gobble.

"Honee," I said, "wha ... eeee ... if ... somfeen hap-
pend ... in ... bed ... aghhhh ... wif ... us ... ewwww ...
could it ?"

Gobble.

"You ... ver lllllllllonleeee," she said, "isolaaaated writer
... oooops ... mooody ... if it happenzz I'llll undrastan
Lahrrrry ... happenz happenz ahhh ... but lez make ...
nnnn ... effert nnnot to dear ... ewww ..." she said.

I-said-okay-I-slipped-out-I-got-up-I-took-quilt-I-slept-rest-
of-night-in-bathroom-with-door-locked.

The next morning she hardly spoke to me and later that
afternoon she told her loved ones that she had had to piss
in the garden at five in the morning.

I was soon back in my old room and there was a letter
waiting for me from her husband in Germany. In a few days

it was Little Dollie's birthday and would I go out and buy her two dozen yellow roses and put in a nice card for him; he would reimburse me if I sent a receipt from the florist. I am not one to bicker and I know when I am well off, so next day I went to a flower shop in the Rue de Sèze and bought two dozen yellow roses complete with card and ribbon.

I took a Métro to the villa later that afternoon but Little Dollie wasn't home; I stored the roses in a neighbouring shed. At supper time I came out to the villa again, but no one answered the door. There were a few of them in the garden — two Americans, a *clochard,* Woo, the Japanese who lived in a cupboard on the premises. They stared at me threateningly so I gave it up and tried again the next morning but again no answer. By this time the yellow roses were beginning to droop and, as night fell, they went limp and some of them were dead.

"This is silly," I said, "I'm going to fling them through the perishing window," and marched over guiltily and banged on the villa door for a quarter of an hour. The noise awoke several people asleep on the lawn; angry voices came from a small tent erected beneath the terrace; Woo staggered out of his cupboard, completely naked, carrying a small bicycle. I continued to bang on the door; at last a light came on. There were many little sounds above, a shadow or two on the lace curtains, the thump of bodies walking.

Finally, Little Dollie came down the steps to the door, red-eyed, yawning, and I handed her the dead roses and said, "He says much love and happy birthday".

But Little Dollie's face was all wrong : the eyes were menacing and the mouth cruel and tight. There was something both haggard and devouring in the shape of her yawn, a feeling that the beast had been flushed from its lair. She took the wilted flowers (like dead weeds they were) and in a voice easy but still thick with sleep : "Isn't that just like him ? Dead for the dead marriage". And with great justification she waddled back up the stairs where Nicky the African was scratching his belly on the landing.

Five

The following tale illustrates an incident which reveals the Miss Carlyle in question better than any narrative study could. However, some words of caution before we begin. Miss Carlyle, to an overeager and emotive nature, might appear as a very sensitive and moving woman. Actually, and without condition, she is a bitch and a lunatic.

I had arranged to meet Miss Carlyle at a small café near the American Express, in the Rue Auber. She was lovely in a slim, confidential way, with dark plumed brows and the erotic hint of whiskers on lip and chin. Miss Carlyle was at her best when angry and she was angry now and had sent me a quickly scrambled note, scrawly with spite and cigarette burns. I had responded with a *pneumatique* later that morning, cool and offhand in tone. I was upset and unprepared (she had said nothing at breakfast). Upset because I had misjudged her (my fault), unprepared because she had forced a scene during the worst of the Paris spring.

"Yes isn't it ?" She came up behind me, indulging her habit of catching you with the theme of your last conversation. I didn't say a word, but ordered some Vichy water to go with anything else we might need. Her long body snapped into the seat and a little sweat gathered in the angel's cradle of her smile.

"You *are* a bastard. What ?"

"I didn't say a thing. Did I get any mail today ?"

"Shut up."

Miss Carlyle was not beautiful, but she was far more than pretty. Her face was marred by a stale, vague smile that judged, in general, everything it could. I had been living with her for only two weeks and we fornicated about twice as often as one uncorks champagne, but it was her way to build conspiracies in the air, to send cryptic notes, to feel cheated and betrayed and vaguely dangerous. She had a highly developed sense of injury, Miss Carlyle. I do not know the difference between lunacy and fright, but no doubt she was somewhere in between. She was a master at improvising scenes, and frankly she scared the hell out of me.

"Have some Vichy; it keeps you regular," I said.

"I want to call it off." *It* hung in the air like an unmilked breast, and I had a vision of her navel, deep, with a small mole stage left.

"What ? You out of your goddamn mind ? You know what you can do," and I rose abruptly of course and dropped a five franc note on the table. I headed towards the Opéra and down the Avenue towards Delmonico's, eyes front, arms steady. I drank a cheap wine (three francs) and smoked a cigarette and killed another fifteen minutes reading the paperback history of erotica in Brentano's. Then I came back and she was still sitting there.

"Are you out of your mind ?" I said. I sat down and put the five franc note back in my pocket. "You must be crazy, are you crazy ?" I smoked a cigarette while she looked crazy. In a little while she was smoking too and wearing black gloves.

"No."

"Oh for Christ's sake."

"That's all and I don't want to talk about it."

God knows what there was to talk about; you had to fondle and sooth and direct her rage to convenient outlets. But I didn't want to handle her, it was too cold and too unpleasant and I thought the hell with it. At the same time, she had a white Fiat.

Maybe it was this : "If you knew how clumsy this Marie-Babette is," I said, "you'd laugh. She's so clumsy I'm surprised she isn't a virgin by default. I have to put two pillows under her and hold her up. Two-fifths orgasm and three-fifths noise. I've pretty much had it, frankly."

"I really don't want to know."

"Yesterday for instance she fell out of bed; anyway she has hair on her chest."

"I have hair on my chest too, you know. No, that's not true."

"You're lovely, I mean that. Through and through. In and Out. Fore and Aft."

"So ?"

Perhaps a bit of mock lyric would do it :
    "And when thyself with shining flit shall pass
    Among the guests star-scattered on their ass ..."
"Just drop it."

"Let's take a walk." I threw the five franc note on the table again. We hadn't ordered a thing. She walked ahead of me, her long legs jerking awkwardly.

"Where's your car ?"

"I don't want to drive."

"Oh this is stupid," and grabbed her arm with some degree of authority and led her to the Capucines. Now to get there, we had to walk down the Rue Godot-de-Mauroy. I had lived there some time before this, in a dingy little storage room, and I always got a certain mediocre pleasure in revisiting the scene whenever I could. The nicely dressed pros were hustling outside their maison meublée and I had a hard time persuading them not to see me. Especially a tall blonde one, Jeanne, whose face was very Egyptian with a nose like a slip of ivory and thick high lips I had nibbled on many an evening.

"Look," said Miss Carlyle, "if you want to stop here for fifteen minutes (that's how long it takes, isn't it ?) I'll go home myself. Just give me the keys please."

"Look, if you don't shut up," I said, thinking of the total simplicity of the fifty franc lay.

We circled the Madeleine three times and that is quite a walk. Then we marched up the Rue Royale and into the Tuileries. We sat down at the first fountain and I watched the goldfish eating garbage caked on the surface of the water. Her legs were crossed and I squeezed the eight-cornered knob of her knee; it was like stroking ice.

"I've got all day, what about you ?"

"No."

It was quite a nice day. The sand was brown the length of the walk and vendors were selling ice cream in front of the gray arch of the Carousel. That was a long walk and it was a short day, but we made it and I sucked on a small raspberry cone that cost a franc while she sat on a bench, sulking and tart. I wandered over to the arch to visit some words I had once chalked there. Someone had written in English, "Mickey Mouse is a Jew," and below it the grand rejoinder "Fuck Hate."

Perhaps what Miss Carlyle needed was a sense of submission. I wandered back to her and said "I'm not going to leave you, so face it." She was sitting under a statue of a nude with fruit. Mostly bananas and pears.

"No, I mean it," she snapped. The nude had small breasts for a statue.

"Oh hell, what's the matter with you, are you crazy?"

The muscle in her leg swelled to one of those taut sensuous cords; her toes reached for something and locked in a cramp. It was that kind of day.

"Hey, want to feel better?" I sat down beside her again, then again on another bench in a small garden with lawns and hedges remote from the grand walk. She shook her head suddenly and made a sound with her tongue like the pop of a champagne cork; it was as if something were trying to force its way out of her throat; her hands made little fists and she groaned and it got out : a stale, vague smile.

I let her walk clear out of the gardens and halfway to the quai before I went after her. It was becoming a regular Cook's tour for the Golden Fleece.

Perhaps she was seething with jealousy and regret : I had been entertaining her with tales of conquest evenings before — Little Dollie, Catherine Cz, Marie-Babette. It had been such a pleasant domestic scene that possibly I hadn't seen the harm in it; she had been seated naked on her best chair while I, on my knees, had cut and trimmed her toe nails. "I'm not seeing any of them anymore; make you feel better?" She was some distance ahead of me and I had to raise my voice. "I'll say the hell with them."

"Please," she said calmly, "it doesn't matter."

"I'll change; I want to, frankly."

I caught up to her and grabbed the fleshiest part of her arm. "It was fun to hear about the girls, wasn't it," I said. "I thought you were such a little Machiavelli."

"Don't bother," she said.

She wouldn't come down with me to the bank of the Seine (our *second* meeting) so I went down by myself and kept an eye on her from the river; her head and shoulders bobbed from the rail above. A few couples were on the benches in difficult positions and I stood awhile watching them. Sometimes you saw some real sights but today everybody was unoriginal.

I climbed the steps back to her and soon we stood unhappily in the square fronting Notre Dame.

It was time to press a new argument : "You're absolutely the best woman I've ever had," I pleaded softly, "you have an instinct for it. Look at me just thinking about it. Will you look at that, darling ?" I stimulated an erection by thinking of the whore, Jeanne, whose fine little organ made whistling noises. And Miss Carlyle's wasn't bad either; her body when first seen had been a bitter disappointment to me, but, once over the disenchantment, she was quite a decent experience : jerky, spastic, mechanical, yet sanitary and honest.

We walked into the gardens of Notre Dame and sat down on a dirty brown bench in front of some swings. Children ran around us with pails. A fat woman sitting far off crossed her legs and revealed a huge fanning thigh.

"I don't want you anymore," she said. "Why don't you find some moist little virgin and leave me alone."

"Little virgins aren't moist; only big virgins."

We walked out of the gardens and over the Petit Pont into the Rue St. Jacques. We walked slowly towards all the corpses in the Panthéon. We were wasting the afternoon. I didn't know what to do. "Let's have some Chinese food."

She didn't answer me and finally she had to sit down and her face was very pale. I ordered some wine but she wanted a coke. Then she wouldn't drink it and had to go to the toilet. She came back looking worse than before. It was an old toilet with just a hole in the floor and she couldn't bring herself to use it.

"What's wrong, dear ?"

"What do you think. I'm sick today."

"Your first day ?"

"Yes." She closed her eyes and looked sick.

So that was it. You had to laugh, such a proud little bitch. "Will you be okay by the weekend ?" I was now so angry that I wouldn't hold her hand; after a while I took it and she peeled off her glove for me and I kissed it like a fawning fool. The pain must have been really bad and she shouldn't have done so much walking and the whole day was shot for me anyway. I was relieved though. "Drink your coke and we'll go home."

"My car's in the Place Vendôme." Her eyes were closed and she looked terrible. She went back into the toilet to vomit. When she came out again, I took her hand and kissed her on the forehead. "I'll put you in a taxi and bring back the car later," I said; everything was all right now.

"Is everything all right now ?" I asked.

"No, it's not all right and it's not going to be all right."

"Yes, well, I'll get a taxi," and got her a taxi and helped her in. She winced sliding into the seat. I promised to come back in the evening, probably late, to give her the keys. The hell with her. When she was gone, I got another taxi and hurried to the Place Vendôme and started the car with my own keys. It was already four in the afternoon and I drove like mad through Concorde and into the Rue Royale. I parked the car and headed down the Rue Godot-de-Mauroy checking the whores on each side of the street and finally found Jeanne against the wall of her maison meublée discussing the new Eddie Constantine film with a friend. "I think his pock marks are sexy," I heard her say in French, then she saw me and made a very professional motion with her belly. "Entrez pour l'amour Larree ?"

"All right, sure — but nice and slow this time honey, I got problems."

II

Tales From The Quarter

One

Never mind why I came to the Quarter. I took a Métro
from Auteuil one morning, very tired and very nervous, full
of a bad experience. I had wanted to stay near the Bois but
something had gone wrong, had inexplicably jammed and
fallen neatly out of place. My life in villas and white Fiats
was dead and buried, and gone for certain was my metaphor
for opulence, the clean white sheet, the scent of lavender,
the texture of silk. Yet I made a last attempt to stay near
that quiet, fresh world; I was not yet lunatic enough not to
want the flowers and fountains of St. Cloud and the clean
stretches of road that wound through dense and shallow
wood to restaurants impossible to afford. So when the villa
was gone, and that lovely shaven armpit into which I had
snuggled my nose many a night had suddenly foliated and
coarsened in rage, I stood with my luggage before a small
hotel in the Rue Michel-Ange a few pleasant blocks away,
thinking oh the hell with it, and went in. After all, wasn't
this the best thing? to stay in the easy life and know nothing
but the nicest smells? The concierge was a splendid bitch.

"How much are your rooms?" I asked in my best resi-
dential French; I had been taught inflection by the better
people.

"What is your room number?"

"No. I *want* a room."

"Is it eight, number eight?"

"I don't live here."

"Marcel, come down. The American makes trouble."

"No no, I come from outside. I'm Canadian."

"You want to leave without paying."

"Look. I come from the outside. From the street."

I went outside and came in again to demonstrate.

"Marcel, check room eight."

"No no, oh God."

"What's your name, how long have you been here?"

"Garber. I don't live . . ."

"Jarrbay. Not Stevenson?"

"Look, please, from the street. I come from the outside to the inside. Out to in. I no live here. I live villa before. No here. There."

"Pig American. How much do you owe on the register?"

"Oh God."

"Stevenson, is that your name?"

"Garber. G-A-R-B-E-R."

"What? S-T-E . . ."

"You here. Me there. Street. Outside."

Marcel came running down the stairs to report that Stevenson was in his room shaving.

"You don't have a room here?"

"No no no. I want know *price* room. How much room."

"Oh."

So I took a Métro from Auteuil, struggling with luggage through passageways and up stairs. The train rattled and had a bad smell.

Two

Some people live their whole lives in the Quarter with their trunks in the hall. It's the illusion of transit that's important. Don't use up all the drawers, leave your clock on the suitcase, pay by the day, store books and ties in the Gare St. Lazare.

I came to a hotel on the Ile de la Cité, within crawling distance of Odéon. That was important. From the Pont Neuf to the quai I could steady myself by clutching the bridge wall, and from there it was downhill into the Rue

Dauphine. The Rue Dauphine led to the Café Buci, the pavement was smooth and wouldn't hurt my knees, and by the time I had puked down the Rue de l'Ancienne Comédie and had restored myself in a cheap grill called the Bar Pyrénées, I would be able to reach the Carrefour de l'Odéon safely where I could decompose at will. Besides that, the Square du Vert-Galant was nearby where the island came to its sharp final point. The tree of spring was there, and a little park with benches; and for those suffering from that sickness unto death there was the cobbled bank of the river itself. So it was settled.

I took the last room on the top floor in the farthest corner, wedged between the flatness of two walls. The windows looked out onto the prospect of three drainage pipes, and the outer walls went down on every side like the shafts of a well. There was a window across the way, within the shaft directly opposite, and at first I had the illusion that it was a mirror in my own room. Behind a netting of transparent gauze, I made out the figure of a girl lying in her little bed, face slightly raised and peering down as if reading the embroidery on her pillow slips.

I dropped onto the bed fatigued. Very little sun ever came to this room and it was in semidarkness now, heaped with the outlines of furniture. I stripped to my underwear, propped up a roll of pillow and fell righteously asleep. Naturally I dreamt of being trapped, woke up, quickly dressed, and found I couldn't unlock the door. I had been given two keys which one used in mysterious combination, but I couldn't do it. I turned on the light, but it only made the problem yellow. I shuffled around, muttered a few endearments, bled my palms. I was tremendously hungry and the hotel had a small café with a wonderful view of some workers widening the road. I had to get down there and eat something so I could move my bowels. "Hey," I said, "I can't open the door." I rattled the knob a few times. "Hey, this door is stuck." I decided not to call for help and fell down on the bed again. The girl behind the gauze netting had hardly moved, but she seemed to be reading her linen more carefully now. She had a small nose and light hair, eyes too close together, red worn fingers. It was impossible to see how tall she was. If she would only stand up, so I said "Hello kid," and stood up myself. I walked to the window and pulled it up. "I'm sorry baby, but I'm locked in my goddamn room here." She didn't answer; she was busy reading her towels now. "Look I'm sorry honey, but I'm ... listen, why don't you go down to the desk and send up the old broad ... or maybe just you come over here ... room 32 ... see the knob won't budge... of all things." Her head came up but she stared right through me. "It's ridiculous," I said happily. Her head went down again like a drop of water. She inspected the pillow, then the vista of her quilt and top sheet. "We'll go down the Bar Pyrénées for the big *saucisson toulouse,*" I grinned, with just the spice of an edge on my voice. She had begun to sniff some of the woodwork near her mattress. Her head disappeared. "Come on sugar, don't you want one of them big *saucisson toulouse's* ? hunh ?"

"Rape," she said.

"Wha ?"

"Don't," she said.

"Oh wait say look I think I can open the door," I said and worked the keys desperately and was out in the street in no time.

When I came back, she was still there on the bed sniffing fabrics. So I learned to be quiet. Whenever I made a sudden noise, or stepped on a bad floor board, her head would go down out of sight. In the mornings when I shaved or rattled a glass, she would scream "Pillage !" or if I accidently wound my clock she'd howl "Enough ! Enough !" I caught on quickly : I hid my pencil sharpener within the week, and my shoehorn too.

Three

The myth of the Quarter was not the Paris myth I had come to find. It was the fairy tale myth I wanted, full of things I had been reading all my life, much of it in translation. I wanted the grand cliché with all its legendary trimmings : wild drunks in Montmartre, jumping in fountains near the Ritz, riding on vegetable carts through Les Halles, watching the world go by at the Dôme or the Select.

But the myth had withered to a purple dust in my absence, jumping into fountains only got you wet and arrested, and the party in the Rue Férou was long over. Ah, to get into the index of somebody's biography, I would have thrown it all away for that; but time left me nothing to bargain with and the only choice now was to ferret out some kind of personal mythology and make do. Should I throw a brick through the window of a Wimpy Bar ? maybe swim across a goldfish pond in the Tuileries ? start a May Day riot in front of Le Drugstore ? These were the only myths available, but of course they had no taste.

Sometimes, I'd go on scavenger hunts : bring back a hair from Alice B. Toklas's stubble, note the stains where Toulouse-Lautrec vomited down a wall in Pigalle, put some air from Napoleon's tomb in a bottle. Why I could almost hear Huysmans, all agiggle, performing a black mass in the towers of the St. Sulpice, and Oscar Wilde was laughing hysterically astride Epstein's sphinx (sidesaddle). But it never worked out, the pilgrimage was all sham.

Yet one afternoon, in the American Express, I almost had what was left of it. I stood at mid-chamber, staring at an enchanting, petite woman, almost a girl. She had whirls of blonde hair tucked beneath a kerchief and she wore sneakers which spoiled the incredible sight of her legs. I was the only person in the American Express that day who knew that she was Yvette Mammri, girl starlet, secretly married. She was leaning against an information desk some yards away, looking dumbly at the floor, biting at a hangnail,

mouth sour in a half pout. Then she looked up. I grinned
and she bit her lip. She fumbled in her straw purse for
sunglasses and, suddenly disguised as an entity, there she
was, oblivious and relaxed, the screen idol caught at rest.
I could see that I was being worked to help her along, so I
reached into my jacket pocket, plucked free my clip-ons,
and adjusted our relationship on the spot. We stood there
for a time, each of us watching ravenously from behind our
points of shelter, then she broke into a whimpering smile,
thin but real. I shrugged my shoulders like part of the
game, and she *drifted towards me,* putting her warm elbow
beside mine on the counter.

"Yvette ?" She didn't turn to look at me, but a bubble
of foam appeared on her mouth and she giggled. It was a
fine soft giggle, a great giggle, a trifle hoarse but clean all
through. We were involved, something was happening, I
was part of the Tales to be told. The vision began to form
quickly : Yvette Mammri and I at Maxim's, and afterward
a carriage ride through Trocadéro and then the boat ride
down the Seine travelling to St-Germain-en-Laye, where
we take a villa for the week. We are romping through the
woods in the country light, scraping the green mould from
the trees, watching the horses train on the lawns, asking the
keepers of châteaux for the key to the red room.

The bubble on her mouth burst and she made a squeaky
sound. There was a café around the corner in the Rue
Auber and I began to build towards that. To take the first
step was to take them all. From the café around the corner
we would begin a life together, documented by Suzy and
sanctioned by Elsa Maxwell (may she rest in peace). I
wiggle through life in a state of grace; we always drink
champagne on the road to Nice; we lie on the beach at
Biarritz praying to the gods of pleasure for supple body and
Ethiopian smile; we are beautiful people and our times are
gay; I make a fortune at the blackjack tables in Monaco and
start a new season at Torremelinos by the sea; I begin to
eat incense and spoil my beautiful talent; Yvette goes mad
and must be committed; I dissipate and disappear in a lovely
lost pose. So there I was.

Then I heard a piercing cry from a deep corner of the place and Yvette Mammri's secretly married husband, bald, with a huge blue ascot tucked to his chin, raced across the floor. "Yves Yves," he said, and it was over. In my vision of St-Germain-en-Laye, a horse manured, the red room was pink with age, the woods smelled of dead squirrel. The myth walked out of the American Express with a fat little man.

Four

The Carrefour de l'Odéon is the centre of the Quarter. Streets run in and out of it in a great rush towards dark corners and deep whispers and cul-de-sacs; anyone who has been there remembers the iron gratings of the shops at night, the flat line of grills and hotels, the smell of urine and sperm, the deep gutters, posters, alleys, garbage, all of it made into a fiction by a maze of shadows.

I was hungry and took a late supper at the Petite Source. There were tables outside, but the weather was bad and the chairs had been piled on the wet table tops. I had some chips and a great black sausage and cheap wine that you try to drink without tasting. There were a lot of people in the Petite Source and no one I knew, so I ate quickly. Then I wandered across the Square towards the Café Monaco where I had vague connections.

The Café Monaco is enclosed within a diagonal cut of the Rue Monsieur le Prince, shielded from the sight of the Carrefour with its Métro station and luminous clock by geography and insight. A few faces were familiar. I entered the place, as brilliantly lit as an extermination centre, and joined the noise. I had to talk. "You order a demi, then you sit forever," I yelled at the first face. But the Café Monaco is a special kind of eternity because it is so small. It does not have the neon grandeur of the Relais Odéon, or the deluxe tone of things ominous like La Pergola. "It nestles like a bright bead of sweat," I said, not yet calm, "a crack in the wall, a slight disorder." At the bar, people were shouting at each other; at the top of the stairs, a woman readied herself for a reckless trip to the toilet; at the windows, faces pressed towards the tables in pale puckers.

"You are attempting inconsistencies of which you are incapable," I intoned by way of introduction. Nate the Accordion, whom I was to know better, scratched his tattoo with some disdain and with his small blue head motioned for me to be seated. There were three others at the table, each of them staring at his own eyes. They were all slightly annoyed. I had to show my style.

"You are Christlike to a fault," I struck again, this time at a tall, gaunt figure — Hugh Brynning — who looked like an underfed gargoyle. "You know what?" I advanced my attack tellingly, "You know what you look like to me? exactly like an underfed gargoyle." Pause. The toying of spoons.

Brynning meantime was an amazing sight to behold; he had a huge gold earring that hung from the side of his head like a hoop. He was a carpenter and a poet and had just returned from the sea with his friend and appendage, Gordon Gilchrist. Gilchrist sat on his lap like a tiny growth. He wore the other earring and to a private vision on the ceiling he extolled the effects of mescaline which he had never had. He was short and square and I said triumphantly, "You know, you look like a rectangle with an internal disorder." He giggled defensively and, bless him, he was hurt.

They were discussing their infamous folly of the week before. Nate, now older than most and a veteran of illusion, shook his head sadly, his body meanwhile dropsical in a slight paunch. Yvonne sat by his right hand as if to cast a shadow and swung her great domestic breasts in sorrow; she was large and Danish and looked like two dwarfs kissing. "Say, you know what you look like . . ." "Shhhhhhhh !"

It was all about the fatal equation and it had ruined their hindsight. Brynning squeezed Gilchrist's elbow and Gilchrist

went "tweak." "And I bought them the blasted beers," said
Nate. "But I agreed with them," said Brynning, "that was
the real trouble; I didn't give them a franc's worth but I
said *yes;* Gordie too." Gordie grinned impishly, but it came
out sublime; his head jerked to one side coyly, balanced on
a thick stump of neck peppered with freckles like tiny
cancers, supporting a perch of red hair flaked with debris.
He looked like a bag of sand.

I ordered a round of demis to assure them of my interest,
and they told me the story in all its tragic beauty. "Well,"
said Nate, "last week two men came into the Monaco and
said they had come upon it. Yvonne asked . . . What have
you come upon please? Truth, they said, Truth proved
mathematically. For a year we've worked on simplifying
Truth to an equation. I am Bill and this is Will. Truth by
fractions, Truth by numbers; it's very possible and we almost
have it. We'll make a million and live forever. Forever?
asked Yvonne; yes, they said, we've just got to put it down,
we're almost there, it's only a matter of time."

"Jesus," sighed Brynning; "sigh Gordie." Gordie sighed.

"I'll admit I was interested," said Nate, "So each evening
in they came with their pencils and pads, Bill and Will,
writing furiously and tearing up paper — but not a franc on
them; so I bought them beers the whole week and at night
we went to the Café Tournon and I bought them sandwiches.
Yvonne said to me it was amazing their love for the problem.
Look at them eat and drink, she said, why we'll all live
forever and be rich. She gave herself to them freely; it was
very touching."

"I want to go to India," said Gordon Gilchrist, "land of
mescaline and magic." Brynning slapped him tenderly on
the neck and evoked a whimper. Yvonne was in silent tears;
her body quivered like an avalanche.

"Oh we believed in them," said Nate, "and then one
Friday night they came in with a sheaf of paper and said
We've done it, just one more decimal point and carry the
two. I bought them wine and we all gathered round; it was
an investment now. Bill said you show it to them Will and
Will got up from his chair and downed his wine and said

here it is and thank you friends and he threw a slip of paper on the table that said $S/H = I/T$ and they ran out of the Monaco and into the street and nobody's seen them since."

Nate plucked at his thinning hair; he stroked his tattoo — a dark orange heart in the threatening shape of a woman's behind, credo *In The Beginning* in sperm white.

"Awful," moaned Brynning. "Let's go to the party." "If I can't go to India," said Gilchrist, "I'll be sad." I tipped the waiter thirty centimes. "All right come along Garber," said Nate.

Five

The party in the Gît-le-Coeur is a quiet fantasy in progress, up some winding stairs where the windows look out onto the halls, into a tiny room sloping eastwards like a runway. Everyone seems caught in a frieze as we enter, an assembly of arms and legs in various poses of rest; and beneath tables and bulbs, on boxes, dressers, cots, stools, there is a settling of white and yellow smoke. Some of the following are present :

Eugene M., known among his own as Bobby E Lee. He is lazy but that is not all. He comes from Manchester where his father is chief of police, and he sells dope. He wants desperately to come from the American south and he has a Louisiana drawl that is quite pleasant. He is a natural pimp. He pimps for cigarettes and he pimps for opinions. "Y'gowatt a cig, Pawla ?" But he is innocent and wears a Huckleberry Finn hat and toeless running shoes. The loves of his life are primarily from Kentucky, young plump girls who have money and find him cute. He *is* cute. He ploughs them for dinners and arranges allowances. However, he is a virgin and he does not exactly plough them, he just pulls at the grass a bit. If his belt buckle could conceive, he would be the legend he craves. It is true that when excited by women his forefinger stiffens. He gives the impression of brilliance disordered, but he is a calculating simpleton. He is lying on the one bed with his head on the one pillow and his arms about the one sheet. When he smiles he looks as if he were waiting for puberty to pass the rest of the way through him. He is likeable but untrustworthy. In the gloom I can see his small eyes thinking. He often tells the story of the man who came up to his place to shoot heroin, mainlined, dropped dead. Poor Bobby E Lee, boy saint, waited till nightfall, picked up the body, staggered to the Quai des Grands Augustins, and dropped it in the Seine. He wears sungoggles.

Sandra Y, white hope of the American Midwest. Her eyes are always sad and no amount of laughter is convincing. Her body is full of wonderful puffs and recesses and there is a latent goddess in her somewhere. Where her brow touches her nose there is a gentle frown line, and when her lips kiss her teeth there is a sucking noise. Everyone is rapaciously fond of Sandra Y for she is an affectionate creature; you feel that if you lit the top of her head she would burn like a candle and form a pool of wax about your feet. She confronts life with a stunned purr and has a talent for feeling sated. She plucks salvation from the slightest pretext and is easily man's best friend. One approaches her with warmth and leaves full of a little talk. A week before, she was passing through Paris on her way to Strasbourg to meet her fiancé; she came accidentally to the Café Monaco and met everyone easily. They took her to a club in the Rue Mazarine where Jules the Seducer plays the guitar and sings through his nose. She was enraptured; it is her way of life. He offered her marijuana in his room, and she thought that would be thrilling and new. It was. She did not come down for three days. When she did she was very different. When Jules held his café conferences to extol and grade her charms, the voyeurs drew pictures, the writers took notes, and Bobby E Lee went straight to bed. At the moment, Sandra Y is sitting on the arm rest of a small chair, somewhat in a daze. However, within minutes, she will run away with a gypsy to Tangiers.

Stephen U, last vestige of Imperial Britain. His face is that of an Anglo-Saxon warrior who has just umlauted. His head is covered with an enormous shock of straw-blonde hair combed straight over his forehead at great expense. He has a car. It sets him apart from the rabble and allows him to be fickle. He has been educated at Cambridge, is a student of the Opera, and goes constantly barefoot. Whenever he speaks, ancient inflections bubble forth. He is by nature a social lion, and he spends his days in an orgy of teas, beers, luncheons; he is on the telephone continuously from the first light of day, arranging meetings, exchanging gossip, contriving noon and evening. He is a creature of rendezvous : the park beneath the Eiffel Tower but not the Champ de Mars, the top three steps of the Sacre Coeur, the pissoir to the south of the Métro Cluny, beneath the clock beside the wall along the soccer field three blocks east of Marcadet-Poissoniers. At his best, he has that restful complacency of the Englishman; he finds women inconvenient, and is "just barely able really" to do his duty. He leaps into love holding his nose. Hate or disgust would be a breach of etiquette : it is the *maître d'* in him. Still, he has moments of hysteria. His car is wanted by the Paris police; he has been hiding it on sheltered sidewalks and cavernous alleyways, but he knows his days are numbered and he is trying to organize an excursion to the Loire Valley. For Stephen U is a paragon of habit : he has been to the Loire half a dozen times, but since he now knows the way nothing else will do. As we appear, he is standing by the window, stage rear, counting the chimneys; when he is finished, he will scratch his toe.

Bonnie, maternal scavenger from some unnoticed place. As a rule I am particular. Cleanliness is next to godliness and Bonnie is filthy. She is filthy in a deliberate way, by way of ornament; her neck is preserved in dry, caked mud and her feet smell like old turnips. The texture of her skin is a study in five o'clock shadow, with the faintest suggestion of moles and berries from mucus to toenail, but she is pretty

and humble and her nostril wings flutter to show compassion.
Her body is not profound. Indeed, she is quite thin and
breastless and possesses a perpetual tremor like that of a
child wrapped in cold water; her face is as narrow as a pane
of glass. Bonnie is a collector of inanimate things; in bouts
of monomania, she walks the streets in search of "something
nice". Her room is a shrine of stones, cans, bits of paper;
there is an ecstasy of old, discarded postcards jammed
methodically into an upright folder, spread or fanned like
a deck of cards. Biweekly, she visits post offices in each
arrondissement and makes a careful study of gutter and
doorway in hopes of a crumpled trophy. Such as, "Dear
Freddie : London odd experience for us. Since only sexual
not good idea. Don't want to see you again. Please don't
write or phone (VAN 2772). What do you think ? Yours,
J." Or, a wiser treasure salvaged from the curb of the Rue
Vignon : "Nu ? Two months not a smell ?" There is
something further about Bonnie that forces men to regard
her not so much as a woman but as a tendency; not her
unhygienic habits or her monomania, but a bland style, a
nice remoteness, as if she were only layers of surface peel,
check points, perforations. She has a fringe quality. Vangrin
the famous writer once wrote a play about two lovers in bed;
he cast the parts himself and chose two transvestites so they
could act as each other's understudy. Bonnie disapproved
and is unpopular. That does not mean that she is not
well-liked.

Trixy, anchorite anonymous. It is curious where prejudice
begins. Trixy may easily have been a fund of mystery and
enjoyment, but Nate says, grabbing my elbow, "If you took
all the faith she has ever had in anyone and shoved it up
her ass, there'd still be room for her to be the whore she is."
So Trixy, smiling demurely into cold space, becomes forever
the epitome of deception.

Fitz, tall and West Indian. Fitz is an abortionist. He is
tall and likes parties. He stays under tables because he is
too tall for small rooms. He steals purses. He will not
steal purses from anyone he does not love, but he loves
easily; he restricts his crimes to the Paris Métros, deuxième

classe. He performs abortions often and uses a sterilized bicycle pump; to assure us of his credentials, he carries a CCM certificate. He is well-liked; we all like him. He wants to go to Mannheim Germany so he can say "Mannheim, Man." He says it now, but he knows it is not the same thing. He pimps for Germans in the Quarter hoping for a letter of introduction. He often pays their way, wine and meals and dancing at the caves in the Rue de la Huchette, but the best he has done is a letter of introduction to a carpenter in Stuttgart. He cures syphilis with herbs gathered at high noon on the banks of the Rhône river. He can be trusted with confidences and, at the Café Buci he sits at the centre of a huge complex of information like a great dark bird settled warmly, wings aflutter, incubating hopes and enmities and dreams. He knows where everyone is and what everyone is doing and to sit with him for a beer is to have entered the medium. He has a good smile and it is said that he is gentle in his operations; he has never lost a patient though he has shredded a few wombs in his time. He is in partial view beneath a table; he wants desperately to go to Mannheim, but he will run away with Nora to Tunisia instead. She will contract dysentery and they will not be happy.

Anne the Pregnant, very and often. She is immense : huge, wide, deep, grand, round and infinite. She bathes daily in a minute porcelain tub, seated on its low partition with the lukewarm water bobbing to her knees, her great arms dangling from either side in an ecstasy of comfort. Her knees are bent in a great span of bone; her toes are well-groomed and curled to a point like isosceles triangles drawn to scale; her thighs are unexpectedly swift, undiscoloured, with no trace of down; her pubis is a thick lump of flesh, rigid in a parody of erection, weaving a vast mat of hair shaped like an arrowhead, as if in mime : "refer to navel"; her navel is a great, puckered cul-de-sac, devouring wrinkles like a tiny mouth closed tight; her belly is more than vaguely swollen, yet hard and globular like a petrified paunch, and under that sheath of stretched skin a hint of something membranous, perhaps a wad of blood and cartilage, or the cold and slippery writhings of a great fish; her breasts drop arrogantly from their cleavage like the bifurcated cheeks of a child's behind, splattered with nipple from forefront to droop; her face is a collision of points and angles and little twitches, medium thick lips, nose sharp and flared, eyes of indestructible black; and so on, quickly noting the heart-shaped skull, expansive forehead, and rich dark hair jerked neatly upright in a bun as if built around a sprinkler. Unfortunately, no one has ever seen her nude and this description has merely been handed down from clique to clique like a faith. She sits in the Café Monaco in an austere, almost royal, silence, a showcase of mystic bulges. There is a dumbness to her that is terrifying because she is so large. Her eyes give you back the stare with a steady cold insensateness, alert as the sheets you die in. "Is anybody home?" but there is no response except occasional silent urps of gas. She likes to stroke the thing in her belly as if to make it grow; some say it never does. Yet she has hired Fitz to tend to her needs. He won't talk. Except, of course, to discuss her dreams; there is only one, recurring monthly, about a pubic hair trapped in a test tube; it coils and lashes. "An' that's it, it just lay there, man, wigglin' round." Is she pregnant? will Fitz fix her up? is her body a miracle? can she talk? Religions die hard. She sits on a low hassock behind the door as we pass in, monumentally boned, impossible. For this is the night that Maynard Duncan conceives his passion; he kneels at her lap, rests his elbow on her colossal flank and smiles. She looks at his essential touch as if it is poison, and makes a chilling motion. He moves off as if burned, and later he sneaks out and races down streets and across bridges towards her apartment; he wants some sign, some relic to cool him down, a talisman. An hour later he comes back empty-handed, shaking, pale. "Holy shit, she got stirrups on her bidet!" he screams.

Emmanuel the Spanish, last of the Gottlieb Furies. He is beige-coloured and blonde-haired, pug-nosed and blue-eyed, sallow-lipped, with big ears and a dumb smile. There is a false tone of violence in the way he moves, shoulders over chest, fists by hips, legs in a lean, wheeling grace; which means nothing. He will fight if he has to and he has to because he is annoying, but he bruises easily. He has the interminable gift of sincerity, a backlog of confessions without end, except that he is not Spanish at all, just a Canadian with tanned boots from Castille. This he does not confess. He speaks in translation, filtering his good English through a school Spanish into another English that is literal, broken and inflected. He wears a black sombrero with a small red feather, that is too big for his head; it casts a deep shadow across his face which he knows how to use. He is the compleat mystic; this is an image it has taken him a year to construct and his sphere of superstition is the Gottlieb. Gottliebs are pinball machines; they are in all the cafés in Paris and are manufactured by Gottlieb and Company of Chicago, Illinois, and not to be confused with the Rogers machine in all the cafés in the provinces and manufactured by Rogers and Company of Philadelphia, Pennsylvania. Emmanuel the Spanish plays the Gottlieb morning and evening, as close to dawn and dusk as necessary, and he has arranged a series of signs and countersigns that foretell his future; it is an exotic kind of palmistry or teacup reading, and he swears by it. If the ball bearing triggers up the alley but rolls back again, that is the worst possible sign : he will sleep for the day. If the ball bearing triggers onto the playing surface but skims straight down the slot, that is almost as bad : he will sit quietly in his room till nightfall. If the ball bearing hits good lights and high buttons again and again in an immortal way, that is an excellent omen : he will follow through his day naturally, with no sweat. If he has astonishing luck with the flippers, that is the best of all occurrent things and leads to free games ("the hand and the flipper are one") : he will allow himself personal relations, vulnerable commitments and sexual congress. He goes into lunatic rages whenever he beholds those who use their Gottliebs in vain by padding the leg of their machines to prevent the tilt and keep the surface level. That sort of infidelity leads to inquisitions and reprisals; for Emmanuel the Spanish, let it be known, is full of honour and a great need to shit. He suffers honorably from Barcelona stomach and claims it as his heritage. He has been arrested several times for discommoding Rogers machines, and he wears with awful pride the cloak of a gendarme stolen from a pill box on the Quai des Orfèvres. However, he is from Northern Ontario. He betrays this virtue by peculiar idioms: everyone is "kinda lovely," or a "perfect guy"; followed self-consciously by the quick return to form, "I tell you of this especial thing without obscenity." He is standing, veiled nicely in cloak and sombrero, one Castilian boot on the sill; he looks out the window, raises an index finger and intones, "perfect gloom".

Cheryl, white beauty from the Carolinas, both North and South. She is tall and gangly like a Long Sam. Her face and body have the eerie whiteness of chalk and her features are uncommonly regular; she is a cliché of loveliness, everything in its ordered place like a finished puzzle. Yet there is something inscrutable and bizarre even in that, as if the castle had been demolished to build the ramparts. She has always tried to gain through love and pity what Sandra Y is about to lose through same; at the moment, however, their lives happen to coincide and there is little difference between them coming and going. She has been used so often and so callously by so many men from Gibraltar to Florence that, in her tragedy, she is beginning to resemble a garbage disposal unit. In Florence, when she had money, she rented a studio where she gazed quietly at walls; she discovered and adopted two jazz musicians, both addicted to heroin and unable to afford it. She succumbed gently to their eccentricities. When the money was gone, musician A committed suicide by swallowing a bottle of perfume and musician B was taken away to an institution for the mentally retarded. Cheryl forgave them their trespasses, bought a secondhand scooter in Rome and scooted alone across Europe. At the French frontier, she veered off the road and lay in the ditch for half a day. The concussion remains, and her image as a woman of the road is ruined. More than that, she is a victim of Jules the Seducer, one of his pet triumphs; she is already his used and discarded project, but she still blushes when he enters a room — an unexpected dividend. She is standing impaled against the wall as we approach her, entrenched in deep solitude; Jules, in a far corner among friends ignores her with ease and indifference. Her sense of tragedy is just right, a trick of the imagination. I'd tell you more, but she has suffered enough.

Six

Our Amusements Are Simple

Cheryl against the wall, Fitz beneath the table, Anne the Pregnant behind the door, Bobby E Lee on the bed : a lovely mosaic indeed. And there were others massed within the tiny room, congealed, immobile : Brynning, Gilchrist, Nate the Accordion, Yvonne, Bugs, Jeanette the hostess, Nora, Burkey and Dalia, two American boys who had slipped in unnoticed, two Scottish girls, Debbie and Briar, who had been brought gratis by Jules the Seducer, Henry Rotter, Nora's albino perched on the eaves trough, Alice and Dan, Blackie and Jackie, E. Bone and Irma, Maynard Duncan, Vangrin the famous writer, Valentine and her whore Dee.

With a proper sense of form, Stephen U tipped bare-toed across the room to greet us, and introduced me to the hostess, Jeanette. She was a tall, frail Englishwoman with a severe, suspicious tone and nobody's fool. The others passed into the party easily, but my way was blocked at the door and Jeanette spread one sinewy arm like a chainlock across the entrance. I exchanged a few remarks with her and stepped over the threshold; but she turned sharply as I passed her, fixed me with a stare, and grabbed my arm.

"Garber, you are glib."

"I feel fine, honey."

"No, you are really glib."

"Feeling no pain."

"You're disgusting."

"You just don't know me dear."

"Can't you take constructive criticism."

"Sure, try me."

"Garber, you're a shit."

I liked Jeanette; there was a wonderful economy about her as if she were trying desperately to save the last parts of herself for something better than she deserved. "Water Conservation," I said. "Don't tell me your secrets yet," she said.

Then I was in the room. Everyone seemed involved in slow suggestive conversation as if advancing their own separate plots. Each mouth was pursed with a private joke; every little secret was swallowed raw. For instance, Vangrin the famous writer (author of *The Case of The Latent Lady*) was explaining it all to Blackie and Jackie, that sweet coy Quarter couple — she in leotards and sleeveless cashmere sweater, he beginning a new beard while wearing a sheepskin vest, sawed-off khakis and plastic sandals. Vangrin was dried up (strategically) like a Moroccan prune, drizzling talk like a small gray cloud, standing at a noble tilt like a figure of speech. You could hear the suction of his mouth as he formed the words. And in the middle of the floor, hunched forward like a major league catcher, was Bugs with a full bag of marijuana grain, rolling joints at great speed and spreading them on a small mat in neat, single rows. His eyes were so narrow they met at the bridge of his nose and formed one enormous bulb, socketed deep as if within a lamp. His jaw was not hinged properly and shivered at the prospect of his decline. He had a small pipe cleaner which scooped out tobacco; his fingers were deceptively agile, such agile fingers were impossible to imagine, they had already deceived the rest of his hand. His tongue emerged to test the air; his cheeks trilled in a resonant happy purr, and grain by grain he stuffed the *Gitanes* full. A long red-nailed toe inquisitively thrust itself into his plans. It had a single hair, looped like a streamer; its rind was composed of six segments, each one individually clean and white; it twitched conversationally, nicely cuticled, but a ball of dirt was lodged in its root. Bugs paused in his craft,

stared awhile, pronounced it intact, then scooped it out and
stuffed it into the cigarette. "Whirrrr," he purred, then lit
the sausage end and honked with glee.

"Burkey wants to meet you," said Brynning through his
long, narrow face. I stumbled over a few people and came
to the wall. Burkey was uninteresting and wore a toupee
and wouldn't talk. But he had a woman with him, Dalia,
middle-aged, kinky-blonde hair, motherly bosom, nice bridge-
work smile. There was that curious two-dimensional quality
about her as there was about everyone else, as if she were
a device or a standard exemplifying some particular wage
of sin. She was suffering; her whole face was a mask of
suffering. Her head was raised and tilted back restfully
against the wall to still the pain, while Burkey held her by
the waist somewhat clumsily. The small thistle of fat at her
throat hung like a pendulum. "Burkey," she groaned, "take
me to a toilet. If you love me you'll take me to a toilet."
Burkey only smiled weakly. "There must be a toilet in the
hotel," I said. Burkey's smile grew weaker; it was his only
source of comfort. Dalia writhed against the wall as if
trying to erase herself. "Not here, Burkey," she groaned,
"not that. No holes in the floor darling; I need a toilet, a
porcelain place. I couldn't go through the other again; don't
make me straddle the hole; it goes down my leg; all the way
down; it's no good. A toilet with a seat, oh please lover,
with a flush handle." "Let's take her," I said to Brynning,
but he gave me the sign. "Not for a while yet," said Dalia,
"let me rest for a little while. Who's that nice man, Burkey ?
Such nice young people."

I passed a brief conversation between Nate the Accordion
and Jeanette. Jeanette's lips were curled in disgust, waiting
to drop their mother lode of malice, while Nate seemed to
skirt the line of talk, artfully dodging to miss the venom.

Somewhere in the lukewarm murk, Yvonne stood, then
sat. Her face was piggish, but had its charm; and she
possessed a certain elephantine grace. The two American
boys saw this and descended on her like vultures. If she
was the ugliest girl there, they figured, then she was probably
the easiest too. It was simple American logic. They began

to make their pitch in low, buzzing tones, circling for carrion. Unfortunately, she was still alive.

Beside me, someone opened a window. The sickly sweet smell of pot spun out into the air; a large hairless leg, at the apex of which a rectum sighed, straddled the sill and filtered the breeze through its toes. That was Nora, brilliant red hair and lips of purple, who had just returned from the toilet and was very wet. She had not mastered the art of the French toilet because she was too tired. Instead she had removed her frayed, crotch-torn jeans to dry. She lived with a seventeen-year-old albino who had pink eyes and hunted mice at night. She had brought it to the party, but, because the room was so small, it had been put out on the eaves trough, and I could see it watching windows across the vast evening gloom.

"I'm Blackie," said Blackie, "and this is Jackie." They were both short, fawning, awestruck people. Jackie had an oval face that kept jiggling with the pleasure of your company; her smile was touched off nicely by yellow teeth and a pleated nose. Blackie was a nice little guy with a bad handshake and it was apparent that they made love with the lights on. "Joris Vangrin," he sang, "this is . . ." "Jarrbay," I explained, "Laurent Jarrbay : of the crack Abyssinian cavalry." "You are a horseman ?" asked Vangrin, shredding a hangnail to make me seem tiresome. "In the Kumar campaign we rode a rare form of mountain troll," I said, "hunchbacked, with a minimum of sweat." "A difficult thing to believe," said Vangrin, his voice careful. "The trolls were put through an extensive training program," I continued, "the object being to dehumanize their capacity for love; they now think they are mules and go south in the winter." "I am not startled," said Vangrin, horrified at the prospect of being conned, "these things happen. Shall I tell him my latest watchword ?" and he turned to the faithful with a melancholic air. They nodded excitedly. "Well then, the bon mot is this : My Tense Is The Present Imperfect."

"Take one," said Bugs, out of his crouch and leaning

forward with a newly created joint. He was making half-strength *cocktails* now, to conserve his depleted store, but even the part-*Gitane* weed went down like pieces of burning glass. "Don't just stare, man, go ahead, it's paid for." I wouldn't keep the smoke in my lungs and fine nets of fume encircled my head like a halo. "Je-zuz, don't waste it!" groaned Bugs, appalled at the sacrilege; he waved the smoke into his own face and inhaled furiously.

There was a faint, amused glaze to Brynning's eye as he watched. Gilchrist hung from his elbow like a bracelet; his smile was rounder, fuzzier, as if his goodness had sprouted hair. In fact, they were all smiling now; it was an epidemic of smiles. Even Jeanette smiled. And Bobby E Lee on the bed had half-closed his eyes behind tinted goggles, and his lids were little puffs of red, worn tissue. He had the two Scottish girls, Debbie and Briar, seated one at each end of the bed like figurines; he spoke to them in his lazy southern drawl, tasting his own words as if they came coated with mint julep. The girls were young, perhaps nineteen, and Briar had long tanned legs, brisk in the calf, and wore no stockings. They were not smoking, but they were watching Bobby E Lee go under with surgical interest; there was a cold sense of mockery between them, a nasty pact that little girls make in the face of something threatening. But Bobby E Lee was too charmed by his own circumstance to notice it, and he plied them gamely with revelations, inducements, fake interest. They would listen to him awhile, wrapt in the spectacle of his idiocy, then catch each other's eye and begin to giggle; Bobby E Lee would mistake this for embarrassment and indecision and flute his voice soothingly. The thing was, he wanted to see their navels; he was a master of navels; he had seen every navel in the room; he was an extraordinary judge of them; it was a hobby. Debbie was heavy set and large in the leg, so it was Briar he wanted with her tiny button of a navel all sewn-in and shy. "Wi gowtta cowm-pahr," he said; "itzza rewl, y'all see?" Briar at the foot of the bed tied his shoelaces together; he was some fun.

"Now that isn't nice, girls," said Jules the Seducer, as if

it *was* wonderful and we all knew it . "Poor Bobby," he said, as if stroking every leg in the room, "such a sweet guy." "I'm Debbie," said Debbie, twisting her girdled buttocks to make a place for him. He had an injured look, did Jules. "Debbie" he said, deep in thought for he had brought them both, "Debbie. Why you must be Debbie," he said, "which is probably short for Deborah, a lovely name." "From Tayport," said Debbie. "Ahhhh what a typical product of Scotland you are," said Jules, but refusing the place beside her. "Well hell, Jules," I said, coming up behind him "it's a pretty underdeveloped country." Debbie froze, then disemboweled me with a look of stone. "Don't mind my cynical friend here," said Jules, putting an arm around my shoulder. "My daddy used to say to me, son (he always called me son), the trouble with cynics is they're not close to nature." Debbie agreed on the spot. I said something to Briar but she returned it with a blank, un-inquisitive look. Jules walked away still leading me by the shoulder and we put ourselves against the wall. "Look Mac don't cut into my action okay," he said, fallen from grace into something cold and steady. "Hell, her ?" I grinned. "It's exercise," he said, "so cut." "Sure okay sorry Jules."

Dan, the rich boy from Boston, and Alice, who needed his money, were being enjoyed by a few people as they conjured sweet nothings near the mantle. They were both nasty, practical people who would not waste time with anyone but each other; and, in a sense, they were lovely people to watch. He played the unmoved mover, and she was a Shylock of more than flesh. Their eyes on each other were blank and remote without a hope of pleasure; and their insular arrangement was envied and mulled over as if they were the demigods of *Photoplay*. As if parodying them, Jeanette was talking to Henry Rotter, the great good friend of Jules the Seducer. Her head was bowed with attention as Henry half-whispered, half-rasped, his face tight, contorted, as if trapped forever in a bubble of pain. But Jeanette was softer with him than she had been with Nate; her voice rose in scale to gentleness. "And Henry," she said, unburdening herself of some philanthropic warmth, "you've got to stand on your own two feet : don't play the patsy; you're no wide-eyed fink; you've got a great deal to offer : offer it." "I know I know," said Henry Rotter. "Oh I know."

For the first few hours the party was very slow and dull, the heavy smoke and the small closed-in room, the hot sweaty faces and the sluggish posing creating a dumb, un-eventful mood. But nearer to midnight it went faster and all the people went faster so that finally it was like trying to crush a moving escalator beneath your foot to keep any equilibrium with the smoke inside and the smoke outside and the smell everywhere. The shapes of the heads changed and then the smiles on the hot sweaty faces grew cavernous, gleaned of stock responses; the noises trebled and merged, terrifically pitched and grating; whoops and crashes and shrieks upon shrieks, like a sound bank, released themselves in thunderous, quaking volume to cut towards the little seed of sober doubt still functioning. The hot sweaty faces, armed with their hot sweaty red noses and their wet reflecting jaundiced foreheads, floated above the innumerable shoulders as if scrambling for air; lisps and farts and squawking questions tangled for leverage in the humid, stale room. Briar : her face at a middle distance was such an open charming face with sharp tiny nose and slabs of beige ear that pierced her hair; and the closer you got the more of a tunnel it became; a trick face becoming a corridor as you pursued it; the malleable, shifting flesh conning you into the slot. What was needed was a subtle approach, a smooth even margin of finesse and no hesitation. So "hi-having-a-nice-time-my-God-I-feel-good-how-bouts-you-Briar-that's-it-what-does-Briar-mean-in-the-long-run-Briar-Briarrrralalalala-I-gonna-be-sick-help." I leaned over for she was at a decided angle and grabbed her leg so nice and tanned; she was warm too, she must have been in a warm climate, and that long hair oh so nice; I stroked that too and she didn't move, didn't stop me but didn't move, maybe a little on the numb side, it happens; so I bent down and kissed her on the lips very chapped and not too thick, very pink, and nibbled on the lips umumum; that did it apparently. Oh I felt good, oh that was good, could I sit down, just shove over Bobby E Lee's legs, poor Bobby E Lee, and now a better angle flush on the mouth and kiss her throat and take a bite of her throat, nice and brown too like French fried potatoes, no I'd better not say that, look, "I need you." She jerked her head back, moved around like a pig on a spit, oh so warm, such a brown warm Briar, and kiss her again, take one giant step, she tastes like milk or toothpaste, am I growing yet am I coming up yet, I better; oh she's kissing back or just trying to keep from falling and her hand on my neck pulling my hair my lovely nape hair, okay that's it. Stand up with her and hold her deep, right up against it, is it there, Jesus I can't tell, I'm all numbed up, its got to be there; reach down and see : oh brother, thank God thank you God. How about against the wall, just move her back to the wall, out of the glow into the shadow, out of the light into the whispers. "Briar smell so nice," such nice haunch ewwww I can feel her muscles, ladder on her buttocks, vaccination mark, and her supple ass too, I touched her supple ass. Whump whump, "Briar here Briar right here," no I can't do that here; I'll take her into the hall no into the toilet no too many stairs just into the hall. "Oh Briar is that you," Jesus teats are small, nice small Scottish teats. "We're going outside just outside the door," so take her out, whoops, "Sorry Bugs," poor Bugs with no broad, but I got one I do believe Bree-orrrr Brey-er Broor Braaa-ear Booray-are. It's dark out here I want to see, why doesn't she say something, "I'm Larry," oh my darling; am I still intact, good; do it quick or someone will come up the stairs and for god sakes Garb put on the light just press the button and there was light amen. Oh her eyes are closed why won't she kiss me, "oh darling don't leave me," her hands are over her eyes; I'll just do it, stallion bull stud, oh those bare legs just stroke that haunch, one-two, one-two, how can I keep her skirt up, she won't hold it up, "hold it up," well pick up her skirt, oh my darling rubber panties, what does it mean. Hey am I getting soft, no fair God, don't go soft God; so rubber panties big deal. Put your hand down there, fuzzy wuzzy baby, who would have thought she was so hairy when she's so quiet in the face; teach you something about human nature; can't pull them down she won't help me, "help me my little Tayport squirrel," I'll pull the elastic over so I can touch it, hey its dry, oh shit, but that's okay, "Briar oh Briar," spread them apart Briar, oh this is difficult. She's dry I got to hit the button first time, no slipping in, oh where is you darling; I can't undress so zipper gonna hoit her crotch, so what you care, I don't care; can't find her, all tight, legs won't budge, wham wham, oh Briar help me sweetie, "is it as good for you as is for me," whoops, no that's not it, I'm all numb can't feel a thing, it'll hurt me if she's dry, just put it to her standing up, that's it baby, ow ow ow ow, I feel a song coming on, something bee — oot — iful gonna happen, hooked into a piece of her, not much angle, oh this is no good oh shit, if I could . . . *"Listen who-ever you are, not in the hall!"*

My excitement popped like a bubble. Jeanette stood there, sparkling with rage, catching us exposed and locked; Briar's organ had me gripped fast — so unsatisfactory in other ways, yet at this superb — so we stood there like a Pigalle poster splashed on the wall. Jeanette had a good look; it was a cool, measuring gaze that was neither embarrassed nor approving. Its effect was, of course, to sober me on the spot. When the three-minute light blinked off in the hall, I worked my way out of Briar, unscrewing counter-clockwise. *"Inside,"* said Jeanette like a sibyl in the dark. *"It doesn't matter what you do, you people, just do it inside."* Briar still had her hands over her face; there were small spastic tremors in the joints of her body; nothing ecstatic — nerves probably. Jeanette had pushed the light switch again and was watching us; again her look was completely disinterested, almost schoolmarmish in its strange concentration. "Briar darling," I whispered as I zipped my fly with my stomach to the wall; I grazed her forehead with my lips. She stood there without moving. I had stuffed a corner of skirt into her closed, rigid elbow and it remained raised in that squalid manner; her panties had been violently shifted to one side and were obviously torn : a shred of fabric hung down one thigh. I adjusted her panties as best I could and let down her skirt. Jeanette waited until I had passed her, then she followed me into the party proper and slammed the door to with a vengeance.

When I was back in the room, the smoke hit me in thin waves of incense. My stomach went for a ride and settled and tried to heave again. "Give me a joint, Bugs old pal." Bugs felt around on the mat as if it were patterned in braille and gave me the cigarette. "Take it slow with that one," he said. "We just got hashish now; I gotta start on the hashish." "Oh sure," I said, "that's okay Bugs."

I began on the last joint feeling a bit queasy. I had come down so quickly that I was suffering from a case of the bends. Moving from one frequency to another has its pain, and this was a siphoning kind of horror as if my insides were being sucked out of me by the action of a straw.

"I leave in little nooks and corners of the world," Vangrin was intoning, "this single note : To Whom It May Concern : I Am Not Concerned."

Anne the Pregnant still sat silently by the door, body convex in a pose resurrectional.

I crawled under the table on a hunch, and waited. Nothing happened. Eventually Jeanette stooped to me with a smile like the snap of a rubber band.

"What are you doing down there, you glib little bastard ?"

"Looking for legs," I said.

"Green with envy, brimmed with snot," she sang.

I didn't have to take that noise. I emerged from beneath the table to demonstrate my full height. The joint was between my lips, crammed in a flat oval at the corner of my mouth. People were leaving. For private parts unknown. I was filled with that very tight despair which is the result of a hopeless evening. I kissed Jeanette approximately on the mouth but caught her upper lip instead and found myself nibbling on a few coarse bristles. I put the flat of my palm on the cords of her throat and stroked against the grain.

"Save it Garber," said Jeanette, "I'm not interested."

"Oh Jeanette, how come ? huh Jeanette, why Jeanette ?"

"I don't like men as a rule, Garber; not extreme farts like you."

"Don't like men, Jeanette? awwww poor Jeanette. Like women, Jeanette? what do you do with women, huh Jeanette?"

"Not *that* anyway," she said, and I saw something. "I wouldn't go over there," she said. "Let them alone."

"But Duncan's watching."

"He's a friend."

It was Valentine and Dee, undressed in a corner, wrapped together in a sensuous bind. Dee looked like a little boy, but Valentine was big-boned with a lovely body faintly worn and slack. It was like a pornographic slide seen from a bad light; their skins were orange and scarlet, with a suggestion of bruises. Every once in a while, timed to a frequency, they shifted and rolled; they had a spoon, taking turns with it, a spoon, putting it to each other, jabbing, gasping. The smell was incredible.

I wheeled about in a brief stagger. The room was almost empty.

"Where's the party?" I asked.

Maynard Duncan had left his vantage point beside Valentine and Dee to look for a fork.

"I guess I missed the party," I said.

I could hear Dalia moaning behind me and when I turned to see, her hands were on her belly as if to hold up her guts and bowels and bladder. "Oh Burkey Burkey," she groaned from the pit of her emblem, "I need a toilet, oh darling."

I went over to pay my respects. "Did you see the party?" I asked. "It must have passed this way. It was wearing a red hat and sunglasses, but it didn't say a thing."

"Tell that man he's very funny Burkey," said Dalia.

Burkey smiled weakly.

"I may have to laugh," said Dalia. "I don't want to laugh, Burkey, it may upset my bowels. Oh why aren't I regular?"

"Oh you're a regular all right," I said. "You're a real regular, you know what you are a regular?... you're a regular..."

"Leave her alone!" came the voice of Jeanette like a scrap of doom.

I went for a walk to the river; the lights of the postcard Paris were flaked on the water and the smell of fresh urine wafted to the bridge. I could hear the water suck and kick and groan against the quai wall, rolling its tremendous tongue. French river, I thought to myself, vicious, dirty, amused; French water, swelled with glut and dead things. If they ever drain the Seine, I added, what a sight that will be : corpses and bones, dead rats and crawling river lice, great mounds of debris, swamps of fungus, and tiny red monsters living off the poisons.

When I got back to the party, Jeanette had disappeared. The little room was almost deserted now; there was an unbearable stillness to it.

"Oh Burkey !" screamed Dalia, and this time her voice was shrill. Burkey stopped her from sliding to the floor and Bugs rose for the first time. He was taller than I had planned. "I got it," he said, his face animated like a cartoon, "let's give Dalia an enema." Dalia fell all the way to the floor this time; her skirt jerked to her thighs. She began to squirm on the rug and rolled onto her stomach; her legs kicked back and up.

"A enema," I said. "Yah ! Leave us give old Dalia a enema, oh good."

"I'll get the equipment," said Anne the Pregnant in French.

Seven

Albino In A Snowdrift

Meanwhile, from the eaves trough where it is perched, the albino spots a single garter strapped to a bedpost. The garter is blue, a not uncommon colour. So is the hand that plucks it. So is the leg that prods it up. But the albino is at a disadvantage. It cannot see the middle-right portion of the window across the way, and so all life maneuvers out of range. The albino whimpers. With its tiny chalk face and little fingers, it makes circles of steam on the party window and its thin purple lips press and contort against the glass. It sees the faces moving inside, the people moving and the feet moving; it hears the music, hears the laughter, hears the talk-talk. It curls despondently in a fetal crouch. Now the albino has been put on the eaves trough by Nora because the room is so small; Nora forgets where she put it, looks for it under a table and finds the West Indian Fitz instead; she is too tired to notice the difference and runs away with him to Tunisia. So the albino is left outside to brave the cold and the loneliness and the vast height of the hotel. It is simple, young and petted and everyone's favourite. People take it for walks along the Quai, keeping their backs always to the sun. It purrs; it whines; it peers into the air in search of objects. Buy it a beer and it goes to sleep; tell it a joke and it cries; draw it a picture and it eats the paper. It is a fine conversation piece and Nora has had it in her room for some time. It lies, stands or sits on her floor like a piece of fleshy driftwood; at night, it sleeps in a little blue wardrobe case and breathes lightly. On the eaves trough, it begins to shiver and grow restless. It hops and wiggles in the trough and scampers up and down the gutter making noises. Every time it sees someone leave through the grease and mist, it gets excited and taps meekly on the pane. Its cry is that of a little dog, a high muted squeal. When it sees a funny thing, it stops its whimpering for a time and sniffs with the fascination of a child; the cold turns its cheeks as pink as shrimp. It sees the woman prone on the floor, sees the hose and the porcelain pan; it hears a shocked, high-pitched scream, hears the accompaniment of cruel laughter, hears the after-sigh; then it watches the people leaving and all the lights turn off and the quiet. But hours after Nora leaves for Tunisia with Fitz, the albino is discovered by Jeanette. Jeanette is a venomous, frail woman; she hates men and locks the albino in a closet for two days. The albino does not die because it is too tired, but it scrapes and whimpers a great deal so Jeanette, who wants to be popular, brings it out and feeds it Pablum. It is no secret that the albino likes Pablum, but it misses Nora something awful and throws up because it is too tired to swallow. A trinity of fog, albino and silence enters Jeanette's life but she cannot accomodate it. Still, she is inquisitive; the albino appeals to her sense of hate. She rapes it, then buys it a hat.

Eight

Cliques in the Quarter seemed to form, hemorrhage and regroup at the rate of almost once a week. Once I had settled into the routine of people they would all fade away and go somewhere, leaving behind them not a trace of anything pleasant; in a few days their faces were forgotten or exaggerated and fitted into a fiction, and then suddenly they were back again and confused by the new routines that had bloomed in their absence. This turned them hostile or made them ingratiating and soon there was a lot of overlapping among the different groups, some of the worst sticking like burrs to the good old times. Eventually, nobody liked anybody very much.

Now, Nora and Fitz had run away to Tunisia and Sandra Y had disappeared forever with a gypsy to Tangiers. Worse than that, Brynning and Gilchrist had found jobs in the country and were commuting infrequently; as a result, their performance lost its edge. Dalia had gone to take (rectally) the waters in Montpellier, though it was not a port city or a spa, and Vangrin the famous writer had barred all people from his table at the Café Buci while he painfully considered his month's bon mot. Bonnie had taken a night train to Strasbourg in order to carry tragic news (and a bag of stones) to Sandra Y's fiancé who had been waiting prickishly on the station platform for twenty-five consecutive hours. Nate the Accordion had turned remarkably sour and incommunicative since the love of his life, Constance Funn, was about to arrive from London. Emmanuel the Spanish was having strange difficulties with his Gottlieb, winning games yet losing friends. And Burkey, that strange, quiet, gentle man, had tried to take his own life by coating himself with vaseline as if intending to soften to death.

Others who neither left nor changed, like Jules the Seducer or Cheryl or Anne the Pregnant or Bobby E Lee, had their hands full just being consistent : it was a constant vigil. And then everyone who had gone soon reappeared, some to vanish again unmissed, others to stick around until they became abhorrent, monstrous albums of what they had been. The shifting and sorting kept everyone occupied, and every day there were little survivals.

The one thing constant was the circuit : two or three cafés where one rendezvoused religiously and in ritualistic order. The Café Monaco was the anchor; it was small and intimate without the possibility of strangers, a modern, fluorescently lit café with permanent views of the street, and faintly sloped. That was for the afternoons and the hours before supper. At mid-evening, the grand shift was to the Café Buci at the foot of the Rue Dauphine. The Buci was narrow with a long bar and a superb Gottlieb; Emmanuel the Spanish swore by it and so did Fitz. Its great value was that it could be seen from hotel windows in the Rue de l'Ancienne Comédie. After midnight, the triangle was completed at the Café Tournon in the Rue Tournon near the Luxembourg where Maurice the waiter was very good at measuring the quality of your stance; to fail with him was a serious matter. The Tournon was a vast café with corners and L's to it — even a latticed partition for cards and chess — spacious and public and open till the early morning.

So, every day I followed the circuit. The art of waste is a bit like a concussion that forces the same moment to endure forever. In a week you are whittled down to a single catchword, in a month you are a reputation. You become accused of things you never did and take your permanent place among the gallery of myths accumulated at the tables. What is worse, you agree with the rumours, and finally you begin to believe in them. An evolution takes place in which you lose the obsolete things that make you hard to figure and as your new simplicity hardens, chronicled by incidents and ordained by gossip, you quicken to the mould; and become damn thankful. It seems that I had swum the Seine from the Vert-Galant on the island towards the Left Bank; the glut of the river had pulled me down like gravy and I was actually drowning when suddenly I yelled : "Hey I ain't gonna die in this shit," and had thrashed my way back to the quai where a Frenchman who had been watching for hours asked me if the water was cold. I heard this story so often that eventually I took it as truth and began to tell it myself. In fact, for a while I kept coming to the Café Buci dripping wet to hear Gilchrist say "Oh my God, he done it again !" As compensation for this gift of personality, you had to go along with everyone else's line too. That was no trouble at all, and before you knew it everybody looked full of danger and promise and cunning.

I was seeing a lot of Cheryl in the Quarter, though at first without results. She was a beautiful girl (picture a saint, quiet and pale, with skin so clean that dirt ran off her like rain from an umbrella) though she always had a headache, and Brynning was usually with us a few times a week. We formed an easy threesome for a while and read the same magazines and ate at the same table in the Bar Pyrénées and paid *service* for each other in the toilets of the Coupolade, which was the ultimate pledge.

One night, and there were several, the three of us bought some wine and went into the streets to kill an evening. It was too early for the Café Tournon, so we stood awhile watching a few people jump into the tiny urine-stained fountain fronting St. Michel. Then we walked on into Les Halles. We built quite a stride in spite of the dull hours coming; Cheryl had long splendid legs, buttoned together by the crotch of her jeans; her heart went out to the world and dripped a bit down her shirt on the way. Brynning sucked at the air like Dracula, his great gold earring hooked and dancing on his narrow head. When we had come as far as the restaurant-café called Le Chien Qui Fume, we opened one of the bottles and took two swigs apiece. Cheryl took hers last, for that was the particular impact she wanted. Then we began to stride again, looking for another place to stop. Les Halles was dimly lit by street lights and headlights and the light of neon signs. The streets were jammed with crates and three-wheeled go-carts, men scurrying and swerving, veering their loads into alleyways and stalls, and drowning out with their voices the great rattle and thunder of the huge trucks wheeling in from the provinces, a trail of cabbage leaf in their wake, their grilles stained with tomato seed and oil.

We were wiping wine from our chins when a shadow stepped out of the light and stood in front of us, dressed awkwardly in blue dungarees and a wool cap. It held up a dark furrowed paw and we stopped dead on the curb. It moved into a slot of light beneath a lamppost, a swarthy half-shattered face, bleeding from the eye, a large yellow bruise from cheek to jowl.

"Hey you my fellow Americans right; I'm from New York City, name of Tony; gimme a hand; lend me a franc. I'm here and on my own and it's tough for me, okay?"

I didn't like this and tried to walk around him, but Cheryl uncorked the other bottle. Nobody likes violence and I could feel it coming; his hands hung loose like slabs of meat. His name was Tony and he was a New York Italian. He looked over our heads and then behind him, but I couldn't see him give anyone the high sign. I could see other shadows shuffle a block down the street though.

"I'm Tony from the army," he said and took a fierce swig from the bottle; the juice of the grape ran from the corners of his mouth and he scooped at it with his tongue. The stubble on his face was gray. "It's good to see guys from where you live; I'm nowhere so it's nice to see a face, I tell you."

He took the bottle again, then passed it round; I put my sleeve to the lip of the bottle as it came my way and gave it to Brynning; Brynning put it inside his jacket pocket. When this happened, the man fell against the wall and opened the top of his shirt to let the air in. He was quite a sight : the bulk of him oozed with sweat and grizzle, there were little marks on his chest. He claimed he was a sergeant in the American army and had been AWOL for eighteen years. "I can't go back," he said, "they put me in Leavenworth, I go back. Oh Christ. I gotta keep working; I clean the streets around here, see my push broom. Soon be twenty years I been out of it."

He was stocky and his jowls bunched in pads of flesh as if his mouth were stuffed with cotton. He tried to smile around his battered face, and as the wine worked in him, his eyes turned glassy and his speech went through a funny change.

"One day I come home inna door; you Tony home Momma, you Tony back from the war Momma; yes you be proud you Tony, he come back a sergeant of the army Momma. I surprise you Momma, who you think this is? This you Tony Momma. Where Poppa? He no like his Tony bad Tony. Run away from army bad Tony no good. No Poppa, I come back. I no bad Tony, I you good son Tony, I come back lots of medals, I been sergeant of the army." He stood starch at attention and snapped a salute at the air. "I Tony accept you medal General; make my Momma happy. See Poppa I get medal. I listen to officers, do what they say. You clean shit wop, so I clean shit Poppa, I scrub out the shit. I good boy of the army. Hey you wop shine you boot. Yessir, I shine it up quick, and wop take dat garbage, oh sure sir here I go. Andrea my sister, I give her kiss from good Tony make her proud okay. Hello Andrea hello Momma yes Poppa I come home now to stay. Lots medals. I good man now."

It was a performance and I was getting nervous about the time when he would break from the cliché and make his move. Down the street, the shadows got larger and they came up on us and grabbed the wine from Brynning and sucked down the last of it among themselves. They were all tall men, bad teeth, well-dressed. "Who are they?" I asked. Tony broke out of his trance and watched them retreat to the other side of the street. "Queers," he said. "They look after me, I don't have money. Look I ain't no queer, but I ain't got money, I gotta go along with them.

They beat me up bad, see my face all fucked. They beat
hell out of me. It's no good."

He stood at ease. "You Tony no queer Poppa; he no
bad like that." He fell against the wall again, gasping for
the clean air just above his head. "One day," he said, "I'm
gonna kill them. I promise that. They kick me around
pretty good." He licked at a shred of skin hanging from his
lip. "They do bad things you Tony Momma. Terrible
thing. You no look at this thing. I wipe them away some
time, you see." He shook himself out of it and pushed
himself from the wall; he shook our hands and gave Cheryl
a wet kiss on the knuckle, then watched the four shadows
move towards him. "Okay, thanks Yanks," he said. We
walked away up the Boulevard Sébastopol, and he walked
back to his queers who were waiting for him by the road.

Nine
Vangrin

Vangrin the famous writer had a peculiar value in the
Quarter; he was the only published writer, and he had both
prerogative and seniority. His name was known the length
and breadth of the St. Germain and rumours of his coming
made uneasy the established guns of the Ile St. Louis.
Vangrin. The name was full of mystery, and the 'n' was
silent as if it were French. *Joris* was the diminutive of
Gerald, and he had loved his first woman under that alias
in the fall and winter of '52. That had been an unfortunate
and hideous affair, but from it he had written his first book
for the Voyeur's Companion Series, *The Case of the Latent
Lady.* From the quick success of that work, he had constructed a brilliant myth about himself, and Joris Vangrin,
as one approached him in his fortieth year, was full of
mystery and the wish to fall ill. He was said to be epileptic,
and had once had a vision in his late twenties while waiting

for his mail in the H to R queue at the American Express. Apparently, a naked woman, gleaming with the purest spring water, only her eyes veiled from the light and rather Joycean in build, had risen from beneath the letters counter and had beckoned with her fingers. He had left his place in the line and had wandered entranced towards that pale spectre, his knees spastic with love, his eyes bright and terrible. "I tell you I was like Dostoevsky stunned into madness by the sight of the decomposing Christ," and as he came closer, the vision receded "not away, but into my mind as if the very sinews of my soul were being spread for a seduction," and as it faded at last, eluded his touch, "I reached out with the tips of my fingers swollen with hope and felt something very pure and warm, with the texture of gentlest silk," and gentlest silk it was, albeit moist, for he had grabbed the blouse of an elderly clerk, Mrs. Wainder, who had asked him for his name and passport. He was in the S to Z section. "The luminous spectre, now snuggled in my mind's eye like a pod, whispered a name, a sound, and it was *Vangrin*." There was no mail for him, of course, and he never received another letter. But that was how the wise man got his spots.

Ten

Henry Rotter was a short, curly-headed kid from Liverpool; his eyes were always mounted in a half-blink as if they had been slit with a razor, and his lips were thick and chapped. He always looked vaguely unshaven but he was never bearded; it was the most incredible thing, and he would walk around with a day's growth day after day. No one knew how he did it, but it was obviously a strenuous discipline because he was always tired.

Henry was the great good friend of Jules the Seducer.

Jules was seldom liked for himself, but in the company of Henry he looked good, like a man with a dog, and he knew it and they went everywhere together. Henry believed in the cult of Jules the Seducer and was awed by his legendary skill and style; there was a certain pride of ownership here, a faith that Jules could do dangerous and terrible things. To know that he was a mere part of Jules' technique was enough to give him a certain stylish self-possession.

But beyond that camouflage, Henry was awkward and found it difficult to live a private life. He stuttered when it counted most, but aside from that he could not make small talk well, and with women his only hold was patience. He was at his best in the midst of things happening, because among that easy noise and traffic he could look like a notion of the way people should be.

In the evenings, he and Jules would walk into the Café Monaco together, Henry a few steps either ahead or behind, strutting like a private parade; they always took up their positions at a table fronting the only Gottlieb. Jules liked to watch the women playing and he took notes in his mind on the way they pressed themselves between the flippers. He and Henry would order their demis and watch the Gottlieb for a while and entertain their friends passing from and towards the bar. They sat cross-legged and perpendicular to the table. Then, after a while, Jules would strap the guitar to his back, swagger quietly to the Gottlieb, and jam a twenty centime piece into the slot. He'd be playing for no more than five, six minutes before everyone was watching him : he had those sad eyes and looked like a tall harmless dupe, but everyone knew differently and they were intrigued. He could always snowball that notoriety into a few conquests; he played bad pinball ("terrible and swift is the wrath of the Gottlieb," he'd whisper hoarsely), the mock martyr easily judged, and while they were needling him, his eyes would roam the café sadly to select a few new victims for the night. A lot of girls were eager and no trouble at all; but there were some who could not be taken easily and then Henry would wander over and play his role. He was such a *nice* person, quiet spoken, decent; his voice was so full of respect and hesitation, tremorous, concerned : there was kindness here. Manipulating the new virtue at hand, Jules was able to perform miracles. Henry would look after his guitar until he came back.

Contrary to certain malicious opinion, Henry was not Jules' pimp; he was his manager. He took a professional interest in Jules' well-being, made sure he ate enough, got his pants pressed, created a fine and lasting impression, was always on good terms with his women. It was a fiction that Jules fed regularly. Jules tended to use and discard things, and was inevitably suspected and disliked; Henry was able to counter this by acting as a kind of apologia and giving good advice. There was a certain grade B romanticism to their comradeship and people who went twice weekly to the Cinéma St. Germain understood that in any given war with Lloyd Nolan and Robert Taylor, they would have fought side by side, full of risk and laughter. In the Quarter, Henry made sacrifice a part of his stature. When Jules was playing guitar in a small café in the Rue Mazarine midnights, Henry would make a lonely round of the circuit gathering customers. Jules got paid by the head and, where his success was concerned (for it was ultimately Henry's too, that was the faith), he was able to swallow his clumsiness and draw evenly on something a bit like pride to see him through. People thought it was a beautiful thing for Henry to do it and they wanted to be part of that beautiful thing. They came in droves and Henry and Jules split forty-sixty.

It was hard to know him. But he was extremely well-liked, and so easily typed as the proverbial sidekick that all his difficulties were accepted and played upon. Anne the Pregnant found him one of the few people worthy of her self-pity. And I can remember a party in the Rue Gît-le-Coeur when the tall thin Englishwoman Jeanette took him by the arm and told him with rare emotion what a fine, clean soul he had, and how much of a favourite he was among them all. He was. Jules posed dark and mysterious like a gutter Satan, but Henry was half-saint and half-child and he liked to assume the truth of everything you said. "Look Henry," says Nate the Accordion, "I humped me a nun last week, pink, shaven and oiled, and damned if she didn't poison my testicles." "Oh that's terrible," Henry replies, stunned by the sudden probability of it, and Nate, grateful to be believed, becomes instantly a friend.

Henry tended Jules' affairs in one way or another as if they were pet frogs in a bottle. When Jules was either bored or busy, it was Henry who took them out for meals at La Crêperie, walked them home on nights when the mists were thick, comforted their doubts and misgivings with a generosity of spirit that was part betrayal and part love. He could be seen with his hand cupping their elbows, shepherding them through the streets of Paris, the lonely devoted guide. But he was less a pimp than a cicerone, and as trustworthy as a eunuch in affairs of the crotch.

Once Jules the Seducer was seeing a tall, dark girl (she had vacationed in Portugal) called Nina. He liked to insult her in public — that was his particular policy here — made her drink beer when beer made her ill and enjoyed discussing her sexual talents to vicarious groups in the Petit Bar. Nina was a high-strung girl, and so involved with Jules that she considered his every spite an achievement. But each achievement had its toll, and Jules exacted a very pretty price. She might come down in the mornings to join him and his friends (they had been promised a scene) for café au lait; Jules would make room for her across from him and next to Henry.

"Sleep well, honey?" "Yes." "You were a little slow last night." "I'm sorry." "Did you shave your legs?" "No." "I told you about that last night." "I'll do it later." "Have a beer, *no* a beer honey, I've already ordered it. Waiter! Un demi! Look, you want to insult me in front of my friends? Come on, drink up." "Bastard," someone would mutter. "A bitch deserves a bastard," Jules might retort. Long ago, Henry had furnished him with all the right rejoinders.

It went like that. Afterwards, when Jules left to make his rounds playing guitar along the quais, Nina would take Henry's arm and together they might disappear up the Rue St. Sulpice and come to the fountain in front of the church.

Nina might wash her face there, splashing the cold dirty water on her neck and arms, or vomit up the beer, while Henry sat on a bench practising the cords of his own guitar which he did not play well.

I insist that Henry did not want Jules' women; he would not have taken them for anything, everyone knew that and respected him for it. They were trophies of a game he could not play, would not risk. He was simply the defender of the faith. But Nina, once certain that Jules had grown tired of her resources, became frightened. Eventually, Jules hardly bothered to make love to her at all. By the end of their second week together, he refused to take off his pants; he even kept a cigarette in his mouth for the effect. Nina became quietly hysterical. She was possessive without owning a thing.

And so one morning in front of that fountain in the St. Sulpice, she would confess to Henry that it was turning sour

"It's only his mood," Henry would reply sheepishly, not looking at her eyes. She'd see this.

"Tell me what's wrong Henry please."

It would be a sunny, fresh morning; there would be the smell of fresh bread and the drone of cars on the St. Germain.

"It won't last," Henry would say, stammering to give it the lie. "We'll all be good again Nina, I promise." His face would suddenly become strained with something known.

"You know him Henry, is it me?"

"No no, don't think that, it's everything this week, he'll snap out of it."

"I don't think he will Henry."

There would be a silence and then Henry would come across the apron of the fountain towards her and touch her warm shoulders and the down on her arms. "It'll be all right though," he would say and that night Nina would go into his room and for nights after. Jules would immediately find himself another woman and soon there would be four of them spending lots of time together; two couples enjoying the life of the Quarter. That was the way time passed between them and, as Jules shed each woman in her turn,

Henry would take the leavings of the Seducer and everyone believed it was to save her from loneliness and despair. Nina, Sandra Y, Cheryl, Florine, Maria... it was Henry who believed in them finally, one by one, as they came his way.

It was a solemn trust, we all knew that. But one day a girl from New York came to Paris and gathered Jules up like a Kresge's notion. She was an old friend, selfish and cold, with a bitch streak that shone in the dark. She knew Jules the way the fish knows the worm, and nothing he could do or say meant anything; she packed his bags, sold his guitar, and took him back to Manhattan.

He left a void in the Quarter which was never really filled again. Now delightful little creatures, all breasty and coltish, wandered through the cafés unmolested, and the playground which had cut down the naive in their tracks became a kind of sandbox. We did our best, but we were no match for that sort of innocence. It wiggled past in high skirts and worn sandals on its way to two months in Israel, all tanned teats and red toenails; it sat down at tables with big brown eyes and soft brown shoulders, waiting for the cheque from Daddy; it scratched its legs and tossed its head and sighed in heat. But without Jules to humiliate it and teach the trick a trick, you got exactly what was coming to you, and it was a terrible feeling to know that you couldn't beat the world anymore as it passed by on its way back.

After Jules had left, a lot of people were happier; but his absence took something from the conversation, and there was a certain amount of bitterness among those who had grouped about him like fungus on a mandrake root. For a week or so, his room in the Petit Trianon became a shrine for the curious and Henry, who had the keys, would let them up to see the bed. A lot of his conquests were said to be suspect, but the bed bore out his reputation. It was a narrow cot with a heavy mattress; the mirror above the sink was extended from its nail in a downward tilt to reflect the action; when the sheets were removed, the mattress proper revealed spots, trickles and runlets of bloodstain; on the wall, hidden by a Modigliani print, was a series of neat X's, 116 in all, framed by initials in a loose rectangular box. He had left his mark all right, albeit in pencil, and the longer he was gone the more affection one felt for his style.

Henry had stolen one of Jules' sports jackets as a kind of memento and for weeks he wrote it, wore the sleeves right through, then put band-aids on his elbows and wore it still. Without Jules, he was something different and people went to a lot of trouble to put a new value on him. I never knew exactly who he was this time round : for a while he was someone who missed Jules, from that he became someone who was alone (leave him alone), then a man sardonic, then him unapproachable. He had nowhere to spend his patience anymore, and women began to walk around him as if he were a puddle. The tall thin Englishwoman Jeanette stopped inviting him to parties and Anne the Pregnant excommunicated him from her dream of the test tube and the pubic hair. He sat at a new table in the Monaco, deep in the nook of the L, and his dark, grained jowls calcified into a dyspeptic droop. He was not missed.

One night, Henry, myself and Bugs are standing in the middle of the Monsieur le Prince where it meets Odéon; it is three in the morning and very quiet and empty. Bugs admits sadly that it has been over three months since he's had a woman. "Three jesus months," he says, "I'm going out of my skull." Henry turns to him with much kindness and says, "Bugs, let me give you a word of advice. Friend to friend, okay ? Never say you haven't had a woman in three months. You don't say things like that here; it's not the thing to say." Bugs is embarrassed but he is grateful too, and he knows who his friends are. "Okay Henry," he says. "Anyway, I was only kidding."

Henry turns on him with as vicious and triumphant a look as I've ever seen, *"Yah Yah !"* he says.

Eleven

"God, I don't know why that nigger don't bath," said Irma lovingly as her lord and master E. Bone sauntered gracefully towards the door. E. Bone was a phantom of a man, black as a turd, with the lazy and beautiful habit of dragging his left foot; he was no walker, E. Bone, he liked to amble. It took him a little more time than most men to get down a flight of stairs or cross a bridge, but he was a pleasure to watch. "I like it smooth," he'd say, approaching a table at the Café Buci in an agony of slow motion, "Irma-thing and God knows I'm smooth; just like a hair through jello." He was too.

E. Bone was taking notes. Every night he took notes, took them in a Prisunic brown scribbler. "I don't know what my lover's writing, but he sure is serious about it," white Irma sighed; for night after night while his generation struggled over the hump of the evening into daylight, E. Bone typed his deathless prose, four words to the line, eight lines to the page. But before he sat down for the night's work, he'd dress slowly in his best manner, dark pin-striped suit, cuff links of muted amber, neat patent leather shoes; he'd flip on his Chrysler wrist watch, adjust his tie clip, zip up his fly and march casually, no, cunningly, towards that small green portable Hermes that sat on a low table overlooking the vast Quarter smell. No one knew what he wrote when he sat down, but he was a feast for the eyes, E. Bone; with semi-religious quiet he leaned gently over his smooth machine and stroked its keys, his fingers slipping off like frying butter. As the night wore on and became worrisome to those down on the street, visitors would begin to mount the hundred stairs to their room. Irma in blue shirt, short pants and straw sandals would let you in to watch the spectacle. Only for a few minutes; it was too painful to watch for long : he was so leisurely, so completely at his ease, hunting for a letter, tapping at a key carefully selected with such conserve, smiling down on the Prisunic brown scribbler that had been forced neatly, tenderly through the roller. Tap-tap. Tap. Ta----p; the sounds were so unrythmic, yet one's eyes were for a short time mesmerized by E. Bone's curled forefinger locked into place and pouncing at the truth in brown sleek movements. Although there were hours to the line and days to the page, his achievements were hypnotic; he was entranced by time as his own device, and he let it escape his fingers very slowly and very steadily and with much respect for its due course.

There was Irma to watch too. A very white, blonde girl with little red pimples on her chin which she picked and prodded daily. She treated them regularly with a pink cream that turned an unhappy purple when dry. She was neither sad nor ecstatic; there was a certain dumbness about her as if she were submerged in a medium that was not her own. Yet she was quite a wonderful woman, Irma was, big-boned, sturdy in the hip and leg. I especially liked the white luminous polish she put on her toenails; for she sensed things with her toes, Irma did, and loved to rub them against various textures. The textures were not pleasing but she accepted her surroundings without complaint, high in the deepest room of the cheapest hotel in the Gît-le-Coeur; and she would have suffered more than that for E. Bone whom she loved and trusted because he was so slow. There was no malice in a man that gradual.

Irma's favourite recreation was sitting. During most of the day, she sat on a small, backless stool reading magazines; when the weather was good she liked to loop her legs over the sill and run her toes along the eaves trough. Despite her remoteness from everything but her lover, she was generally a happy girl; she took to poverty like someone who has had everything but deprivation. Over the months, she developed a spread and the flesh of her thighs grew lax; but that was a sign of being settled and content and certain, and mute proof of E. Bone's manhood.

Now it cost money to be clean in the Quarter, but Irma showered every noon for a franc. In everything else, she knew how to swallow her pride, sperm and all; in fact there was a special playfulness to the way she rose above it, as if she were playing a game called Degradation, complete with dice and tokens. But she needed to be clean. It was a minor quirk and E. Bone humoured it. Every noon, she went to the shower stall in the basement, a dark place filled with rats and noises, and scrubbed herself with expensive soap until she smelled as fine as a May day in the provinces. She always shaved herself with loving care, clipped her toenails, powdered her appendages, and nipped her pimples in the bud. It was a continuous war against some principle, probably the survival of the fittest; "My body is a garden," was the most serious thing she ever said.

Certainly, all such ritual made even the worst things bearable : the stench of pot re-smoked, the doorless toilet on the second landing, the filth toe-high everywhere. But E. Bone never washed. He always put on his freshly laundered clothes over his unclean body. She might chide him for it, but she loved him for it too, and one smell eventually outlasted the other.

They were a very lasting pair. One was kind to them because they were so permanent. They weren't people you saw once, you saw them again and again, year in and year out, as nice a couple as you'd want to meet, with a pretty sense of balance between them : she knowing what was right and he knowing what was wrong. During the winter, they were terribly cold up in the room, bundled in overcoats and boots, their eyes stinging from paraffin. So their winter pastime was to ride the Métros; within the centre of the vast Métro complex they found warmth, and it was very nice besides to speed carelessly through that subterranean world. Irma's favourite Métro stop was Franklin Roosevelt because it was so chic with its window cases and translucent brightness; she liked intimations of luxury when they were that tame and distant. They explored every line for heat and they were very cheerful about it too; they had their favourite routes and peculiar mystiques and it kept them going in the bleaker seasons. They travelled from Neuilly to Vincennes, Clignancourt to Orléans, Place d'Italie to Porte de Pantin, in and out and around Paris, through, from and to it, beneath, above and sometimes on it. So in the winter, their life was dull and well-heated. But in the summer, life was good to them and they were certainly worth a visit or two a week. E. Bone's conversation was soothing to say the least; it consisted mostly of agreements, endlessly tasted, as if he were preparing the words for his digestive tract. Of course, every day E. Bone, and sometimes Irma, were in the Café Buci or Monaco without fail. E. Bone would sit at his accustomed place and pass the time of day in easy humour, getting a little sun, moving over his thoughts like a great tortoise. He would even listen to André of the French Foreign Legion (who was made mostly of wood) by the hour, a terrible fate for an ordinary man. But E. Bone never complained or apologized about people; he respected trivia with a politeness that was almost saintly.

E. Bone made his money in the Quarter selling drugs and hemp. Afternoons between the hours of three and five and after midnight, you could buy the best quality stuff in his room. His marijuana was from North Africa, very high grade and unmixed, and he sold it wrapped in newspaper neatly folded, the corners sealed to prevent the grains leaking. E. Bone spent a lot of time preparing his wares and he certainly knew his business; he was terribly fair with everyone, no one was ever cheated by E. Bone. Irma kept the books on people.

Once a year, towards mid-July, Irma and E. Bone took a trip to Ibiza to buy their annual supply of hemp. They spent a very nice month on the island, relaxed in the sun and saw a lot of the American colony. Irma developed a sincere tan on the beaches and by early August the pimples on her face vanished till the fall. They always left before the American riots in the late part of the summer. While they were gone from Paris, someone had to move into their room to keep the trade moving. That summer it was Bobby E Lee. They had more or less adopted him; they liked the way he smiled, his Huck Finn hat and toeless running shoes, and whenever he blew pot with them he was always amusing. They got a vicarious kick out of his doomed escapades; his style was an endless joke between them. "He's a nice kid,"

Irma believed, "little pecker and all." In his guise as orphan, Irma and E. Bone would have him up to dinner a few times a week, and when he was sick — which was as regularly as possible — they always sent him down some soup. He lived a few floors below them in a cell-like room that had a bed, a rack and a chair. Dog-eared paperbacks lay on the floor and dresser and his filthy underwear fluttered from the doorknob like dark brown ensigns. At night he moaned sometimes and Irma would rush down the stairs with a morphine capsule or a thin broth to ease his trouble. He was endearing, you couldn't deny that; with his mock southern drawl and his faint boasting, he was like a cartoon figure. The simple colour and line of his mind seemed easy to figure and that made you feel safe. There were so many weak links and perforations in his life that he felt if he just folded on the dotted line it would all come off like a coupon and buy him in. "Ah'm just a kid," he'd say. So when Irma would visit him in his bed, he would ask her deliriously for favours, groaning through a mild induced sweat; little things, he would sigh, things that wouldn't make much difference to her, like could she unzip her fly and let him take a peek, or could she let him touch her in there for a second, oh he was so hot and unhappy and did she see the sweat on his face he was going to die and what did it matter such a small favour when E. Bone probably did it and worse too. You had to like him.

During July then, Bobby E Lee moved upstairs into their room and maintained the trade. He lived — as best he could — a charmed life. He invited his friends up every day for a little of this and that, and there was always free pot for those who admired him for his courage and variety. He locked up the savings in a high drawer, and arranged the stock alphabetically in little green bags; he bought a cheap, tin scoop to ladle out the merchandise, began to wear a gambler's eye shade, and put a red shade on the light bulb. It was towards the end of July that that incident occurred about which he was to speak for ever after : *The Death Of The Man Who Mainlined In My Room And Who After It Was Dark I Dropped Into The Seine.*

As dispenser, he realized a certain power; and the notoriety that came with the territory, he accepted without complaint. But in his new role as someone necessary, he forgot what he was for and made mistakes. For instance, he was told by E. Bone never to give credit to anyone while they were gone; Bobby E Lee followed his instructions to the letter, except he let people postpone payments and then every sale became inevitably a pursuit through the Quarter.

"I ain't got no money now, boy," he was told late one afternoon by a complete stranger, huge but lopsided like a slightly defective engine. "But you're Bobby E Lee right?"

"Right," said Bobby E Lee, dancing tiptoe on his name.

"Well hell come round to the place in the Rue du Dragon tonight; we pay you there Bobby."

"Sure okay," said Bobby E Lee, tripping towards the door to let him out with an envelope containing five morphine capsules, two matchboxes of hashish and a supply of light green hemp from E. Bone's best drawer.

"You're Bobby E Lee" — he was becoming proud of that all right, so about eight that evening he took Brynning and myself to the Rue du Dragon and rapped heavily on a night club door. "Now y'all see," he instructed us wisely, "sellin' stuff in the Quawtah is lahk a marriage, ts'all faith." They wouldn't let him in and he waited an hour for the party in question to come out. They finally did because he began inevitably to call them names through the door. The stranger was wearing a tiny felt hat with a gold feather in the brim and he held in the perpendicular of his elbow the large, coarse meaty hand of a woman called Paula. She was syphilitic and red-eyed, but what caught your attention in the end was her feet. They were monstrous things stuck through the remains of great straw sandals; the painted nails were chipped like corroded plaster and the toes proper were wrinkled and hairy. Her hair was held high by a strip of towel. A man might have taken her out of sheer spite, or the occasional need to wallow; certainly, she dwarfed the commonplace.

"You the one just called me a shit head?" asked the stranger, gently adjusting Bobby E Lee's Huck Finn hat.

"Wasn't me," said Bobby E Lee, "any of you guys say anything?"

Brynning and I denied it at once. Paula had her eyes trained on our belts.

The stranger flexed the bone of his thumb. His arms looked like legs and his legs looked like people. "Well someone out here just called me a shit head," he said coldly; "anyway, what do you want boy?"

"You owe me fifty francs," said Bobby E Lee, scared right out of his drawl, "from this afternoon."

"Oh yah," said the stranger, "what makes you so bright?"

"Really," said Bobby E Lee, "five capsules, a couple matchboxes . . ."

"You're a funny little snot," said the stranger, "I ain't got no patience with you."

"Look Harry," said the slightly effeminate Paula, "make him strip down and cut his balls off."

"Oh I'll take good care of him," said Harry.

"Make him eat shit, Harry," said Paula.

"Have we got time?" asked Harry.

"No, it's near ten, we gotta go," said Paula, and they turned and sauntered up the street towards the St. Germain, crossed the road and took a table at La Rhumerie.

Bobby E Lee followed them at a sad, patient distance. He stood staring at them from the curb; his drawl came back and with it that quality of innocence and surprise. A shank of hair fell over his eyes, he stropped his fingers nervously on his hip. Eventually, Brynning and I left him, and the next morning he had a long dry cut under his eye, his clothes smelled of piss and his face was puffed from crying.

Dear Irma, he wrote, Could You Send Me Money As I'm A Little Short But Everything Will Be Straightened Out In A Week Or So. Can I Come Down And See You And E. In August And We Can Travel Back Together? I'll Rent The Room And Etc To The Two Scottish Girls Debbie And Briar Who Live In My Room Downstairs Now. My Back Hurts. Love Bobby E Lee.

There was no answer. Bobby E Lee began to live on Oxo bars and oranges, and a very slow life it was for him.

He smoked up his merchandise every night with friends, and lay on the bed in a sickly pot daze until he became so entranced by his own image on the ceiling that he could actually feel himself growing taller and more beautiful. People came up to his room daily, by way of pilgrimage; they sat in carnivorous circles on the floor and passed around joints of pot till they were glutted with it, then lay stunned and grateful. Three people actually lived in the corner for a week; others threw parties and met friends.

Boot was one of them, almost unnaturally good-looking, a Puerto Rican. He had women all the time, it was no problem, and he struck one as being some dark angel of grace. There was something of the Bobby E Lee in him, for he took from others the necessary qualities he lacked; there was something of Jules the Seducer about him too, in diluted form, and even, on his effeminate side, the quality of sorrow which Cheryl so successfully expressed by way of silence. Bobby E Lee was both fascinated and repelled by Boot; he saw in the kid, who could not have been any younger than himself — except by discipline — all of his own devices elevated to the point of complete achievement, the facility and ease which Bobby E Lee could chart for himself only in fantasies and concocted tales. He saw at once that Boot was his natural enemy.

Everyone had a good time while it lasted. Bobby E Lee didn't mind being used this way, he just didn't want to be used up. Boot was the first to discover this, so Bobby E Lee was made the nominal centre of everything happening, the gift horse on the bed with his mouth wide open. Boot even had the sense to know why he was there and he performed among them like a projection of Bobby E Lee stripped of defects.

Once in a while, Bobby E Lee would motion for someone to come talk to him, and then beckon for attention with a limp, unhappy finger; if you gave him your ear, he would claim in a half-whimper, his breath fouled by sleep, that he was making it with both Debbie and Briar. It wasn't true, of course. He had got them to compare navels as forced reparation for the good time they were having at his expense, but the whole episode had been, for him, a tremendous letdown. Other maneuvers had failed. The only revenge left him was to discuss their sexual prowess in remote detail; mind you, his fiction was healthy : Boot had given them the finest references, knowing the appeal for Bobby E Lee of a perfect lay.

So he lay on the bed for a month, an almost Proustian figure, but popular at last. He soon had two or three old friends camping permanently on the floor of the room, but he was too tired to complain and very depressed about Irma and E. Bone who had abandoned him.

He did get a postcard near the middle of August which said that Irma had a nice tan and E. Bone had bathed by accident in a rock garden near Málaga. It was a pretty postcard and Bobby E Lee stuck it on the wall longingly. It showed cliffs and water and some figures kneeling in the surf.

Twelve

One night I walked into the Café Monaco : early evening, sky a sea blue, wind thumbing the gutters for paper. A storm was coming and that is not an easy thing to accept. The air had turned a phosphorous green, the smell of the river came up to foul our beers, neon signs rocked and groaned. The general angst of bad weather brewing, like salt water in the nose, had delivered me from an hour's walk and the fierce swill of the river beneath bridges. I came to the Monaco against the possibility of a deluge.

Within that uneasiness, the Café seemed bright and close and comfortable. André of the French Foreign Legion was gesturing in cape and glove before a mirror; Cheryl and Hugh Brynning were peering down the toilet stairwell at Gordie Gilchrist who had flushed not wisely but too well;

Anne the Pregnant plucked a rose from her cleavage and the air whistled through her breasts; the sight of Rose the New Zealander rising drunk and unbuttoned from the floor drove three Americans into the street and down the Métro; and Dixie (whom I did not know then) sang a song of *Neem* along the frost of his demi. Everything brightened and echoed as the rain began to fall.

I sat at a table by the window with Nate the Accordion and friends. Bonnie was standing near the bar, one timorous leg on the rail like a tendril, and I waved her over and made her sit to my left to ward off the draft from the door. She had a pleasant smile that night, blue veins revolving in her nose as she breathed, but her head was so tiny that her grin seemed to cut her jaw like an enormous scar. Nate was talking carefully about the weather and it was obvious to everyone who cared that he did not want to talk about anything else. He was grizzled and solemn in his middle age; he was a lean, worrisome man still in the archaic posture of youth, and his presence had the texture of a lizard that had never molted. The woman of his life, one Constance Funn, had arrived by ferry and boat train from London two weeks before and he had recently locked her in his room at the Hôtel Dieppe. It was a rare expression of love, but Nate the Accordion was like that; he made love to her at noon and after supper, but at all other times she was eternal behind lock and key. To mention her name in his presence was tantamount to rape, seduction and intrigue; as a result, conversation became difficult. Still, one respected his taboos.

"So look Nate," I said. "How does Constance like Paris?"

"Shouldn't she? What's on your mind?" He fluttered his nostril wings angrily to reveal dark thistles of hair and refuse. He was amusing. The thought of Constance Funn at *his* hotel, in *his* room, perhaps at this moment straddling and dipping in *his* bidet turned his wizened groin to jelly and his swarthy face to a light urine amber.

"I'll bet she does like it though," I said, "singing and dancing and running about."

"Do you know something?"

"No, just she seems to be enjoying herself," I said.

"Enjoying herself? Garber, is there something going on I don't know about?"

"Probably not," I said.

With Nate was Yvonne, of course, who accompanied him on guitar in the streets, and a fat man called Bunny Zenner. He was more amusing than Nate and knew it, so that even when he sat back quietly his mouth hung open, accomplished and anticipating. He was funny enough to keep us amused for hours, but not funny enough to make a dime out of wit or presence. He was ugly without being professional and he had recently come to realize that everyone liked him for his failures. It was really the only joke he could not do without. And he had a big wart on his face. It seemed to curl and sprout everywhere. He was an amiable person if you could forget about that wart, but he kept bringing it into everything as if it were a talisman and whenever you met him it became at once an article of faith between you. It was a fairly ugly wart too.

"How are you," you said as a rule, and "What's the good wart," said Bunny.

But not tonight. Tonight I said, "Bunny, that was some routine you gave us on Monday, by God."

"You said a wartful," said Bunny.

He was with his wife, Honey, a thin, bandy-legged girl who might have had no thighs at all.

The lights dimmed gently to the sound of thunder. Conversation swung round to a freethinking discussion of Nate's work in progress: an agonizing reappraisal of all the cafés in Europe. He was now writing about La Pergola, haunt of the well-heeled lesbian, and he had in mind the American market for this particular segment: perhaps *Harper's Bazaar*. "It's definite food for thought," he argued defensively, "the free love of the Pergola, no one can say it isn't. Your Wimpy Bars are nothing compared to it for style, and all one needs is a woman's magazine to give it the proper frame and mood. We're all so lesbian conscious these days, it's such a featured source of comment, why *Harper's* or *Vogue* would eat it up like that..."

"Lickety-split," suggested Yvonne.

"Yes, that quickly," continued Nate who knew her troubles, "I tell you it makes me optimistic, I admit it willingly; and it might provoke a new taste in currencies of habit, build a future for the woman who goes her own way with sponge and dildo. I'm going to concoct the thing as a series of vignettes, with the same people recurring like motifs on an outhouse wall; obeying the laws of time and evacuation insofar as my mood permits. Keep it to yourselves. And this too : I was talking to a Max Goob Thursday last about a possible scenario on La Pergola, all quite decent and in colour . . ."

"You're liable win an academy awart," said Bunny.

Nate stopped. Constance Funn's navel lay revealed to him as a luminous smile in his bière Strasbourg and the joy went out of him marvelously quick; dread — selfish and particular — brimmed him in its place. We were in for an evening of his old haunts and fears. He introduced the ghost with lunatic dullness to prepare us for the business at hand. "But no, you know how I feel about that, it's no good pretending the mere pretense, *if* we're all doomed and gone in that order . . ." The italics were his, for he bit into his words now, and with that precise tone of gray, began carefully to build his babel.

The rain unfurled in streamers of green and rust, spanking the windows, the piled chairs, the road. It was a lovely, warm rain; the drops were solid, almost penciled. Yet the sky whelmed above us, vast and bleak; it was as if we were strange gilled creatures at the bottom of the sea, speaking in ever-diminishing echoes.

I suppose any one of us could have stopped him — it was Nate's old shudder about the world's end and the end of man, about how we had cheated death by refusing to believe, by staving off the memory of the bomb and the holocaust — but we were all in deadly pursuit of the evening, and no one was going to cheat us of that. At the same time, no one was going to cheat Nate either; he needed this : it was his private device.

"No," he said, speaking in a weird falsetto along the

strings of his throat, "I can't reconcile the good I'm feeling
with the sense that *I'm gone* ... I'm trying vaguely to
remember what I was doing at the time ... If I could, of
course, I'd disappear ... perhaps it was ... no I'd better
not ... we're too blind to see it, all cooped up in our
hope ... I tell you if I could remember the thing dropping
and the end of everything we'd disappear *poof* ... something
I've been considering for a long time : the permutations
and combinations of the entire mirage ... I'll put it to you
this way : if I believe I'm still alive, with reservations, then
I can go on working and playing my instrument and eating
and the rest; I can have Constance twice a day, soft thing,
and make my way ... whatever we do is what we've wanted
to do all along, like the Quarter and the café and the rain
(but who's responsible for that I couldn't say) ... much
too dangerous to go into now ... to know you're dead
without being specific is to succeed, that's the thing, for
then there's nothing we can't do if it's a dream see ... but
you have to be patient, you can't jump off buildings and
float in the air and walk on water because others don't
believe it yet ... it all has to be made clear at the centre
first ... a reorientation, a horrible business, but we do have
forever if we put our minds to it ... I haven't aged in the
last two years, that's what first struck me ..."

"Why don't you spread the secret, wart of mouth," said
Bunny.

"If Constance, in my room, were to think this instant and
remember that she isn't in a hotel room waiting for her
happiness, but a bag of bones at the bottom of the sea no
bigger than a peace button, or debris scattered in the
atmosphere, why she'd disappear and join the other corpses
... now haven't you noticed that Paris is less crowded,
fewer traffic jams, people off the streets by one, business
failing ? ... people are thinking, then popping off ... every
time I think it's coming back to me I shiver inside and feel
myself decomposing and breaking apart, but I pull myself
together and leap into life at the last moment and make
the mirage noisy to push the other away ... but it comes
and goes like a bloody twitch and there's no telling ...

Bunny tell us some jokes . . . I don't like the way I feel this
is awful . . . you've got to put out of your mind the holocaust
and the smoke and the fire and the water and if necessary
yourself . . . *Bunny say something will you* . . . people's faces
like rubber and plasticine . . . disintegration, you've got to
hold it back, breathe heavily, smoke a cigarette, fornicate
at whim, move your bowels by rote if necessary . . . *Bunny* . . .
we were listening, is it possible, to Mrs. Gond-Horne discuss
peace and economy for a dollar a day with membership
button and motor trips to Glasgow, and then I'm drifting
through the entrance of the Museum Tavern in Bloomsbury
with a roar in my ears, a terrible noise, and I fall apart arms
and legs and my accordion makes a bad sound and floats
off in a series of filaments and there's a rattle in my throat
and I'm am sores . . . *Bunny for god sake* . . . I'm all quiet
and torn apart and several gases equally diffused and a
little blood, and silliest thing I see Mrs. Gond-Horne upside
down dangling from an upper window a run in her stockings
farting and snorting to get free . . . *Bunny am I beginning
to fade ? . . .*"

"Wart off these omens, kid."

"So clear, so horrible, I've let it slip damn . . . someone
lash me to the mast . . . and there are chunks of flesh on
the spears of the Museum fence, the roads are covered with
vomit and faeces and indescribable deposits, the stench goes
right up the nostril like burning toast . . . *Bunny, please,
describe your nose* . . . no, it's too late, this is bad . . . what
about Constance . . . I may vanish at any moment . . . I've
got to walk it off . . . I'll be back if I can, am I beginning
to fade ? . . . *Garber, am I still here ?* . . . somebody hold
on to me, about the shoulders, Yvonne grab my legs, keep
pinching, Bunny draw some blood . . . goodby I have to go
unfortunately . . ."

He leaped up, his mind's eye dimmed by a nervous blink,
overturned his demi on the table, dropped his accordion to
the floor and was off, out of the café and running in the
rain. Bunny and I exchanged looks and ran out after him;
he was headed towards the Hôtel Dieppe. Bunny hobbled
on his fat, warped legs, but I dashed as fast as I could

towards Nate who was galloping through Odéon screaming, arms extended; the rain was warm and heavy; Nate seemed to stop for a second outside his hotel doorway and pinch himself in terror just to be sure he was presentable, then he jumped into the place as if falling from a plane and had already disappeared when I got there and was by now several flights above me; I swung through the entrance myself, flushed with embarrassment, and mounted the staircase and pursued him five floors to his room; the door slammed behind him as he kicked in the lock and went in and then there was sobbing on the other side and little noises of forgiveness and terror. There were other crashes too as Bunny swam up the stairs on his belly like a dolphin, face sweaty, wart like a beacon before him. I opened Nate's unhinged door to see him kneeling with his head on the bed and Constance perched naked on a large white pillow stroking his sparse hair as he bit the blanket. A lovely scene and worth remembering.

Bunny took a peek himself and then we walked down to the street together. "He's crazy," I said, somewhat stunned by that tableau of the dream we dream.

"Listen, with an epic streak like that," said Bunny, "he ought to call his book *Wart and Peace.*"

Thirteen
Vangrin In Love

It was not love and it was not pity that caused Vangrin to marry, it was his sense of formal design. He had been corresponding for some months with an Israeli girl in Haifa, and had experienced stirrings of a social nature, perhaps humane. The girl's name was Zippi, he had both snapshot and signature to prove it, and she was well into her twenties. One could gauge her style by the way she erected her name : the Z was disproportionately large and its foot cut the other

letters in a bold rise as if they were all sacrificial t's. The
snapshot was even more conclusive; Zippi was fat, sloppy
and coarse. In subsequent photos, she could be seen dancing
in a traditional circle with her friends; they looked like a
herd of cattle.

But if it was not love that prompted Vangrin to break
the mold, it was not lust either; and it certainly wasn't fun.
It was a gesture of principle. They had a dead friend in
common, an adventuresome parasite who had been miraculously killed in a border incident. Zippi had rifled the
pockets of the corpse, found Vangrin's address and avail-
ability, and had sent off a quick note of condolence. Vangrin
had responded with a Tract On War, and from that moment
there was no stopping it, the cascade was on.

Their correspondence thickened. Vangrin kept duplicates
of his letters and watched his ideas grow and transform into
principles of non-violence; he became genuinely enthralled
by the rounded transition in his thought — why, it was close
to art, it was art : sequence, motif, *progression d'effet,*
interior monologue — it had everything. It was a fine,
esthetic feeling, but Vangrin mistook it immediately for
something he had done; so when Vangrin, in this roundel
of emotion, got to the part where he became a pacifist, he
sent off a letter (surface mail) to the effect that under no
condition should Zippi allow herself to be drafted into the
Israeli army. "My darling little Zippi, ma petite bête, the
dogs of war are nipping at our heels, and they'll nip us,
God they will — yet God willing they won't." Vangrin
began to revel in this new interest; detachment, selflessness,
beatitude, concern — a touch of the missionary altered his
aspect. "If war is hell," he said, "I am the devil's advocate
and no mean Beelzebub in the case."

His philanthropy manifested itself in a grand design : he
would marry her by proxy; she would come at once to
Paris; they would get quickly divorced, become instant
friends, drink café crème, go to parties, converse at length.
It was a popular plan, and Vangrin became celebrated and
wise. He became briefly rustic too and tramped the Bois,
indissoluble in rain like the paragon. Zippi, accordingly,

arrived in Paris married through lawyers and every inch the coarse, sloppy bride. Consummation was another thing; in the original draft of the Affair Vangrin it had not been a detail. And for Vangrin, who fed on visions, it was an unpleasant thought. Zippi was not only coarse and fat and sloppy, but she had bad teeth as well, several wavering chins, and acute abdominal bulge; what was worse, Zippi was ingenious and witty and made Vangrin look bad. She was oblivious to attack and had a certain coquettish wisdom as if something very beautiful had been poured into the wrong husk. Her eyes sparkled, her nose glowed; within the bovine, apparently, a soul sang. Vangrin was not amused.

He found her a small flat in Neuilly, miles from the Quarter, wrote her *pneumatiques* twice a week, and visited her every second Sunday to discuss his plays. She was not sympathetic to his work; in fact, she knew what was wrong with it. He came to detest her. In vain, he countered with descriptions of the way she smelled, how obese she was, how neurotic, deranged and obsessive. Her one response was to correct his grammar. A divorce in Paris was prohibitively expensive, and he could not raise the money. He wrote her poison pen letters : "I will slit your skin into little folds; I will peal back their edges; I will fill your sores with molten wax." or, "Cher Cochon, I live in the rooms diametrically across the park and each evening I watch with disgust as you undress at your window. Never have I seen such putrid flab, all blue, yellow and orange; never have I seen such odious habits, such scratching, farting, wiping. Isn't there a maintenance law against animals in your building ? I will inquire. In the meantime, you are despicable and foul; beware the Ides of Flab."

Zippi didn't mind at all; adversity was her game. Vangrin contemplated murder. However, he realized that until he knew her carnally, the marriage was not sanctioned by the state. This gave him hope; especially when she began to sprout a mustache. But most flesh is weak, and Vangrin's was sickly; she seduced him in an extraordinary way, there is no way to describe its brilliance, and the word was made flesh. For weeks, Vangrin prowled the streets in an orgy of self-disgust; he took a few Les Halles whores, began a collection of pornographic snapshots, knit himself a hair shirt, placed tiny rocks in his bed, even contemplated emasculation. But in a month he was back and Zippi was waiting, her coy style made only a little less ridiculous by something already domestic in her look, settled. And she wasn't half bad in the sack; she was downright inspired.

So Vangrin accepted her as one accepts a dirty habit, picking one's nose for instance, and he began to take a certain, measured pride in her fat, sloppy ways : it was a measure of his endurance. He revelled in her wiles like clockwork, twice a month, and began to construct an aura of mystery concerning their relationship. She became some obscure mentor, hidden away in a Paris suburb, unavailable for public show, unknown, unfathomed, a study in devotion. Even the domestic side was argued for : he was a married man, he had a wife, his range of experience was now complete, compatibility was a special faith, the articulation of the soul was blossoming anew. He certainly knew how to varnish a trap. "Her thoughts," said Vangrin, "are translucent and dropsical, with the relieving fulsomeness of weighted turds." "Naw," said Bugs, "she just fulla shit."

Fourteen

Brynning had a rather disturbing effect on women : he was not simply good-looking, there was a prettiness about him which caused endless embarrassment wherever he went. His girlish, narrow features suggested something fragile and delicate, while his green, densely unmoved eyes did nothing to alleviate the impression he often gave of being a mannequin or a contraption run by strings. His bony, disjointed kind of grace lent him the air of a clown, enviably tragic;

there was more of Rouault than Barnum there, and something apparently irresistible in his habit. Actually, he was attacked from all sides, as likely to be propositioned by your meekest homosexual as by your most brazen slut or virgin. He had developed several stances to ward off these assaults whenever they occurred, but they filled him with horror nonetheless. There was, of course, his celebrated loyalty to little Gordie Gilchrist with whom he had been to sea and for whom he apparently sacrificed, without regret, elements in his nature usually left unhampered. Obligation had long ago given way to habit, so that eventually an interior warp had finalized his relationship to Gilchrist, the way a crooked finger will school a glove. They were inseparable, but there was very little of the parasitic between them; most Quarter friendships are expedient, to say the least, but Brynning and Gilchrist gained nothing tangible from each other. Their great gold earrings symbolized some dreadfully naive contract, observed with apparent cynicism by those — the Seducer being one — who knew how to market a feeling. Certainly, there was something quaint about their friendship; its darker corners — if they indeed existed — were made obscure by the sort of cavorting, eager distribution of gaiety which was their special mark. Just what sort of influence Gordie exercised over Brynning, or why this rare emotion of fidelity to one so obviously harmless and inert should have made Brynning so inaccessible to a wider range of pleasures, was a gnawing problem — especially for those who had never had it easy and had to settle reluctantly for their own level.

Although Gilchrist was the greater puzzle. He was generally considered to be an idiot, someone who lived in a complete, childlike soliloquy. He was a short, rambunctious kind of imp, on whom the gold earring — half the measure of his head — took on far greater consequence. It seemed part of his devised armour against the encroachment of detail; and the jewellery swung from his lobe like a talisman warding off alienation, thought, and anything stronger than lots to drink and a few practical tricks. Whether he was as oblivious to the situation as he seemed always to be, only Brynning knew, and he wasn't saying. "We're from Dundee," was his only explanation. Maybe it was that simple.

It was certainly no one's business, and — except for the necessary gossip — no one gave it much thought; they were expected to be around. Brynning was sharper than anyone had a right to expect from one so obviously precious, and when Gilchrist wasn't with him, he seemed fairly alert, even the epitome of coolness. Yet when Gilchrist was on the scene, they were like uninhibited vaudevillians, noisy with a kind of music hall patter, and always concerned with a few familiar jokes as predictable as the time of day : how to keep Gordie comforted was one, and it had endless variations. But without Gilchrist, Brynning regarded the atmosphere with suspicion.

For a brief time, Brynning, myself and Cheryl formed a kind of midnight threesome. Our comradeship was never certain and, of course, in the presence of little Gordie it became immediately nonexistent. It didn't take long for a split to occur; it eventually revealed something about Brynning, already suspected admittedly, which made me swear off his company for good. The split — or rearrangement — happened very quickly. One day, both Cheryl and Brynning disappeared. I had been half expecting it in a despairing sort of way, but the extent of the loss or the details of its nature were not known to me for some time after. Rumours circulated in ugly cycles up and down the circuit, beginning with a sense of amazement that Brynning had actually succumbed to someone so elementary as Cheryl, and arriving in due course at the more comfortable conclusion that something decidedly perverse was going on. After all, little Gordie had vanished too. Before the speculation had had a chance to develop into more bizarre theories, however, Brynning and Gilchrist left Paris for a job in Normandy and began to commute weekends only. But Cheryl continued to lay low for some reason, an irritating business since I had had plans for her myself.

I tracked down Brynning one Saturday evening, perhaps a month later, at the Tournon. He seemed genuinely indifferent at my arrival on the scene, so I asked at once about Cheryl.

"She's no good for a man," he said.

"What do you mean ?"

"Exactly what I've said : she's difficult to take."

"Could you be more specific ?"

"All right. She wants to touch me all the time. She wants to . . . you know."

"Copulate ?"

"Fuck; yes."

"I don't see anything wrong with that, Hugh."

"Well, you wouldn't."

"What's the harm in it ?"

"It shows a lack of consideration. She's like all the women I know; the men too for that matter."

"Where is she ?"

"Probably in her room. Hôtel Windsor. I don't know."

"What did you say to her ?"

"I told you : I said that she was no good for a man."

"But it isn't true, is it ?"

"I always say that. It makes them go away. It gives them something else to think about."

"My God."

"Well who says because you're tall and beautiful you have to be a sex maniac ? I don't. I prefer to think."

"I see."

"Why should I put up with it ? I'm not here to service people. I'm not something to clean people out with. I can't go out alone after dark. It's shameful."

"What about you and Gordie, Hugh ?"

"Go to hell."

"I can't believe this. You mean you always tell them they're no good as women ?"

"Usually."

"But I thought you liked Cheryl."

"I did. I told her not to touch me so often. I'm very private. But there's no stopping them."

"Who else ?"

"Well, you see that girl ?"

"Yes. Trixy. Deceitful little bitch, I hear."

"Trixy, that's right. Same thing. She followed Gordie and I around for weeks. I told her she was no good as a woman; didn't do any good. So I got ahold of Nate and we created this line about her : 'If you took all the faith she has ever had in anyone and shoved it up her ass, there'd still be room for her to be the whore she is.' "

"I've heard it."

"Now she minds her own business."

"What's she like ?"

"How should I know."

"Don't you care ?"

"Well, Nate had a piece of her; wanted some more permanent arrangement but she refused; he's been broadcasting the line ever since. It's not my fault."

"Hugh, do me a favour."

"What's that."

"Get Cheryl out of her room; maybe you can set something up between us; I want that girl."

"That's your problem, I'm no pimp."

Fifteen

Boot Enters The White Slave Trade

When Boot first heard about how much money they were making he looked in the mirror; the mirror was in the vestibule of a shoe store on the St. Michel and over the back of his fine reflected head he began to see them swimming down the Boulevard like gaped fish suddenly, their tails revolving like pinwheels. He stretched the pad of dark muscle under his eye and his eye went red, but other than that he looked awfully good. He had one of those neat snub noses that amateurs usually draw, and some premature gray powder in his hair; his neck was stemmed like the stalk of a rose and tanned besides. But there was sure more to him than that, so he went down the list.

Check, his pitch-black eyes

Check, his sperm-white dental caps

Check, his thin steady mouth tricked like a contracting orifice

Check, the twitch of his nose

Check, the flap-flap of his eyelids

Check, the high swallow in his throat

Check, the bird-light gestures of his bones and body

Check, the look of pure unhindered puzzlement

He put the network through several tests; everything was in working order. He would have to shave some of those grains from his neck, but goddamn, he was well-equipped and looked natural and functioned fine, not like your Seducer who "was probly a rank dud" when it came down the line to sheer technique, or Brynning who just wasted it. But how many of them had he wasted himself, now that he knew? Who had he taken and then let go? Sonofabitch idiot.

So everywhere he walked now, he saw them in a different light, standing or mobile in new attitudes. He sat for a while on the terrace of the Coupolade nursing a beer as he watched them stroke out of the Rue Soufflot, then he came down to the Rue Champollion and saw them in the dark alley outside the cinemas moving and shifting about like bothered maggots. He even tried his very good style and picked one up outside the Select-Latin, an *au pair* girl from California. Her skin was different shades of pale as if she had just pulled loose a series of scabs, and her freckles gave her the air of a pinto pony. ("You look like a fuckin shrunk Indian," he said, hooking her on the point of his wondrous smile. "Yah? Eat crud, spic," she said.) He let her go because she was no test at all, and he missed two others because he was impatient now and walked the few blocks to the Hôtel Stella.

"You member me," he said through the door on the second floor, "Boot the Café Buci this saft." The large man stepped out into the hall, leaving the door somewhat ajar so that Boot could see a few of the faces in distant profile through the dim. They didn't shake hands and the big man caught Boot by the shoulder blade; not in a friendly manner. Boot was wearing his boat neck silk because he had that good tan on his arms and throat; the man gripped the shaft of bare bone and squeezed and rolled it so that he was half in pain the whole time. "This saft," he said, "in the Buci."

"Sure," said the big man, "what do you want ?"

"Well," said Boot, "I contact easy."

"Yah ?"

"Well I never did nothing cept fuck them before; but I got this style."

"Go home."

"You wouldn't believe the way it is with me; I don't panic none and I got no feelings. I'm money in the bank."

Boot took a deep breath and tried to peer round the bulk of the man, but the monster had his thumb in the slip of his clavicle. The big man was a funny man in a café, but he was no fun now.

"Well look maybe I'll see you round," said Boot.

"I see you again I'll stuff you down your own vomit," said the man.

Boot went back to the street. He wore his good clipping boots with the new reinforced heels and he seemed to roll off his own hip striding into the Place St. Sulpice. I got to clean my fingernails though and he held them up and scooped a bit with his thumbnail.

He wondered how it was done because the big man Harry that afternoon had not been too drunk and had only mentioned prices and seaports; he had heard him talk about thousands of francs and Marseilles and dummy cabs and had learned a few addresses, but he didn't know about contacts or the different ways it could be done or how the money was made and where. He had heard them talk about the club in the Rue du Dragon, but he couldn't go there now.

He went to the billiard parlour above the *tabac* in the Rue Buci. Michael, who was French and unfriendly and knew plenty of people, was playing three cushion pool and Boot sat watching for a while and asking questions. Michael thought it was funny that this completely stupid Puerto

Rican would want to know about white slavers. He, of course, knew one or two.

"I don't know a thing about it," he said, "it's all a myth."

"I heard them talking today," said Boot.

"Everybody talks," said Michael, "it is the tendency. Look at all the people in the Tournon who say they blew up bridges for the OAS. Did you see one bridge blown up? If there had been as many explosions as talk, we'd be living in Florence."

"I don't understand," said Boot.

"Naturally," said Michael.

"Where do they take them?" asked Boot, lifting a cue from the rack and spinning it across the flat of the table.

"Who what?" said Michael, "it's a fairy tale. Who could seduce women into that? You're a child."

"Well no you're wrong," said Boot, setting up his shot; the cue ball kissed and spun and kissed. Boot sighed at the ease with which he had done it. "I had a girl last week would have sucked goddamn cock in the Métro for me. I got this tremendous effect."

"Go home," said Michael.

Boot put up his cue and went downstairs for a turn at the Gottlieb. Then he went out and across the road to the Café Buci to sit on the terrace. The wind flopped his hair into his eyes and he sucked the top of his lip as if it was candy and watched his snub nose wrinkle.

"Shit."

Then he waved at some people he knew who were crossing the road and followed them up to the St. Germain. One of them was the coloured boy Isaac-and-Jacob who was friendly the way some people are sick. "Hi Boot," he grinned and crackled, spanking the air with his tremendous beige palm, "we going to the Tournon." So Boot followed. Isaac-and-Jacob kept on in his patented friendly way, his mouth and face beveled, one hand coming down on the back of Boot's very fine neck. They called him Eye-Jay and his only two emotions (hurt and affection) stunned and warped his stride. His right eyeball which hardly revolved except to take in details just beneath him, only saw the dark cracked pavement of the Rue Tournon, so he moved around Boot and slipped his hand and wrist into the kid's elbow and studied his own manicure awhile. He did favours as a kind of penance for some natural guilt which weighed him down; he did not especially like Boot — hardly anybody did — and he hoped that the favour would be a small one.

"What's the matter kid ?" he asked.

"Eye-Jay," said Boot, "I got a skill."

"You mean with women ?" said Isaac-and-Jacob, full of accommodation, "I know sir."

"But it's never done me any *permanent* good," said Boot, his flat voice breaking as they came up to the café itself; Eye-Jay brought out self-pity like rain brought out worms.

When they went into the café, Eye-Jay waved his friends to a table and took Boot to the bar. He was full of concern now, still hoping that the favour would be a small one, for he had larger debts hanging fire. His eyes watered and his breath went fast and some sweat came through his shirt. This was his allergy and his cross. His bad eye fixed on the zinc bar.

"I've got a cold centre," Boot was saying, his eyes tightening so that the centre was hard to see. "Human cunt don't bother me like some. I contact easy."

"Sure," said Eye-Jay, full of relief at catching on, "I know that too."

"Well if I could just get in," said Boot, "goddamn."

"Into whom'siz ?" asked Eye-Jay. His bad eye trailed down the side of the bar and took hold somewhere near the floor line.

"No no," said Boot impatiently. "The white slavers."

"Oh yah," said Eye-Jay, quickly, "right."

"See if I could make a connection, I could get them all sort of pussy. No sweat."

"Do seem a shame not to," said Eye-Jay.

"It's just slipping through my fingers, I can't touch it. Eye-Jay ? Do me a favour."

"Anything," said Eye-Jay.

So Eye-Jay talked fast, working it between his other

favours for four in the afternoon; his bad eye came up so fast from the floor it almost scraped his nose.

"You bring her round about four o'clock tomorrow the Old Navy," he said, "I'll work something out." They shook hands on it, though Boot didn't like to be touched by people like Eye-Jay; people like that had a soft, wet touch and left a stain in your palm.

Now Boot knew that one night and one day wouldn't do it. Everyone had heard of the seduction of Dinnie Waters by a man in a boat neck silk in the Mabillon. And that had taken two months. He had spotted her in the courtyard of the Alliance and had taken the trouble to court all her friends with beers and winning conversation. He had sat on the terrace for weeks without a word passing between them, only looking and smiling and offering her his seat on a busy night. They had been introduced a dozen times before he took the liberty of laying her and it was more than a month after that before he had asked her to come to his villa near Marseilles. The rest was common knowledge. She was now turning over a buck in some cathouse in Morocco and he was working out of some jazz cellar farther down the St. Germain. So a night and a day wasn't going to be enough and Boot mused on that for a while. But that had been a *seduction;* on the other hand, you could dope them up and kidnap them in no time at all : one quick screw to check them out, then hustle them to the docks. Boot decided to get some sleep before evening.

He went home and slept the sleep of the dangerous and in the evening he raised himself carefully from the bed so as not to strain his organ and dressed in black. Black seemed the proper colour now. He washed out the premature specks of gray from his hair and darkened it with polish. He laced a small whip to his wrist and tied a curtain tassel to his belt. He applied talcum to his armpits, lotion to his sphincter, and picked the day's debris (like tiny shrapnel) from his testicles. "Boot, you are love," he said and counted his money.

It was already dark before he found one to his liking. He followed her to a small hotel in the Rue Bonaparte, and waited across the road, leaning against a post, smoking a black Sobrani. He let the expensive albino ash grow, then amputated the turd in one deft flick of the forenail. She came out of the doorway dressed as before in purple bell bottom trousers and small spiked heels; she carried the matching jacket on her arm and wore a sleeveless Persian lamb sweater, striped orange and black like a beehive. He followed her out of the Rue Bonaparte. She had black trimmed hair and black eyes and a black belt on her trousers. She goes with my outfit, thought Boot.

When she came to the Brasserie Lipp, she scrutinized the terrace carefully; she was petite and she rested her entire weight on one buttock. When she was satisfied that there was no one in the Lipp, she made for the other side of the street. Boot got there first and came across the street again towards her; her nose was a little crooked when seen full face. He slipped his arm inside her elbow as she passed him and turned her around gently. The air from the cars passing made little currents through his very fine hair.

"Weren't we going to meet at the Lipp?" he said.

She didn't say anything and then she said, "I suppose so; do you know Eddie?"

"He's sick."

"Isn't he always though," she said.

"I thought we might have some supper and then maybe go to a party in the Gît-le-Coeur."

"Fuck that," she said, "let's go to bed."

She led him back to her hotel in the Rue Bonaparte and up three flights of stairs to a small square room with no linen on the bed.

"I'm Boot," said Boot, locking his smile.

"Just get undressed," she said and pulled the beehive sweater over her head.

When she had pulled off all her clothes, she dropped to the mattress and stretched. Boot took a morphine capsule from a small pocket above his belt then, and held it in front of her.

"You want something nice?" he said.

"Say," she said, "You want to make it or not?"

So he made it. He worked on her like some dark graceful menace, moving his celebrated cock at various speeds as she milked him through the night.

"Okay, relax," she said as dawn broke.

"Jesus I contact easy," Boot thought and went off to sleep.

Their bodies dried about noon the next day and the chill woke them. Boot dressed smiling. He broke open the capsule and dropped the powder into a glass of water. He came back to the bed and lifted her head and put the rim of the glass to her parched mouth. She swallowed some of it and then she coughed and wiped her mouth with the back of her hand; her face had a bitter look.

"Did you put the morphine in this?" she asked.

"Eddie's treat," said Boot.

She shrugged her shoulders and got dressed; this time she wore pink bell bottom trousers and a Persian lamb sweater that was striped mauve and gray.

"What are you," she asked, "part nigger?"

"Puerto Rican," he said.

"You fuck like you're part nigger."

"Happy darling?"

"Cut the shit, I'm hungry."

They went to the Crêperie and had crêpes and jam and a flask of cider with flies in it. The morphine didn't show in her eyes or any place else so he broke another capsule and dropped it in her drink. She made the same bitter face.

"Did you put some more morphine in this?"

"Eddie said nothing was too good for you."

"I've got to piss."

He took her to the Coupolade for a beer after that. She walked straight as a die.

"I want you to meet someone," he said at a quarter to four.

"Who?"

"Friend of Eddie's. Tremendous sensitive guy."

"Does he fuck?"

They walked down the Rue Monsieur le Prince to the St. Germain and along it to the Old Navy. Eye-Jay was sitting on the terrace breaking toothpicks. When he saw them coming, he jumped up and came into the street and led them back to the table; he gathered up the shreds of toothpick guiltily and stuffed them into his shirt pocket. Boot ordered the girl a drink and signalled to Eye-Jay for a private conference. They went inside for cigarettes.

"What's happening ?" asked Boot.

"I hired a car for you," said Eye-Jay. "It's parked near here."

"Good," said Boot. "And ?"

"And ?" said Eye-Jay.

"What else ?" said Boot.

"Well," said Eye-Jay, feeling the favour getting bigger, "we just drive around see."

"Until ?" said Boot.

"Right," said Eye-Jay, straining his inventive powers to the limit, "until I get the word. That's it."

"Then ?" said Boot.

"Then," said Eye-Jay, straining so hard he could feel his hernia shift, "once I get the word, we're gonna be joined in the Bois by some guy called Black Jack Fischer."

"Black Jack Fischer ?"

"Right."

"What happens after that ?"

"Okay. After that, see, you going to drive with him to Marseilles and meet the big man and deliver the goods."

"The big man ?"

"Name of Orland Turk."

"Orland Turk ?"

"Right, Orland."

"Sounds good," said Boot, "but I got a problem."

"What's that ?"

"Well, I gave her a capsule this morning and another one an hour ago and didn't get no reaction."

"No reaction huh," said Eye-Jay. "Better ply her with drinks and don't let her piss."

They bought her cognac and beer chasers for an hour. When she stood up as if to make for the toilet well, Boot took her by the neck and steered her into the street. Eye-Jay

led them to the car, which was an old Ford Vedette that
he had borrowed from Stephen U for the day.

"The two of you sit in the back," he said.

"Where we going ?" asked the girl, no more drunk than
she was drugged. But she saw that they had money.

"Thought we might take a drive in the Bois," said Boot,
"maybe go to one of those swank cafés on the lake."

"I got to piss," she said, but he put his mouth on her
lips, not kissing but holding her lips together with his teeth.

They drove along the Quai, down into the tunnel then up
again onto the Avenue de Versailles. Boot held her lips in
his mouth most of the way, but she struggled free as they
came to St. Cloud. Eye-Jay didn't want to think about the
Bois; he thought what they would do would be drive around
for an hour looking for a Black Jack Fischer and then come
back. Some people pushed his favours to the limit; no
consideration but what they forced him to improvise and
contrive. The imp of concern was killing him.

The girl's eyes were hard and stony. Her legs were
crossed very tightly and she had three fingers pressed on
the crotch of her bell bottom trousers. Her spiked heels
dug into the floor mat making a slight impression. There
was something cold and brutal in the way she would not
pass out.

They drove through the Bois for hours, cutting in and
out of sandy roads, passing the lake itself and the tiny
fences around gardens, circling the racetrack, nosing through
laneways where the trees soared high above them, passing
the gray stone institutes. Finally, Eye-Jay turned off onto
a small path, narrower than the span of the car, and drove
deep into the woods; twigs and branches shivered against
the impact of the old Vedette. When Eye-Jay had found a
likely landmark — a wooden bench beside a twisted wicker
basket — he stopped the car.

"Listen, what's going on," said the girl.

"Nothing," said Boot and stole a quick look at Eye-Jay
who pretended to search the landscape in hopes of Black
Jack Fischer.

"Something's going on," said the girl.

"Shut up," said Boot and hit her across the mouth with the small whip on his wrist. He saw a line of something dark weave out the side of her mouth; blood; he put his forefinger up to her burst lip, fascinated by the warm fluid. He hit her again, across the eye this time.

"Oh," she said, "you guys want to assault me." She pulled her sweater up over her head. "But I better piss first," she said.

"Let her go piss," said Eye-Jay. She put her sweater on the rear ledge of the car and unlooped the black belt from her trousers. Then she opened the back door and went out. She seemed to stumble forward like a diver; she disappeared into the thicket.

"He ought to have been here by now," said Eye-Jay, "goddamn that Fischer."

"He'll come," said Boot, feeling her blood on his finger go dry. He felt a cool affection for the whip.

Somewhere in the dark, they heard the thud of piss where she squatted over the ground. Then after a while it trickled and stopped and they heard the rustle of cloth being yanked to. Her footsteps beat a track towards them. There was a pause. They heard a series of crashes as she fell and rose and fell again.

"Oh no," said Boot, "the stuff's working on her."

"Call her name," said Eye-Jay.

"Don't know her name," said Boot, scrambling out of the car. "If this Black Jack Fischer comes, keep him here," he said.

"Will do," said Eye-Jay. As soon as Boot had gone, he started the motor and reversed the car out of the side road and was back in the Quarter in no time at all.

Boot broke through the thicket. It was pitch black now. He could smell the grass but there was no smell of vomit anywhere. He clenched his small wrist whip. He was feeling good and brutal. "Hey baby," he called.

It took twenty minutes for him to become thoroughly lost and another ten before he saw something moving on a bench in a small clearing. "Baby," he said, "hey."

"Babee Babee," came back to him like an echo from the

bench and he made out two figures standing, waiting for him.

"Oh," said Boot, peering through the gloom, "one of you people Black Jack Fischer ?"

"Feeshir," came the echo.

"Well, I'll tell you, she's somewhere around here," he said, "and Eye-Jay's waiting in the car."

"Iyyy-Jai," came the echo again and with it a sort of wicked laughter. Boot came on, rolling off his own hip as always in that very good stride. His mouth was open and he was going to say something that would prove him in the trade, some special watchword like "I contact easy," or the one about human cunt not bothering him at all. But the two figures waited for him to get close and then moved towards him from either side, circling like wolves, their mouths open too and thick with spit. Boot let out a scream then as it triggered in his mind and made a dash for the woods, but they brought him down by the legs and pinioned his arms on the grass. They tore off his wrist whip and the curtain tassel on his belt; they wrenched him free of his shirt and pulled his pants down over his boots and chucked his underwear to his knees. He couldn't scream now, something empty came out of his throat. One of them sat on his face and raised his legs, holding them apart, while the other slipped himself up Boot's posterior. Boot ripped and farted. When the one was done with him, they changed places carefully and then rested and did it a second time. After that, they let Boot's legs drop but still kept them spread on the ground and took turns kicking him in the groin. They took his money from his wallet and threw the wallet back and then they left. Boot lay unconscious for an hour and after that he lay with his eyes closed pretending that he was unconscious still. He did not want to wake up to see what they had done to him.

Sixteen

Bugs was a natural worrier and lived on the debris or by-product of people around him. He looked like a cross between a basketball player and a Hindu mystic; he had a lemon-shaped head with large red ears and a crew cut; through the transparent hedge of his hair one could make out several scars on his skull, trophies of an athletic past. He didn't talk about that much, but he still kept the natural graces of an athlete and could be seen most any time shifting and faking down the corridor of the Rue Tournon. He was called Bugs not only because of his eyes. He was a natural pest. He carried with him the burden of events as if he himself were the final judge of something historical, as if, in fact, it were his own fabrication; no detail was too meaningless, no incident too unimportant but that it had to be chronicled in his own inevitable hand. Not that Bugs could write; that was for those who observed; Bugs did not observe, he calculated. He was everywhere, wherever the minion gathered, taking rapid notations or storing in his mind the cumulation of what was said and done. He enjoyed a mild notoriety as a voyeur, but there was nothing sexual about his pursuit; women he might have occasionally, but only by way of cleansing himself, as the intermittent depletion of waste material. No, his real strength was drawn from a unique awareness of what was happening. And his real art was the art of the statistic.

He loved statistics. It was his key. He would divide the number of rapes by the approximate litres of available semen, or multiply the periods of general angst by the fraction of the combined pregnancies of two arrondissements over the discarded condoms in any two mile radius. It was his private gauge and it gave him a feeling of control. He had also devised a system of averages by which he could know you. This was his prime statistic. It pried the individual from his mask, and he swore by it; it solved discrepancies in the atmosphere and made everything simple and rewarding. This average was compounded of several variables; it took into consideration one's weight, height, agility at the Gottlieb, number of arguments won in any three month span, frequency of i) induced, ii) spontaneous orgasm, range of prowess both seductive and cerebral, number of consecutive rebuffs and their particular quality, intimidations suffered and perpetrated, decibel of coolness possessed under a) trying, b) mediocre conditions. There were various other tests known only to Bugs, and above all there was his own special instinct for rendering synthetic the clues of the day. It was an annoying habit. He was as busy as a plague.

"The Seducer gained ten points this Half, incredible."

"Garber, I am trying to locate the owner of a defective condom found at the corner of the Rue Madame and the Rue du Four; it's upset my goddamn calculation."

"Anne, did you have your period this month ? Anne ?"

"Now think, Cheryl : how many verbs do you normally use under pressure ?"

"Enemas this season : 3 medicinal, 1 esthetic."

"Trixy. You averaged .256 this Third. Room for improvement."

"Bobby E Lee, folks, is on the injured list."

"Hey, we broke the Quarter record this year. Angst over Cool : No Sweat."

But his greatest triumph had to do with Emmanuel the Spanish. The Spanish lied so well that he could deke Bugs' system any time he wanted. Bugs, as a result, treated him as an unknown quantity, an untouchable. Still, it was a serious gap in his percentages and it gave to his averages an inherent taint. He was not allowed to forget this, because the Spanish liked to taunt him for hours with incorrect data; he would fabricate information with a sense of logic that was difficult to break. More than once, he had forced Bugs to work round-the-clock to meet his deadline.

Then one day, as they were sitting in the Monaco, the Spanish revealed to all that he had once again outlasted Yvonne in their tireless battle on the bed. "I withheld my true essence till the woman had succumbed and proved valueless; thus again the prize is mine."

"You're wrong," said Bugs, uncommonly excited, twisting about, face flushed.

"Wrong?" said the Spanish disdainfully, "I am not wrong."

"Wrong wrong!" said Bugs with righteous ecstasy, trembling as he bent to the floor. He produced a small tape recorder and put it anxiously on the table. "Oh are you wrong!"

"Prove this thing immediately," said the Spanish.

Bugs worked the tapes furiously. Then he flushed again and folded his arms with imperial calm.

The voice of the Spanish came over the tape. "I will tell you of a terrible thing," it said. "In my drunkeness I will confide. Yvonne has a function beyond my worth : she is too vaporous."

"See see!" said Bugs, shattering his attempt at calmness. "Oh isn't this wonderful! I can't stand it. And I'm stealing a computer next week. Ain't nobody safe now. The age of Bugs is here!"

Seventeen

The person talking in this tale is Valentine. She is medium height, with dark straight hair, large in the hip, incommunicable. She is often seen with her whore Dee in the Café Monaco, large hands pressed to her forehead and her eyes narrow. At midnight, she is at the Café Buci or on the St. Germain, and at two or three in the morning she is at the Café Tournon for the late crowds. Dee never leaves her side.

I took Dee up to the man about one o'clock and waited myself by the first floor landing. There was no light, I wish there had been a light. Outside there was a slight drizzle.

The streets were damp, but the moon was large. I did not take off my gloves for it was chilly; I had a checkered black scarf wrapped about my neck, but the tail of it was wet and I felt it wet against my throat. At one-thirty I came back up the stairs for Dee. The door was closed but the light was on, I could see it under the door. "Dee?" The man came to the door and let me in. Dee was wiping herself with a green towel. The man was naked. I sat down. The single bulb had no shade and was beside the bed on the floor. The bed was low. The man had been taking pictures with a new camera; I saw it on the dresser. I lifted the camera and underneath were six pictures of Dee. "No," I said, "that is not included." The man shrugged his shoulders. He scrubbed his body with a hairbrush. "That will be fifteen francs extra." The man took the pictures over to the light. He made two piles, four in one, two in the other. "It is fifteen francs either way," I said, "for one or all." He put the pictures into a drawer and climbed into bed under the sheets. Dee went to a corner sink and emptied the pan of water. "Doesn't she speak?" asked the man. Dee put on her clothes. The man took the money from beneath the pillow and I took it from him. "Not once did she say a word," he said. I took Dee by the arm and we left him.

On the way it was damp and the rain went inside our shoes. "We should have worn boots," I said. We stopped off to have some *chocolat* on the Boulevard Clichy. Dee took off her coat and with her short hair and little chest she looked very much like a small boy. Her fingers were short and yellow. She had tiny bee lips in the form of a heart. The bar was bright and shiny, I can't tell you how shiny when seen by the rain and the dark night. The *chocolat* was warm; I watched Dee sipping slowly and getting a little foam on the corners of her mouth. Her little face was pale as chalk and her eyes were not open wide. I gave her the cigarette and went to play the Gottlieb. I smelt the marijuana ash behind me and I soon won a free game and then another. The Gottlieb was orange and purple and it rang as the ball of silver dropped through the slot. Dee came up to it and put her hands on the glass.

We walked through the streets and down the small slope from Pigalle. At St. Lazare we went into the Métro; Dee and I stood in the Métro car. There was a lady sitting there with an accordion and a cup; she had two glass eyes. We got off at Odéon and walked all the way to the Café Tournon. That was very brightly lit and the Gottliebs were noisy. Emmanuel the Spanish was playing and swearing; he rocked the Gottlieb with his arms and stomach like a lover. Maurice put us at a table in the back. He had a thick nose. I ordered two omelettes and Dee asked for another cigarette. Jules the Seducer came over to talk, then Florine and then Emmanuel the Spanish and Trixy. Emmanuel said that the Gottlieb was upset; if the Gottlieb is good to you then everything is all right, but when the Gottlieb gets angry then you might as well sleep all day. He said he played the Gottlieb every morning for a sign. Georges told us a joke.

Four or five men were sitting a table away and one of them smiled at Dee. She was wearing trousers with little blue buttons. The omelettes came and I wrote on the napkin in English, "Woman's Voluntary Service," and passed it down the line of tables. An American came back with the napkin and asked if she were male or female. Dee's eyes were almost closed, like those of a little cat. The smell of the cigarette made me dizzy. "Female," I said. The American was not convinced and bent over to look into her face. He went back to the others and I could hear them talking and deciding not to take her. We ate the omelettes slowly. Maurice came over and joked with us for a while. He wore a white waiter's jacket and an apron. Had we heard the latest story about that idiot Vangrin the writer? He wrote a play yesterday afternoon in the front of the Café and in the last act the actors had to bring a cow on stage and slaughter it. Everyone told him that was silly, what if it was a successful play, how could you kill a cow every night? It was an impractical cow. So he rewrote the last act and in the revision all the actors had to do was bring on hunks of fresh meat. Maurice waited for a tip and then joked some more. Did we know that he had given that idiot

Vangrin the writer twenty francs because Vangrin had promised to put him in his novel? "Maurice," Vangrin that idiot said, "for ten francs I will mention your name in my novel, for twenty francs you will get to kiss the girl in my novel, and for forty francs I will put you into bed with her on page three hundred and twelve." He is taking money orders now, and when he has enough money he will write the novel and put in all the names who paid for it. "I can't afford to sleep with her," said this Maurice, "but I can afford to kiss her on page two hundred; he promised it will be a long kiss and will last four pages." Dee liked to hear him talk. Her lips were so very tiny and pink. Her eyes were tiny too. The darkness and the cold outside made all the sounds louder. Dee took me by the sleeve and spoke softly telling me things. Little Dee. She had tiny puffs under her eyes and wore a brown shirt unbuttoned at the throat. Her arms were very nice. She finished the cigarette and dropped it under the table. Cheryl came over and talked. She was worried. Anne the Pregnant waved. Cheryl said goodby. Lots of time passed. Many people we knew played cards and joked. The new person Dixie blew bubbles in his wine and made his funny monkey sounds. Dee rested her head against the wall. I saw little freckles on her nose and throat and on her arms. There was no business tonight, but there was nothing to be done about that. I played eight games on the Gottlieb with Emmanuel the Spanish and lost; he said he would wake up the next morning instead of sleeping all the day; he thanked me for this good sign; the Gottlieb loves its own, he said. I played five games with Brynning and won.

The glare of the lights in the cafe gave me yellow spots outside on the wet street and in the dark air. We walked awhile and then walked to our hotel. Across the way the Café Buci was noisy and the lights glared. Fitz waved from the corner and his friends watched Dee pass into the hotel doorway looking sick and tired. I came after her and we mounted the stairs in the dark. I could smell the rooms. We climbed the stairs to our room and I put on the small light. Outside I could see the other hotel windows and the shadow of chimneys. Dee undressed and went into the bed. I opened the windows; it was so very cold, I could hear Dee groan and whimper. I turned a little gas on from the stove to make us drowsy. I took off my clothes and came into the bed. Dee curled her back into my chest and stomach and lay facing the wall while we waited for sleep.

ighteen

There is a grotesque in the Rue de Rivoli, not far from the Ritz and the Rue Cambon, whose facial skin has long ago been burnt off and replaced by a bright, pink scab. She has no nose and her lips are reinforced with rubber. She has two glass eyes, blue, that stare at you like a trick portrait — they draw a bead on your movements that is inescapable. Her face is stuffed with putty and glass, rubber and hair; one hand is no hand at all but a stillborn wing or a soft claw or a pink bone; her legs, where visible, are a boiled scarlet and taper from thick scaled calves to ankles as narrow as a vertical pin. She possesses a facade of scorn and distance carefully arranged, for it is part of the market value, and if you are susceptible to guilt you may have to buy your way past. Deep in the bowels that have survived, there is an instinct for intimidation that is unfailing. At best, she is a bad memory.

"A bad memory," said André of the French Foreign Legion who is made mostly of wood, "but I have seen worse, and will mention them day by day as our friendship increases."

To say that André of the French Foreign Legion is made mostly of wood is misleading; he is made of other things too, metal plates, wires, cement, gold, string, paper, safety pins, silver, reinforced hair and zinc. The first time I saw him was in the Café Buci where he sat nightly against the

far wall, his head resting on the ledge of the mirror behind
so that his own image seemed to be leaning against him for
support. André's face was clear and white. Nothing surprised him, nothing upset him; his face was free of meaning,
everything in its proper place, lip and brow rigid. His black
hair was parted in the middle and sleeked down on both
sides so that his skull resembled two sloped roofs. His arms
seemed wired to his sides with both hands palm down on
his lap except when he bent carefully for his expresso. Then
in four stages the arm and hand moved. On command, the
appendage raised itself by the hinge of the elbow to table
level, remained stationary (as if in gear) until released;
next, the hand lowered towards the cup, fingers locking
about the handle; then, the hand pulled upward while the
elbow, maintaining the angle of descent, beckoned the
apparatus to the mouth; the mouth sipped awhile to a frequency; the elbow then released the arm proper which in
turn placed the cup successfully on the table. All the while,
his head did not turn : it jerked, like the head of a bird.
Its range of movement was the four points of a square, and
the whole man was like a diagram which tested itself again
and again, putting its uses to the proof, raising an arm,
arranging a leg, flexing a bone. André always wore black
gloves and an officer's cape; otherwise, he was in civilian
dress, suit and tie and pocket hanky.

"Most days," he said upon introduction and by way of
preface, "I will wile away my noons wandering down the
Boulevards. When I am not working it is a great pleasure
to notice these grotesques, it uplifts me. There are five blind
musicians on the Capucines who play amusingly off key.
They walk in single file like elephants joined trunk to tail
and it is wonderful to see them chat among themselves and
laugh occasionally, which is a burlesque of ordinary people.
Of course, it goes without argument that if it was not for
their blindness they would be fools. I am still more intrigued
by the lottery people on the Boulevard Haussmann at the
corner of the Rue Caumartin. They have subtle handicaps,
it is a wonder to see. I have noticed their bodies covered
with scabs and boils and secreting through the cloth damp

acids. I personally know a man who was cut purely in two by a team of German doctors. From the navel down. He was in a test tube for years. Like a plant. Now he rests on a cushion, in a little wagon. He is surrounded by pouches and sacs for his waste matter. I am particularly interested in this case."

André of the French Foreign Legion was unable to walk : he marched. I never saw him outside the Café Buci, which might have made all the differences in one's attitude, but it was possible to see him marching in goose step once daily and twice nightly towards the toilet well. He never smiled; it would have been a savage reversal of everything he believed in if he had. And what he believed in was so easily acquired by those who had the time that it did not seem like a belief at all, just an odour.

André was in appearance and effect a kind of initiation into the Café Buci; everyone at one time or another became an offering to appease his sense of public, for he was like a minotaur, killing with conversation the victims fed to his monster. He had a need to transfix you with the importance of his wounds; it was a determination and a bore. That first evening, Brynning led me in like a vestal virgin, deposited me at his table in the form of a small offering and ran like hell to the nearest Gottlieb. André wet his mouth in an orgy of preparation, then chewed his words as if they were cleansing his breath.

"Take rape as an example," he proceeded *in media res.* "I was guilty of this crime in North Africa; sometime in July; I will not name the place. Now if I may be permitted I have in my possession certain photographs of sexual and miscellaneous atrocities which you might find instructive." In three stages, using his forefinger and thumb as projectile, he produced four pictures of such horrible proportions that I could barely smile. "Photograph A," he droned, "was taken in the kitchen of a rather pleasant house. Note the small green twigs for the stove. And the condition of the quilted rug. These incidentals are the savoury of the situation that prevailed. The body upper left (the left foreleg is merely out of range, not dismembered) is that of a girl age

19 in possession, I must explain, of a rather small orifice proper which led to her death by bleeding."

"I'm gonna have a cheese baguette, André, what about you ?"

"Not for me thank you. Photograph B as designated," he continued, and didn't stop until, pale and trembling, I rushed to the toilet only to find it occupied, as always, by Gilchrist. A small trickle of digested cheese crept from my mouth like a thread pulling my stomach with it.

"Take me away," I said to Brynning at the bar.

"The trick is not to eat beforehand," said Brynning casually.

Escape was not simple. André was a legacy of pain and boredom which had to be passed from hand to hand like a de Sade heirloom. One had to find some new, unsuspecting dupe and arrange an introduction; only then was desertion allowed. No one actually made the rules; but no one defied the general consensus either. It was Bugs who said that André's presence helped to measure cycles.

I was developing, in the meantime, a tragic need for Cheryl, though she seemed almost impossible to trap, and my time was valuable. She had recently emerged from a self-imposed exile in her room at the Hôtel Windsor, taking the alternative to complete abnegation, and was around. I had planned a grand confrontation that very week. Still, the next night, André beckoned me again and, not yet having found an offering I could send in my place, I wandered unhappily to his table and sat down. André was sitting with a woman this evening who faintly resembled the open-mouthed horror of Photograph D as designated. André rose with a jerk as if a noose had just yanked him into death and introduced Penelope, a woman of probable middle age, although the condition of the body made complete identification impossible. She meant things that were beyond imagining, I was certain; nothing less than lunatic could have fathomed the contours of that smile. She was all pleasantness and light concealed, one hoary innuendo. Her gaze on your mouth made you feel weak in the knee and privates, and you began to question your own disciplines when you

could siphon such perversity and promise from a look like
that. Apparently, she had scurvy.

"Penelope," said André with imagined warmth, "is a
valued friend to whom I commend your patronage."

Penelope showed me what he meant by a baleful twitch
of the lip. She made an unfair noise sucking on the moisture
of her mouth.

"She is not," André said, "unseldom at my beck."

Penelope slavishly complied by some rearrangement of
her clothing. Her mouth, briefly opened as if she were
surfacing for air, looked like the inside of a purse.

"Perhaps," said André, continuing the tale of his evenings,
"you have wondered what I am possibly doing out of
uniform. Yes ? No matter. I have retired from the army
you see : officially. I was in the hospital for some time in
North Africa, a country incidentally where I witnessed rape
and murder; sometime in July. Perhaps, if I may be permitted . . ."

"I've seen them," I said.

This news made the rest of the evening impossible for
André : he had miscalculated the date. He extracted, with
mechanical agility, a calendar and concentrated on it for
some time in stony silence. On his face was reflected the
laborious shifting of hook and screw.

"Does Mr. Garber want to come back to the house with
us ?" asked Penelope, as if the Photographs A to D entitled
me to a small privilege.

"Doubtless not," said André, fixing the button of a glove.

He was right, of course. But there was a sickly lure in
the vision of her honed and curly pubis dripping poisons
down each flank, the great Transylvanian shadow of her
organ rearing for an easy kill.

Next evening, André sat in his accustomed place alone.
His look was almost evangelical, there was even the pre-
monition of a smile on his face. His voice seemed to under-
mine the noise about him.

"Now to continue," he said, "I was in a hospital for some
time. No, I will tell you exactly how long : a year and two
months; naturally, I cannot tell you where. I had some

thoughts of import in the hospital; I will try to relate them to you in order of their occurrence; rape and murder and the pillage of sundry goods was consistent in my mind, of course. I had suffered too much, I had seen and done what it grieved my mind to recollect. In the tranquillity of illness, I asked myself, What about the future? My mind was at a crisis. My injuries were sorely great, I cannot tell you. Sorely great indeed. I had had no training but the war, and a man like myself who has been a party to rape and murder and miscellaneous torture holds life cheaply in the palm of his hand or at other junctures of his anatomy. He becomes somewhat cynical of people, impatient of weaknesses. Particularly in the dark races. I was disarranged. Great were my burdens of guilt in certain directions. I read the philosophies of the world, exposed myself daily to the great musical works. The conclusions I drew were not happy ones. I found in the flowering of genius the germs of demented souls, obsessed, unsound. Hope lay elsewhere, surely. But where? The hospital staff put me together, but it did not put me together, you see. One must put one's self together or remain for ever apart not a part. You see the difference?"

Yes, I said, I saw the difference, but there was Cheryl wandering into the Café Buci, looking around in that somnambulent way which seemed to carry her dreams before her like a carrot. She saw me, pouted with sympathy at the company I kept, and left through the same door without so much as a gesture of conspiracy. But she would be at the Monaco within minutes, I knew this infallibly, and suddenly I put my hands on my stomach and gagged, I reared up in my seat and howled. André quieted; quarts of intimidation flushed his moving parts. I raced out of the café in search of Cheryl whose pant bottom was still miraculously visible, sneering counterclockwise down the Rue de l'Ancienne Comédie.

Next evening, I brought Cheryl with me to protect my interests and André at once proceeded in a tone ironical which for him constituted the nth degree of charm. This changed, however, to the tone confessional in no time at all.

"With manifold possibilities, I studied my future and

found a variety of avenues open that could benefit extraordinarily from my skills, experience and cleanliness. Put
whatever has been the past behind you, André, I said to
myself thoughtfully; condition, discipline, are easily sufficient
for a good life."

He took hold of our eyes *en masse,* making severally sure
they were in place. Meanwhile, Cheryl was not happy by
any means. When Cheryl was not happy she shook and
the currents made tiny resonances in the air. The atmosphere
vibrated with her unhappiness. This set off a wonderful
agitation in us both, the first stirrings of what was to become
an unimaginable week in the country.

"And well," said André, "and what am I doing now?
you and the young lady who is too charming might well ask.
I am doing very well. Do you possibly know the Harold
Winsines of Butte, Montana? They have a supreme apartment in Trocadéro. Three times a week, exactly at eight
o'clock in the morning, I arrive: Mondays, Wednesdays
and an occasional Sunday. Three times a week, promptly
and efficiently, I clean house: wax the floors, wash the
walls, dust the carpets and perform chores of a less specific
nature. It is noble work. It is a philosophy of work, gained
from deep thought in hygienic institutions. I am building a
credible reputation as a dependable among the American
families of Paris. It is ennobling labour. It is an ethic of
duty. Mrs. Winsine has said of me: André, you take your
work seriously and that is important; you are an excellent
cleaning man, meticulous and tasteful. Mrs. Winsine, I
reply when spoken to thusly, I am a man of honor and do
my duty. Discipline and self-control are needed for such
work as this, and I am proud to serve you in such a
capacity."

Now that the secret was out, André allowed his face to
tire; the sheets of grafted skin deflated into zones and
hollows. He was still wearing his gloves and he pulled the
fingers, smoothing them into the gnarled shape of his hand.
Apparently, he was going to give us time to consider his
ways; he rose with measured triumph, and marched in a
hardened goose step to the toilet.

I had never truly spoken to Cheryl, except in that comic give-and-take one hesitates to bridge. I had assumed that André would give her a certain kick, but he was no laughing matter and her face was very pale. When it was that pale it was frightening, for she was exceptionally beautiful; her features were hauntingly regular, with lips in an inverted half-moon to designate sorrow. She made you wonder if your feet were clean.

"He's awful," she said.

"He's pathetic," I said.

"We used to talk to him when I was with Jules," she said.

"He's a racist," I said.

"Jules used to make him show me photographs," she said.

"He's a fascist bastard," I said.

"Jules would make me sit with him for hours alone," she said.

"He's a baby raper," I said.

"But when I first met Jules, he was so kind and gentle," she said.

"That André," I said.

"He was playing guitar in the Rue Mazarine, his curly dark hair and his eyes. He talked to me all evening and he told me he just wanted to hear my voice," she said.

"He's a fucking parasite," I said.

"And that first night he took me to his room and I hardly knew what was happening; but he was nice," she said.

"He's a whoremaster," I said.

"No, he just doesn't feel anything for most people," she said.

"André ?" I said.

"Jules," she said.

Our first intimate dialogue ceased with the return of André; he had applied some powder to his cheeks and chin to simulate a five o'clock shadow; he looked lovely. He maneuvered himself into position and waited with reserve while his system reassembled. His head jerked with exact precision by way of greeting.

"I would say it is agreed that we are friends," André began, tracing nervous circlets of expresso on the table top, "and so I will presume to ask of you a special favour." He examined my eyes as if to rally to his aid all available good will. "You seem, Mr. Garber, a discriminating person, who would not have for a friend someone unworthy or suspect in the least. And so I will presume upon your trust in the matter."

He slipped forward like the shuttle of a printing press.

"If you could possibly write for me a letter of recommendation to certain authorities in the American Immigration Office in Paris, explaining my qualities as I have outlined them, I would be happily in your immense debt. Could you say that I was a fit and proper person to reside in Butte, Montana or any other place of their choosing, a tireless worker with assets of character and qualities of mind and a thorough training in especial fields? And could you ask for an immediate personal interview with a Mr. Rowlins or, that failing, with a Mr. Freeman? I will personally tutor you as to your performance at such a meeting so that your sponsorship will appear adequate to the Department. And please do not think that my intentions towards your services are not honourable, nor that you will take these troublesome duties unrewarded. A Miss Penelope Herig, whom you met under pleasant circumstances the other night, would be as grateful as I, and willing I'm sure to accommodate any fancy or recreation you are prone to. She is inventively friendly. This failing to interest you, I will personally sign a cheque cashable at any Crédit Lyonnais in Paris or Belgium. As a gesture."

"I don't know how to tell you this André," I said, relieved by this chance at honourable exit, "but I'm a Canadian."

"Canadian? What does that precisely mean?"

"It is the northern extremity of an attitude prevalent in New York."

"New York! Good, then its settled."

"Well, not quite André. There is something else. This Mr. Freeman, of whom you speak, has had a vendetta against my family for years, dating from our paternal lines in Lithuania. I make his bile turn blue. And unfortunately, he has passed the word on to your Mr. Rowlins. Whose hobby is guns, by the way."

"A Mr. Morris Freeman ?" asked André, visibly shaken, "a Mr. Terence Rowlins ?"

"That's the ones."

"You would not possibly consider a disguise ?"

"Sorry André."

André was very upset. I could sense him counting the wasted hours.

Cheryl and I rose quickly. "I'll write you care of the American Hospital," I said and I clasped his hands and wished him all sorts of luck and discipline. He seemed unmoved by this concern, and collapsed upright in his chair like so much dead weight.

Outside it was weatherless. Odéon was sparse with people, and many of the lights were out. I put my arm about Cheryl's waist, the way one holds a basket against one's hip, and swung her chin to my shoulder. She was rather tall for his and had to buckle her knees. But she was mine after a fashion, I could feel it as we walked. André was only a bad taste, but we were together and the hell with grotesques and monomania and whoring. I led her down to the tree of spring; we sat on the cobblestones with our feet dangling over the water. She rolled up her trouser legs and her toes turned dark where the water touched them. Some Algerians were sleeping under the trees on flattened boxes; someone played the harmonica far off in the darkness under the bridge. Her hair smelled of fresh flowers, and I could smell the sweet soap on her neck and arms. So Cheryl. I counted her fingers tenderly, closing them into a fist. Her arm was soft and white. She stared at the middle distance, out across the flat river, and her face seemed to exalt and transform into forbidding marble; like the exaltation of the dead. I touched the furrow of her spine and the cool muscle. Well Cheryl. The waters of the Seine were still as a pool. Whispers carried from the little park. I kissed her shoulders. It was good to be with this girl, in this place.

"I didn't mean for you to be upset about André," I said.

"He's cruel," she said.

"Just pathetic," I said.

"He's got no feelings, like a machine," she said.

"Never again," I said.

"It's hard to forget, when you've been with someone for a time and loved them," she said.

"Jules ?" I said.

"André," she said.

Nineteen

Cheryl, age 20, walked into the bedroom of her studio flat in Florence. One of the men she was living with was picking his nails with a scissors and inspecting his sleeked hair in the mirror. "Cheryl-Erryl-Barrel," he said by way of greeting; he then raised himself from the vanity chair, left the room and went about his business. Cheryl's face was as remote as memory, unable to conjure even disgust at the sight of the bed, the smell of the room, the noises Foncee made drawing his bath. She was dressed — by now habitually — in dungarees, buttoned cardigan and checkered shirt. The sunlight tapering through the window made a prism of lighter colours on the wall. Cheryl sat on the bed with her hands hanging loosely between her legs; her fingers were coarsened and red; there was some ingrained dirt around her knuckles, and amber streaks of nicotine. "Herb," she said, as if trying to catch her breath. It made an empty sound. Her face froze briefly in an attitude of remorse and self-pity, as if in mime : Harlequin Disgraced. She kicked some balls of crumpled paper under the bed, then wandered with a slightly intoxicated bearing into the studio proper. Herb was not there; she moved along the perimeter of the room as if to measure its opulence. "Herb ?" Foncee came down the hall wrapped in a great white towel that had Gran Hotel sewn in blue down his hip. His legs were bowed and hairless and one big toe was scarlet red. "You going to

scrub my back, creature ?" He put one hand over the hallway arch and the other against the wall. "Come on Cheryl-
Erryl, the wad-ah's getting cold and old." He didn't seem
to expect a reply, but stood nevertheless for several seconds
in a frozen, pigeon-toed stance. Cheryl had her haunch to
the wall and was gazing distractedly at the dead centre of
the room. They held this impressive still life for some time,
in fixed and vacuous concert, then Foncee turned on both
heels like a Raggedy Ann and whistled himself to the bathroom. Soon he was making his little splashing noises in the
tub. Cheryl slid down the wall to a squatting position on
the floor; the sun planted a disk of light on the carpet and
she tried to settle within it. She sat there being slowly
cooked for an hour. When she rose and went into the
bathroom, Foncee was already dead, having — for no good
reason — finished off an entire bottle of perfume. One arm
hung limply over the tub and the towel from the Gran Hotel
was wrapped carefully in Marat style around his head.

Cheryl, age 21, sat at a table on the terrace of the Petit
Bar in Paris; her hand, in a clutch of fingers, rested on the
bare forearm of Jules the Seducer. It was a late Sunday
morning. Jules sat in the shadow of the café awning and,
grouped about him with their backs to the sun, were three or
four of his newest set already fashioned into attitudes of
reverence. Henry Rotter sat at his left hand. Cheryl seemed
contented; the standing pallor of her face was almost flush-
coloured now, as if all her resources had at last been fathomed.
Jules, on the other hand, smiled vacantly, with a certain nice
disinterest; he disengaged his arm from Cheryl's hold to touch
the flat edge of his hair. "Henry," said Jules, "what was
it my father said about boxes ?" Henry didn't know; he
looked away then back again. "Son, my father used to say
(he always called me son), a box is for collecting things :
you really cherish something, you don't put it in a box."
Henry smiled painfully. Jules raised both arms, opened his
hands to heaven and make a small appeal to the god of
boxes. There was an instant of nervous laughter around the
table. Florine, an unpretty blonde with raven lips, passed
the salt. "Are you happy, baby ?" asked Jules, turning

abruptly to his right and planting a wet kiss on Cheryl's
nose. "You ought to be happy, kid, I worked over you five
hours last night," then let his head jerk full circle for the
hooker, "and missed my goddamn dreams." "He missed his
dreams !" howled Bugs, choking on his giggles. Florine
laughed loudest and sucked in a lip. Jules trained his
professional eye on her mouth for a while; she kept it tight
for him until he had finished gauging its prospects. Cheryl
smiled stoically and Henry stared at the drift of the river
under the bridge. It was a dark green that morning and
glutted with leaves and pods of leaves. "Henry," asked
Jules, "what did my father used to say about itches ?"
Henry didn't know; there were bits of yellow dust on the
leaves. "Son, my father used to say (he always called me
son), an itch is like the devil's own invention : the more
you scratch the more you scab." Florine released a deep,
hungry laugh. "You itchy, Florine ?" asked Jules. "I don't
want no scab Jules," said Florine. She brought up a nervous
hand to steady the cords of her throat. Jules broke into a
lopsided grin; he leaned back in his chair and brought his
mouth up to Cheryl's ear. What he whispered was whispered
very loudly, but it got no visible reaction from Cheryl. She
got up to leave the table, and walked away from the terrace
towards the Petit Pont. Jules gave Henry the high sign and
he followed her at a quick distance.

Cheryl, age 21 and 3/12 (it was evening), submitted to
the sight of André disrobing. He removed teeth, hair, foreleg, waste pouch and various metal cylinders. "Whom have
you had to this point ?" he asked, disguising his tremendous
shame behind an enquiry of mild interest. "Has it been only
Jules and those poor unfortunates in Italy ?" Cheryl cringed
at the sight of his gradually diminishing body as further
objects were detached and shelved. "Or has it also been
Bugs whom you have taken ? and the Spanish ? and Fitz ?
And prior to these, Henry Rotter ? And more recently
Maynard Duncan, Nate the Accordion, sundry others ? I
had but to inquire to be furnished with the information."
Cheryl closed her eyes, not yet doubting her own love for
this man who had courted her with his talk of honour and

discipline and creed. "But I am not jealous; it is a wasteful emotion; I prefer to tolerate." He removed some flesh-coloured tape from his forehead, unscrewed his left ear lobe. "Doubtless you made a wise decision in taking me up, as they call it. I will instruct you in the art of temperance and steadfast purpose. We shall be happy, I can assure you." He unbuckled a very complicated back brace, and something metallic dropped from his jaw. He applied a screw driver to several parts of his torso. "We shall make what I call a separate peace, dear girl. I know for a fact that a certain charitable element lies behind your actions; well, we shall build on that. It will be truly wonderful, of that you have my guarantee." When he was finished disseminating himself about the room, he swung by the aid of chairs to the little cot and lowered his remaining parts. "It is late, and rest is renewal. Come to bed, so then." Cheryl opened her eyes and came quietly towards the bed. He made one final adjustment, then raised his appendage to receive her. She looked down; except for his spartan smile, there was nothing there.

Cheryl, age 21 and 7/12, followed Brynning and Gilchrist into the Rue Jacob. They apparently preferred to ignore her, but she moved easily behind them, like some vindictive ghost, and when they emerged out of a labyrinth of streets into the St. Germain, she was still there, silent, pale. "Take a look, Gordie," said Brynning. "Is she still there?" Gordie turned and squinted. "Yes. I'm scared Hugh. What's she gonna do?" "Just keep walking Gordie." They walked west along the St. Germain; they ducked into the washrooms of the Café de Flores, but when they reappeared, she was standing at the curb like some haunting spectre, so they continued to walk. "I don't like her, Hugh," said Gordie, "she's scary." "Say tweak," said Hugh. "Tweak," said Gordie. "Feel better?" asked Hugh. "I'm scared," said Gordie. When they came to the Seine near Concorde, Brynning stopped. Cheryl stopped too; she stood in a distant doorway, her sad eyes trained on the slim beauty of Brynning. "Go down this stairway, Gordie," said Brynning, "I'll be there in a minute. Go ahead." "Are you going to give her the business?" asked Gordie. "That's right," said Brynning. "Why can't

I fucken hear?" pouted Gordie. "Gordie!" "Okay, but don't be long; make it a quick one." Gordie Gilchrist ran down the stairs and onto the paved bank of the quai. He stood with his hands sheltering his eyes from the sun and tried to see. When Brynning took a quick look over the wall to see if he had arrived safely, Gordie turned abruptly and pretended to watch the water. Then Brynning came towards the doorway where Cheryl waited like some abandoned rite. "Go away," said Brynning, "you understand." Cheryl put her finger to his brow and traced the line of his nose and mouth; she had never seen anything so fine. "You bother me," said Brynning, "so get lost, you silly slut." "Hugh," she said. Brynning slapped her hand from his face, swatting it as one swats flies. "I don't want you around, hear!" he said. "Stop following us." Cheryl stood there, looking at his fragile face and lean graceful length; she said nothing. "Okay," said Brynning, "I better tell you the truth. You're no good for a man. You're defective. You're not a woman. You're not satisfying. You're inadequate. You spoil what you touch. You're useless. You got awful breath." There was a brief silent impact as vagueness countered vagueness. The impasse held. "Ready yet!" shouted Gordie from beneath the quai.

Cheryl, not much older, sat quietly in my hotel room on the Ile de la Cité; she sat on a hard-backed chair a few feet from the bed. I was on the bed. My head was propped by two pillows so that I could watch her; I had never seen such a vacant, inert look. It was as if she were unexpectedly recovering from a frontal lobotomy. Every time I met her, I had to lead her by the hand, plant her on a chair, amuse her before she passed right out of this conscious world. I was a little tired of this grand tour of her soul and had reached the ceiling of my patience about midevening. "Cheryl, want some wine?" I took a bottle of the cheapest from under my pillows and cleverly withdrew the cork so that it made a dull, squishy noise like you know what. Cheryl seemed to enjoy this, though she said nothing. It was like toying with an amnesiac for whom you had to go over the fundamentals of life every morning; it always took a few hours to bring her up to at least simplicity. "You'll have to bring over the glass," I said, "because I am slowly dying of a rage to live." She stood up (the lights were off) and lifted a plastic cup from the soapcatch above the sink. "Rinse it out," I said, wanting a little time, "I gargle in it." Cheryl's tall shadow bent over the sink gently as if she were baptising the plastic; the tap water groaned, then spurted. "I-gotta-de-vino-babie-ifa-you-gotta-de glass," I said enthusiastically. She came to me in a lean stride, holding the cup high like a small prize. Her new jeans were so tight she looked as if she were trying to swallow her pants. "On-you-kneez-babie," I said, "so I won't spill the wine, Cheryl." She stooped beside the bed and I took a deep sniff of her hair as I leaned over. "I-ken-finda-de-cup-babie," I said, groping with the neck of the bottle as comically as possible; she brought the cup up closer, so I nailed her on the mouth with a small kiss. The skin of her lip was dry and warm. "Cheryl Cheryl," but I had to say it through my nose. She laughed and I let her pull away, then filled her cup to the brim with the vin rouge ordinaire. She turned round in her crouch, using her ankles as a kind of turnstile. "Don-go-babie-stay-wida-me-a-few-min," but she was already up on her long legs and walking heroically to the chair. She hardly ever bothered to cross her legs; she spread them in front of her with boyish disregard. I forced the sigh of a man who is remembering. "Please," said Cheryl, "say something funny." "Well, I'm not in the mood," I said. "Just anything," she said. I swallowed loudly. "Okay : you know Bunny Zenner's nose ? Well, when it's troubling him he doesn't go to an ear nose and throat man, he goes to a chiropractor." "Thank you," said Cheryl. She stood up in the dark room and dropped her jeans. I could see I'd have to get her out of the city for two three weeks minimum.

Twenty
Into The Valley Of The Loire

What follows are impressions, or entrails, of a week in
the country :

The first evening we drove to Chambord and walked
through the park of the Château without entering. There
was a smell of dried leaves and the noise of crickets as we
walked into the woods and out again. The northwest facade
was frightening in the summer dusk; the vanishing light had
taken with it the sense of depth, and the Château stood
shorn of its dimension without volume or fold, one dark
massive wing, the towers, the galleries, the arcades of a
flatness that seemed to move and palpitate. When we walked
back to the car through a labyrinth of footpaths, the Château
welled up at our backs in deadly pursuit. Across the vast
stretch of lawn, Stephen U and Bonnie still stood beneath
the turret, talking quietly.

We bought some pâté and baguettes in the village and
prepared to spend our first night in the open. We drove
the car along the banks of the Loire until we had found
ourselves a small circular clearing that sloped slightly onto
an apron of rocks and bushes. When enough time had
passed, we spread our blankets on the grass. Some two
hundred yards down the river and midway across, there was
a small island; when it was completely dark, a mansion
perched on its rising base suddenly burst into a myriad of tiny
lights. "We could swim over," said Emmanuel the Spanish,
"those are the lights of a great festivity." But we only
looked, lining ourselves along the bank in the darkness. We
were all strangely fatigued and, worse, already longing for
a café.

Stephen U built the fire. The flames did not shoot up,
but to one side, and the smoke settled around us, choking
off the fresh air. We ate the pâté spread thickly on the
baguettes. There was nothing much to say; we remarked
on the lovely weather and on the river so different from the
Seine and on the island like a jewel ("an electric jewel,"

I said). We felt, each of us, somewhat embarrassed to find ourselves among strangers. After a while, Emmanuel the Spanish went to the car and brought back a bag of pot and some cigarette paper. "I have a longing," he said. The wind started up and the fire began to right itself. We passed the joint around the fire, sucking down a drag each in turn; the wind took away the smell and the fresh air kept us from getting high. But it made us very tired. "Perfect flake-out," said the Spanish, his eyes squinting. So the blankets were spread at three corners of the clearing. Yvonne scrambled up the small hill to the car and came back with a towel about her shoulders; her behind wobbled like cold jelly as she passed into the darkness. Emmanuel was waiting for her, his boots protruding from the folds of his own special sheet. Stephen U stood on a rock in his pajamas, staring downriver toward the island lights. He struck a monumental pose, leaning on a staff of branch wood; the night wind threw up his pompadour and, slowly, with deliberate majesty, he raised his staff and pointed towards the east. He held this tableau until a small wild pig scooted through the thicket. Bonnie screamed. Stephen U immediately turned his gaze from the river, leapt solemnly from his perch like a carnival St. George, and charged the beast. He jumped through the thicket, only the yellow and pink of his pajamas visible; then there was a high girlish shriek and he bounded out of the thicket as the pig squirted through his legs and up the hill to the highway. He stood in the centre of the clearing silently for perhaps a minute, trying to salvage sufficient aplomb to continue; he stood erect with his staff by his hip, then paraded regally towards his special sleeping bag. Bonnie followed in his wake, shivering. "All right," I said to Cheryl. We lay down at either end of our blanket and slowly rolled ourselves towards the middle. When our legs touched, we fumbled for a hold. Cheryl moved her head into the hollow of my throat. But we didn't make love; we didn't even talk.

We woke at the first light, surrounded by a herd of cattle licking our faces and dropping manure piles at our feet. Emmanuel the Spanish lay a short distance from his blankets, blue with cold, and naked except for his boots and a small towel spread over his middle. Yvonne was hidden amid a cloud of blankets, folded and partitioned in an odd complex over her porcine, heaving form. Stephen U and Bonnie were already back at the car, stuffing their equipment into the trunk. "How are you feeling?" I asked Cheryl who was beginning to stir. She released herself from the blankets and stumbled down to the river to vomit.

We drove into the small town for our first *café au lait* served up in huge soup bowls. There was no one there except the proprietor and we gulped quietly until the sun rose higher. Everyone was trembling and miserable. After the croissants and jam, we used the toilet, then we went back to the car and onto the highway.

When we came to Blois, we parked the car and crossed the river by a low bridge. Blois was built on a hill, peaked by a château. The colours of the Loire here were orange and blue and the streets of the town were steeped and cobbled. We decided to visit the Château at noon and, in the meantime, sit in a café. They were just beginning to put out the tables in the Rue Denis and we trooped up the flights of steps onto a plateau of the village. While five of us sat outside in the sun and drank beer, Emmanuel the Spanish removed himself to the bar to look for a Gottlieb. We sat cross-legged, basking our chins. Cheryl was bundled in a long cloak. Bonnie was starting a letter in pencil.

"We've got to organize," I said. General assent.

"We'll buy a Michelin and do the thing in style," I said. Everyone said that was fine. Stephen U stood up and took off his shoes and socks.

"We want to go to that *Son et Lumière* at Chenonceaux, don't we?" I said. It was agreed.

"And what about the gardens at Villandry?" I said. That would be perfect. "So let's buy a Michelin." Dead silence. "Yvonne, you want to take a walk and buy one?"

"The Spanish is a pig," said Yvonne.

"What's the matter?"

"He's a fucking pig."

We were all very quiet for a while. In the Quarter, Yvonne was always smiling and displaying her dimples. Now she was scowling and her dimples were gone. The flesh on her bare knees drooped and puckered.

"What a lovely city Blois," I said. "Did you see the colour of the river ?"

"If he comes near me," said Yvonne, "I'll kill him."

"What did he do ?" asked Cheryl.

"Come to the washroom," said Yvonne.

"All right," I said when they were gone, "Bonnie, let's you and I look for a Michelin. Want to come Stephen ?"

"I've actually been here before," said Stephen U.

We left Stephen U at the table to look after things the way he wished he could, and took a walk. Bonnie was good company. She always walked a bit behind you, as if waiting to pounce on anything you might drop.

"I think the Spanish is nice," she said. The shape of the Château de Blois rose beyond the roofs and steeples of the city.

"He's not Spanish," I said, "he's Canadian."

"What's he doing being Spanish ?" she asked.

"It takes up his time."

Her thin face displayed a look of surprise. I turned around to see it; the look of surprise went from her mouth to her nose, but everything from her eyes up remained the same.

We found a *tabac* at the other end of town where we bought the Michelin and some cigarettes.

"You know what the trouble with us is," I said.

"Yes."

"You do ? What's the trouble with us ?"

"It's uncomfortable sleeping on the ground."

"Oh Christ ! The trouble with us is, we're too goddamn self-possessed. Everybody's at the larva stage."

"Is there a circumflex on *Château* ?"

"You got to stop hoarding information, Bonnie, you're becoming unbearable. I'm not going to tell you."

"A circumflex is like a little tent, isn't it ?"

"You get nothing out of me."

On the way back to the café, Bonnie spotted a small church in a quaint state of decay. "Oh let's see," she said, scampering over the steps and pushing back the door. Inside, the place was barren; benches were piled haphazardly along a dark corridor.

"Are those groined vaults ?" she asked excitedly.

"I'm warning you Bonnie."

"Oh look, stairs," she said, keeping up the impulsive quiver in her voice.

The stairs mounted to a low balcony without railing; it looked like an elevated stage. "Come," she said, holding out her hand. She raced up the stairs with a forced hoydenish appeal. "Isn't it lovely ?" she gasped, hardly able to lose her breath.

"It's a rundown church," I said, "what's lovely ?"

"The atmosphere," she said, "it's kind of a deserted atmosphere."

The only thing of interest was a microphone on the undraped altar.

"Oh I love this !" she exclaimed. "What's that ?" She pointed to the microphone.

"You know too much already," I said.

"And the smell," said Bonnie, "it's like, well, like an antique shop smell ! Isn't it ?"

"You've already reached your limit," I said.

"There's a bit of trouble," said Stephen U when we were back at the café. Emmanuel the Spanish was standing in the doorway, one hand on his hip, the other gesturing grandly.

"These machines are not Gottliebs of Chicago," he said when he saw me moving towards him, "they are Rogers of Philadelphia. That is not the true machine."

"So take it easy," I said, *"prenez la facile."*

"It is a proven matter of heresy," said the Spanish, "I will not accept this matter of heresy."

The proprietor stood just inside the threshold and behind him stood his wife, watching with a frozen glance of disgust.

"Heretic," said the Spanish. "Infidel."

"He tilted all their machines," Stephen U whispered.

The proprietor was beginning to build a fierce logic in his mind as to what was to be done and I tried to guide the Spanish away. This only made him more vindictive.

"Obscenity of thy father's tusk !" he shouted, making the sign of the cross over his private parts.

"Oh," the Frenchwoman groaned; her husband ventured into the street.

"Bring up thy heart," said the Spanish, "and thy liver also."

The proprietor gave him a somewhat inquisitive push, but the Spanish was short and powerful and stood his ground. He had a taste for violence and obviously he wanted this. I could see that I'd have to play the ace up my sleeve.

"Come on let's go," I said, and added the final hooker by calling him by his rightful name. He showed alarm for the first time. "Hersh," I said, "for Christ sakes." His face went white and he put an arm on my shoulder and led me away. "Okay," he said. He turned to the proprietor and his wife and shrugged his shoulders and we all walked towards the quai and over the bridge to the car. Nobody bothered about the Château.

We ate a small picnic lunch near the main road, and afterwards picked some apples in a large orchard. "Let's skip Chaumont," I said, "and drive to Tours, pick up some wine, and have a good supper." So we drove past Chaumont. "Check one château," said Yvonne, and then as we left it behind us, "check one wooded environs." In Tours, we bought the wine, eight bottles in all, and ate a bad supper at a cheap grill. When we found our clearing for the night, it was already dusk. We parked the car near a small wooded area and moved down a slight embankment to a small beach where the river was wide and the sand seemed soft and deep. To our left, there was a bridge; along the shoreline, small pieces of driftwood rocked in the water. We built the fire, a much better one this time, and between us we drank five bottles. Afterwards, Bonnie and Stephen U went up to the car. The Spanish stayed by the fire with Yvonne, who was still angry, and boasted of his prowess. "I will tell you of this especial thing, that I have great equipment and much endurance in the performing." That's how we left them.

Cheryl and I wandered down to the shore and along the

shore to where the river deepened and the shore became a
bank. We cut through a small forest along the bank for
perhaps half a mile; there was no weather, no lights, nothing
but a musty gloom where one could smell animals and straw
and hear tiny field mice breaking through the leaves. We
came to a large rock shaped like a saddle, the horn itself
submerged with part of its prow poking from the water.
"Why don't we take a swim," I said, sensing the dimensions
of a dream. We sat on the rock and took off our clothes;
we piled them neatly with all kinds of concern, then wandered
downshore for some shallow break to the river. There was
no moon, we were in complete darkness; our hands touched.
Against the shadow of this toy wilderness, our own shadows
formed lighter shades of motion through the foliage as if
cut out, superimposed upon the stillness. It was very unreal.
When we came to a place where we could wade, Cheryl
moved first into the river and stood there knee-deep, thumb
on spine. She finally crouched in the water, shivering, then
spread herself full length and submerged altogether; her hair
floated near the surface, spanned like sea weed; her ankles
spanked the calm flow of the river. I made out the cleft
of her behind cutting the water like a small iceberg. I put
the ball of my finger to it and shuttled her back and forth,
hooked to me like a swing. The ridge of her back showed
a bit pale now as one grew to see. I slipped into the water
myself and we swam towards the middle of the river which
was very cold halfway across, then back again and along
the bank to the saddle rock. I pulled myself onto the rock
but Cheryl stood belly deep in the water for a time and I
watched sadly where her breasts were faintly coned and
sagging. She was staring with mindless wonder into dead
space, victim to an old ghost, and I felt the awful pain of
wanting something good for her. "Come to me," I whispered,
"Come," and while she struggled slowly onto the rock, like
a child after candy, I took our clothes and refolded them in
the grass. She mounted the rock : with some difficulty for
it was smooth as glass beneath the water; her ass, rising
clear, made a fine splutting noise as she jockeyed for footing
on the ledge. Her hands gripped the horn of the rock and

she pulled her weight out of the water, her arms and legs producing a kind of leverage as beads of water streamed down her back. Her leg thrust itself over the brim, her toes clinging to the slippery, pocked texture. She came free of the river in a slow arc, her head and knee meeting above the scoop of the saddle. When she had raised the other leg up, she hovered in mid-motion, then lost her balance and fell forward with a crash, bruising her knee as it glanced the horn. "Darling." I turned her onto her back like a turtle and kissed her wet face and stroked her squeaky hair. It was still too dark to inspect thoroughly the units of her body; but that didn't matter. I propped her up, revolved her carefully and bent her back so that her head rested on the sharp prow of the rock and her abdomen lay cupped in its shell. Goose pimples bristled on her shoulders and neck. I sat on my knees between her legs and kissed her eyes, nose and throat; I sucked briefly her toughening nipples, clenched my hands under her tight buttocks and raised them until her legs crossed like a scissors under my armpits and around my back. Her spine scraped the crust of the rock. When I slipped into her, she began to contract at once, creating that nibbling sensation that waits for no tide. "Oh," I said. Her head, perched awkwardly on the sharp cushion of the horn, began to bob uncomfortably, slipped, yanked, banged against the hard stone. I tried to build the rhythm slowly, for it was her due, and as she began to move against my motion, her toe stubbed itself. "Cheryl," I said. I adjusted her ass and tried to prop her head in my hands while she pumped wildly, a bit off centre now and slightly to the left of my gravity. I had to shuffle the whole complex further down into the saddle without missing a beat; I abused my balance and popped out of her with a sting into the cold air. Her legs were tired and came down heavily from my back to rest spread-eagled over the lip of the boulder. I sank into her slime again without much difficulty and churned and stabbed to pick up time; her head lay in the saddle now, and her toes touched the grass and her legs were spread so wide I could hear her pelvis crack. "Now," I said. Her belly slapped against me hysterically and carried me onto another frequency; my own knees were on the lip of the rock, shredding painfully against the grain, and I didn't know if I could hold myself up. I clamped both hands forward onto the husk, and she kicked out, and I said again "Now," and she said "Ouch," and there was a great explosion.

It came from the sky. The whole sky burst into colours and clapped like thunder. Missiles of coloured flame shot into the night air, exploding into spindles of falling light. "Shit." I fell onto the grass and Cheryl leapt down from the rock and stood by a tree rubbing herself. My scrotum ached. The colours of tapering flame zoomed and hissed over the river, bursting into spools of pink and blue and crimson. Cheryl stood shivering against the tree; her body was bathed in a variety of colours. "OAS ?" she gasped, on the mute point of panic. "Fireworks," I said hoarsely. Jets of fire swooshed directly above us, erupting into a flower of sparks that showered down on the Loire; meteor-like tails climbed higher and released their lodes of gold and silver. A few stray pellets fused and kindled at our feet. Cheryl climbed back onto the rock suddenly to stand majestically in the line of fire. Where her body reflected the dyes of light, the hair on her groin stood erect and dazzling, a pocket of glaring, almost angry fur. The noise accelerated into explosions that were deeper, more sustained. Cheryl stood on her toes for a while then went flat-footed as her knees gave; she made a whimpering sound and settled helplessly into a half crouch; she began to jerk forward in little spasms. The muscles of her belly heaved like a top. She put her hands to her forehead as if in horrible disbelief, then down to grip her crotch. She pumped, then gasped, then stopped. "Oh for Christ sake," I said.

When the last plume of light had shot itself out, we dressed and walked back silently to the clearing near the beach. Cheryl went down to the shore and sat on the sand; she couldn't cry but she seemed terrified and ashamed. I moved beside her and put one hand (open, palm down) on the top of her head. "How do you feel, kid ?" I asked. She shrank a bit, and released some air through her teeth. "That's never happened before," she said, "I never did that before." "You want to finish it off, darling?" I asked. "It's already finished," she said.

"Oh for Christ sake," I shouted. "Know something? You're no good for a man."

"This has gone far enough, I want to see one of them châteaux," Yvonne said the next afternoon. We were sitting in one of those barren little cafés by the main road, and I began to wonder again about the Yvonne I had known in Paris; she would often go into a paroxysm of giggles there until you thought that she might expire in the midst of her attitude. But on the trip, she hadn't giggled once, and there was such a seal of discipline to her responses that you could almost hear the wax hardening. "I'm sick," she said, "of these cafés altogether." So we drove to Villandry and saw the gardens from the road; the hedges were neatly arranged in squares and oblongs with flowers bordering the walks. That's all I know of Villandry.

That evening, Emmanuel the Spanish explained the wilderness to us. He always travelled with his own private ash tray. "The forest is full to a fullness of spooks and pagans and only the true smoke of the hashish weed can outline them clearly. I tell you for a truth that this is so." "I don't need no goddamned spooks," said Yvonne, charmed by his folklore, "you're a spook." "I have especial powers from the smoke of the hemp," said the Spanish. "It gives to me a great sexual profoundness." "Go profound your ass," said Yvonne.

Every day we passed the same boy scout troop on the road, moving at a steady clip; no matter how much distance we covered during the day, there they would be by forenoon, trudging in double file through the dust. Their leader was a short, compact scoutmaster, probably in his mid twenties, with horn-rimmed glasses, bulging legs and not a trace of humour on his grim countenance. His troop were in their middle teens, without exception model youths of Germany, light-haired but for one, and completely untouched by the valley. "It's because they're virgins," said Yvonne as we passed them one afternoon, "they don't know what a valley's for."

We swung into Azay-le-Rideau, parched with thirst and having missed another château a few miles back. Everyone was getting along now and the atmosphere was full of plurals; the straining for rapport consisted in finding levels of interest where we could all indulge. The level agreed upon was fairly low; we would all submit to group paranoia, warding off together all kinds of imagined intrigues designed to relieve us of our sanity. It seemed ridiculous later, and it was ridiculous then, but it kept us going and everyone was grateful. And that's what made Azay-le-Rideau seem so mystical and bizarre. It was an amazing thing, but everyone in town was fifteen years old and everyone looked alike. The streets were filled with people all about five foot four, wearing variously coloured slacks and exuding an air of almost cynical disinterest. "It's a bloody Utopia," said Stephen U wheeling blindly down an alley and out the other side into a small square. I put the problem rhetorically : "Are these children the sad result of allied infiltration ?" "That is an absurdness," retorted the Spanish, obviously in his element, "they are spooks and pagans; do we have a cross ?" The sight of older people who might have ruined our thesis was properly ignored; for the sake of group harmony.

The café was large. There was a restaurant in the back and an elevated floor for dancing. A juke box with coloured bubbles stood by the bar and several Gottliebs lined the wall. We ordered beer at the bar and snails in the restaurant and discussed the phenomenon of the village for as long as it would hold. We spent the rest of the day drinking beer, planning to get up and go to the Château, but savouring the energy compounded as we sat. Stephen U spent the afternoon treating a calloused foot. He lanced it with a safety pin, then wrapped it in a sock. We watched him, half mesmerized by his little squeals of pain. A deadly spell fixed us. It was worse than boredom.

But at about seven in the evening, the glass door of the café swung open and in marched the boy scout troop, dusty from the road, but looking brisk and healthy nonetheless. The scoutmaster with the horn-rimmed glasses ordered them

four to a table in German, then stood in the middle of the
dance floor to survey his work. He put his hairy knees
together to reveal a slight warp. He had a lisp and a nicely
tooled vandyke. Except for him, every boy in the troop
looked fifteen years old. They had bright blue eyes, crew
cuts, soft clear faces.

About nine in the evening — we had by that time put
away several demis apiece — Yvonne noticed that one of
them had a guitar and another an accordion. The scoutmaster was glancing nervously at his wristwatch. The troop
were amusing themselves and drinking orange soda; whenever they laughed, their voices cracked. The café was filling
slowly; a few couples, easily fifteen years old, were putting
centimes into the juke box, but the music didn't carry and
they didn't dance. Yvonne thought about it awhile, then
wandered across the floor to the boy with the guitar.
"Spreckle English?" she asked. She rested her bulk on the
edge of a chair. Her face flushed.

"Sure," said the boy, "I speak this perfect, please."

"Play 'House of the Rising Sun'," said Yvonne, touching
off an image by running her fattish fingers through the strings
of his guitar; she smiled toothily to set off her dimples.

The boy blushed quietly and began to play. It was not
"House of the Rising Sun", but it was something that
Yvonne knew because she sang in a low murmur of a voice.
She coaxed the other boy to play his accordion. "Good,"
said Yvonne, "now someone dance."

The couples that had been by the bar were already
standing hesitantly on the floor; one of them kicked the
juke box and it burst into something furious with drums.
"La la," groaned Yvonne, her head flung back, her tongue
curled through her teeth, "la la la!"

"You can to dance?" asked one of the scouts, standing
very tall by her chair. It was not only that he was aware
of the others, he was totally fearless. One of those people
who achieve a margin of sexual courage quite early in life.

"La la," said Yvonne.

"So we dance," and he took her arm and led her cockily
to the floor. The other couples were already in formation.

"Ewwww, I like," laughed Yvonne. The scout moved her gracefully through neat swoops, regimenting his steps; he threw knowing, wicked glances about the café.

The scoutmaster looked around uneasily and moved up and down the perimeter of the dance floor like a prowling jackal. He finally came to our table and shrugged his shoulders helplessly. "We must for sleeping," he said, then without waiting for a reply, he made another tour of the room and came to rest against the bar.

"Buy those boys some beer !" I shouted to the Spanish. The Spanish came swinging into the room with a trayful of demis and passed them out among the tables. The scouts were very polite and finished them off in one guzzle. "More !" I screamed. The scoutmaster, perspiring like a pig, made his way to me and gripped my elbow.

"Please not to drink," he said in a dry, clipped voice.

"Why the hell not," I said, "it's good for them. Good." I made a small, blue muscle to show him how good.

"No this is no good," he said.

"It's good enough," I said. "Feel how good."

He smiled weakly like a man who has lost his wife at cards, and pronged his thumb and forefinger to feel my muscle.

"Not so good," he said.

"Emmanuel more drinks !" I shouted.

He removed his hand from my elbow and turned slowly and walked back to the bar. He began to speak in German to his troop, trying to organize them into an obedient mood; but by now they all had a few beers under their belts and were putting their own money on the tables.

"La," said Yvonne, "Ewwwwla !" She had her chest out and her rump high; she kicked a leg back to reveal flashes of yellow chunky flank. The Spanish grabbed one of the fifteen-year-old girls standing by the juke box. They moved in a stylized flamenco. Bonnie approached the scoutmaster with a demi and thrust it mistakenly at his nose. Foam slopped on his vandyke. Then I smelled something bad. The Spanish had rolled himself a joint somehow, and he was rolling more and placing them on a beer tray; the girl he had with him was puffing furiously with her eyes crossed. "Emmanuel!" I shouted. "No!" He only grinned at the prospect of his wickedness and began to hand out joints to the scouts. Matches flared nervously, then they were puffing and coughing. The sweet smell rose to the lights and began to sift; there was a din of noise like that of croaking frogs. Stephen U had left at the first smell of pot.

The scout with Yvonne was a gentleman. "You are quite effeminate," he said, "I like." Yvonne purred, her cheeks swelling.

"How old are you?" she asked.

"Twenty years," said the boy.

"No, no," said Yvonne, her dimples popping, "how old?"

"Fifteen," he said, "but much older to look, yes?"

The guitarist had stopped and the accordion lay on a chair. The scouts sat sprawled in their places with the oddest looks; the scoutmaster had loosened up and was looking nearsightedly into Bonnie's jerking dogface for a sign; there was something truant and perspiring in his gaze. The smell of pot was really bad and had created an unmistakeable mist. Worse than that, the scouts were squint-eyed and turning green. One of them threw up on the floor. It touched off a chain reaction; their smiles turned into rasping grunts; there was a sudden epidemic of glassy-eyed spewing. "We'd better get the hell out of here," I said, and Cheryl and I danced towards the door where the Spanish was already waiting with his hand on the knob.

We walked out of the café leaving Bonnie and Yvonne behind us. Outside you could hear the hacking noises; a rising stink of vomit wafted out the door. Halfway across the square, Bonnie caught up to us.

"Yvonne's still in there, it's awful. They're all being sick."

"I know; where's the car?"

Stephen U was asleep in the front seat. "Where's Yvonne?" he wanted to know. "She's still in there," I said, "we'll drive by and pick her up on the way."

When we stopped in front of the café, Bonnie raced in. The smells coming out of the café were unbelievable. In

a few seconds, she came out with the news that Yvonne
had left.

"Where in hell did she go ?"

"I don't know; she's supposed to have left with that boy."

"We'd better drive around. How is it in there ?"

"Awful; you wouldn't believe it; those boys are really
sick, there's puke all over the floor. The one with the little
beard peed on the juke box."

"Are the police coming ?"

"I don't know, but the proprietor was on the phone. That
scoutmaster peed right against the juke box."

We drove out of the square again with our lights dimmed
and moved through the streets. There was no sign of
Yvonne.

"Maybe she went in an alley," suggested the Spanish,
"she likes it in an alley."

"You wanna look ?" I asked.

"No, I'm not going in no dark alley," said the Spanish,
"I do not have the grace for these scenes in the alley."

We drove along the streets. But it was no good looking
from the car. "I'll get out and take a look," I said. "Park
the car here." When I came to a gravelled lot with a few
cars parked on it, I knew that's where they'd be.

"Yvonne ?" I descended a few steps.

"Here we are," said Yvonne. She was sitting on the
fender of a car as if she were riding the headlight. The
young kraut was standing forward with his knees against
the grille. He had one hand on Yvonne's knee and he was
smiling politely. He didn't like it one bit as I approached
them.

"We're leaving," I said.

"I'm coming," said Yvonne. "Now be a good boy and
let me go." She slapped his wrist playfully. When the boy
moved back to let her go, I noticed that his fly was undone.

"See you around," I said.

"I will be in Tangiers next week," he said very slowly to
Yvonne, "if you will come I would like."

"Tangiers; okay." said Yvonne.

When we were walking along the street, Yvonne began to shake and chuckle.

"He wanted to screw me," she said.

"Sure he did."

"But he has nothing," she said.

"You checked huh."

"Nothing at all," she said, "he's a child and he wanted to screw. That's a good one."

But when we returned to the car, I noticed that the scout was behind us.

"Look what's happened," I said. "Tell Emmanuel and Stephen to get on out here."

I walked back to the boy.

"You don't know what to do with it, huh ?" I said.

"She must finish," he said, not smiling.

"She's tired," I said, "she'll finish in Tangiers."

"Now," he said, "she must finish up."

I waited till Stephen and the Spanish were behind him, then I slapped him hard across the ear.

"Get the fuck away from us !" I shouted.

His face turned red, but he was a tall strong kid. He closed his hands ominously. "Grab him," I said.

They pinned his arms back and I slapped him again. He clenched his teeth and jerked his elbows, carrying Stephen U with him as he twisted away. The Spanish wouldn't let go though; he caught the kid round the neck and put a hand over his nose and mouth. I hit the boy in the belly twice, then the three of us ran to the car. The kid fell to his knees and brought up a trickle of beer.

We did not see the château at Chinon, nor had we seen the one at Ussé. Yvonne's month had come full cycle and she was feeling mean again; Cheryl seemed on the verge of the same mutation. They spent their time gathering leaves. Meanwhile, we sat daily in cafés. Emmanuel the Spanish worked his daily Gottlieb like a high priest pressing pinballs to his service, and Stephen U gazed toward the towering, ominous shapes of châteaux he had seen before. Which left Bonnie, a rather jerky organism that collected dust in its nostrils and went scavenging about the streets for paper, sticks and general refuse. Which left no one. I ate snails and walked the back roads. Whenever I encountered Bonnie, her arms possessed of pails and corks and bits of string, I nodded and walked on. Once I came across Yvonne and Cheryl at a pharmacist's shop and stopped to chat. The Spanish was fine, I said; Stephen U was well too, although he seemed to be developing a cold. I bought apples and wine and sat in the square in Chinon eating, drinking, waiting for my bowels to stir. I watched the town clock. I counted the benches. No license plate added up to more than twelve, no chimney was orange, bicycles stood neatly in racks of eight.

Another day or two passed. It was hard to tell how much time we spent in cafés, on the streets, waking up or bedding down. The pot went. We were always tired and looking for a place to sleep. We decided against any more châteaux although we did drive to the Abbaye Fontevrault; but it turned out to be a prison where criminals slept in the ancient cells of nuns. We tramped through a few landscapes, but that only fatigued us more, so we gave that up too. Not a word now passed between Yvonne and the Spanish, and I had lost my taste for Cheryl.

Late in the evening of the seventh day, we were outside Chinon again, in a clearing by a desolate side road. Ashes had been spread everywhere and the ground was burnt black, and prickly with weeds. Our tour had deteriorated into an endless hunt for places to urinate. We parked the car on a steep incline and arranged ourselves on the ground. The woods before us were deep, a barren path trailing into it and out of sight. The fields to either side were flat and windblown, waves of dark shadow transpiring over the sorrowing heads of wheat, moving and spreading them with vast, cruel motion. The night was cold; rain fell. The ground turned to mud, the mud softened and bubbled. By morning we were sick, incommunicative. We walked about in the mud in a vague, incredulous stupor. We pushed the car up the steep incline, using bits of wood to get it through the muck, onto a road that was no better. Our noses dripped needles of crystal; our breath was stale. The rain had soaked us to the skin, so that we shivered as if palsied. No one said a word. When we had cleaned the mud from the tires, we made a strategic turn and drove towards Paris.

It was a lovely trip back as we sped past the grand châteaux and finally left the river where we had found it. No one spoke for almost an hour. The silence prevailed against coughing and the circular shifting of backs into temporary postures of rest. The Spanish was watching the sun; in an hour he had set the stage : "Perfect sky," he announced, "it has a loveliness." Suddenly, he was the same. His blonde hair, snub nose, bull neck covered the rear window like a splat of egg. The curious mechanism of his smile managed to raise one lip in greeting. "Kinda lovely," he said, "perfect sky." His fingers warped themselves about the arm strap; they fluttered with a tenuous grace. He was all grace, the Spanish. And Yvonne, in the front seat with Bonnie, followed the line of the road, her bloated face set in a scowl. Her arms were wrapped protectively about her own body and her hands squirted out beneath her armpits, the fingers rooted with dry dirt. She hadn't bothered to wipe the mud from her legs.

"Listen," I said, "I liked this trip; it was good."

Bonnie was stacking her spoils in the glove compartment; she had found a few stones that she fancied and was using them to weigh down a freight of paper, textiles and what looked like petrified dog shit.

"You're not going to put *that* there, are you ?" I asked. I could smell its acid tang permeating the car with a raw, unholy stench.

"Why not ?" she asked, somewhat innocently, still tucking the stuff in with an eye to neatness.

"It's goddamn dog shit," I said.

"It's a memento," she said, "I slipped on it in Chinon."

Another half-hour went by. Everyone was testy, anticipating : as if Paris, with all its steeples and terraces and boulevards and interiors, would suddenly loom up over the rise in a single dimension revealing the insides of villas and the traffic on the St. Germain. Still another hour went by and, without quite meaning to, attitudes accelerated. When we

were within an hour of Paris, I had to chuckle. I had
thought of a funny thing, Stephen U in his pajamas the first
night, running from the pig like a carnival St. George.

"Were you really scared ?" I asked.

"Scared ? I was damn petrified."

"Jesus, I'll never forget it."

"And what about me," said the Spanish, "when I tilted
all those machines in Blois ? Infidels; it was a judgment."

"That's right," said Yvonne, "and you wanted to pull the
plugs out too. You were gonna castrate the machines."

"Beautiful," said the Spanish.

"Or those fireworks," said Cheryl, "oh God that was
funny."

"Or that church," said Bonnie, "with just a microphone
on the altar, that's all."

"You knew it was a microphone all along ?"

"Sure."

"That's magnificent."

"But the boy scouts, that was the best," said Yvonne.

"We ruined them," said the Spanish.

"When they began to vomit, oh God," said Bonnie.

"And that little boy who wanted to screw me in the car
lot, and you had to fight him," said Yvonne, "God you
were good."

"I was lucky," I said, "I caught him quick and that was it."

"Or what about being bored in Chinon ?" said Stephen U.

"Boy was I bored," I said, "that was something."

"Or what about that spooky night near Chinon when it
rained," said Cheryl, "we were so depressed."

"And I pushed the car out of the mud," said Stephen U.

"We all pushed," everyone said.

"And you put the dog shit in the glove compartment,"
I said, "is it still there ?"

"Sure," said Bonnie.

"Beautiful," said the Spanish.

We came to the flat yards outside Paris, the factories,
then the small trawlers and the cranes on the river. We
drove through Auteuil, onto the Avenue de Versailles and
finally down into the underpass. Yvonne was giggling madly.

"It was all good," I said, "I can't remember anything like it."

"I was thinking," said Cheryl very quietly as we were coming up into the light again, only a few minutes from Concorde, "about our evening. The colour of the sky and the water. The way you held me and how I felt, so different. I want to go back there with you, to the same place. I keep remembering the hot bowls of coffee in the mornings and the lovely walks, and then the river and the fireworks. I thought it was the OAS and you held me under the tree and we lay on the rock; it was such a nice smell. We swam in the river and it was all dark, do you remember? my hair floated in the water. Then the evenings on the ground, everybody together, and the châteaux, château country. Do you think we can go back again?"

"Sure."

"It's like a dream. I won't ever forget it," she said.

Twenty-one

"Look," said Cheryl one evening, wearing a dark empress dress high in the breast and long in the leg, "let's none of us ever leave each other, let's not lose it." A week later she was gone and I never saw her again, but that night we were going to the opera to see the new ballet *Daphnis and Chloe,* with sets and costumes by Chagall. We took the eight franc seats where you saw half the stage for half the money; the right hand side of the ballet was beautiful.

Afterwards, we strolled down the Avenue de l'Opéra. The lights of the Avenue were brilliant but muted, with the dark shape of the Hôtel Louvre high in the distance. "What a perfect night," said Cheryl labouring for a perfect night. The remark was derivative, but I let it pass. When we came to the Rue Daunou, I put my palm on the bowl of

her hip and steered her gently into harry's new york bar. She moved forward with that fathomed, accommodating vagueness one expected and we sat by the back wall and talked about the Loire. The tables were made of varnished wood, low and bare; on the walls were plaques and pennants and foreign money. "Coming back to Paris is so much nicer than living there all at once," said Cheryl. I let that one pass too. We ordered two beers and two hot dogs and I put my hand over her spreading fingers and said something funny I had been saving up to give her; the distance on her face from laughter to the blankness which covered it so quickly was so minimal and rapid that it became almost suspect. So I said : "Darling, you know that you are absent by your conspicuousness ?" It didn't mean a thing to her, but she caught the modulation of my voice — with the talent of the blind — and that set off an even, senseless smile. There was, however, some fast conversation beside us. A celebrity — she was unmistakeable in her tight, flesh-toned skin — was seated a table away with a man some years younger than herself; he was toothy and slick and somewhat large in the forehead. He looked as if he had groomed his hair with butter, and it was parted down the centre to give him age. I listened; this was obviously the big leagues.
Slick :
"Kate Kate, you look damn beautiful, you know that ?"
Celebrity :
"Thank you darling boy."
Slick :
"Every frigging head snapped back tonight, no kidding. Kate you're once in a lifetime."
Celebrity :
"I'm feeling lovely already."
Slick :
"So what do we do now ?"
Celebrity :
"I'm going to bed, bucko."
Slick :
"Alone ? or it that an invitation ?"
Celebrity :

"Without benefit of animal or clergy, honey."
Slick :
"Aww. And here I thought I'd make you . . . *confortable.*"
Celebrity :
"No bucko, there's no Santa Claus tonight."
Slick :
"Why not Kate ? We're adults."
Celebrity :
"I may be adult entertainment, sweety, but you're strictly afternoon matinee."
Slick :
"Okay Kate. I'll come over tomorrow noon for lunch."
Celebrity :
"Bring a bib, buck."
Slick :
"You're absolutely great Kate, know that ?"
Celebrity :
"But remember, honey, I'm the daylight-saving girl : always an hour behind."
Slick :
"I'll set my clock."
Afterwards, Cheryl and I walked back to the Quarter. You could always learn a lot from the famous; they certainly knew how to talk and were never disappointing. Close to the river, Paris smelled like an old shower room, and crossing the Pont Neuf we could hear the *clochards* nestled about the statue of Henri Quatre, grunting under their cardboard blankets. In the summer, it was easy for the *clochards* to sleep; they could be seen any time, curled on the benches by the river or bunched beneath the monuments in Concorde and Pigalle. But in the winter, they stuck to the ground and had to wrap themselves in tissue and flat boxes; the choice spots during the cold nights were above the Métro gratings where the warm air came up to heat their bodies. If they froze to death, they had to be scraped free of the pavement with shovels. That was no great loss either. They were no more than the bad jokes of a very beautiful and cruel old city.
"I mean it," said Cheryl when we were safe in the Café

Tournon, "if we just stay together and laugh like we did on the trip . . . I know, tell me that joke about Nate." Later that night, everyone came in. And in a week most of them were gone and new ones took their place. Cheryl went to Edinburgh where she was arrested on a morals charge and deported. Bonnie went to Geneva owing me money, Jules the Seducer was abducted by a bitch from Manhattan and taken to New York by ship, Stephen U returned to London where he resumed his life as a wine steward in the West End. The others remained more or less around, but they drifted slowly away from the centre of one's action, fading by stages into remote and ancient catchwords. After a while, it was embarrassing to run into them, as if we had all been part of some shameful conspiracy and now carried each other's diseases.

But that night we were still thick in the conspiracy and damn thankful too. We sat grouped around Jules the Seducer; he was attempting a young Irish girl, fresh from Dublin, and Cheryl, who had been one of his earlier victims, wanted to watch. The Seducer must be re-explained because he never changes. He was tall and curly haired, with a slightly broken Roman nose and a clever hunch to his shoulder; he played guitar in a little café in the Rue Mazarine when everyone else had to play in the streets, and his hotel room was rent free. The amazing thing was that he was not an interesting person; someone said that he was the dullest schizophrenic alive, because both sides of his personality were exactly the same. Cheryl looked on wistfully like an outpatient. He had trapped the Irish girl in a corner (where he could watch the mirror) and he was unloading a barrage of clichés as if he had primed himself with laxatives. The Irish girl, to be fair, was already curious and frightened and still wearing her mother's corset. Jules wanted to take her into the country for a weekend.

Jules :

"Son, my father used to say, (he always called me son), stay close to Nature and you'll never go wrong."

Girl :

"I suppose that's true."

Jules :

"Son, he used to say, take a friend; you'll never go wrong with a friend in the country."

Girl :

"Oh."

Jules :

"Make friends Jules, he'd say, (sometimes he called me Jules bless him), a good friend in the country, close to Nature, is a wonderful thing. And you know something, Shebwawna, I think I've found her and I don't mind if my friends hear it."

Girl :

"I'll go, I'll go."

Afterward, Cheryl and I took our traditional walk to Pigalle to see the fire-eater. Cheryl didn't like to see him eat the fire or drink the turpentine, but she liked to hear his jokes. He would skip about the paved island across from the *Follie-Pigalle,* spewing tremendous insults at the crowds, scratching his bare chest, waiting impatiently for his hat to be filled with French coin before beginning. When he began, we moved along the boulevard, past the fat whores in the alley, to a book shop that sold dirty magazines. I liked to thumb through them in the back of the shop while Cheryl glanced over my shoulder, nervously anticipating the police, or expecting at any moment some lecher with a green, skin-less nose to take her from the rear. Beside us, ranged three deep, customers shuffled quickly through their favourite pages. Cheryl didn't make them feel much better. Her presence seemed to stalk their sense of indecency. "It's ugly," whispered Cheryl, pointing, "why don't they shave down there like models do. It's obscene." This remark detonated a hum in the first rank of readers, even a few suppressed smiles of delight. Three or four men walked out of the shop in a hurry with their hands deep in their pockets. When the proprietor saw them leaving, he came to the back of the store to recount his merchandize.

I bought us some Italian ice cream for a franc apiece, then we walked down the narrow, unlit Rue Pigalle. We came to the Rue St. Lazare still nibbling on our cones, down the Rue Tronchet to the Église Madeleine, into the Place de la Concorde. A *clochard,* busily asleep behind a buttress near the obelisk, jumped up hysterically as we passed. She was covered with fruit netting and fell entangled onto the sidewalk. "You don't see that everyday," I said. We had no end of fun, Cheryl and I.

In the Avenue Matignon, near the twin fountains of the Rond Point spurting their geysers of light, army trucks and pill boxes were filled with soldiers; sentries stood spaced under the lampposts.

"Well, I guess we can't jump in the fountain," I said, "it was going to be a surprise."

"That's all right," said Cheryl.

"But I'll take you for a drink to Fouquet's; a pernod."

A pernod at Fouquet's was all I knew about the Champs, so we sat down on the huge terrace. I counted my money and ordered two pernods with straws and a souvenir umbrella for the lady. The drinks came with tiny papier-mâché umbrellas; Cheryl reacted with predictable gratitude. Two lesbians passed, dressed like fashionable mannequins in tight slacks and wide-brimmed hats. It was amazing how the cliché was made flesh in this city. An aging French actor, going gracefully blind, walked by with his Seeing Eye starlet. An entire generation of French boys came next, looking like dolls of another country, their hair slanted and brushed into neatly heaped coiffures, all with duplicating *tweest* shoes and pink hankies. We sat a while longer, ticking the ice with our straws. Cheryl looked owned. When she looked owned, the discomposure vanished and the agitation with it, leaving a vegetable nature that neither thought nor even wanted for itself. That was her ghost, and once you understood that there was nothing to her except a sense of being owned, there followed a cushioning of her impact on your drives. That was a bad feeling because it had to do with pride; it was almost shameful that it couldn't be dispensed with, because she was so beautiful. And the day you ditched her, some other prick would begin the same process of acquisition. Pricks were people who owned the things only you should have.

"And now for the real treat of the evening," I said. "We are going to the Hôtel Prince de Galles and sit in the lobby."

"Oh Larry."

The lobby of the Prince de Galles was not large but it was rich; we could sit in deep cool chairs and stare through glass-topped tables. I went into the bar and bought (for eight francs plus, but what the hell) a club sandwich. We ate solemnly in our best style and watched the money go by on its way to the elevator.

"Did you ever think when you were living with those queers in Florence that one day you'd be in a hotel on the George Cinq?"

"No."

"Well, you can't say that I'm not good to you."

"I know."

"Or that I beat you."

"It's true."

"Or that you suffer unnecessarily."

"Thank you."

"Want some mustard, I'll ring for the mustard."

"This is fine."

"How about a funny joke."

"I'm happy as it is."

"How about some disreputable fornication?"

"Whatever you want."

"Maybe I can get us a room here for the night, what about that?"

"Oh Larry."

"A small room with a large bed and a view of the city."

"Larry!"

"You're right, it's too much. But I'll do it."

"But I haven't taken a bath; I'll ruin the sheets."

"Good."

"Maybe I can take a shower first."

"After; they always take a shower after."

I went up to the register and asked politely for a room. The hawknosed Frenchman looked at me, at the company I kept, at the clientele entering the lift, and said No.

"We'll be back in an hour, should any vacancies occur,"

I said, "in the meantime, the Countess Schlitz-Fag and I
will stroll through your city. Can you suggest a suitable
pissoir for the relief of bladder ? The Countess would not
be unmoved by your sympathies."

I made a suggestion with my forefinger that was unnatural,
then we walked out into the Avenue George V which smelled
of freshly cut grass and expensive cigarettes.

A whore drove by in her little Renault and pulled into
the curb ahead with a screech; she opened the car door and
began to bid for a tall, gaunt gentleman who carried a cane
with a white wolf's head handle. He was above the whole
business and swung the head of his cane over his shoulder
like an artillery piece. The whore raced the motor without
closing the door and the car took off with the open door
flapping wildly; when she made a sharp left turn into the
Avenue Montaigne, the door slammed shut by itself as if
faithful to some prefigured rage.

"If I was your pimp, I wouldn't let you walk the streets;
I'd buy you a nice little Dauphine."

"I know you would, Larry."

"I'd check everyone's urine for possible bacterial deposits."

"Darling."

She slipped her hand inside my arm; an annoying depen-
dency. We walked out into the Champs again, with the
slightest consoling wind at our backs. The pavements were
immense and people passed four and five abreast, pressing
toward the Étoile as if it somehow summed their evening.

As we walked by the Drug Store, two Italians fell out of
the doorway carrying hot dogs and little tubes of mustard.

"Hey you wan' bite ?" one of them said to Cheryl.

Cheryl took a taste.

"Hey Pietro, she like to bite !" He pulled his friend into
the conversation. "You take bite him too," he said.

Cheryl took another taste.

"She like everything bite, eh ?" he grinned, fingering Pietro
in the ribs. "Ewwww, I like this business for biting."

Pietro wasn't listening; he was jumping on one leg with
one hand inside his pants belt.

"Later we all have a big bite," he said and grabbed Pietro by the arm.

We didn't see them again until we were crossing towards the Arc de Triomphe. They were standing beside one of the pillars, their arms spread secretively against the brick. When the guard in front of the eternal flame moved through the arc to the darker side, they moved stealthily into the shadow of the arc itself, straddled the flame and unzipped their flies. A great surge of piss spurted from their dangling equipment and made a hissing noise, but the flame only crackled and spat. The Italians grinned as the gendarme flailed them with his billy club; another gendarme caught them as they staggered around spraying the pavement wildly; they were dragged, still grinning, into a small room in the shaft of the Arc and the door closed.

Once we were through the Arc, the crowds thinned. Benches and strips of lawn lined the walk. It was dark and warm where we sat, watching the apartment lights flick on and off like matches in a stadium.

"When I go to Edinburgh for the festival, will you come too ?" asked Cheryl.

"I'll meet you there," I said.

"Won't that be lovely."

We rose and moved on.

"I'll have all sorts of jokes saved up by then."

"Funny ones ?"

"All kinds."

Which was one of the last things I ever said to her, alas, walking beneath the trees of the Avenue Foch.

Twenty-two
Vangrin Pursued

Vangrin should have known better, but impulse was one of his most prized and studied virtues. "I am emotional by a habit that is without compromise : I never merely *am;* I *do.*" When he *did,* it came after months of slow fermenting rage that finally kindled into a quick ten minutes one afternoon in his room at the Dieppe. Now, at a party, or on the terrace of cafés, Vangrin seemed impersonal, unbothered; nothing could shatter the shatterproof glass of his innermost disciplines. But Jackie secretly plagued him with her sweet, coy leotards and cashmere sweater, her indelicately buttoned nose, her large wet lips. And she seemed wasted on Blackie, that nervous, eager little version of himself; if Blackie was made the clumsy recipient of her innocence because he paraded as a lesser Vangrin, then why not Vangrin in total ? Vangrin Himself ? His mind concocted fantasies of a bestial nature. "Where she has previously hiccuped, I shall make her belch," he said. It was not difficult. Jackie was astonished by greatness, certain in fact that his was already documented and wonderful. Everything that Vangrin did had for her the glitter of divinity; she sat popeyed and in speechless wonder at his relevant feet. At the same time, Vangrin was unsure of himself; sexual codes were not his forte. If she should refuse him in the face of his dispensation, there would follow the quick melting of his image, the subsequent ridicule of the mob, the slow weeklong reconstruction. He overcame his fondest doubts, however, and in no time at all she stood before his bed while he read to her sonorously from his *Lesbos In Transit,* "my transvestite work in progress please sit down." The cashmere sweater that had kept him sleepless with its promise of soft timid purity was soon unbuttoned to reveal dugs of a rougher texture, and the leotards so sweet and coy were yanked down to reveal what he had suspected all along. Vangrin did his duty with detachment and pride and a few other tricks he knew, and in two day's time he came down with a dose of clap.

The day his piss turned green, he received the following letter : "My darling V. I've got the money and am leaving Harold. Should arrive in Paris, my lover, next Tues. You know Harold's problem. I am desperate for you, so please save yourself. Until we come to know each other again (in the biblical sense), I am, your F."

Impulsively, Vangrin flew into a panic. He collected himself at last (with the aid of several villanelles), wrapped his organ in cool, life-giving gauze, and attended a series of conferences at the Café Monaco with Fitz the West Indian. Fitz was the Quarter abortionist, a kind and selfless man under pressure, and he was celebrated for his cures of venereal infections ranging from pubic lice to madness. Vangrin would not reveal the source of his disease; "it is, let us say, an immaculate infection : it evolved itself at the pissoirs near Notre Dame."

"First the herbs," said Fitz.

Vangrin sent him, with living allowance, to the banks of the Rhône river where he collected the necessary leaf. In two days, he was back. F., meanwhile, was on a boat within three days of Marseilles. Fitz cooked and treated the herbs, baked them to a dark ash, stuffed them into cellophane wafers, and applied as directed like roll-on deodorants. The infection grew worse. Vangrin's urine still burned and the strange crystals that bloomed on the tip of his penis were pebble thick.

"You are thinking too much, man," said Fitz.

"I am soul and cock united," said Vangrin, "but I will try."

Fitz next concocted a special liquid to be rubbed twice daily on the swollen parts and drunk each night before retiring.

"It burns when you rub it on, but it's good to drink," he said, "and leave you mind a blank, man, so it won't get stuck in the upper regions."

Vangrin followed this practice for another two days, but it didn't help. By some gross miscalculation, it turned out to be an aphrodisiac; Vangrin suffered the pangs of hell.

"I may have to operate," said Fitz.

The day F. landed in Marseilles, Vangrin lay on his bed, propped by the arm of the bitch Jeanette, while Fitz boiled his instruments on a hot plate. He prepared and sterilized a CCM bicycle pump, three hangers, a thimble, two marble puries and a large fish and chips basket with an aluminium frame. He drew a circle in blue chalk around the area of concentration and set to work. With mauve and agile finger tips, Fitz tampered and delved. To no avail.

"Are you thinking, man ?" asked Fitz.

"Not that I know of," said Vangrin.

F. wired Vangrin from Marseilles early on the Tuesday morning, and by midafternoon he was taking hot whirlpool baths. He raced through the fresh air in the Bois, exposed himself to the healing sun, but the smarting green-gilded rash remained. So within an hour of F.'s arrival, Vangrin packed his belongings and left hurriedly for the Spanish frontier. The note pinned to his door was this : "My darling F. I have laid a surprise for you, but it being somewhat delayed, I must now go to the Spanish coast to seal the bargain. Meet me in San Felíu de Guixols, in front of the garage by the fountain. I wait erectile and enduring, your V."

F. caught the first train to the coast, already half wilted with anticipation; she stroked the bony flat of her knee, she gripped her small parasol in sweaty clutches. When she arrived at San Felíu, Vangrin had already been to three doctors and was just boarding a bus for Villanueva stuffed with antibiotics and special creams. The note at the garage near the fountain gave her directions and she followed immediately down the Costa Brava. At Villanueva, Vangrin took a small hotel room and unpacked his supplies. He had already eaten enough antibiotic capsules to put him in a mild stupor, but now he applied the salves. The irritation was now concentrated in a small hard pimple. Coated with salve, he promenaded on his balcony overlooking a wonderful vista of the sea. The sun warmed his troubled brow, but hardened the preparation into a caked shell. He was forced to break this plaster sheath with a lamp end; it skinned him in the worst way. "If I but had more time," he said, "or even spatial distance."

By four that afternoon, he was on a train bound for Madrid, locked in the toilet compartment with salves and pills and some stray herbs he had packed in his kit. F. again found his note instructing her to meet him there in two day's time. She was now quite bitchy and nervous; her hand shook when she tried to eat and the rocking motion of the bus had ruined two pairs of panties. But F. was adamant and steely; she had refused a sailor in San Felíu and a German in Villanueva. Yet at night she chewed through her seat pillow and lurid visions of Vangrin (prodding his equipment with lethal grace) had imposed themselves upon her tense unsettled mind.

She did not wait two days in Villanueva; she had developed an hysterical rash on her nose, so before her condition worsened, she took a plane the next day out of Barcelona for Madrid. Vangrin had found a room where he could suffer quietly, but when she phoned him from the terminal, he immediately moved out.

"It's so good to hear your voice," he had said.

"Oh V.," F. cried, "I'll be right there."

"Make it two hours," said Vangrin, "I'm not quite ready."

He rushed out of his hotel, panic stricken, his burgeoning suitcase leaving a trail of T-shirts on the Calle Mayor. In three hours, she had tracked him down. He was undressed, furiously bathing his cock in a pan of warm water, when she burst into the room.

"Oh my darling," she gasped, "let *me*."

And then there were two.

Twenty-three

It was about this time that I became friendly with Dixie Glukicz and his girl Iris. I had known them before this, but it was not until the early clique had wilted like a trick flower that I began to see them frequently. They brought others with them. There was a sullenness about this new crowd, a strange dyspepsia; they were grimmer company. It was as if some distrustful and restless bargaining — conducted daily — forbade them to take pleasure at their games. You were always conscious, in their company, of being bought or sold, no matter how trivial the gain; which resulted in a new kind of reticence, and it was soon fashionable to mock and belittle even oneself for the sake of dark, ulterior motives never made clear. That was important : the more clouded your resources, the deeper their assessment. It was a simple law and reputations were fed daily with self-imposed humiliations.

Dixie Glukicz : The first word he learned in French was *piscine* and the sound of it drove him wild. He liked sounds that had resonance to them, and for hours he would play with the nasal sense of words. *"Piscinnnnnnnne,"* became an early watchword for him; soon he would narrow his eyes and blink his nostril wings till they popped, then turn quite gently to the first available patsy and exclaim divinely, *"Neeeeeemmmmmm."* This sound was a variation on *piscine* and he came to regard it as his own. One could watch him sit for hours and days discovering the different intonations it had for him. After a while, he learned to alter its sound according to his mood so that *Neem* (short) was a judgment short and curt, while *Neeemmm* (long) expressed a mild and simple joy. When he and Iris were at their happiest, you could detect him purring, all through the day, his ecstatic vibration, *Neeeeeeeeahahammmmmmmmm.* This was the resonance in its purest form. It could drive you crazy.

Dixie Glukicz claimed that he had been around. His father had been a union organizer in the thirties in Detroit, an incoherent man like Dixie himself. His only legacy had been an ability to take punishment, and that was something Dixie knew and understood. He had been in and out of a dozen schools in Michigan and Ohio, and in his late teens had been picked up on a narcotics charge and sent to a military academy for four years. He didn't like it much, but he learned to run with the pack there and he got his hands dirty. He had a certain amount of guts for sure, even a leaning towards brutality; but in Paris he had a mustache and was soft-spoken. When he was released from the academy, he came directly home but his mother had remarried and his father had been blacklisted from the unions and was unapproachable. Dixie kicked around for a while and finally hooked onto a fat prostitute who fell in love with him the moment he said nothing. He lived on her earnings, washed her feet when she came home to bed, but she cramped his style. So he sold her to a friend at Wayne State for key money and went to Los Angeles where he got a job on the set of a movie about the Civil War. His job was to stand behind the starring actor during the battle scenes and hold him up; the star liked to drink. He went the round of Los Angeles parties, bought a car, indulged in that fringe world which celebrates itself with gossip, pot and innuendo; he was even threatened by a phalanx of gangsters (he was proud of this) for making a pass at a blonde starlet, and he was once propositioned (in a gold-tiled bathroom) by a producer who was going to make him the Huntz Hall of his generation. Dixie enjoyed everything that became habit or style, and the L.A. life was fast and easy and he was well liked and took things as they came. It was there that he developed a case of seductionitis. "Weird," he said, "had to have every woman I saw, couldn't help it, it was awful, I'd walk down a street and there'd be this broad maybe ugly as sin, didn't matter, and I'd follow her around the city like a bloody sex maniac, slaver at the mouth for hours. See I'd pick something out like the mole on her neck or the way her stockings went or some mud on her leg, and I'd train on it and wouldn't let off. Nasty scene." To complicate it, he also had a case of prostatitis, rare in a man so young. It hurt something awful when he had sex and he kept meaning to have an operation. "The only thing is," he explained, "I kinda like it when it hurts like that. I'm doing fine with some chick and out of nowhere I get this wild drip, burns like hell, and I go ew-ew-ew-ew, and all of a sudden we both go straight out of our skulls." But there was more than the masochist about him; he took everything on faith, even a pain so bizarre as that, and his loyalty was incredible. Incredible, because one did not ask for it where he had been or where he was going; it was a virtue like chastity which meant nothing here or there. Nevertheless you could count on him. Except that he had an unaccountable streak of violence which surfaced like clockwork once a year, a

clean well-timed eruption. It seemed to purge him of suspicion and the more nibbling guilts, leaving him ready for
newer propaganda.

In Los Angeles, he discovered the arts; but more or less
the way a bear discovers civilization at the zoo. He returned
to Michigan (a whole lot wiser, he said) and became involved
with some pretty sordid people. He knew for a fact that
they were sordid because they told him so. He tried university, but he was thrown out of Wayne State in a year. He
and his friends bought a house in Detroit where they drank
and threw parties with the professionalism that comes of
wanting to do permanent injury. He developed a middling
taste for orgies and acquired a morphine habit that made life
more interesting and taught him responsibility. And, oh yes,
he wanted to be a writer. Perhaps the saddest thing about
Dixie was that he had no talent; he was irrepressibly likeable,
knew his way with women, had always been careful to live
a fairly unpredictable life. For a man of twenty-four he
was almost a boy of twenty, and he had done more than
most of us would see in a lifetime : but he couldn't put it
down on paper, and that, more than anything, drove him
mad. At any rate, it drove him to Europe where adventures
he couldn't describe and people he couldn't peg happened
to him all over again. In England, he had stumbled across
a great and ambiguous critic of English Literature; Dixie
didn't know who M. was, which seemed to delight M. no
end. So Dixie found himself living on a farm some distance
from London, chopping wood and shovelling shit and listening to the table talk of great wits. M. was an old man with
a great white beard of almost mandarin fineness and a young
wife who needed more than that to prime her senses. M.
allowed her to keep a lover, an Atlas type who kicked sand
in your face, with bulging biceps and ur-thoughts. This was
obviously a sophisticated kind of supply and demand and
even Dixie got a piece of the economy. In time, they tried
to teach him to think. At first he was hesitant, because
discipline was inhibiting. But M. and his wife encouraged
him and he was at last exposed to a series of debates. He
joined in; one night they were discussing disarmament and

Dixie mentioned that his father had been a foreman in a munitions factory during the war. They threw him out at once and he found himself alone in London. He spent four wretched days at the YMCA on Great Russell Street where the fags threatened him in the shower stalls. He walked up and down Oxford Street for twenty consecutive hours. He came upon Soho by accident and drank a gallon of coffee in an Italian bar. He wandered down to Trafalgar Square in a light rain and the breeze drifting across the fountains soaked him to the bone. He took the ferry to France and the train to Paris.

One of the more amazing things about Dixie in Paris was that he never left the Quarter. He arrived at the Gare du Nord, took a taxi to the Carrefour de l'Odéon and bedded down at the Hôtel Petit Trianon indefinitely. He never saw Pigalle or Montmartre, the Champs Élysées might have been in New York for all he thought about it and the Louvre and most of the right bank was some dark hovering spectre across the river, shrouded in the necessary mist and left untouched like some foreign menace. He soon fell in with the Quarter rituals, played his morning Gottlieb for instruction, walked to the American Express for his mail in the early noon, sat at the Cafés Monaco and Buci during the daylight hours and ate faithfully his meal of saucissons frites in the Bar Pyrénées. He was nicely balanced — lunatic and self regarding the way a Dixie ought to be — and so easily typed by those who needed to break his riddle, that he became a mild sensation, if not a downright asset. Jeanette said that he was really a giant dwarf whose six feet of height only disguised something truly diminutive and grotesque. "Fuck off, you skinny little bitch," I said, but there was a certain nicety in that judgment. Of course, Dixie was no prick; he had nothing that wasn't coming to him, that he hadn't earned in one way or another. He was no saint, but there was something of the jolly monk in his manner; raving soon put a stop to that though.

The first thing Dixie asked me when I met him was about writing; he was awfully embarrassed about the subject, as if we would immediately take him into a locker room and work him over, but he wanted to know if it was true that most writers smoked pot and got visions. He had been trying this but it had done no good, and he certainly couldn't write. He had seen a lot, I soon found out, but he couldn't trap any of it on paper, and he was beginning to feel that his life was a terrible waste : if you couldn't document your life, what was the use of living it.

I promised that someday I'd write him up in a paragraph. I'd give him epilepsy, I said, and I'd give him innocence and he'd end up marrying into the Rothschilds and instituting a Glukicz Prize for quality pot. So he told me things about himself, personal things that he wouldn't even tell himself until it didn't matter, and I later used them to get Iris. But that was long before we became friends, and during an unfortunate trip to Barcelona, and the whole devious business is better forgotten for a while.

Iris was a Greek girl. She wore her hair long and it was faintly yellow. She had a hard tight face that had about as much expression as a rubber mask sewn to the bone. She had soft ways about her, and tanned skin, but it was as if warm and supple things had been grafted to a sheath of cold and impregnable iron. Her nose ran aquiline over a thin-lipped mouth; her mouth was small; her strong pointed chin was dimpled, aggravating a softness that wasn't there, and her eyes were pure blue, rarely in motion, as if fixed to something already planned and done and set in motion around her. She had run away from a marriage of convenience in Athens and her life in the Quarter was the first leg of a flight that could not end well. She treated Dixie like dirt, like some dispensable luxury suspended from her toe; it was a shame to watch what she did to him so carelessly. She had cured his seductionitis once and for all, he claimed, for he was at last in love, but she had taken something from him too and he didn't even know that it was gone. No man ever satisfied her, that was her claim and her escape, but Dixie seemed to suit the way she lived now, and she lived with him out of a nasty desire to be destructive. It was something she let herself have, giving into it with a taste for killing things that made her feel secure. Dixie took it;

and what was worse, he loved it. Pride was something he could do without; he was better than that; pride was for people who didn't want. "Nasty scene," he would say, drained as dry as an egg shell, but he couldn't leave her alone, always trapped within distance of her light-haired body, set helplessly into a motion of touch, reaching and prodding for brown skin, rose nipple, yet getting no further than the clean, odourless womb and going no further than his cock could take him. Her cleanliness was a constant fascination to him. She was always scrubbed and fresh smelling, and it was partly his own sour sweat that produced in him the docility she used so well. But he had only mortgaged her flesh. When he discovered, at her own prompting, that he could french her without an aftertaste, scoop with his tongue the tasteless vapour of her gum-coloured orifice, he knew that he had been given a gift above all other men (or below when she put him to his knees). He did not have the freedom of her body, only the privilege, and although she hated to be touched, he was allowed to fondle her, allotted his quick period of conquest, then shaken from her body like debris or shadow. Dixie didn't mind; he learned not to mind. If he could not scare up some gentleness and love, he would accept some other propaganda, the understanding that this was a union of parasites, he to shed his seed, she to humiliate. And like the parasite, he glutted himself without mercy or caution, as if he were vaccinating himself against some imminent poison. So she was turning out to be just another disease, like prostatitis or seductionitis, but to cure it would have been to take away a sensation already gained and paid for.

In their tiny room on the top floor of the Petit Trianon, Iris had painted two nude studies on the ceiling and wall : one of herself, arms and legs spread as if impaled on the consonant X, the other of Dixie curled up like a foetus. Dixie, of course, was terribly embarrassed by these pictures — there were also some photographs in a drawer — but Iris refused to wash them out. He tried hanging pennants and flags, but she only tore them down and beyond that obstinacy he would not go. Out of this, Dixie developed a very fine sense of humour that was close to the edge. He was unable to write and he was no longer master of his instincts, but at least his jokes got better. Iris had no wit and didn't want any. She had a quality of receptiveness that demanded complete engagement and gave back in return its own passive and reclining gift. Still, for all her beauty and feline grace, she was very tough and manlike in her thinking. She permitted herself to need men badly, the way one might eat food joylessly or starve; and everything was on her own terms, a price that was easily paid. The awful problem of her inability to experience a man completely was not awful at all, and no problem to her; it was a necessary boycott and maintained the balance of power.

It was on the eventual trip to Barcelona that Dixie told me the whole story. She had been treating him badly, hardly talking to him at all, and driving over the Spanish frontier he was almost suicidal. What was worse, she was blatantly propositioning everyone else on the trip, as if meaning to squash him for good. In Paris, months before, Iris found herself pregnant. Dixie was surprised, then ecstatic, and insisted (with the insistence of an eager child) that they get married. Iris was cold and unmoved, and demanded an abortion. Dixie gave in after a few days that must have been terrifying; the prospect of a separation left him helpless, and Iris gutted was better than no Iris at all. So he bought her an abortion from Fitz. But Dixie was a funny guy. One day walking along the quai by himself, it suddenly struck him with all the nauseating and lovesick force of a man pursued, that maybe Iris wasn't pregnant at all, that maybe she was going to take his money and split it with Fitz and he'd never be the wiser. He insisted on watching. He helped Fitz strap her down, then sat in a chair while Iris had it done. "I never heard her scream before," he said. "My God." There was a lot of blood on the table, and yelling, and the table leg broke. Dixie became impotent.

The one thing Dixie believed in above everything else, excluding Iris even in Barcelona when it was all gone, was the illusion that kept passing itself off as his life. It was as if he were trying to live according to some perfectly remembered dream that had already been rendered defective and untrue. He was always high; he carried about with him a small leather pouch full of pills and drugs and powdered compounds which more and more he administered on the spot according to the tone of the moment. He had to perpetuate the dream of things about him; we were all, I am convinced of it now, figments of his imagination — the highest compliment he could pay us — and he spoke to us as if we were parts of his own anatomy. Somewhere someone was getting everything they wanted and, although each time it was becoming more difficult, he would always begin again with that in mind. I cannot forget easily the image of Dixie standing in front of the Pensión Toledo in Barcelona in the early morning, still haunted by the night's revels : he looks about him quickly, sucks in the tail of his mustache, says "It Didn't Happen," and goes up to bed.

Twenty-four
The Symposium

One evening as I was betaking myself to some mild festivity near Invalides, I was hailed by a group of persons seated on the terrace of the Brasserie Lipp. How extraordinary, I thought (while passing), that they were not in their accustomed places, ranged in chairs near Odéon. I would not have stopped but for that and, even then, I had meant to loiter only for a little while. It was not yet evening; the sun had only recently settled and the air was still soft and freighted with a certain lazy quiet. A block away, La Rhumerie was bustling with early customers, seated on the raised, wooden terrace sipping their concocted rums; vendors outside Aux Deux Magots hurried cheerfully about their business and the mood everywhere was light and frictionless. Traffic moved calmly up the St. Germain, cars slicing smoothly through the summer wind. "Come join us," exclaimed one of the persons at the table. I made my way across the road (for I had been wavering on the other side) and was surprised to discover that each of them was known to me. Rose the New Zealander was the most recently acquired of friends, a portly, brusque but goodhearted woman; Bunny Zenner was an old acquaintance, cheerful yet genuine, with a large protruberant nose topped by a dark, not unbecoming wart; seated by his side sat his wife Honey, a slim, bespeckled girl, whose attitude of pliant shyness endeared her to one instantly; Nate the Accordion was there as well, an older man with a clear and pungent wisdom, rightly celebrated for his accomplishments in the musical field. Seated near him was his woman friend, Constance Funn, a charming and devoted companion who took a deep, abiding interest in our modest ways. I took a place next to Rose and greeted each one in turn. The night breeze seemed infectious with its promise of ease and companionship. We ordered baguettes and cheese with some vin rouge to wash it down, and when all this was set before us we set to with hearty appetite, hardly pausing to exchange our views. But when our repast had been concluded and the table cleared, Bunny Zenner asked if I would settle a point which they had been discussing just prior to my arrival. It concerned the varieties of love and affection and, although I found the subject to my taste, I protested that I should have to leave them for festivities already mentioned. But when they clamoured in good humour that I could not possibly leave a feast which I myself had started, I acquiesced; and so commenced the conversation.

Garber :

Let me begin with an extreme. If by the end of the evening this extreme has been softened into something better, good. Otherwise, let is stand to our peril.

Bunny :

Agreed, bubie.

Garber :

Love is sweat and calculation. It's sheathing yourself before and wiping yourself after. It's putting menstrual rags in cans and buying creams from the chemist. It's depilatories and crud extractors. It's ten hours of hustling for ten seconds of give and five seconds of take. Love is no sooner in than out; no sooner out than cold.

Rose:

What are you? some kind of fucken pervert?

Garber:

Let me put it to you another way. Love is just another dirty lie. Love is ergoapiol pills. Love is quinine and quinine and quinine. Love is that dirty aborting horror. Love is insides all messed up. Love is half catheters and half whirling douches. Love always hangs up behind the bathroom door. Love is ...

Constance Funn:

Excuse me but isn't that from Hemingway?

Garber:

Oh. Yes it is. Which may prove my point of course. It's the monologue of a woman just before she masturbates.

Constance Funn:

No it isn't. It's a woman arguing with her husband.

Garber:

Oh. Well Hemingway did a lot of rewriting.

Nate:

If you're so disgusted, why do you make it?

Garber:

Let's say that it's the only game in town.

Rose:

I think he's a fucken queer.

Bunny:

Wo. Let me get a wart in edgewise. To me, Honey you listening, Love is having a big laugh, enjoying yourself like with a punch line. I'm-a-fat-man-see-with-my-face-they-broke-the-mould-who-was-that-lady-I-saw-you-with-last-night-I-just-wanna-say-it's-wunaful-a-be-here-see-all-your-shining-faces-I-know-you're-out-there-I-can-hear-you-leaving-you-say-you-fed-a-quart-of-prune-juice-to-a-bull-elephant-then-couldn't-find-a-cab? For instance, if I'm walking down a street with Honey and I see something wart mentioning, something funny like, I build it into a big joke and then we laugh together. That to me is Love.

Garber :

What if it isn't funny ?

Bunny :

Then we don't laugh.

Garber :

But if you don't laugh, then it isn't Love, right ?

Bunny :

Hold it. You telling me I ain't happily married ?

Garber :

I didn't say that.

Bunny :

Then mind your own business. I mean just because a man's fat . . .

Nate :

I'll tell you young pigeons what Love is. When I am separated from a loved one, I go into an agony the likes of which is intolerable and gives me headaches. Love isn't giving, it's keeping; and when I do not possess, I am empty. I know a lot of you have been censoring me quietly, behind my back — Yvonne told me, don't deny it — because I keep Constance locked in my room at the Dieppe. But I think you'd better look after your own affairs before you begin to meddle in matters you don't understand. Yes, I do lock her in the room, but that's an act of faith, and it's all part of a special game between Constance and I called *Frieze.*

Constance :

Nate, don't.

Nate :

I will if I want to, so just shut up.

Rose :

We don't want to hear none of your fucken secrets.

Nate :

Well you're going to hear them. I racked my brains for a way to explain to my Constance the source of our gift together. What did it mean and how was it to be exchanged between us ? So here's what we do. All day long while I'm out on the streets with the accordion, I think of her in my room all locked up with the windows

shut and the curtains drawn and a slab of towel under
the door. I think of her carefully and I squeeze everything
else out of my mind until there's nothing but her image
in my brain. My mind scans her face, or pans to the
objects in the room; sometimes I even try to knock over
a book and I strain myself to see it wobble and fall. In
the meantime, Constance in the room is supposed to be
trying to construct me too; from the minute I leave in
the morning, she traces me down the stairs and into the
street and follows me walking away towards the Beaux-
Arts. No jumping in time, every minute in her mind
takes sixty seconds; she sees me playing under the bridge
and she looks at the faces of the people on the quai and
sometimes she even tries to count the money Yvonne
collects. This is all day long and whenever I'm out. And
I keep in my mind's eye the sight of her sitting or walking
about the room, undressing or washing or using the
chamber pot. And then I hit upon an image, something
frozen like a picture, her in motion or a still life, and that's
our Frieze. I keep this in my mind without altering it in the
least and I strain to communicate it to her while she
strains to watch me going about my business. Once I had
an image of her navel in my bière Strasbourg, or that
famous time straddling her bidet, or just kneeling on the
bed waiting for my head to rest in comfort near her lap.
When my day's done, I race up to the room with the
vision clear in my mind, trying not to alter it one bit
because that's the sin of the world attempting to get
into my thinking part and ruin what is customary and
abiding between us. So if I have it that she is posed by
the curtain with one hand on a frill and the other placed
by her belly and her legs placed so, as if walking with one
heel spun up and the toe resting on a crack in the floor,
I accept this as an act of faith and believe that she knows
now what I have been constructing all day long as she's
been watching myself for a sign in her own mind. I open
the door to the room and look for her. We keep the light
off because we are pandering to magic, and when I find
her in the Frieze dead stiff in some lovely guise of her

very own making, I compare it with my own and find it exact. It has never failed to be the duplicate of what I have wanted. Last night, I came home earlier than I usually do, with the kept mystery of her sitting on the dresser, legs crossed and feet resting in the open top drawer; I made it very difficult by having one of my socks in her mouth as if gagged, and I put her left forefinger in a glass of cool water. When I came into the room, there she was as if by contact, perched like a lovely white bird on the dresser, chewing a piece of sock with the top drawer open and her toe sniffing about in my linen. When I saw that she did not have her finger in the glass, I left the room, somewhat shaken I admit, and wandered about for a time and when I came back she had the chamber pot up there with her and was lapping the water from it like a cat. I left again, straining in my mind to make her see the glass of cool water, trying to have her lift her forefinger, and I walked for a good hour knowing that if she didn't do it that would cause a rift and a block between us. And she too; because she rushed around the room touching objects and trying poses, thinking she had done wrong and needing and wanting me and trying to be faithful and true. She sat on the dresser again and put her feet in the drawer and shoved the sock in her mouth; she found the ashtray by the sill and moved it slowly counterclockwise till her palm itched like torture. But she could see me walking along the Quai D'Orsay deeply troubled and perturbed and she knew — for this was the sum of it — that it was wrong. I could see her sitting there, the room all dark, her eyes jerking for a sign, suffering soft thing, and I gave her the sign again and again. Many maneuvers followed, some indelicate, most too deep for pity. I won't talk of them. I went as far as the Quai de Grenelle and when I came back with everything in the balance to be judged, after much pain and trial and even bloodshed, there she was miraculously on the dresser as in the Frieze, with her lovely left forefinger dipped in the glass; in a pose of love and forebearance and duty. Oh Constance.

Constance :
Nate.
Nate :
Constance.
Rose :
That's absolute bullshit. You don't get me up on no fucken dresser with my fag end in a pot of piss. What are you, two fairies ?
Garber :
That's very interesting. You both see love as a vision located between reality and some undated zone of quiet. Love may easily, in your sense, be a psychically determined state; but I'd like to put some questions to you.
Nate :
Yes.
Garber :
It seems to me that yours is a contact of souls, each fully responsive and engaged. But you say in your touching example that at first the sense of engagement was weak, deterred by some preconceived current that proved false and inadmissable.
Nate :
That is true.
Garber :
Now obviously what is demanded between you is a total commitment without cessation of time, without even moments of grace. The mind must be instantly freed from the debris of what is extraneous and temporal. As if, out of some ultimate and irreducible logic, there is salvaged only the clot that concerns you both alone; everything else remains undefined, irrelevant. Only *your* scab exists.
Nate :
Agreed.
Garber :
Good. Now, there is one thing that still puzzles me.
Nate :
Go on.

Garber :

When the Frieze is not exact, it admits impediments.
The wave between you is being disrupted by something
that is curiously stronger. I find it curious, at any rate.
Perhaps some hypothetical transference from another
source moved Constance towards the chamber pot, the
ashtray. And until you know what jammed your reception,
can you ever be really *engagé ?*

Nate :

Do you know something ?

Garber :

Come again ?

Nate :

Is there another man breaking in on our frequency ?

Garber :

Well, of course, that's a hypothetical possibility, yes.

Nate :

You mean someone else wanted her to lap water out of
the chamber pot ? To humiliate her ?

Garber :

It remains a possibility.

Nate :

All right, I'm just going to say one thing : if I ever
catch anyone trying to produce static between Constance
and me, I'll kill him. And if I ever catch Constance
trading Friezes with anyone else, I'll cut their hearts out
and consign them to hell.

Bunny :

A good wart of advice. My nose bleeds for you, kid.

Rose :

What are you Goob, some fuckid Mort Sahl monster ?

Garber :

Garber.

Rose :

Well, just let me get an assword in here. I got a crud
husband who just left me, buggered off last week. When
we came to Paris, the asshole wanted to buy a houseboat
so he could piss in the Seine like a big hairy. That bloody
contraption cost us everything, but we got it, right near

the Pont Alexandre where all the fricket traffic goes by.
Okay, let him have it. We been married four years and I
said go ahead you stupid scum sucker, buy the bloody
thing so we can sit at home and vomit up our fraigen
guts. Then he says we got to have all these frikon people
up for parties, make it like a poncy French salon. Fake
you, I says, but we went ahead and did that too, had all
these snaggle-assed little perverts in for beer and crap.
When I married the prick all I wanted was a good shit
and a little fun, but he wanted to travel and get *ejucated;*
he's a little guy but he's built good like some stunted
Greek job and he always knew what to do for me. He
wanted to be *decadent;* be decadent up your pearly ass,
I says, I don't need no impotent little bastard scrubbing
my back; go scratch a turd. No, he says, we gotta be
decadent and go with the fraikid crowd; everybody's
decadent, he says. So we have the boat for a while and
a few *parties* would bore the ass off Erryl Fint, and then
one day : we got to make it *notorious,* he says. Squash
yours. I'm gonna write poetry, he says, on the boat in
the daytime. What you gonna write about, the frickle
traffic ? Every day, he's on the deck chair scribbling this
shit about *decadence* and flowers. Then, he says, we
gotta go a little queer. Wha ? I says, I'll queer your
jelly. No, he says, we got to *experience,* because all I'm
writing about is cars. If you think I'm gonna go down
for some froggy little dyke, I says, you are mistaken as
green shit. It's just *temporary,* he says. I'm not your
filthy whore, I says, and if I catch you with one of them
queers I'll cut your frilic balls off. That's *emasculation,*
he says, see how much we got accomplished already ?
First off, he says, you got to dye your hair blood red,
and I want you to start swearing something awful, and
also don't wear underwear anymore. What ? I says.
You've got to *acquire a reputation,* he says, quick as you
can so we can become the centre of everything. I says,
Thank you very much Oscar Wilde, you want me to dye
my snatch too ? Hey that's a good idea, he says, hey.
Maybe turquoise, I says; and I'll drill another hole for if

company should come. That's *mutilation,* he says, see how easy it is. I told him no, I wouldn't do it, I wasn't some filthy little slut you could maneuver like some friggit checker. Love lay deep, I says, but it don't lay for everything walks by. So for over a month we don't even pass a fart between us. He sits on the deck chair writing this crap like Arthur Ramballs and I sit in the hold waiting to shit. I loved that little twatmaster, but he didn't even come in to sleep at night; he just lay on the deck there without even a franek blanket. Anyway, one day I took a walk and I come back with my goddamn hair dyed this Chinese red and you could see I wasn't wearing any underwear the way I sweat. I love you Rose, he says, you are my Rose. I'm your funic whore, I says. And that's how I met those pimply Danes. That night he goes off and brings them all down to meet his wifey; she's *amoral,* he says, we're both *amoral,* it's something we got. Well you know Robbie, that tall blonde spider? and his spooky friend Jan with the fonnet mustache? They all come over for the big party, and they bring their girls, and one Australian broad Daphne; with glasses. This is Daphne, he says, meet my wife. Up your frigget crinoline, I says. See, he says, she's *amoral* as sin. I wouldn't have nothing to do with any of it, not the way they were, and Robbie begins to play with my husband; goo and all. You get the funt out of here, I says, this isn't no cathouse for freaks. I'm bisexual, says Robbie, any end will do. Go squat on a medicine stick, I says. Afterwards, my husband was real pissed off. Goddamn you went and did it, he says. I got enough material for four day's work, he says, and you ruint it. If you're queer, I says, that don't mean I am. If you want to make time with some facry poove, just let me know and I'll leave you. Go ahead, he says, get out, you're no help. The shit. So the next night, they all come over again and I don't say a goddamn word and I let them do what they want because I loved that man. Daphne with the fracken glasses tries to make a pass at me and I don't say a word, I let her play with it, the dirty little fruck, mucking around like I was some pigeonshit slot machine for chrissakes. Rose, he says later, I will love you forever Rose because you are true, and I'm gonna write a poem about us Rose. By now the word is around and every night we have these big parties and I'm swearing all the time and coming across big for everybody, one big sack of goo like some goddamn Lady Fintroy. Rose, he says, we are getting a reputation, we are almost there. Where? I ask. In the eye of the tycoon, he says, in the darkest part of the soul, he says, it is always three o'clock in the morning. Install a light, I says. Then last week, he says Rose I'm gonna leave you. Why? I ask. Because I've never done it before, he says. I've *outgrown* you Rose. You couldn't outgrow a cretin, I says. I'm planning on a heroin habit in Spain, he says, I'm counting on it. Go count your grebes, I says. I don't know when I'm leaving Rose, but one night I'll be gone. If you read *The Razor's Edge* you'll understand, he says. Somershit Maam, I says, what's he got to do with it? One day Rose, he says, you'll understand; I need to gain *rapport*. Then he was gone. So now they're lined up all along the franklin quai waiting to get to me.

Nate :

Why aren't I invited?

Rose :

You're invited.

Garber :

That's quite a story. Are you sure you want to talk about it?

Rose :

You're invited too, monster. You *anal fixated?*

Garber :

Sometimes love is a vicious testing ground. As if there were some deep interior goblin that is not satisfied with the more forward urges, but must continually renew itself in acts of outrage and contumely. Love often drains off its own existence by driving toward some extreme and unhallowed proportion that overreaches its very meaning. Ruskin said that the greatest artists never stop until they reach their point of failure. So does Browning in a way.

But when love goes beyond its definition, it dies and
becomes resurrected as something else, something impish
and inert like decaying food on a samples counter. May
I ask you something?

Rose :

Oh fuck off, Grubs.

Garber :

Garber. What strikes me particularly about your touching thesis, is that you succumbed only slightly less
willfully to the whole business. The imp is a two-headed
goblin; its janus face is deceptive and betrayed you into
the impossible equation that to render was to withhold.
And now that you've succumbed, you're trapped on the
other side of the colon. It happens.

Rose :

Yes, well I'm not finished with that ass-bleeder yet;
don't think I'm so frickit *succumbed* up to my dent that
I can't do nothing. I'm going to show that fart a wind-
storm; he'll know what fancken love is; I'll find him and
shove love right up his queer.

Garber :

At least you still care. That's something I wouldn't
have suspected. "Forked man has yet his charm," I see.
May I ask you something else?

Rose :

Be my crud.

Garber :

In all your talk, you didn't once mention what one
supposes to be the essential in love : that membraneous
illusion which manifests itself in affection and sacrifice
and the nobler graces. Spiritual commitment : the webbing
of the soul that catches Time and holds it prisoner and
fashions it to its own unsuspiring mould.

Rose :

Goobs, I think you're a friggled ass-man.

Garber :

Garber.

Nate :

Weren't you listening to me at all? Constance and

I have above everything the spirit between us. The spirit that moves in and out and gives us Friezes.

Bunny :

At your age, wart else ?

At this happy point, the conversation ceased. All eyes reverted to the street and there ensued much rejoicing. For both Brynning and Gilchrist were making their eager way towards our table. Dusk had descended now. The tribulations of the day slumbered in warm shadows. The lights of cars winked and flickered up the St. Germain. The cooling breeze of the river chilled us briefly, then wafted past into the deepening, lovely gloom. Brynning and Gilchrist were sturdy, faithful fellows, beloved by all, seeing to each other's every need, devoted, loyal. They made a strange, yet gladdening sight. Brynning was the taller of the two; he had a long, thin face and wore a gold friendship earring. Gilchrist was short, rounded; his face was swollen, childlike, and he moved like a little bear, swinging the duplicate earring to the delight of all. They were certainly welcome additions to our talk, and room was made for them instantly. Brynning sat down cheerfully and little Gilchrist sat down astride his lap. This to the amusement of all.

Garber :

I trust you're both in good spirits.

Brynning :

Great.

Gilchrist :

I feel sick.

Garber :

Ah, instant dichotomy. Friendship, they say, is an admixture of indissolubles. Now don't laugh or I shall think the worst of our motives. But mock me if you will, I cannot swerve from my sincerity. Don't say it Rose.

Rose :

Bunny :

We've been discussing the varieties of love and affection, boys. We just got to the point about the spirit. Garb says we oughta have it. Nate says he's got it. Rose says she had it. I can do wartout it. So say something.

Brynning :

I love you Gilly.

Gilchrist :

Me too. I'm in love with your pickle.

Brynning :

Give me a kiss.

Gilchrist :

Can I pull your string?

Brynning :

Just once.

Garber :

I detect a note of cohesion here . . .

Brynning :

I got to wash out your ears when we get home.

Gilchrist :

Yah. And I'll pull your string right off the spool.

Brynning :

Scrub-a-dub.

Gilchrist :

Hey get away from my grisby.

Garber :

A true friend is a second self, I suppose. Beyond what is sacred into what is complete and self-enduring.

Brynning :

Gilly and I grew up together in Dundee. We'll never ever part.

Gilchrist :

Nevah.

Brynning :

We look after each other like little mothers.

Gilchrist :

He even wipes me.

Brynning :

That's cause he's got short arms. When we were kids, Gilly was a little tiny guy with lots more red hair than he got now. I was the tall kid but I was too beautiful, nobody liked me. (I *was so* beautiful.) So Gilly and I used to play together, just the two of us, and take the ferry to Tayport. Remember Rolfe? Limey Rolfe used

to wheelbarrow us by the legs, but we fixed him once in
the boiler room; I poured hot water on his head and Gilly
took a bite right off his leg. And he swallowed it so Rolfe
couldn't get it back. We had this society; with secret
pledges and initiations. Shall I tell them? We had to
drink little thimbles of each other's spit. Then it was
sucking toes. Then it was true love we had all right. Why
when I had a girl, Gilly would follow behind and hide in
the bushes and make little hoots. I love that little guy.
Like we were the same person. Say tweak.

Gilchrist :

Tweak.

Brynning :

Again.

Gilchrist :

Tweak.

Brynning :

Why I had a girl Kora-Lynn. We always went to the
films together holding Gilly by the hand. If we wanted
to do something, he'd always wait outside somewhere,
then we'd say it was all right, so he'd come running back.
Say tweak.

Gilchrist :

No.

Brynning :

He doesn't want girls so much. He likes to play doctor
with them. Once when he was a little kid, some older
girl done it to him. Let's play horsie, she said, you
be the rider and go up and down. And he didn't even
know that she had done it neither. That's why he's so
cute : he doesn't know. He come up to me later and he
told me *I played horsie*. But he doesn't like it unless he
doesn't know. You've got to pretend or he won't do it.
Just a little teddy bear aren't you Gilly? Don't pout.

Gilchrist :

I'm tired.

Brynning :

Want to play doctor?

Gilchrist :

I haven't got my instruments.

Brynning :

I wouldn't touch nobody but Gilly. We even snore the same. We sleep in our bathing suits. When he's asleep sometimes, I pinch his little cheeks cause he's so small and warm, a little ball all furred up. When we ran away to sea and become carpenters, Gilly was sad; he was all homesick. So we bought these earrings and I said Gilly we got the same head so one on each ear and you are the only little person I love. Tweak.

Gilchrist :

Now you told them everything.

Brynning :

Tweak.

Gilchirst :

They'll think we're hermansensuals.

Brynning :

Tweak.

Gilchirst :

Tweak.

Brynning :

I even know when he's got a pain in his little belly. And I give him a bath sometimes and I got to pull his pickle or he gets sad. Nobody can say I don't love you Gilly. I even gave up girls cause it makes him upset; he doesn't understand. He thinks you do awful things cause he doesn't know what you do. What do you do with girls, Gilly ?

Gilchirst :

You pull their pickles.

Brynning :

See.

Garber :

Excuse me, but do you actually commit the sexual act *per anum ?*

Gilchirst :

Don't tell.

Garber :
I find this, within the touching context, extraordinarily beautiful. Yet you are delimited by the very qualities that make you free. Apparently, you're still capable of having women and still you impose upon yourself the conditions of a purer alliance; won't this sacrifice inevitably rear upon itself and cause your latent normality to spring ?

Gilchirst :
Oh don't answer : he's a psychansophist.

Rose :
They're a couple of frottled cock suckers.

Garber :
I should like to pursue one final point. Cloacae notwithstanding — a sore point I'm sure — there seems to be nothing traditionally perverse about your relationship. Or to be more succinct, I fail to detect, within the complex of your values, anything of that proverbial ugliness so often associated with queerness. (Sorry, that was an unhappy phrase.) Can you, at any rate, enlighten us as to your sublime holds on pleasure.

Brynning :
Razz

Gilchrist :
A

Brynning :
Ma

Gilchrist :
Tazz

Nate :
I'm not about to sit here and watch everyone make admissions while you bait them, Garber. It's your turn. I'd like to know what your puny experience amounts to.

Bunny :
Yah, put your two cents wart in, kid.

Garber :
Love and affection. I have personally known this thing in all its tones and shades and modes of light. What you have all said is enough to convince me that the truth

should be heard, because in all its varying and peculiar units it somehow exists among you. When I sat down I was not prepared to admit this, or go any further than your own devices. But now, of course, I must, if you will be patient and bear with me in your attitudes. I knew a woman once; her name was Cheryl, a very tall, a very long-limbed thing, filled to the brim with hesitancy and forbearance and a quality of rare acceptance too. She loved to laugh, Bunny; oh god how I can hear her laugh. And she had her rituals, Nate. Every afternoon in those free and golden days, we would sit outside the Monaco and read *Time* Magazine; it was the Atlantic edition, I remember. There was a keen sense of pain as she bought it, for the cover was important in her life. She knew that she'd have to live with the colour and texture of it for a week, plumb its glossiness until it faded and turned worn. Would it be a graphic photograph? an Artzybasheff nightmare? a Koerner? a Vickrey? some startling mural unimagined, not foreseen? She would creep up to the little stand on the St. Germain, hardly able to look at what the week had brought, at the torturous vision already there. We read the advertisements first. All of a Wednesday, we went through an agony of detail, letters to the editor, letter from the publisher, the listings, the masthead. It was as if we were hoarding some response, like a small flame that would burst and winnow from us in some easy ecstacy at last. But we would not go beyond the Wednesday matter; that was doctrine; and when, in the night, I could feel her tense and unreleased, wanting to turn *now* to the *People* section, fighting against an imp that would make it all meaningless, I would stroke her feverish skin, prickled with heat, tremulous; I would fetch for her glasses of water, bathe with a mother's care the blanched and swollen mouth, the throat give water to, all cracked with dryness, unable to sound. Then, with more a lover's care, sweep up the gauzened cloth, stroke the legs with cool tempered sponges, watch them strain and member, the toes locking into anxious cramps, the forebone luminous. "Gossip," she would whimper, "there will be lovely gossip." "There there." "There'll be pictures of Maximillian Schell and Princess Soraya," she'd half cry, frigid with it, racked into something mummified, the mortis already rigoured. "Don't think about it, no no don't," I'd say, and by morning it would be all right again, for that was the way it went with us. As day succeeded day, we scanned minutely the *U.S.* section, *The Congress, The Presidency,* all the things we needed to build our hopes towards what we knew would come. And when it did, with the inevitability of our little death, after days of *The World, The Press, Art, Crime, Religion, Science,* the inevitable letdown sprang like fungus. *Cinema,* that was what she believed in, even when the rest of it was gone, yet she only glanced at this, as if it were a talisman only to be touched and verified, some barren and lonely act of faith without content or substance. So when the anticlimactic *Books* section had been attained, and the slow-mounting pleasure of the week drained off, we seemed to be surrounded by the holy debris of our week, a wreckage. That was when it all meant something, Rose, for Love is a coincidence of points and pain is the sum of its arc. That was when Love was best; we walked the quais in the night, hand through arm and arm on neck, feeling it seep off as if suffering were an eaves trough, letting it go, watching it go, and the cool wind whipping the river, anointing our bodies with a soft, affirming breeze. Paris went on for some time and meant a great deal. You know how it is when the city starts to counterpoint your life and makes the good things good and the bad things bad. Each Wednesday it would begin again, the slow wait, the mounting pain and anxiety and hope. But one night she broke and I could do nothing. She leapt from the bed, her hair spurred back, her arms flailing and tangled, and she took the magazine and turned to the *Cinema* section, an act premature by four days; and then it was over. I knew that I would have to get her out of the city. We could start up fresh in the provinces, perhaps get the *New Yorker* and build to the *Profile.* We would see the Loire Valley and the river of the Rhône, wander through châteaux and live in the villages where it couldn't touch us. It was difficult; she didn't want to leave Paris. For Love is linear and knows only one direction, Hugh, a straight unbending curve that will not boomerang. To begin where one has ended : that is the sexual irony. But Paris receded like a bad thought and we picked it clean from our teeth and were gone. We went alone, that much we had to do; and purging was easy once it started. The ritual died among the valleys and towers of the Loire; and once effaced, as if by some magical slate, things became fine again. We camped by the river and saw the châteaux and had coffee in the mornings served up in huge soup bowls. There was Chambord with its whitened mass and its grand staircase; Blois with its gothic gateway, its symmetry of windows with their carvings and standards, the great staircase climbing spirally in its octagonal well; Chaumont with its painted rafters and fireplace and carved wooden door; Chenonceaux in the night with its moats and canals and the Italian garden; and then Villandry at the height of noon with the sun planted like a kiss upon the geometric gardens. We saw it all, we were there. You know Cheryl, soft and pale, clothed in her own quiet and yielding shame, Cheryl of the Sorrows. Well, the valley changed that; her lips were red now, as if she had been sucking berries by the bank, her cheeks swelled with colour, by joy abscessed, and there was a good taste on her tongue. And there was one night among the nights. Love, when it is like a neon sign, blinks swiftly and you cannot fetch its light from shadow; but that night we did, as if the sign had frozen in a frost of light and we scanned at last like the Song of Songs. We went swimming in the river, Constance, and when we had raised ourselves from the water and were resting on a great rock, the sky suddenly erupted into colour, jets of fire swooshed high above us, bursting into a flower of sparks. Meteor-like tails climbed higher and released their lodes of gold and silver; spangles of turquoise and ginger fused and scattered, their bright dead ashes showering the river. And suddenly we were part of that volcanic prism. The rock was scooped and prone

like an altar, for Love is a sacrifice, Gilly; and homage
was done with wafer and cup. She lay beneath me, all
teat and twat and belly mobile. I held her, pumping with
a slow and membered grace, distended now up to the hair
and beyond, into something yawning, moist, almost lifelike;
she groaned, sobbed, convulsed by hiccups, rounding my
organ in a loft that womped and thudded. I seemed to
move through her as if she were myself again, traced on
cellophane, as if my penis had impaled her on the rock
like some collector's bug. On and on we plumbed, into
the night and long after the firelights had faded; in the
morning, the dawn lit her face angelic and white, and it
was not over yet; midmorning came and still I strove and
still she staved; by noon the sweat had dried on our bodies
like some gelatinous and protective lotion, but we lay
sustained; afternoon passed with its angular shadows, dusk
settled upon the river and yet we remained, heaving,
spurting, caught in waves of our own making, renewed
by the tight slavering motion. Night fell. Stars and moon
headlined the sky, streaks of darkened cloud hung like
banners over the river light. And still we came and saw
and conquered, winning the battle again and again without respite, accumulating the gift like hydras regrown.
All that night we worked our separate peace, and only
with the second dawn did we rise at last from the little
death. Her eyes that day were stunned and crazed, like
those of the epileptic before his vision; she walked with a
martyr's limp, yet there was a cleansing tonic in her belly
now. And she moved her bowels thricefold, as never.
Minor words to describe the phenomenon of that
journey into flesh. For I was not absent from her damp-
ness. So Love is a fountain welled without depth, spurting
its salve and its balm, threading us from orifice to soul and
back again to cock triumphant, a desert where hope turns
to water and rains upon the sterile root, a camel with
brimming hump, a bird that finds the garden sprinkler,
a dog harboured to its hydrant; smells changed to odours,
stink transformed to wafting pleasure, corruption turned
to holy chaffing. Love is an apple.

Bunny :
I don't know wart to say.
Rose :
If he fucks like he talks, you're liable get a colon up your crud.
Constance :
It was beautiful and so true.
Gilchrist :
I bet she ruint her pickle.

And so we parted with a good feeling, for we had done something truly rewarding and had learnt each from the other a future course of conduct that would serve us in good stead. We agreed that we should meet again soon and renew our little talk. Each was quiet, still deliberating upon the evening's modest lesson. Thus we went our separate ways, in good faith, the way brothers part each to his own house in solitary gladness. But when we had reached the St. Germain-des-Prés, Constance could not withhold a last enquiry. How withdrawn and sincere she was, hardly able to put the question to us; and how eager we were to help, gently urging, and chiding her in good fun for her tardy comment.

Constance :
There's just one thing I don't understand.
Garber :
Yes ?
Constance :
What's the difference between *decadent* and *debauched ?*
Bunny :
Debauched is when you do it in the rain.

Twenty-five

Prior to the Barcelona trip, I was seeing a great deal of

Rose the New Zealander. Rose had the foulest mouth of any woman I had ever known and her judgments were monumental. "Garber," she once said to me, "you are a fuckid Mort Sahl monster," and that piece of insight stuck to my vanity like flypaper. When she made up for this in her own inevitable way, she was like a great cow licking her own spilt milk; for that was the way she took it back, and every little foulness in her talk led invariably to the bunk bed (six by three) a few feet below the river line.

Rose had a tremendous bosom; it was by reputation much bigger than she thought, and it drooped in a series of bulbous folds. She seldom wore underwear, it made her itch, and on windy Paris mornings she was on the itinerary; people would walk for blocks to see her standing on the gnarled deck of her small blue boat with her fingers staunched at the hip, the breeze off the Seine whipping cross deck to slap and unfurl her skirt, revealing to those who waited the wilted discoloured cheeks of her behind. "Two three times a week I fart like hell," she'd say, "the rest of the fanic time they can watch it gratis." She also had an extremely ruddy face — she always looked as if she had been eating jam — and everything she did, she did loudly and with abandon. She had an insatiable appetite for men and food; she could not distinguish the one hunger from the other, and watching her eat her way out of some confused, suggestive meal was a sight known to turn the stomach. She liked the gravy to ooze from her mouth like hot lava. "It's just sewage," she'd say, "I got sewage everywhere." And in bed she expected a nine course meal or God help you; she'd serve herself up boiling and blotch-bodied, medium rare with the juices just below the blood and the eye of the fish trained on you from start to finish. She was never, in all that time, completely sober in bed; there was a drunken curiosity to her prowess, a vague, demented clutch. She liked to occupy you like an army; if the proof was in the pudding, the pudding was endless. And she was obnoxious. It was one of her skills. Someone once gave me some extraordinary advice, "Closed Mouth Gathers No Foot," but Rose's mouth was one of the vilest animals in captivity. It was a wet, sloppy beast that stored insults in its cheeks like a dyspeptic squirrel; its lips were dried a perforated pink, almost blue, with an ichor of gray silt. Emanating from the sullen, misshaped maw was an odour only half beer; the words and curses that spilled unhappily over the hump into the air were freighted with a stink that left no room for argument. Of course, she was never wrong.

Her most charming feature was a houseboat in the Seine. It was docked quite near the Pont Alexandre, a very wealthy bridge, and day and night there was the steady unchanging hum of traffic as cars moved over the paved ramparts of the Quai D'Orsay. That noise was the only constant in her life, and she hated it. Not within the memory of man had that boat ever floated on the river; it merely rested against the quai day after day and threw parties. Before Rose, the boat had belonged to Vincent Van Gogh Motes, a Quarter artist with both ears intact and a stubbly red beard. He was said to bathe his stubble in tempera red and he had a whore on the side and a few friends who disliked him. Motes's whore gave him money for equipment and he kept up his rent by chalking biblical scenes on the sidewalk in front of Cook's. Every day he returned to the same picture on the pavement of the Capucines and put another margin around it so that eventually it stretched a good block away, and one summer it went all the way to the Ritz in the Rue Cambon. Motes had the theory that Van Gogh was not dead, that He was hiding in the hills. So he painted like Him in order to gain His confidence and patronage. Except that painting like Van Gogh cost money; when he saw that he could not keep it up, he underwent a sudden expedient revelation and changed his name to Henri Matisse Motes and began to work with water colours. This saved him all sorts of coin and he spread the happy rumour that Matisse was not dead, that He was in fact a waiter at the Café de la Paix. But by this time he had no money left and his whore was in the hospital having her ovaries mounted. So Motes put the boat up for sale and in no time at all along came Rose.

Originally, Rose had bought it for herself and her husband, intending that they should live in it forever and watch the

city from the shore. Her husband was a pleasant little man
with thin wrists who loved to idle; he was grateful to Rose
for the boat and he did his best to keep up the sinecure
and provide for his wife a spectacle of riot and glamour. No
man, however, could live with Rose indefinitely, it was
against the laws of gravity. Her sexual habits were more
cavernous than artful, and she measured everything by the
noise it made. Rose allowed you anything but the illusion
that you were free of her bite; if she told you to heel, you
heeled, and if you could salvage your dignity while heeling
that was your business. Her husband ran away to Portugal
or Spain.

Because she was now husbandless and inconsolable, Rose
was to some extent easy game. She liked to wallow in self-
pity, it was the privilege of the deserted and she knew it.
She allowed herself to cry publicly for the little man she had
finally driven to lunacy and flight; the tears would curl down
her great red cheeks like scraps of tinfoil and her mouth
would open to receive them, and from her throat a noise
unlike a rattle would heave and burp its tragedy into the
night. The sag of her bosom would rise in the intake, then
decline and fall; her beer belly, now dropsical in a slight
paunch, would inhale courageously, then bloat, spill, collapse.

"Goobs," she would sigh, "you're not listening."

"What is it Rose?"

"Up his ass," she would say almost quietly, all atremble,
"just up his pimply ass."

So Rose was two people, which I suppose is getting off
easily. When she had overwhelmed you with her fat-assed
dominance, she could afford to reveal her sorrow and loss
and gooey pride as if they were a gift to those she had already
trapped into patience and fright. Yet even when she bawled
and whimpered (the snot precarious on her nose), she never
let you forget that she could break your back. You picked
the thorn from her paw, but you still had the lion. Her
weaknesses were not reassuring.

Her husband did not leave her empty-handed like a thief
in the night. He willed to her keeping a legacy of friends :
the Danish set. The set was composed chiefly of three lovely

people, Robbie, Jan and Daphne. Robbie was a tall blonde boy with blue-tinted glasses and pimples so ingrained and old that they passed for freckles. He was the centrepiece of the group because he was belligerent; he dealt for his people out of a savage sense of trust as if they were his property and his burden. He loved violence of any kind; when alone and bored, he often stubbed his toe. He began visiting the boat out of love for Rose's husband and ended up in love with Rose; he fawned in her wake, basked in the gloom of her booming voice, fed off her indifference in the hope that she would drop his way a few indifferent favours. Whenever she was drunk enough, he was rewarded : she would pass out, the gruel like fuzz on her mouth, and he would proudly exhibit his strength by carrying her all the way from Les Halles to the Quai D'Orsay. He'd arrange her in her bunk and make love carefully so as not to rouse her from her drunk, oblivious stupor. In the mornings, when the crowds gathered below the bridge to catch a glimpse of her wind-blown posterior, Robbie would emerge instead, bare-chested, zipping up his fly, unwinding the hairs in his armpit with stately calm and self-assurance. "She's all fine," he would say, "she's sleeping now." Daphne started coming to the boat because she was in love with Jan, and eventually because she wanted Rose; Jan had come because he did not care and had a car.

There were a series of parties on the boat which the Danish set threw and hosted; they were not good parties because the Danes were rather pompous, but the boat was like an oasis in the midst of the city and people came for the sheer novelty of being rocked and swayed silly, and for a sight of Rose in her bulky T-shirt and green Arabian trousers.

"Get these fuckend spastics out of here," Rose would growl at Robbie.

"They're my very good friends," Robbie would answer, his throat throttled out of respect for more woman than he knew was necessary. "Just a little longer."

"Any fuckle longer," Rose would say, "and it'll be out my sweet and fanic mouth."

I can remember emerging from one of those parties thick with smoke and noise, twenty bodies already piled into the hold. The deck was peeled brown, curled into strips of rotten wood and muck. There were a few quiet voices by the bow; a few signs of struggle near the bank. Enclosed within the greater darkness, there was nothing but the boats and the lights of Trocadéro and the water; the soft hum of the cars dipping and swerving to avoid instant death down the quai, the dull click of footsteps on the cobblestone and weed. I could look far across the Pont Alexandre, past its rain-green Neptunes, and see the island wedged to a point in shadow. After a while there would be a few screams from the cabin, then someone stomping up the ladder; then a great trembling arm, bare and salmon pink, would wiggle through the hatch, a sullen voice would say "Where's my funt monster!" and down I'd sink into the boat again.

Although she was probably worth it; that's hard to say. One of the many services she performed for us was the trapping and draining of rich Americans in the Quarter. Her dishevelled kind of wildness seemed to promise a great deal to someone from, say, Cincinnati, and she got us more drinks and meals per square Yank than anyone else. She wasn't beautiful by any means (imagine a large pink girl), but she was promiscuous, there was something damp about her, even moist. Robbie lived a full month on her leavings, and there were those who could count on at least three meals a week, and by August drinks maybe once a day. She usually found her marks in the regular places : outside the American Express, on the terrace of the Café de la Paix, in the lobby of the Grand Hôtel. Rose always looked good to them and they were hospitable and soft-spoken and waited patiently like jackals for her equilibrium to fade. She came down the street with them while the word went round, one meaty hand directing their elbows like a tiller. She'd bring her latest conquest (some middle-aged Sammy nervously measuring himself against the advent of her buttock) into the Café Tournon, seat him at a large empty table, and wave us over. We'd move in like vultures, order our evening drinks and meal and leave *l'addition* for the good time Charlie; he seldom had a good time, and he never had Rose.

This made Rose invaluable on certain levels. But there were other times when she was not much fun and a few instances where she was downright dangerous. Once, she broke Trixy's nose (a right hand over a left jab) on the apparently false assumption — duly suggested by Nate — that Trixy was acting as her unofficial pimp.

"She's simply diabolical," Nate had whispered in her ear, "there's no telling what the bitch will do if given enough leash. That deceptive little beast actually approached me the other day with a wax impression of your cabin lock and some written particulars of your body. I was to pay a certain sum. Insufferable."

"Where is that moth-eaten whore !" screamed Rose.

"At the Café Buci, third table from the left as you enter; but don't be hasty, will you."

The rest had been subsequently witnessed by several people enjoying their quiet café crèmes. Rose had burst into the Buci, her face a sickly, sausage red. Trixy was sitting alone, the very picture of sombre concentration. In her hand was an edition of the *Ancren Riwle*. A fresh flower had been carefully arranged in her hair.

"You !" Rose had bellowed.

"Oh, hel . . ." was all Trixy had time for. The blow sent a spray of blood across the floor; the petals of her lovely flower scattered wildly down her face. She fainted, and was carried out.

However, that episode had been due, in part at least, to Rose's menstrual cycle. The first day was a particularly difficult time. It always brought to bear upon everything else the full force of her predicament. It flushed out secret haunts which habit ordinarily suppressed; it disturbed and made intolerable a mode of action usually unquestioned. Because the fact remained that Rose desired a simple life; glutted, indulgent, vulgar as she was, stronger feelings of guilt pursued her whenever distractions failed to deter them. So during certain painful interludes, she found her conduct to be inexcusable, a sexual travesty, a dirty joke. Her monthly periods served to remind her of an essential function which she had somehow abused. It was astonishing, really, that she was capable of such feeling; but it was an interesting sidelight. And whenever the flow began, transforming her temporarily into a baleful Hyde, she would put forward some crazed remark, often self-mutilating in its implications. "Next time I'm gonna stitch the goddamn thing for good," was certainly her favourite.

Rose liked Dixie and didn't mind Iris; she knew Dixie was crazy but she liked his style and Iris was too beautiful to matter. Dixie liked everyone — a defect which caused him endless trouble — and he thought that Rose had character. Iris reacted to Rose as if she were a stray hair and to most men as if they were mouth rinse. I got along with all three, although I found it trying. Dixie was not in good shape, although it was hard to tell what *that* might have been; he was, as always, anxious and likeable and the constant foil. Iris' abortion had taken place hardly a week before and he was still not sure whether his condition was irreparable. Iris, on the other hand, was certain. And because we did not know, and would not know till Spain, what lurked between them was a mystery, perhaps some natural and ingrained sense of malice.

Dixie loved to sit on the deck of Rose's boat alone in the late afternoons with his shirt off and a comic book (vintage 1940) on his chest. About five o'clock, he would wander along the Quai to the Rue Dauphine, the suppliant *Neeeem* low in his throat, and up to the Café Buci for his Oxo soup and celery. Iris, Rose and myself, and perhaps the Danes in fawning attitudes, would be seated on the narrow terrace. He would take his place and eat quietly; sometimes breaking wind to relieve the tension. "Come on," he would eventually say to Iris, screwing up his head to relieve himself of a resonance, and they would cross the road and disappear into the Petit Trianon. But they would be down again in half an hour to resume their accustomed silence; not a pleasant word would pass between them and one could only surmise that they were tough and sullen lovers.

"I feel like I'm at some fantid wake with them," said Rose afterward. "What do they do up there : shit ?"

"That's the way they are," I said, "but it's different with us Rose."

"I'll say," said Rose. "You given me piles with your fancy funts."

A month after the old Loire Valley group split up, I received a letter from Stephen U. He carefully explained where he had hidden the car and authorized Bobby E Lee to sell it as best he could. Bobby E Lee was at this time depressed and abandoned in E. Bone's room, prone on his back. Accordingly, he decided to take it to Spain and push it over the Pyrénées.

Twenty-six

"They got everything," said Dixie, "look at that."

Dixie was looking across the street from the Café Monaco where Dan the Boston Brahmin had just parked his Porsche; he was now walking counterclockwise round the car in order to help Alice unwind from the front seat where she waited instinctively and without joy. Then he opened the low door; Alice swivelled calmly, right leg forward like a tendril, and raised herself free to the road the way some people avoid puddles. The move was designed to expose a minimum of flank and a sudden flash of trimmed forcleg; Dan's corresponding elbow was designed to accept, with unsuspecting grace, the fingertips and dainty weight of the woman already acquired.

"I can smell them from here," said Dixie, *"Neeeem."*

It was the mannered smell of blossom and plum lotion settling before them like a protective shield and leaving in its wake a small gift from their bodies. They came over.

"They got a toilet right in their hotel room," said Dixie quickly, "behind a purple curtain; right in the room."

"Have a cracker with your cheese," I said.

"Naw, I like it raw."

We were sitting outside on the small terrace enjoying the warm air; Dixie was toying with a tic of ice at the bottom of his glass.

"This *is* nice," said Dan. "Dix I think you know Alice."

"Nerm," said Dixie.

Alice smiled cunningly for the exercise.

"Why don't you sit down," I said.

"No no, we've been sitting all day; drove to Chartres last night and back this morning."

"Pleasant trip ?" I asked.

"Dix," said Dan, "what are you doing about four o'clock ?"

"No thing."

"Good good," said Dan, "come meet a train with us."

"Sher."

They signalled goodby, much joy, and disappeared up the Rue de l'Odéon.

"Why do you bother with them ?" I asked.

"They got style," said Dixie defensively; his mouth moved around other words stashed like cud, but they didn't quite make it.

"They're spoiled shits," I said.

"They just live good," said Dixie.

"Dan gets an allowance from his father, doesn't he ? and they live in the Hôtel Voltaire, don't they ? and keep their luggage in a room at the Windsor, right ?"

"So ?"

"I'm telling you then, they're rich phony shits."

"I got their confidence," said Dixie.

Dan was writing a novel. He had 150,000 words done and fifteen characters and he divided the 15 into the 150,000 and got 10,000 but he didn't know what to do with that yet and had given himself a year in Paris to figure it out. The novel was not about Alice whom he had met at a party on the Ile St. Louis; it was about a friend of his who had committed suicide at Harvard in the spring and fall of 1959 and who had so far taken up 50,000 words. The rest of the book was concerned with ethos and syndrome and the cumulation of Quarter motifs as they occurred to him each morning. At the precise moment of his fading up the Rue de l'Odéon, he was going through an agonizing reappraisal of the multiple 10; with the multiple 20 he could have had 30 characters; this thought was a watershed in his development. He wondered if he should ask for a hike in his allowance and follow it through. Otherwise he might have to give up Alice and divide by 12.

Dan's hair was ginger coloured, curly, set off by a bright blue ascot tucked like a drape into his shirt; he wore tight dark trousers and light brown desert boots, wrap-around sunglasses, lightweight tropical jacket with suede patches, white gym socks and Alice on his right arm. Alice wore a cool print dress, a white ribbon in her hair, pumps pink in colour and Dan beneath her left wrist.

As they passed by and into the distance, their walk seemed to become a series of hitches and gimps, a leg drawn up too fast, strides a trifle dissonant, a toe spinning forward to tilt them like puppets. It was as if a network of strings were tugging at their centres to give them the casual and disjointed walk of dolls. Which was, of course, what they wanted and worked at. Like athletes who come from the showers covered with heroic bruises and sporting aches, Dan and Alice made a promenade of their privileged moments together. Carefree, flamboyant, the sunkist cavalier, Dan put his hand to his *aching* knee, rubbed the joint with mock *alarm,* whistled prettily. Charming, electric, all sensual cool, Alice stroked the nape of her neck with a childish, disapproving *pout,* gracefully *scolding* a life like their's. It was a bid for something lyrical (which took up all their time) and cheap at the price.

When they came to the Boulevard St. Michel, Dan made a decision. He would keep Alice after all; but he would not wire home for more money; he would keep his self-respect too. He would reorganize and subdivide the novel and add some new information. He would make use of Dixie; he would write a mid-chapter entirely in italics.

When he and Alice had achieved the Luxembourg, they sat at a café table across from the Gardens and ordered two lemon cokes. Those who knew them circled enviously, yet at a distance : there was something private about these rich and beautiful people, fragile as tissue paper and not too absorbent.

"What do you think of this, Licious," said Dan.

And he told her how he would devote an entire chapter to Dixie, develop an isolated rhythm, break the foremood of the novel by way of tragic relief, juxtapose the pattern proper, then move their luggage into the Dieppe and save two francs a day.

"Sounds good to me," said Alice.

They sat quietly on the terrace for an hour. The sun at three o'clock pierced awnings and withered shadows; it made a golden, or tin disk of Dan's face as he prepared his triumph with pen and paper, rounding out fractions till everything was even; rewriting was the difficult part, all right. Alice hitched up her dress to catch the refracted glow of sunray as it bounced off her pale knee.

"He's a real character, Dixie," Dan was saying. "I think he's a real find."

"Sounds okay," said Alice.

They finished off another lemon coke apiece. They liked lemon coke because it looked like rum. People who drank rum in the afternoon had tragic pasts.

"I think I've pretty much mastered the art of balance," said Dan. "What I want is a series of fragments joined to the hip, so to speak; something architectonic. Dixie's going to be tremendous."

"I like it," said Alice, "sounds okay."

In half an hour, they left the café and wandered especially into the Rue de Fleurus past Gertrude Stein's *atelier* with the floodlight over the doorway. They came round to the Café Monaco via the Boulevard Raspail and by a quarter to four Dixie was walking with them to the car.

"We can all sit in front," said Dan, "I want to talk to Dix."

Vivien Goodleigh was arriving at the Gare du Nord on the 4:20 boat train from Calais. Dan wore his trench coat.

"Oh there she is. Vi !" laughed Dan, running, springing forward, putting his arms around a tall, blonde girl who stood erect and smiling behind a porter.

"Vi Vi Vi *Vi*," he laughed.

"Isn't it *weird* to be in Paris again," laughed Vi. "You look *good,* Dan."

"I *feel* good," laughed Dan, "that's Alice laughing over there."

"Oh Dan, she's *lovely,*" laughed Vi.

They came off the ramp, arm in arm, preceding Vi's luggage at a nice distance.

"Alice Vi, Vi Alice," laughed Dan. "Let's go get a drink, the car's outside."

The two girls sat in front with Dan and Dixie sat in the back reinterpreting a hangnail.

"Who's *he*?" asked Vi, bending forward secretively as if confiding to the clutch.

"You mean Dixie?" said Dan casually, "I'll introduce you later; he's crazy, a real Quarter bug. *Dixie?* where shall we go?" Dixie imitated the action of the tiger by relieving himself of a tremendous yawl.

They decided to have drinks and a little supper at a small cellar bistro just south of Montparnasse. It had a five piece band in the evenings and an elevated dance floor with a brass railing. When they had found their table and ordered their drinks, Vi, Dan and Alice began to talk about Terry who was at Yale.

"Oh *Terry*," said Vi, "he's fine."

"Is he all right?" asked Dan.

"Oh yes," said Vi, "he's fine."

Dixie meantime screwed his eyes together and evoked a small vibration. He knew how to be simple when necessary.

"Dixie," said Dan, "this is Vivien Goodleigh, Vi Dix."

"Hello there," said Vi.

"Neeeeeeeem," said Dix.

By seven-thirty they had him talking and a little high.

"He's marvellous," said Vi. *"Wherever* did you find him?"

"Dix is always in the Monaco, day or night. I met him on some slob's houseboat once. Dix, do your motorboat."

"Ahummmmmmmm."

"My God," said Vi, spreading long white fingers, "you people are really living *the* life here."

"It's quite a crowd," said Dan.

"But please tell me about your book," said Vi. "Everyone *but* everyone wants to know."

Dixie ordered the Chateaubriand with potatoes and buttered sprouts. He got a little butter on his nose.

"What does he do?" asked Vi.

"Nothing," said Dan.

"But isn't that wonderful!" said Vi.

"He's got this girlfriend Iris : she had an abortion."

"An *abortion!*" said Vi.

"Dix," said Dan, "tell Vi about the abortion thing with Iris."

Dixie told them.

"And afterwards," said Dan.

Dixie added the rest.

"You mean he *can't*," said Vi.

"Nope," said Dan proudly.

"Oh that's awful," laughed Vi. *"Poor* Dixie."

She put the ends of her fingers on his cheek and her thumb in his mustache.

"Anyway," said Dan, "he's got prostatitis; whenever he does it, he gets this burning drip. And he lived with a prostitute in Detroit."

"My *God*," said Vi, "you've come a long way from St. Louis, kids."

"They try it every day," said Dan, "it's lovely."

Vi shook her head in mock disbelief. Her nose was shaped like a small, inverted arrow; she was entirely blonde and pale, true to her publicity, with lovely spots of purple on her face when the skin flushed. It flushed when sufficiently excited.

"Dance with Vi, Dix," said Dan about nine o'clock after most of Dixie's past had been exhausted. "Do your little gorilla step."

Dixie rose and walked along the railing to the dance floor. He turned half-drunkenly in the dim with his arms spread and his eyes crossed.

"Go on Vi," said Dan, "he's harmless."

So Vivien Goodleigh, full of fun, placed one hand on the

base of his spine and with the other clutched his wrist and held it like a perpendicular branch between them. They circled and dipped.

"Do you take dope ?" asked Vi.

"Nermmmm," said Dixie.

"Dan says you have holes in your arm," she said.

"Piscinnnnnne," said Dixie.

"Swimming pool ?" laughed Vi.

He pressed his flat groin against her skirt.

"Now now, naughty," said Vi. Purple spots blossomed on her cheeks; her nose crinkled frivolously.

"Tell me about this Iris," she kept smiling, to keep the spots in place. "Is she terribly bohemian ?"

"A Greek girl," said Dixie, attempting suddenly and without warning to trap the corner of his mustache with his distended tongue.

"Is she angry at you because of, you know ?"

"Neem," said Dixie at the ready, swaying off to the left, sailing towards an object unseen as yet, diagonal, feverish. He pinwheeled and bowed, charged like a bull.

"Gorilla," shouted Dan from the table.

Dixie turned on his heel, metamorphizing quickly, shifting back, cutting at once into the slow, musing rhythm, spreading and hunching his arms, extending his swollen gray tongue and emitting as he waited in mid-floor the snort, grunt, chirp that was expected of him. Vi was satisfied and led him back to the table.

"He's not in really good form yet," said Dan. "Dix have some more cognac. Did you bring your pouch ?"

By ten-thirty, he was in exceptional form. He blew bubbles in his drink, aped the sounds that flew past his head, spluttered, burped. Dan pumped him for humorous details of his life with Iris and took notes down the red margin of his notebook.

"Why does he make those funny sounds ?" asked Vi.

"If I knew that, I'd know everything," said Dan.

"Oh I must write Terry about this," said Vi. "Dan, you've *really* arrived."

At midnight, they drove him home. He lay curled up in

the back seat, one hand and wrist projected through the window like an automated signal. The resonant *Neem* fluttered through his closed lips like a low snore and tickled the neck of Vivien Goodleigh. Dan drove especially fast and took each corner on three wheels, but he could not revive the tranquil, fading Dixie. Who, filled with cognac and Chateaubriand, buttered sprouts and peach melba, cheeses and apples and the sounds of the dance, lay tucked peacefully in a corner of his own mind contemplating the noise of bees. "We better drive him to his place," said Dan, the fun over, and he turned into Odéon and through it into the Rue de l'Ancienne Comédie. When they arrived at the Petit Trianon, Dan opened the door and sprang out quickly. "Just push him out," he said. They dragged the soft, breathing object out of the door by the arms, the head hanging between. Dan raised it up and pushed it to the doorway; he laid it down on the steps, then propped the thing against the wall. The head slumped forward as if severed to a thread and a bubble of air popped from the mouth; something trembled in its nostrils and broke free in a sharp, vibrant hum; the arms and legs jerked and kicked free, then shrank back towards the body resting.

"Delivered," said Dan.

Twenty-seven

So the three of them were sitting there and feeling very good about it. Leonardo de Crud'homme-Pervert (known reverently as the Crudhead) was sitting in the middle; he pulled a wormy mucus from his nose. The other two, Al Scythe to the right of him, Lyle Voyd to the left of him, sprawled in their chairs like protective gargoyles, alert and flanking. Flies buzzed and settled on their faces.

Leonardo de Crud'homme-Pervert had the beard of a

Stoic, the mane of a lion, the eyes and beak of a condor vulture; his baleful, terrific glance cut a tension through the vacuous noon. He ate chips. Al Scythe was gaunt and spectral; he had a small unsuccessful vandyke that gave to his chin the appearance of a stillborn pubis; while his sleeves might billow, his head tapered; he grouped his legs experimentally. Lyle Voyd was fat and pink, relapsing distantly into his own tonnage, armlets folded severely over breasts; his solemn, warning gaze was like a safety lock that kept him in; his distended belly, rolling thighs, tiny leg shoots, seemed to have only recently emerged from some secret and intestinal fête. So they sat there, these imperial three, maintaining the faith on the terrace of the Closerie des Lilas; where no one saw them.

One thing was certain : Lyle Voyd was the *epitome;* he took it in his stride and was not unhappy; he sacrificed himself as the unquestioning and devoted metaphor; his body was of many colours like the rainbow. Al Scythe was the *genre* though he kept it to himself; the patched fuzz on his jaw seemed to mirror (hopefully) a whole generation of despair and deadweight. But Leonardo de Crud'homme-Pervert was their *fulcrum,* and it was He, the Arch Crud, who finally meant everything they said. *Epitomes* might change and *genres* might expire, but *fulcrums* were eternal. They waited.

The talk of Al Scythe was bony; it was nervous and pitched, almost flutish; he spoke compulsively, in frenzied hyphenation, swallowing the little words like an anteater, his tongue displayed. He uttered commonplaces under strict decree. The talk of Lyle Voyd suggested the softness of pudding; it was slow and thick, a veritable drone, the words wet as if dripping out of a monosyllabic dream. He was permitted only foolish thoughts. But the talk of Leonardo de Crud'homme-Pervert was nostrilized and booming; it was deliberate, heavy, resounding against eardrums like the crack of a chastizing whip; it worked fear and havoc among the meek, its piercing staccato more terrifying than any dialectic, its triumphant verbs commanding. He alone spoke to waiters.

In matters of habit, Al Scythe abstained. He ate little and felt less. Weekly hormone injections were his only vice. His ravaged exterior belied a soul wasted away by constant guilt. He rarely slept; his fingers were scarred with the sign of onan. In matters of habit, Lyle Void indulged. His body was a symphony of noises; the deep flesh rehearsed its senses, basking in a riot of feeling, sensitive beyond belief to sound and touch and odour. The mouth was an organ of perpetual taste; there was no crudity it would not perform, no bestial act beyond accommodation. The mouth alone was catered to; in everything, the mouth was fed. But in matters of habit, Leonardo de Crud'homme-Pervert was the compleat function. The self-perpetuating myth was legend. Stronger than ordinary men, his sexual organ the reported cause of many a hemorrhage, he assimilated experience without effect. Men quaked in his tremendous presence, women prayed and tingled in his wake. Impossible to poison, not really susceptible to disease, objects of his desire succumbed obediently everywhere. He was leviathan of the mind as well; alert, omniscient, he had forgotten more than he could remember. And generous too; whenever he took his fun, Voyd and Scythe were allowed their little games.

They sat. In the loggia of their minds (airy, cavernous), several things wavered on the brink of thought; yet superceding traffic, sunlight, people, their patience weighted and sank the atmosphere. Nothing was, for the moment, said. The Crudhead basked his profile in secret wonderment and gratitude. Al Scythe prodded the separate hairs of his jaw. Lyle Voyd secreted warm impulses. Two to three hours they sat, keeping the vigil, each in his ordered legacy. Immobile, proud, the very fixture of the terrace itself, the Crudhead scrutinized the horizon, its line glass-domed, metallic in the sun. No sign beckoned, nothing stirred. "All Is Vulnerable," he said. He crunched his chips. The arid Montparnasse and the arid St. Michel became one before them. Pigeons flew. Awnings fluttered. Time passed. Then, contemporaneous with their watch, a distant object stirred and shifted.

"Jesus, here comes one," said Al.

She came from the fountain, out of the final peninsula of

the Luxembourg. Her name was Billie Balene and she was
bright-eyed and a little simple. She came across the octagonal
towards the Closerie. Her bell bottom trousers caught the
perfect muscle of her rump and held it like a sculptured ball :
preceded by her beehive sweater, followed by her jet black
hair. She passed close to the tables and sent them an
astonished glance across the terrace, up the steps. They
were ready. But she was still walking, now almost past them,
moving in the wrong direction.

"Shit, she's getting away," said Al, trying to hook her
with a hairy smile.

Lyle Voyd contracted.

She was already completing her turn into the arid Montparnasse, moving through the separate portions of her body
like a cat or train. She wore spiked heels. She kept them
in view, pausing for an instant, then cantering on, then
pausing as before, until only her cuffs were finally visible
pumping like clockwork out of sight.

"No no, she's gone !" cried Al, one hand still between
his legs.

"Death And Destruction !" boomed the Crudhead rising,
"Come Sit Down." So she came right over.

"I thought we had lost this one sure," said Al.

"Interesting," said the Crudhead, "Feline Too."

"I figured she was gone for certain," said Al, "am I
smiling ?"

"A Little More Tooth," said the Crudhead as she came
up the steps.

"I'm Billie," said Billie Balene.

She was more than that, Felicity Wilma Hyacinth Balene,
who seemed to pursue her own breath at a distance, who
spoke sharply as if to cut down the margin. She sported a
cut over her mouth where the notorious white slaver Boot
Chavez had whipped her; put a finger to the crisp, dead
tissue; picked.

"Billie," said the Crudhead ruminating, "Short I Suppose
For Williama."

"No," said Billie.

As she sat down (facing Leonardo de Crud'homme-Pervert

thus completing a perfect phalanx), she placed a heavy, large straw purse on the table filled with various pastries (the Crudhead wisely observed), a map of the Paris sewer system, six postcards of a highly erotic nature, a can opener, the remains of a boat ticket on the Danube, a pair of slippers, an umbrella sheath, a pack of used Italian condoms, wads of tissue, a tube of mysterious salve, a rubber diaphram stretched out of all proportion, needles, thread, and a currency chart in a plastic folder.

The Crudhead recognized her immediately for what she was.

"Do You Perform Coitus In The Vernacular?" he boomed.

His eyes passed among the host; they began to adjust themselves to their probable image. Al Scythe sucked in his cheeks, creating a wondrous hollow and giving to his jaw a certain sharpness and to his vandyke a kind of apse-like threat. Lyle Voyd, as if to counterpoint the gaunt and spectral Scythe, released himself, allowed himself to flow in a bacchanalian surge of rounds and domes, his face massive and his organs small, his belly, paunch and guts peculiar taking one giant step towards his lap or knee. But Leonardo de Crud'homme-Pervert remained constant like the truth itself, mesmerized by his own intactness.

"Do You?" the Crudhead repeated.

"You mean screw?" asked Billie.

The Crudhead paused. Here was no ordinary victual.

"Yes I Mean *Screw*!" he thundered, his voice oceanic.

"Oh sure," said Billie.

"I See," said the Crudhead, "What About Fellatio As Designated?"

"Which one's he?"

"And Are You Equally Favourable To Cunnilingus?"

"Sure, anyone."

"And No Compunctions Concerning À Trois? Soixante-Neuf? Quatre-Vingt-Cinq Or Huit?"

"I don't like the French, but what the hell."

"You Intrigue Me."

"Well let's go."

"Not So Fast."

The Crudhead, with suspicious ire, turned to his cohorts. A conference ensued. Al Scythe interrupted a private maneuver, Lyle Voyd withdrew his tongue.

"There's Something Wrong Here," said the Crudhead quietly, "Something Facile."

"I'd just as soon forget it," said Scythe.

"Her ass too small," said Voyd.

"I Will Pose The Problem," intoned their leader. He turned back to Billie who was waiting calmly.

"Are You Prepared," he said, "For Sexual Depravities Probably Unimagined ?"

"Okay."

"Aberrations ?"

"Guess so."

"Copious Perversions ?"

"Sure."

"Necrophilia ?"

"Sounds good to me."

"Oral-Anal Stimulation ?"

"Why not."

"Blood Fetish ?"

"Right."

"Coprophagia ?"

"I'm game."

"Costumes ?"

"Oh, a party !"

"Does The Name Gilles De Rais Ring A Bell ?"

"Ding a ling."

"This Is Serious : I Don't Think She'll Do."

"Thank God," said Scythe.

"I just so fatigued," said Voyd.

"Then It's Settled."

Leonardo de Crud'homme-Pervert put both massive hands on the table. The joint of his thumb cracked playfully.

"So you guys want to make it, or not ?" asked Billie.

He broke the news.

Twenty-eight

When Trixy first came to Paris, she spent her afternoons in the Cimetière Père-Lachaise. She loved to walk among the dead for she was somewhat haunted herself and the Cemetery, with its stone tombs like little huts and cottages, gave her a quiet, settled feeling. The first day, she bought a map of the place and trailed down its silent streets to special graves. Afterwards, she sought out favourite benches, shady trees, vantage points where the view was awesome. Sometimes, she bought a lunch and watched the families tending plots; children played handball against the stones, lonely men carried pails of water; sometimes, she helped by weeding gravesides or watering plants; sometimes, she sat in the little huts alone, contemplating the sculpted heads of the departed. Often, in a slab of onyx, there would be a cameo picture of a child or woman. It was the smell of the place she loved : not the sharp smell of decaying flesh, but the smell of roses and grass. It was the idea of the place she loved, everybody lying horizontal under the ground. She loved the gaping pits under reconstruction, the crumbling roofs of ancient sepulchres; she loved the little grave of Auguste Comte, obscured in a small wayside thicket with only a headstone to mark it, and the ascending stairs that led to other plateaus, like the streets above Pigalle. When it was sunny, she walked; when it rained, she retreated into little huts and lit candles to the ghost.

Of course, in the Quarter she went to parties. She was not a bad looking girl and, although she was petite, she gave one the impression of height. Perhaps because one saw her from a distance.

So Nate, one evening, put a hand on her lap and asked if she could sing.

"I need an accompanist, you see, to ply my trade; I play the accordion."

"That must be wonderful."

"It's a good living if you have the wit. Since Yvonne met

her tragic end, I won't discuss it, I have been at a great loss. I can't allow Constance on the streets, she can't be trusted. I'm always fair to my little helpers; and I'm not a fiend to be with. Ask anyone. Well ?"

"I sing only hymns, I'm afraid."

"What about 'House of the Rising Sun' ?"

"No, I can't sing Japanese."

"Are you joking at my expense ?"

"**Oh no.**"

"I'll give you ten percent of the take; that's certainly fair. Ask anyone at all."

"I don't believe in personal gain."

"My you have a crackling wit; a fresh blast of it is always welcome. Anyone will tell you I have a comic sense."

"You're very pleasant."

"Thank you. Does my hand disturb you ?"

"Please don't."

"I see. Well, what about my proposition ?"

"I'm sorry, but I mustn't."

"Well, I've never heard anything so snobbish. Most women would give their left breasts for a chance to work with me. And don't think I haven't noticed you and Brynning in the corner. It's obvious to me exactly what you are. I've had experience in the field. You're a recent example of my thesis; I can be dangerous if roused to anger."

"Please don't."

"It's a mere finger, madame. It's not as if I were raping you on the spot. I'm thought quite a catch, you know. No need to play the virgin with me."

"It hurts. Please."

"Do I nauseate you ? am I a dirty old man, do you think ? I have never been exposed to anything so disreputable as your responses. I warn you I may take necessary action."

"Help."

Later in the week, Trixy was sitting alone on a bench near Notre Dame. She was reading Fuller's *Sacred and Profane State*. The nail in her shoe was hurting exquisitely. She had not been to the Cimetière Père-Lachaise for several days; the thought of Nate's coarse hand still filled her with disgust; she was not worthy yet to visit that place; she was impure.

As a bookmark, she used a worn, well-read letter which she had received a few days before. The sender was anonymous. In red crayon the words "If You Took All The Faith She Has Ever Had In Anyone And Shoved It Up Her Ass, There Would Still Be Room For Her To Be The Whore She Is" were scrawled childlike in an uneven circle across the page. She cherished it as a token of her venal thoughts. It gave her pleasure.

"There she is," said Nate, tramping across the Parvis Notre Dame with a retinue of odd types following. His accordion was slung across his shoulder and made a whining sound as he moved. "There she is," he said, "that deceitful little bitch. I want to give you all an object lesson in faithlessness and vanity. Hello?"

"Hello."

"Do you deny that you indulged with Brynning? possibly others?"

"Excuse me?"

"Note the pale hue, the angelic askance. Note the grandmotherly dress, the plaintive voice."

"Is Hugh here?"

"Want it badly, don't you? But I've heard his story. How you used him ruthlessly, threw him off like a hangnail, went to others while he pined with remorse. I'm merely a more current example of your cruelty. Bitch, whore, sycophant."

"But we only chatted; he looked so pretty, like Christ."

"Ha! What a devious wit you have: the better to eat you with my dear. Do you know our methods with girls like you?"

"Beg pardon?"

"A gang can be a horrible thing. The rapacious mob, you know. Will you reconsider?"

"Please don't."

"What was I doing? A mere finger, for god sake. This is a public place, do you think I'm crazy?"

"Help."

Trixy lived on the Ile St. Louis; her room had the exact dimensions of a cell. It was always dark. She had put a wool shade over the light bulb and the drapes were always drawn. The floor was made of cement, not wood. There was a crack in the door; it was a crooked fissure. At night it admitted a thin light from the hall, sometimes curled like a mouth, sometimes tapered like a worm. The room was narrow and sloped; beneath the sink pieces of old tile, loose and making a sound when stepped on. The slope of the floor ran downhill from the door; it levelled again near the window so that sitting on the bed in the dark, the centre of the room looked like a pit. The centre of the pit seemed far away, but it rose to meet her when she walked across. Often, footsteps passed along the hallways, shapes blotting out the light coming through the fissure. When people paused in the hallway, not talking, but silent, as if waiting for her to break, she wouldn't break but held together tightly. Eyes often tried to peer through the line of the door, feeling with their fingers for the gape of the fissure, but the darkness discouraged them and they went, their footsteps sounding along stairs to other places. The room was widest near the door, narrowing in a sharp V towards the window; the window was small, like a misshapen porthole. The dark bureau had a mirror; the bureau door would not shut, and the mirror would swing to reflect her bed and the window behind it and the sink. Trixy seldom undressed. She slept in her clothes for fear of waking in some dread place that she did not know. She did not dream of wandering forlorn through streets and alleyways; but when she slept, she sensed the new place, as if she were already there, lying in the midst of some terrible quiet. The room was always different when she woke. Sometimes, it was reshaped, the V inverted, so that she had to stumble through a tunnel for the door. Sometimes, the window was in the door itself and faces passing in the morning peered in to see her on the bed. They whispered excitedly to each other, all trying to see, moving about like a nest of snakes; so she couldn't undress.

She didn't know what was the matter. She had come

across an ocean and half a country to live in a small room; that was wrong and something horrible was happening but she couldn't help it.

Not that she was crazy. She was sick and it would probably go away if she didn't break. So she never panicked. It might even be a practical joke done with mirrors and hypnosis; although she preferred to be ill, because practical jokes were embarrassing.

She had liked parties and even people, but that changed and she couldn't understand why she didn't go to them any longer. She had liked men, but there were no men in the little room and not even thoughts of sex; she didn't know where that had gone either. She could want these things without having them or needing them; desire was there but it had no feeling, like a dead finger. She could see everything from a corner of her mind and not wish for any of it, yet know all the time what was right. She was not repelled by the flesh, for Brynning had aroused her; but being aroused was enough now; and it had not really aroused the flesh but something else and whatever it was, it was wrong and horrible to think about. But she kept calm.

She had taken to reading religious books and medieval tracts on virtue and character; she didn't want to read them. Yet she read them all the time and put away childish things. Nate had asked her to accompany him in the streets with the accordion and she had said something about the wrongness of personal gain, but she didn't believe it. It was as if her old self — the one that went to parties and used to giggle and had no shame — were trapped behind her eyes, pounding fists against the wall of her skull. When she said something that was not true to her old spirit — the one that danced and was coy and loved its pleasures — she would try to break through the cold words and warn them. But the one was too loud and the other hysterical; so to keep calm she let it pass. That was the way to hold together. Then one day she bought a book about anchorites who had sealed themselves into little rooms forever. It filled her with horror and she tried not to bring the book back to her room, but there it was under her arm and then on the bed and she was reading it. She read it through and despised it; but in a few days there was a new lock on the door and a key somewhere and she knew that soon she would lose the key and never leave. She fought it. She clutched the key, put it round her neck on a string, took forced walks into the Quarter, trying to keep awake so that she would not find herself alone in the room, sealed off for certain, gone for good.

In the Quarter, people were unkind. A rumour had started; she was accused of things. They played it like a game, never taking the rumour seriously; yet she was toyed with and never let off the hook. But she wouldn't leave; yet she felt it slipping. It wasn't happening to her, it was happening to someone else; she held on.

Nate was in the room. She needed the sounds of people to keep it going. Perhaps she had invited him up. He sat on the bed beside her. She had lost track of the day but she knew where they were now; she tried not to fall off again; she kept the room in mind and she clutched the key.

"Do you think all I think about is Sex! adjust your thighs," said Nate.

"What?"

"Believe me Trixy, all one needs is a small act of faith from you. To counter these stories circulating about. I'll have them revoked in no time. A bit wider."

"What?"

"Constance understand is another matter; that is love. This is merely a sampling of the will : effort to be true and not deceive. I find your change of heart refreshing."

"What What?"

She was moving out of it again and she tried to steady things. The trick was to hold onto what was happening and not let it skip. Her hands moved calmly but her dress was not there, she was sitting naked from the waist down, her legs loosening. Nate was looking between her legs. Nate held a clutch of pubic hair.

That went away and then it was another night and she was alone in the room; the key was still there and she was clothed again. She drifted off. She felt herself walking. She came to the Quarter and made a turn and was back in the room, trying to leave the door open; she slept between the door and the bureau, one leg holding the door ajar. It was morning; you could always tell by the crack in the door. It was dusk. She was in the Cimetière Père-Lachaise and then she was in the Café Buci reading the *Ancren Riwle*. It had some funny parts; was she going to laugh? Nate was there. He was being caustic.

"Nothing to boast of. Like taking a corpse. Deceitful to the core, that way. Proper response necessary to warrant my respect."

Nate was plunging a finger up her anus.

"Self-respect through humiliation, proper Christian act."

The room was smaller. The window immense.

Père-Lachaise, dawn; raining.

Boulevard de Strasbourg.

"Un wimpy, si plait."

The key touched.

An eye peering through the fissure.

She was pinching herself to stay awake. Nate at the accordion under the bridge.

"The money! What have you done with my money, you whore!"

Sleeping, but filling the void with pain, not letting it go. Then it was gone.

"What?"

Comte's grave.

Vomitting up something pasty.

"Help."

Wrapped in blankets, because the walls damp rubbing against her back and belly.

"Please don't."

The key in her mouth. The key in her hand. Cold against her throat.

She put a flower in her hair.

"Don't close the door."

In the Cinema. Outside.

"I can't hold on."

Nate at the Café Buci in a rage. She was reading the

Ancren Riwle again, awake thank God. Perhaps if I stay
in constant pain. Nails in my shoes. Hair shirt. Sharp rock
in my hand. Violent jolts were good; they kept her there,
in one place. She could remember if the flesh was felt.
Where the flesh hurt.

"*What ?*"

"Oh, hel . . ." A moment later, Rose the New Zealander
broke her nose.

Twenty-nine

Concerning Billie Balene. How she met and received
Anatole Antishaft, notorious peeping Tom. Whose singular
devotion to craft led to partial blindness. Whose last vivid
recollection was that of Billie by her window. In a state of
undress. Innocently exposed. Telling also of his nightly
ritual. His superhuman patience. The art of the Venetian
blind. The mysteries of the telltale drape. His ladder which
allowed him to peer *down* rather than *across*. The reper-
cussions of this geometry. His modes of operation. Tele-
scopes, plastic panes, stools of varying heights, shoes with
retractable heels, light deflectors, elements of camouflage :
all these divulged. Also, his greatest triumphs revisited.
His adventure of the roof top, straddling shingles above the
city to witness bohemian orgy in the Rue Jacob. His many
female disguises allowing admittance into toilets and shower
stalls. Of his diving bell, too, whereby he glimpsed through
portholes. A blur of nipple ten feet below the Seine, his
finest hour. His secret invasions of privacy. Awful sex acts
committed in cubicles of light. Considered his most cherished
memories. Of how, the night coming on, his person elated.
The metamorphosis determined. He sits in little room,
surveying prospects. All directions weighed for possibilities.
His final choices adamant, and tenacity of patience ensuing.

His fortitude and heroic quiet. Many the time all for nil, naught achieved. Yet much worthy to report from year to year. His philosophy encountered. The vast metaphysic of his projects. His ideas seen to be sound, the humanitarian principle held to. To see man in his subnatural state, stripped of guise, in bestial raiment sighted. To witness the habits of the insect. Leads to Knowledge, Truth. Arousal of the Good. His conquests do no harm. This discussed at length. His Apologia For Seeing Too-Much. In what way this improves him as a man. How reality may be encountered without danger to the agent. His credo found sympathetic. Moreover, his methods not wanting in taste. Witness to the flesh and grass of the body, a permanent science. Yet his work takes its toll. Occupational hazard sadly discovered. His sight diminished. Years of self-imposed darkness, a toil that extracts its due. Objects become hazy. Uncovered flesh indistinct from curtains. The horror of misreading windows. The end in sight. External light to fade. The soul its own dark place. How, discovering his fate, actually takes a woman. Fastens field glasses so seen through long end throughout experience. Eavesdrops on himself. This not unrewarding. But his sight wastes away, unreplenished. His art in state of decay. Leading to his last visual encounter. His final project unfolded. He rents room in Rue Bonaparte. His apparatus assembled for best possible effect. Billie Balene as seen from street. Described in florid detail. The appeal of her beehive sweater, bell bottom trousers. How he is enamoured of her spiked heels. Their grating sound announces her coming. His room light extinguished hurriedly. Ladder carried to window. Its fourth step found most appropriate to his ends. Her window light still dark. His patience brought to bear. He smokes many cigarettes in sink. Wanders back and forth through darkness, gathering strength. Feels momentarily caged. His doubts conquered finally. Her light pops on. A quickening of his heartbeat. Aids metabolism. Wheels telescope to within range. Units of space quickly measured. Changes shoes. Wears black shirt to blend with gloom. His face smudged with polish. Curtain raised 6⅔rd inches by special pulley. Takes spoonful of cough tonic to insure silence. Part in hair recombed to camouflage bright scalp. All chinks in atmosphere neutralized as well. No motion detected across way. Antishaft peers from a professional lean. His dire squint. His heavy breathing muted. He undergoes religious experience just prior to action. Immolation against pangs of guilt. His science reaffirmed. Now trains his vast skills on room sighted. Takes in dimensions. Records position of chairs, bed, bidet, sink. Bureau within field of vision. Probable fulcrum of scene to follow. The first flash of shadow across frame. Quality of detection noted. Degree of mobility quickly figured. The second flash of shadow in fleeting motion. Certain attributes determined. Telescopic sights adjusted. A rising sense of what is to come. Gradual excitation of the optic nerve. Third flash of shadow at a much slower pace. Subject obviously considers bed. A final check of gadgets. Subject scratches crotch. Everything tested for performance under pressure. Subject pauses at window. Hand on string of Venetian blind. Peers ominously out. Antishaft's response to this : a prayerful position assumed on ladder. Knees on fourth rung, hands folded piously on foot board. An incantation delivered, personal in nature. Subject decides to leave blind open. Antishaft sighs, gives thanks. His heart dangerously quick. His breath threatens to mist up window. Special non-coloured sponge applied. Transparency renewed. His hot panting breath directed downward. His trauma controlled sufficiently without detracting from its resultant pleasure. Subject moves away from window. Towards chair. Antishaft given to understand clothes will be placed there. Vast consequences of this easily apparent. He concentrates on keeping calm. Applies eye drops. Subject takes a glass of water. Subject wanders to and fro. Familiar litany of waste motion. Subject disappears momentarily into hallway. Urination femina, recalls Antishaft, takes three and one-half minutes; evacuation femina too complex to determine. Stopwatch carefully studied. Subject returns in one minute, thirty-eight seconds. Probable constipation. This adds immeasurably to personalization of project. Rapport growing. The serious business

begins. Early stages unbearably exciting. Subject combs
hair. Subject removes earrings, hair band. Hair allowed to
flow in dark continuity about shoulders. A lingering shot
of subject standing before supposed mirror to acute right of
window frame. Thereby offering to Antishaft a much-needed
respite. His eyes dimming. A mucus forms. Produces a
fatal glassiness. Eyes gouged with cotton pad and special
plungers. Renewed sight. Brief double vision. Subject now
in titillating still life, gazing distractedly. Subject at brink
of shedding action. Antishaft gasps. Moment of truth at
hand. Penultimate adjustments made. "Oh God." His body
growing tremulous and lax. As expected. He plunges finger
into special circuit outlet. Body charged and jolted. Renewed
rigour. "Oh dear God." Blinks to wash debris away. Subject
chucks beehive sweater over head. Arms struggle. Head
squirts through top. Breasts exposed. Antishaft achieves
self-wisdom. Subject with hands by side. Antishaft encounters
visual difficulty. Dimness encroaching. The strain weakening
his ability to mark and judge. Makes out, vaguely, the cli-
mactic gesture. Subject apparently unhooks button, releases
clasp, pulls zipper, draws string, unholes button, loosens
band. Trousers fall to buttock, revealing white rubber
panties. Antishaft hysterical. A general haze fast approaching. Hue and contour merge. Should subject tarry with final
accoutrement, project will fail. Without evidence of threatening pubis, bestial element incomplete. Panties snapped playfully. Panties stretched. Panties considered objectively by
subject for texture, size and colouration. Panties lowered.
Navel a quickly diminishing point of reference. Antishaft in
total darkness. Emits scream. Asks mercy, in the name of
humane practices. Cites examples of his work. Recounts
past achievements. A last glimmer permitted. A mixed dispensation, however. Detail is all important. The milk of
his endeavour. Each pore its own exemplum. Each hair
and mole the proof made flesh. No longer there. The
Utopian moment receding. Subject in pink nudity now only
shades of shrimp and shadow to his weakening eye. The
final apocalyptic vision marred by fading light. Irregular
motion sensed, much flurry. Subject made out clothed in

nightie. Thus cutting off all source of strength. The Truth veiled. Its Judgment hidden from worship. Antishaft in his sudden blindness falls from ladder. Lands loudly on his belly prone. Receives instant hernia. Ingorges dust without restraint. Telescope smashes. Stools collapse. Pulley wrecked in crash. Electric outlet shorts. Pandemonium of the mind ensues. All is lost. Yet I sing also of the following day. Of how Billie Balene redeemed the event from utter chaos and dire consequence. Whose sharp eye made out the peeping Tom. Who took pity on his lowly state. In which way she relieved his anguish. Her methods examined and found charitable. Her theory of perpetual motion adhered to. Her deep ways accounted for. Also, Boot and the Crudhead seen in perspective. Their devious styles exposed. Billie Balene tainted by their guile. Yet essentially good. Emerges unharmed. Thus her compassion and relief. The simplicity of Antishaft's needs compared. A comfort to her. Whereby she is enthralled. Her maiden modesty regained. Her bluntness softened by repeated subtleties of mind and body. Antishaft fast learns the art of sexual ingress. Its value as an aid to the handicapped discussed. His sufferings thereby alleviated. He makes do. Concluding with a treatise on the fortunate fall.

Thirty

Bobby E Lee fell down the stairs one day; he collected himself on the first floor landing, adjusted his Huck Finn hat, laced his toeless running shoes, then collapsed down the final staircase and into the hallway. He slumped forward into a sitting position, his hands on his knees, contemplative, ruminating. When the front door of the hotel opened, a quick lethal spade of sunlight froze him to the spot; he had not sensed sun or weather for a month. He crawled from

the gloom of the hallway into the bright sunny vestibule.
Several people, girls among them, stepped over him on their
way to the street. They had spent many days in his room
chewing, smoking, swallowing his merchandise; they stepped
over him politely. He spread his legs towards the door and
placed his arms, palm up, beside them; to be oiled. After a
while, a small motor began to churn inside his belly. It
warmed him, secreted life-giving responses, and finally filled
him to the brim with easy laxative powers. His eyes squinted
and opened; beneath them, like dark puddings, the bags
flattened. His joints cracked, then hardened as he prepared
to rise. He lifted himself to a squatting position and, with
the aid of four fingers screwed to the floor, stood. He walked
on tiptoe and with the aid of walls; he entered the ground
floor toilet well, fumbled for but did not find the light,
yanked down all his pants and lowered himself toad-like
over the mouth of a pipe. After much effort and with eyes
serenely closed, a liquid trickle emerged cautiously from his
behind and dropped vertically into his trousers. He smiled,
pulled the chain above his head, resumed his trousers. He
walked with a popeyed, heavy motion into light again; something swished. He stood patiently in the hall awhile, figuring.
Then, unaware that his fly remained unbuttoned, he reentered the toilet well, zipped himself up by rote, and
urinated. He was now prepared. He shuffled through hallway and vestibule into the open air of the Gît-le-Coeur; he
could not afford to squander his thoughts, so as he moved
carefully towards the Café Buci he trained his eyes before
him, maintaining the thing on his mind. He walked past
the Buci, signalled. No one waved or followed. He put a
limp finger to the pocket of his shirt, fished for and retrieved
his sungoggles, one plastic lense already shattered. He
wrapped the elastic band around his head and walked
through green and yellow streets; his thoughts were green
and yellow too : he was alive.

Bobby E Lee found the car in a small alleyway near
Sèvres-Babylone. The windows were closed tight, but the
doors were not locked. Bobby E Lee opened them with a
key. Inside, the vacuum was unbearable. Bobby E Lee

crawled into the back seat and reclined belly-up on the seat cover. He snapped the door shut with his leg, then fell asleep. He had a little dream. When he awoke, it was because he could not breathe; the stench of manure and recent piss clogged his lungs. He took a few mental notes, then wandered back to the Café Buci, intoxicated by lovely visions and thigh deep in his own refuse. He sat alone at an inside table. He wanted people to join him, but the stink was terrific, so he sat there alone writing letters to E. Bone and Irma, figuring on the backs of envelopes. When the sun went down, he rose. Dixie was playing his evening Gottlieb. I was seated with Rose and those parts of Iris that were conscious and communicable.

"What did you do, shit in your pants ?" asked Rose.

Bobby E Lee smiled under the shadow of his Huck Finn hat, his lips and jaws still numbed, his eyes glassy, dazed with the remnants of hemp.

"Ah've bin thinkin," he said.

So it was arranged that we would drive to Spain within the week. Dixie and Iris had their own private reasons for wanting to go and Rose said she would come as far as Barcelona, then head towards the interior in search of her husband who was reportedly somewhere in the country.

Bobby E Lee explained that he might push the car over the Pyrénées, then travel by sea to Ibiza where E. Bone and Irma were buying hemp for the winter. Most of the stuff in their room was about gone, much of it going free and for lost causes, and Bobby E Lee was depressed and lonely. He could not bear to see it gone and no money on the books and not a venereal memory worth repeating. He would arrange to give up his old room; he would talk to the two Scottish girls, Debbie and Briar, who lived there now; they might move up into E. Bone's place and keep an eye on the clientele; he would then have to arrange to have someone else move into his old room to keep a constant vigil on his dirty underwear and diary. All this would take four days. The whereabouts of the car was his own secret and could not be divulged until the last moment. I said that I knew where it was and so did everyone else. He asked us not to break the faith. We agreed.

That weekend, Brynning and Gilchrist came to town. They were working as carpenters thirty miles out of Paris and living in a small hut surrounded by burnt trees and barbed wire. Whenever they came into the city, the concierge at the hotel on the Gît-le-Coeur always put at their disposal a small storage room in the cellar where they slept on burlap bags and old trunks. That's where they were sleeping on the Saturday morning when Bobby E Lee entered their sanctuary to extract certain objects of interest from his small, square steamer trunk. Gilchrist was curled in delicate repose upon that very article; Brynning lay not five feet away, depressed sumptuously in a sea of burlap. Bobby E Lee stood inside the narrow doorway; the door could not be opened, one had to raise it by strings like the shafts of a dumbwaiter, and he was merely resting after the mute struggle of admitting himself. His face was yellow. In his mouth, he clenched one of the final vestiges of his recent and opulent past : a freshly rolled joint drooping beneath the weight of its fresh gray ash. There were no windows or holes in the little cellar. Bobby E Lee lit a match; it burned green in the dark.

"Y'all rize an shahn," he said.

Brynning only burrowed deeper into his bedding, enjoying the warm bodies of mice.

"Y'gottah git," he said, still leaning in from the doorway, chin clubbed flamboyantly on knuckle.

Gilchrist purred in his sleep and shook his head from side to side as if to tune his earring. Tufts of carrot-red hair lay in a corner where he had pruned himself the night before. His filthy, ingrown toenails, visible in the green light, were smeared with white lacquer and there was a patch of clean skin just below the neck. Bobby E Lee had never seen him like this before. The match flared and died.

"T'ain fayah fellas," he said.

When there was again no response, nor any hint of agitation or discomfort, Bobby E Lee walked straight into the room and stood with his hands spoiling on his hips and the clean ashturd dripping in flakes to the floor.

"Would you *please* remove yourselves at once," he said.

"I didn't know you could talk English," said Brynning.

"Whan ah gits angry nuff," said Bobby E Lee, nervously smiling.

He didn't like Brynning who was so incredibly beautiful with his long narrow head and the thin slip of his nose, looking like a carved gargoyle. Brynning abused his beauty and his own natural grace and his lean sensuous style by being unaware of them; it was a waste. Bobby E Lee would have known how to use them. Brynning's very existence offended him; he coudn't stand it.

"Good t'see y'all agin," he said.

"Gordie," said Brynning, "come on, wake up."

Gilchrist smiled in his sleep; his teeth were still smeared with pink toothpaste and he had obviously taken a scissors to his nose as well : the nostrils were specked with little grains.

"Better let him sleep for a while," said Brynning, sitting suddenly erect like an embalmed corpse to let three small mice escape from his open shirt and pantleg.

"How cum he's sa clean an ahl ?" asked Bobby E Lee.

"You know Briar ?" asked Brynning.

"Suah thing, she an hair girlfren is mowvin ina mah rewm come evenin," said Bobby E Lee.

"What !" said Brynning. "With all that stuff ?"

"Ah trus em," said Bobby E Lee. "Bunch us goin Spain."

Brynning scrambled to Gilchrist on the steamer trunk; he grabbed Gordie's exposed ankle and yanked it forward, the body following as if attached. Gordie fell. His head made a quaint thud as he bounced haunch up on the cement. He opened his eyes sleepily and saw them standing over him, the one limp and dazed, his fresh joint shedding casual ashes, the other excited and erect with the narrow head and gold earring like his own.

"Hugh," smiled Gordie.

"Get up," said Brynning. "Come on."

"You ruined my hair," said Gordie when he felt the wet blood on his forehead.

"Ah jus gowt get zese things," said Bobby E Lee, striding weakly to the trunk, key chain wound by a string about his wrist.

"Don't touch me Hugh," said Gordie, "I'm mad."

"Later," said Brynning quickly. "Come on, I want to talk," and they hustled out of the cellar room, leaving Bobby E Lee alone to scrounge amongst his souvenirs and old forgotten stains.

Once in the street, Brynning grabbed Gordie by the elbow.

"You know the girl you met last night ? Briar ? The one who let you play doctor ?"

"I took out her appendix, Hugh," said Gordie.

"She's moving into E. Bone's room; Bobby's going to Spain; she's moving in with her girl friend Debbie to look after the stuff."

"I seen her pull Garber's pickle once," said Gordie.

"No no, he's going to Spain too : with that pig Rose."

"Tweak."

"Hold it. Listen, Gordie, wouldn't you like to have all that stuff free, anything you want : pot, hashish, morphine, *mescaline*."

"Oh *mescaline !*"

"Isn't that wonderful ? You've got to hustle her, Gordie; she won't talk to me after what I said to her. You've got to fuck her before somebody else finds out."

"No."

"Gordie, it's all right. I'll show you how to do it. She's got, like, two assholes. It's easy."

"No."

"But this is what we've been working for in the country, isn't it ? We won't have to work anymore if we can get it all free. Oh please Gordie."

"No."

"Tweak."

"Tweak."

"Does that mean yes ?"

"No."

"Oh for chris . . . Gordie, she *likes* you. Look, why did you get all primped up for if you don't want to fuck her ?"

"I'm her doctor; I squeeze her little cysts; she's the best patient I ever had."

"You want to ruin everything ?" said Brynning. He stopped shouting and put his hands on Gordie's face, his own face persuasive. "Okay okay, I love you, *I'll* fuck her."

"You leave her alone," said Gordie wrestling free.

"Why."

"She's recuperating," said Gordie.

"Oh for . . . look Gordie, if I fuck her she'll need special treatment once a week : from you."

"A hysteremptimy ?"

"Right."

"No."

"*Gore-dee.*"

"No."

"And you won't do it yourself."

"No."

"I hate you, I really do."

"Poo."

"I'm willing to fuck her for the both of us, Gordie; I'll do it cause I love you and I want to see you happy : having *mescaline . . .*"

"Maybe she won't," said Gordie.

"She's a filthy slut," said Brynning, "sure she will."

"Am I a filthy slut ?" said Gordie.

"Oh Jesus . . . Gordie, I'm going to slap the shit out of you."

"Just try."

The fight took place in an alleyway five minutes walk from the Rue de Seine. The alley was sheltered like an arcade by an adjoining sky ramp between the buildings. A series of garbage cans lined one wall; several broken wine bottles, wisps of scattered weed, heaps of rock and ash, old rag, some rubble, lay strewn upon the prickly gravel. Brynning pulled off his sweater; Gilchrist unbuttoned his shirt. They circled. No one could see them from the street; across the road, a small lithography shop, up the street, purple meat dripping jelly in a window, the Rue de Seine strangely quiet and deserted save for a cat in heat yowling by a fountain. Brynning's nails were long and filed to a point; his fingers were spread like claws. Yet Gilchrist was so short that Brynning would have to stoop to scratch him. If he did, Gilchrist would move in under the claws and butt him in the groin. So they circled and swooped. Brynning liked to move off the ball of his toe in a kind of spin, while Gilchrist stood flat-footed and half-squat, the primeval stalker, his small fluffy head swaying from side to side. There was a short series of quick darts and short retreats followed by little cries. At one point, Brynning hissed and clawed at the air, while Gilchrist responded by dipping low and faking forward. They recovered and circled again, kicking up the dust of the alley between them. This went on for some time, neither venturing a direct assault : they were established counterpunchers. But then it happened. As Gilchrist stumbled forward in a short feint to the left, he held too long and Brynning came down on his cheek like a cat, scratching him from ear to jaw. Gilchrist saw the blood, but he went on instinctively under the fingers and caught Brynning in the groin with the flat of his head, lifting him up and away. Brynning tried to protect himself by reaching for Gordie's hair; he pulled out a complete tuft. But Gilchrist kept scrounging between his legs, butting, churning, until he had him against the wall; then he bit. Brynning stuck his nails like a prong fast into Gilchrist's back, tore away the shirt. He then proceeded to gouge out a line of flesh along Gordie's spine. He began to work on it, skinning the back neatly until a whole strip had been peeled off. He then leaned over and bit to the bone. Gilchrist couldn't take it. He relaxed his tooth-hold and staggered back and, as he did, Brynning brought up his bony, unlocked knee and clubbed him glancingly on the chin. They circled. The pain was bad between Brynning's legs and the wall had scraped his neck raw; but Gilchrist looked worse. He had lost the first exchange and the blood ran fast in many colours on his face and spine. With the first test of strength over, their abandon grew. Brynning skipped, flirted, pawed, his face screwed into an attitude of sadistic vigilance; he slapped Gordie in the mouth, then sidestepped him like a matador, pirouetted on one leg gracefully, and caught Gilchrist in the cleft with the blunt of his toe. Gordie fell forward mawkishly and squirmed on the ground. He regained his little legs without further damage. They recircled. From a crouch, Gilchrist stopped, his eyes trained on something; Brynning took the bait and came in with his fingers fanned. Gordie leapt between them like lightning and went for the throat; his teeth dug and nuzzled. They fell in a heap to the gravel, four legs circling in the dust like the blades of a windmill. Brynning did not have much time but he did not panic right away. Coolly, he stabbed his fingers like a corkscrew into Gordie's half-exposed rump and his other hand plucked out hairs like a tweezer. Gordie faded quickly and rolled over. "Had enough?" gasped Brynning. The blood on his sweater, already dried by the sun, was turning a deep mauve. Gilchrist watched his little belly quail and rise; his cut rump and skinned back slid and twisted in the dirt. "No." They struggled to their knees at the same instant and shuffled morosely to an equidistant spot; each made exactly the same move at precisely the same moment, incredibly mirrored like reflections of springing monsters. Simultaneously, their heads tilted back, then swung forward in duplicate arcs with a momentous crash. Their earrings locked. Nose to nose, they bucked and wiggled, trying to break apart; the earrings held fast. Then the infighting began. Each tried to gnaw the other's nose. Brynning bit Gordie's lip, Gordie pried Brynning's eye. Their heads jerked together, flew apart, banged wildly; the looped earrings jingled. They lowered and butted but couldn't rattle free. There was a pause, then a struggle for leverage. Gordie on all fours tried to pull Brynning with him by the ear, but Brynning desperately grabbed hold of a can with his legs locked as anchor while his earring stretched and pulled. But Gordie had him. His legs slipped weakly from the can and kicked in pain. Cartilage tore; skin frayed and drums popped. "Tweak," screamed Brynning. "Tweak," said Gilchrist and stopped and it was over.

In Bobby E Lee's room in the Gît-le-Coeur final preparations were being made. Iris and Dixie, Rose and myself

were there, assembling before dark to make sure that things
were right. Debbie and Briar were shuffling back and forth
in the process of moving in; they had their luggage in the
hallway and were waiting for us to leave. And I remembered
that evening months before at a party at the bitch Jeanette's
when I had taken Briar in the hallway in the dark, setting
her gently against the wall with the music coming through
the doorway. We didn't talk now; it was as if we were
phantoms, apparitions even, deceased and unmourned : ah,
we knew how to bury our dead, Briar and I. But her eyes
were on me, bright blue like a low flame, with the texture
of the skin still brown as toast and the dry black hair. I
came over to where she stood on the threshold. There was
still about her the quiet, insular mystery; the eyes would not
focus, the mouth was turned down in a kind of harlequin
distress, pink, registering ridges and condoms of disgust.
She was wearing the same black dress, or a dress similar;
it swivelled neatly to her knees like a series of tightly woven
pencil lines and the legs were bare; the muscles flexed and
swallowed, the flesh seemed to gulp. But it was her tan that
I remembered best; everywhere the deep sephardic skin like
singed potatoes. I stood before her with a look of pained,
sardonic ease.

"Hello," I said.

"Not good not bad," said Briar, "and how are you ?"

"Fine fine."

"Thanks for asking," said Briar, "and so and you ?"

We decided to leave in the morning after a good breakfast
at the Petit Bar, little gesture of tradition. "What about the
pot ?" asked Dixie. His own leather pouch was already
filled with variously coloured necessities : capsules, tubes,
pills, aphrodisiacs. According to Bobby E Lee, there were
still two bags of good hemp left and we would take that
with us; Iris agreed to carry it over the frontier in her
underwear. That decided, we began to disgorge out the
door to the stairs. But before we had rid ourselves of the
room forever, there was a small, fat scream and Debbie
waddled in over the threshold with a look of supreme
annoyance.

"They've gone and killed each other," she said, "the two of them."

Brynning and Gilchrist appeared, looking like miscarriages. They were still bleeding through their clothes, which were tattered in the fashion of music hall clowns, and their skins were fouled with dirt and perspiration. Their ears were especially discoloured, and Brynning's gold ring seemed to hang from a loose thread of cartilage; no longer fanned like a shell, but dangling like a thin baiting hook. They were arm in arm, but not smiling.

"You been hustling the fuckid Markee de Sade?" asked Rose.

"Hi Briar," said Gordie, puffy-eyed and meekly winking, "how's your health?"

"I've got a terrible pain right here," said Briar flushing warmly.

"Let me just check," said Gordie, "mmmmmmmmm."

"Wait till later," said Brynning. "You taking some pot huhn?" he asked, watching Bobby E Lee stash the little bags into his satchel.

"We're taking *the* pot," I said, "that's the end of it."

"What!" said Brynning, "Isn't there any more?"

"Nope," said Bobby E Lee, "we down smowked it ahl."

"*Now* do you love me," said Gordie.

"Briar," said Brynning, "you're no good whatsoever as a woman. I mean that."

He walked over to Gordie and kissed him on the cheek and put his hand through the ruined, untufted hair. Briar joined them in this spectacle of love.

"On the table," said Gordie, directing her officiously.

"Tweak," said Brynning.

"Tweak," said Gordie, "you can be my nurse."

So we left them to their own devices and went to Spain.

Thirty-one

Bobby E Lee meant no more to shove the car over the Pyrénées than he could mean anything, and Dixie, who had wanted the trip for himself and Iris, knew already that he was dead and shrivelled. He had begun to take morphine in the evenings as a substitute for piercing pleasures, and he was more surly and incommunicative than ever. It was as if he were caught in a deadly interlude where the first set of illusions had faded and he had not yet built sufficiently the resources of the second. Also, Iris was giving her finest performance as the mythical bitch, and during the joyless ride through the south of France she played off his patience coolly. Whenever we stopped by the road, she would jump from the car, grab me by the arm and race into fields to pick fruit or chew on straw; when we were hidden from view, Iris would drop my hand and slump by a tree, counting the time, wordless, until she was satisfied that the thing had been done. After these fictitious bouts of fornication, she would stumble up to the car, legs dragging heavily, eyes soft with dew, sometimes hedging her pose by scratching her own throat with a sharp stone. But she aped contentment badly, like someone who overrates what they do not know. I played along because there was always the very good chance that I might take her yet : one had to figure all the angles. Even Bobby E Lee was getting some of the preliminary action; he began to strut from ditches like a country rooster.

For a while, Dixie thought that he could beat it. If he became our very good friend, built a kind of camaraderie with myself and Rose and Bobby E Lee, then it would be all right. So he tried to charm us, and he might have done it if he hadn't been so tired and lunatic. Even in his deterioration, he had a gift for rapport; it was easy to see why Iris had settled with him. He was straight, that was his quality, only it wasn't the dimensional virtue one thinks of, possessed by honest, forthright people. Dixie wasn't honest;

he might have considered *that* an affectation; and he certainly wasn't forthright; there were more corners to his style, more false trails and guileful cul-de-sacs, than a Chinese box has walls. He was merely true to his faith, and he never fell off the line. What exactly that faith was, is a little more complicated, even laughable. He was never blunt, so it probably had volume. He seemed to stockpile his pleasures against some rainy tragedy and if you were all right, you became only another pleasure to be tended and dwelt on. He couldn't settle for the short run, and his charm was implicit in that naiveté. Yet what betrayed his style now was that it had not arrived at tragedy at all; he had ended up pathetic.

Anyway, he tried to take us in. He always insisted on fixing the flats himself, drove alone into villages to buy supplies, even shared his great and private store of drugs with us — a sacrifice for which there is no name. His despair, as he conned, lessened in a suspicious way; fronting a mind ravaged with doubt and impotence and the rough edge of Iris's little game, was a winning confidential smile and all the sounds of a good time everywhere. To choose between Dixie and Iris, then, was like choosing between two unskilled facades : sex in the bush or total friendship down the line.

The day after Marilyn Monroe died we were in Avignon, unwashed, unfed, and in no mood for sentiment. Except for Rose. The closer to Spain we came, the more she resembled the emotional slob; her toughness was melting at an unbearable rate and her voice had risen at least one octave.

"So fuckit young," she cried all afternoon, relieved somehow that she had been spared the outrage, and savouring her bloom like the last candy in the bag. "Men such finting bastards."

Bobby E Lee, whose contacts were supposed to be uncanny, claimed to know intimately the Counts of Avignon and their dear mother the Baroness d'Orange. We spent the afternoon sleeping on the benches in the papal gardens, then drove to their town house, anticipating an evening's slumber on the silk and purple. The family was not at home, they had retreated for the summer to their castle a few miles to the southwest. We drove to the castle and found it some time after midnight. It was not a pretty place; there were no gardens there, no lawns; the brick was crumbling and discoloured by whitewash; weeds grew wild over the fields and bushes; there was a stench of chickens and manure in the little courtyard.

"Ah'l jus seef the cownts is about," said Bobby E Lee.

"See about perishing goddamn baths too," said Rose, lowering a window.

He rolled out of the car secretively, like a frogman rolling from his raft, and left us in the courtyard; he entered a small door at the rear of the castle. He was gone almost an hour. When he returned, he was grinning and flanked by twin brothers with identical watch bands.

They walked up to the car in single file. Would we be interested in a late evening's swim ? the lake and its environs were at our convenience. Iris swung out of the car and accepted the polite arm of a count. They walked around the rest of us and made for a wooded path. Dixie released a few obscenities, collected his gear, and slept alone in a garage on the premises. Rose and I remained in the car. About four in the morning, Bobby E Lee rapped on the car window.

"Ah'm beddin down in the cassel; see yah morrow."

"Where's Iris ?"

"They gafe her nace rewm."

"What's going on ?"

"Nothin goin on, Garbs; ownest ta gowd."

"Go to hell."

Iris was not seen again until the following afternoon. We were having breakfast in the court. The Baroness d'Orange was explaining to Dixie that he reminded her of a favourite Manet profile : peasant with brimmed hat. She said she would make him a gift of just such a hat. Iris came out of the rear of the castle at that moment looking calm and fresh. She was wearing her last clean dress with the puffy sleeves and she had apparently bathed and powdered, for her hair was still wet. The twins led her into the sun, identical paws on the base of her spine; their fingers touched behind her back. At the sight of her, Dixie, coated still with dust and sweat, turned from the Baroness and began to make odd sounds, short surly *Neems* of displeasure. He rose and walked to Iris and began to sniff sadly. She smelt of soap.

Thirty-two

A confession; Dixie mumbling stoically, anchored on a rock with a twig held between his legs, tracing a small pattern through a patch of rubble. Iris somewhere sleeping. Rose and Bobby E Lee bent towards the fire. The Spanish chill coming up from the sea; nowhere in sight. The woods quiet, tin cans loose in the clearing. Ashes of previous nights powdering the ground. Iris's leg seen from a queer, distorted angle, seeming to flatten out in the gloom like a fin. Wind through the dry, baked leaves. The car parked on a mound, ten yards away. The Pyrénées looming miles off, blue.

Dixie saying : "See, when I first met her she seem like butter. So I said, We're okay you and I. She just come out of Greece *nerm,* lovely girl with the eyes. I said, Let's make it together, I got some money. I used to have luck with broads, I'm a lover Garb. We moved into the Seducer's old room Petit Trianon, fair place, and we were set *neemah.* Good legs, don't smell, clean as a Jap. Quiet, like I don't know. Something a little deeper, not much talk *neeeem.* I watched her come and go. Glukicz you are a primed soul, you been working ass for this a long time. You can stop right here with this one *neem* kid, and you don't miss a thing. But she was wrong, something broken. She don't come off regular. Cool as a bitch. Listen, I'm telling you this stuff. Let her not give a sweet fuck all, I figure; I got time. But she got her hooks in nasty. Iris, I said, baby, let's

get married, I'll do you some good; I was took good. *Neee.*
No, she didn't want nothing like that : just leave it alone.
I'll never say she's a great lay, but it didn't mean nothing.
I've had good lays; fuck good lays; I been there. Didn't
want nothing else but her. Crazy ? *nerrrrk.* Oh Garb. Then
I knocked her up. Good, we'll get married. I'll settle like
cream. I'll drive trucks. No. Oh shit, okay, but have the
baby Iris. No. Man, she wanted this filthy abortion; that's
got to be hate. *Neeeeeeeh.* Only guy I know of is Fitz.
Meantime she's carrying around my kid like it's muck. Fitz'll
do it at his place, she says. She gonna flush the bastard
down the toilet. We're hardly talking now. When it comes
out, she'll be okay, she says. I'm took man, I'm gone. No
way. Fine, I says. But you know I'm walking one day and
I think She's a grade A bitch — that's what you got — she
don't feel for nothing. I can't trust her *neeee,* I don't know
her, she got me tied in too many knots, what am I doing
here. *Scinnnnnnnne.* And Fitz, I don't know Fitz. Big
black bastard, probably got a huge rod, fast oily nigger. It
figures. They're taking my money. What kid ? They ain't
no kid. That Fitz is an ass man. Bad scene. I gotta see for
myself. That hook better have a fish. Isn't that love though ?
I never saw her scream; but Christ she screamed. All the
time. We had to hold her on the table. Damn thing broke.
We had to ... on the floor, Garb. *Nerk.* Flushed it down
the toilet. Then she wasn't any good. I thought she was
dead. She had her hand clamped on her cunt, we couldn't
stop the blood. Then I wasn't any good. Felt it go right out
of me. I think my cock muscle bust. Couldn't even piss
awhile. Nasty twats; all fulla fucken flies. Now I just sweat
a lot."

Confession over. Dixie sits marooned in debris. A hundred
feet away, beyond the car, there is a small white tent.
Gypsies, waiting to cross the frontier into France. In the
morning, they come outside with their goat and ladder. The
wife has bad teeth and is suspicious, but the man is
friendly and talks about the big money in Paris. He says
he will stand on a corner of the St. Germain-des-Prés and
make his fortune. He puts the goat through its paces. The

goat has dried dung on its flanks. It struggles up the ladder; trembling legs jack-knife at the top; it pisses.

Packing up the gear, immersed once more in the sucking vacuum of the car; travelling hot, dry-mouthed, towards the sea. Everyone filled with sand and smoke. Iris menstruating. So the windows are open, admitting dust. Rose is sweating, her jam-face scab-scarlet. Dixie is driving; the prow of his nose touches the wheel, sweat drops like acid into his eyes. Bobby E Lee asleep; the stink of his caked toes like old turnips, his Huck Finn hat pulled cockily over his eyes and nose and upper lip, still leaving the groove of his throat bare and puddled like a small pool : polluted. Cutting to a main road, still new, soft as pudding as the wheels pull and grip. The engine of the old Vedette boils, whistles. Little geysers of hot spray jet into the thick, fumed air. Everything sticks; as if we are exhaling glue. One more turning, dipping through a rise, deep then high, then the sudden flatness of the sea and the beach. The colours of the coast are pink and blue. The sand of the beaches like gray dust; smoked by the heat, washed by the water. Rock, stubble and weed scattered like refuse near the road. Pollen suspended in the still air like powder. Our skin like the surface of custard, foul as lard. Slightly jaundiced. Bobby E Lee knows a French girl, Marie André-John, who owns a villa in San Felíu. By late noon, we are climbing a cliff; it hangs like a pout over the calm pool of the sea. The sea is not smooth as glass, but frozen thick like deep plastic. I say, "It reflects itself like a masturbating narcissus." The car wheezes, spouts; its funnel of hot vapour flamboyant like a plume. This is no fun.

Marie André-John is short, spidery and whiskered. She stands on the small terrace of her villa in halter and shorts, surrounded by friends. The villa stands in from the cliff on the flat of a hill; a hundred feet off, the cliff erodes into a tapering descent of rock which broadens almost to a beach. Marie André-John regards us with a slow smile; her toes tapping on the stone patio, not overjoyed. We pile out of the car like a troop of thieves, tramps, migrants. The radiator of the car hisses and sizzles and finally bursts into a whine.

The noise quickens like a siren and we are engulfed by the stink and smoke rising in a spiral. Out to sea. We stand like idiots. "Mah-ryah Mah-ryah," says Bobby E Lee, tumbling up the terrace steps like a slavering lap dog. "Marie," says Marie. "Mah-ree," says Bobby E Lee and flings himself over her shoulders like a shawl and tries to plant a wet kiss on her teeth. We are introduced. Marie André-John glances sharply at her friends; she will not come down to the road to greet us; she merely nods, throwing away a brief, hard look. "I need a bath," says Iris. "There is a water tap in the back," says Marie André-John.

But that evening there is a party and, since we are bunched at the rear of the villa in the car, eating pâté pasted on three-day-old bread, we are invited. By a Frenchman with lime-coloured shoes, the line of the toe squared like Chiclets. "Funny," I say, "he don't look Jewish." "Don't be so fuckit raw," says Rose, "I can still beat the shit out of you." Iris and Rose have washed in stages at the water tap and look clean, fresh, reconstructed. It is a polite, well-combed party full of latent boredom; the French arranged in little circles, chirping like birds in a mangrove, fingers twittering, teeth dazzled beneath fluorescent lighting, wine in buckets, beer stacked in the fridge, salads on a varnished table. Marie André-John decorous and sweet smelling; she wears a curious sari, light green with pink print flowers, held in place by the relentless grip of her left hand, falling shawl-like to her knees and containing within its unifold, black lingerie and cooling cream deodorant. "The Americans," she says. "You may eat," and waves a free hand towards pretzels and frilled chips. "Oh," says a goateed Frenchboy, "a *beetneek*." He skips on his slippers, open-toed, vermilion, towards Dixie who hangs from the transom by his arms, swinging for a better view. "And you're just a small Frenchman with a little beard," I say. "No no," says the Frenchboy. "Is false," and pulls up a tuft of goatee to reveal a pimply jaw. Immense laughter. Iris and Rose seat themselves by the table and begin to eat, gorging themselves with salted peanuts, olives, chips, strips of celery. The French giggle and roam and exchange naughty little idioms. But Marie André-John is the acknowledged centrepiece; other women — who do not own villas — skirt her like figurines, forming little semicircles of attention. Marie André-John has recently treated her face for just such a role; it is like a mask of pallid white, set off by pink icy lips. In shadow it remains intact, all of a piece; but beneath bright lights, her skin is thick with congealed powder; crumb yellow. Her contact lenses catch the light as well, reflect like tear drops, and give to her face a look of tragic and astonished grace, a myopic sadness. She is by nature deciduous, fur-bearing and fur-shedding. Beneath the coats of cream and powder, the hairs poke up like nettles on her arm, crawl down the sides of her face like dark fungi, perforate her legs with red pimples where the roots are burned. About her, and within range of her judgments, they dance the *tweest* according to some rigid doctrine, swinging their mechanical asses like tiny pendulums, lips sucked to a bubble. Their faces suggest some deeply felt void; simple, alimentary. Ruthless as innocents at a rally. And Dixie, perched now, squatting free against the wall as if incubating his loneliness, dandruff flaked and speckled on his mustache, releasing a resonance that quivers his lip and hums through his eardrum, scratching the pelt of his thigh, sniffing in the clean, perfumed air as if to cleanse his webbed nostrils. But Bobby E Lee is dancing and being clapped at like some performing seal; they are playing the theme song from *Jules et Jim* and he trips the light fantastic by himself, skipping along the perimeter of the room, cigarette in the catch of his mouth, legs high, sun-goggles strapped to one ear and slapping the side of his cheek. He thinks that he is joy itself and that they have come to share with him his verve and flair for life as he sails on the wing of his arm into tables and people who cringe from his soiled touch. He is laughed at and prodded. Iris and Rose are busily stuffing chips, peanuts, olives, celery into small bags which they plant pouch-like beneath Rose's loose-flowing shirt. This is tolerated; patronizing looks turn the other way, turn towards Marie André-John who draws them in like suction and whirls on one spindly leg. *"Thee Streep,"* giggles the Frenchboy with the false goatee; his eyes sparkle like ale and he wiggles his hips playfully. Marie André-John mounts a hassock, her back to the picture window casting in shadow the immense relief of cliff and sea, and releases the flap of her sari. The French clap and hoot at this mimed erotica; it is ritual. Marie André-John removes her sari and stands in black lace underwear for half a minute, swaying, suggestive of a spider; her skinny thighs depressed like ingrown pads of flesh; then, in a sudden flurry, removes her underwear to reveal a dark green bikini, leaps from the hassock with a shrill scream, runs giggling to the bedroom and emerges shortly in slacks, halter and single strap sandals.

"You want to see *feesh?*" asks the Frenchboy, one manicured paw on Iris's shoulder. "Sure." People rush out to get cars from their fathers; a procession of little sports coupes lining the roadway; we take the Vedette and the Frenchboy sits in back to guide us. Winding down the cliffs in the dark; San Felíu like a bed of jewels; headlights of the cars, eight in all, like fireflies snout to tail, moving in a slow parading silence deeper into the cup of the village; we drop off the mountain road into the streets of San Felíu, which are rivetted by islands of grass; through the streets, moving onto the unlit highway crackling with cinder. We are last in the line of cars and there is no need for a guide at all; the Frenchboy squirms in the back seat and emits an embarrassed squeak of pain; I turn around and see him caught round the neck in an arm lock; Rose; she is pulling off his false goatee hair by hair; patches of pale, bleeding pimples on his chin where the paste still sticks. We come into the small port and park in a straight row by the side of a low warehouse perpendicular to the wharf. The fish have already been auctioned off, the boats are in, coils and fists of rope on the dock; the smell of fish stings the nostril. Marie André-John leading; inside the warehouse, a dead sulking shark strapped to a wheelbarrow, the wheelbarrow hidden in a corner, shrouded by burlap. Marie André-John slips the shark from under the straps, wraps it about her waist, the fins slapping her small, punctuated behind; it is a small shark, bright red eyes, teeth like jagged tin. Marie André-

John in a medium jig, kicking her ankles, prodding with her
toes the sawdust on the warehouse floor. Around and
around she goes, the body of the fish slithering like glass
against her belly, breast and leather buckle. It is taken from
her, thrown high into the air; it wiggles towards the rafter,
the head writhing as if alive, then folds upon itself, falling
with a plop into the sawdust; a dead weight, mouth agape
with dust. Dixie and I steal the wheelbarrow, break it into
portable shafts of wood, shove these into the trunk of the
car. This does not please the French : they are gay but we
are scavengers. Then they are gone, without warning, leaving
us to find our way back in the dark.

Rose and Iris come from a distance away with a plastic
bag of pink shelled shrimp; we have enough vegetables left
from the party to cook ourselves a meal. Into the car again,
the stale smoky odour, the must and crumbs of old baguettes.
In an hour we have found our way back like spawning
salmon; Rose with her yellow pudgy fingers in the shrimp,
toying with them as with organs, crackling the plastic as the
scent builds a succulence in our mouths. When we arrive
at the Villa André-John, the lights are off, the terrace
deserted; sounds of mumbling behind the curtains, a dim
orange fluorescence in the bathroom. Iris breaks through the
screen door in the rear, returns with a small cauldron; we
urinate against the basement windows, then drive the car
higher into the hills, onto a flat weeded plateau. Dixie builds
the fire with remnants of wheelbarrow and dry twigs from
the bush; we build a crude tripod for the cauldron, dice the
vegetables. Bobby E Lee leaves in search of water. This is
the finest enterprise of the trip; bonds of accomplishment,
a grim unified dexterity, each in his functional place. The
fire is lit, the water boils, the vegetables are scattered into
the roseate bubbles. Rose unshells the shrimp, drops them
like pink thumbs into the smoking cauldron. The smell of
cooking shrimp and celery and carrot; Iris drops in the salt
of peanuts, Bobby E Lee spits to give it body. On the edge
of the plateau, at a sheer drop, San Felíu and the sea,
indistinct; the series of cliffs range like shoulders and muscles
down the coast, winding out of sight to leave the sea barren,

expansive. We fan the fire and the sparks fly. "My, thaht smelz awfal gewd," says Bobby E Lee. "Take care," I say; but we fan some more, at one with the night and the shrimps and Rose's plump forefinger prodding a carrot pasted to the lip of the cauldron. Transcendental cooks. The sparks fly; the fire grows, spreading suddenly like the stubble of a beard along the grass, wafting a column of smoke high over the cliff, hanging above San Felíu like a miracle come to bless. Then the field is a sheet of low, buzzing flame; circuited like a snake. We run for water; the smoke billows, thick as fog. In a while it is out, but we are coughing smoke, our mouths glutted with the taste of tar; in no mood.

By noon the next day, we are on the last leg, speeding towards Barcelona. We can see it between the rises and beyond the curves, spinning towards us like a saucer of glass. Dixie driving. The beach is white; within miles of the city it is flat, deserted as advertised. One last pastoral. We stop the car, strip to our underwear; Dixie, Bobby E Lee and I race like mermen into the low waves of the sea; dip chest first into the cold salt. The Mediterranean is unintrigued by the weight of our bodies and the depth is incredible. We thrash and spit. Iris and Rose standing on the shore as the breakers wince about their toes. Iris wears an old jersey, panties; Rose in frayed bra and gym trousers. They kneel, then crawl until they are floating. They ride, ass-up, through the deep water which is lime-green, then black. No one has noticed before that Bobby E Lee is slightly humpbacked. When we are satisfied and have the taste of the Mediterranean on our tongues, we collapse on the beach; the water runs down our bodies, beaded, sensuous. Bobby E Lee runs in the surf alone, along the line of the beach, stoop-backed, kicking up the sand; his Huck Finn dries and cracks in the heat. Iris beside me. Puts her head on my chest; her wet, scented hair crisp with salt; her eyes closed, nostrils puffing; at rest. Dixie : mumbling to Rose; bloodshot eyes; part hero, part dupe; with not that much to lose.

Thirty-three

We arrived in Barcelona by late afternoon and drove immediately to the Plaza Real in the old part of the city. The car seemed to cough and die on the Ramblas and it had to be wheeled to the curb and abandoned; then we wandered. From the port itself where the statue of Columbus looked out to sea, to the Plaza de Cataluna with its bright, painted tiles, the Ramblas stretched busily, smelling of flowers bunched in carts, black tobacco, oils, tar. The Ramblas was cut in two by a paved peninsula and people sat on the benches or crowded in front of newsstands; but beyond the Plaza de Cataluna everything grew larger, busier, and we seemed out of our depth : the streets widened and cut deep into the distance, the trees closed ominously over the horizon, air swam in a larger space. So we kept turning back towards the port like hamsters on a rubber pulley; we walked in twos with Bobby E Lee trailing. Whenever we came to the statue of Columbus, we would retrack in a small, defined circle that drew within a few feet of the dock steps, whiff the scent of water and gasoline, then start up again towards the Ramblas. Whenever we came to the Plaza de Cataluna, banked on every side by neon signs and trolley wires, we would wheel in a tremendous arc around the fountain and move down again on the far side of the Boulevard. It took us maybe an hour to exhaust the sights. In another hour, the route began to spoil. Dixie, on the inside of the track, let his tongue hang out and his breath came in small barks. He diminished nicely; but then so did the rest of us finally, so we sat on the steps of the port and watched the colours of gasoline thick on the water.

That was where a pimp named Connie found us about seven in the evening. Rose was prone on her back, already asleep; Dixie and Iris had taken off their shoes and placed their feet on the cool last step where the oily water lashed the stone; Bobby E Lee was talking about Paris, slowly. Connie stood looking at us awhile, as if we wore tags or balloons, hardly believing his luck; then he came to us, down the steps smiling, and said as how he would take us to a good hotel near the Plaza Real if we promised "to frequent" the Blue Note Café where he took a commission. That was the way he talked. He was thin as a stick with baggy, windblown sleeves and a sharp blistered nose; his mouth was the mouth of a fish and he wore on his left wrist a wide, black leather strap to stress the muscle. I was beginning to see how people overlapped, how, if you took a bit of Boot and a bit of Bugs and threw in some of the Seducer's cruelty, you could make a Connie without too much trouble.

"It all goes on at the Blue Note," he said. "Come round tonight; deal ?"

We shook hands on it — Rose abstaining — and he led us grimly, with the professional quiet of Moses parting the darkness, to the Pensión Toledo. "Okay," he said. "This a good place. Right ?"

He shook hands all around again, like a man trying to imprint an indelible contact on our minds, and left us in the lobby like little dye markers to pinpoint the progress of his day. We took two double rooms; Bobby E Lee was given a spare office in the back with a couch and a view of the hotel court, where paved flowers circled a water tap.

That night we played Connie fair and went to the Blue Note Café and got reasonably drunk and a little sick on cheap Spanish wine. Connie was there, just inside the door, marking them off as they came from the street and climbed the stairs. When he saw the five of us clawing our way along the stair wall, he found us a table by the window, then joined us for a drink. The window was at leg level and looked down into the Plaza through wooden gratings.

"I'm Connie," he said flatly. "Have the rum and coke."

"We'll have the wine," I said.

He waved over the waitress. She was blonde and had no eyebrows; moving away, the hitch of her ass was like that of a man's. When she had gone for the drinks, Connie looked us over. We didn't make a sound and we didn't look so good; even our heavy breathing was gone. We were so tired, we seemed turned on; Connie mistook it for an induced stupor. He engaged us in conversation.

The girl came back and deposited the drinks on the table. When she left, Connie snapped forward as if he were dissecting himself; he propped his chest upright with the aid of his arms; his neck craned above the table.

"She's German," he said; then he paused, tightening his eyes; then he said : "anybody ?"

Nobody said anything.

"Well, any of you Jewish ?" he said. "Some Jews like to take krauts. I fix Jews with krauts all the time.

Nobody said anything this time either, so he took his drink and disappeared, moving as if a cat were an insect.

But he caught up with us the next day where we were having breakfast in the Plaza. The Plaza Real was nothing more than a Spanish Quarter, a great cloistered rectangle or trapezoid, enclosing within its bowels some tables in the sun, cafés, plant life, fountains, and the stench of fried squid and bad beer. It was not hard for Connie to keep his marks in sight, arranging them like a gallery at the tables. He came out of the Blue Note Café followed by a negress who wore slacks, bandana and a look of complete disgust. She was the singer at the Blue Note, Gloria Marlowe; a poster depicting her in action at a microphone was hanging from a stone pillar nearby; she looked frightened on the poster, but she looked downright hysterical in the flesh. Her eyes were like small marble drops, slightly popped. As often as possible, Connie liked to explain her : she was ordinarily a quiet-spoken woman with a very soft and brilliant voice, but she spoiled everything she touched with perverse streaks of humility that took back everything she gave. To the sounds of applause, she would retreat from the stage in grave embarrassment and clumsiness, falling over herself, her eyes averted, her shoes suddenly much too big for her, as if she were a child dressed in her mother's clothes. It was the ugliest part of her performance, but part of her performance no less, and an uncomfortable thing to anticipate every night. But she could not trust her public (who were, after all, only transient and curious); she was constantly intimidated by all those eyes eavesdropping whenever she exposed a little soul. So every evening she failed. Connie, who fancied himself an expert in intimidation, enjoyed toying with her failure; he knew she felt compromised and humiliated in the Blue Note (it was a pleasure to watch), and every afternoon he would be waiting to begin his saccharine lecture on "the requirements of art and ease. Look Gloria honey, you freeze you break down you kill everything you build." Gloria hated things put in the open this way even more than she hated keeping them secret to fester and spoil.

"Why you dirty little pimp," she'd say, "don't talk to me about art or anything when you don't believe and you don't care and, and, sell whores and yourself, and, and."

"That's true," Connie would grin, buttoning the argument neatly, noting his own image intact, "true, very true."

He helped himself to a chair at our table where we were already breathing bad air. He had spoken earlier to Bobby E Lee about whores, and had easily sized up Dixie and Iris. He was spending a lot of time figuring out what he could do for us.

"This Gloria will be over soon," he said, with an exact flatness. "You'll see she's like I said."

He had two ways of talking; he could be articulate and use only the best prose, or he could indulge in idiom to flaunt his professionalism. Either way, the effect was mixed; when he spoke well, he sounded like a pretentious little pimp; when he spoke in the idiom, he sounded like a precious little bastard slumming.

When Gloria came over, they went through their daily dialogue. He spoke for a while, giving her time to build up a little ferocity, and when he finished off with a small speech about the professional in the role of disseminator, she burst finally into something brusque and incoherent. It went off like clockwork. When it was over, Connie left us dramatically and disappeared through one of the arcs of the Plaza.

"He's not much of a pimp," said Gloria when he was gone, "he's too sensitive."

The Blue Note Café downstairs about ten in the evening, after one has slept through the afternoon, eaten fried squid

from a paper cone and drunk a quart of wine and lemon :
the night club proper is in the cellar with a bright chrome
bar as you enter and a small elevated stage at the deep end
of the room. The smoke is loose and coiling, like undigested
string floating over the tables and railings. The light filters
out of screened bulbs. Crepe lanterns swing from the ceiling.
There are a series of small partitions, half-walls, cardboard
arcs slicing up the room like a labyrinth, so that one can
dance in one's very own half-room, glide from depot to
depot, arrive and depart.

Gloria Marlowe came out onto the stage about midnight,
in a tight green sheath, squinting without pleasure through
deep, golden eye shadow. Her splayed hipbones, like crossed
blades, gave to her thin, corded body the shape of a badly
cut diamond. She took the microphone in both hands,
cupping its head as if it were the skull of a child, not raising
it to her mouth but stooping instead. There was no pre-
amble, no introduction; she merely announced the name of
the song, then waited nervously while the band behind her,
lost in smoke, broke into its agonizing whine. She sang
"It Had To Be You" as if it couldn't have been anyone
present that night; her eyes went over the crowd and moved
by habit to something dense and still and nowhere in sight.
Her face and voice were private, as if we had caught her
in a private place and had nevertheless witnessed nothing
grand at all. When the singing was over, she left quickly
for the street to hide for two hours in her hotel half an
hour away. The whole thing left a sour aftertaste, as we
had been warned : the ugly, cheated feeling of not having
been betrayed or deluded into an evening's rapport.

Connie the pimp, who had become our personal vendor,
had gone to find a whore for Dixie and had come back
alone. He found us carefully.

"He's in a bad way, your friend," he said.

"What's that to you ?"

"Nothing; I don't like to mind my own business."

"Gloria tells me you're much too nice to be a whore,"
I said.

"That's not true : I killed someone once."

"You mean the famous killing a month ago here ?" I said.
"Yah."
"The one where the girl was found by the port with her throat slit ?"
"Yah."
"That one, huh ?"
"Yup."
"Kiss my ass," I said, "I just made it up."
"Well, it's true though."

Later that night, Dixie somewhere with his whore, Rose checking all the hotel registers on the Ramblas for her husband, and Bobby E Lee having fallen ill, Iris and I took a walk. I had imagined making love to her in a hundred different ways, for all the way from Paris to the Spanish frontier she had given me little chits of affection in fields and garages. I had grown to suspect, despite Dixie's current talk, that she possessed a golden bun, full of sweet coin and easy butter. We had been in Barcelona two days; I had been used more or less successfully the previous week — only she could be the judge of its effect on Dixie — and now, apparently, I was to be paid off. It was an involved process of acquittal; at least, involved for Iris, who found all motivated acts complex. She had no honour, but she had something better than honour; she knew how to accomodate a debt; without undue thanks or gratitude; in a casual fashion.

We came to the Plaza de Cataluna, then looked for an alleyway. When we found an alleyway, we looked for a doorway. We sat in the doorway. People of a highly suspicious nature walked by at odd intervals.

"Well," I said.

"I suppose it's better than nothing," she said, "unless you prefer nothing."

"No no."

She was wearing a full skirt. We would assume, for safety's sake, that we were being watched. The full skirt, therefore, was an asset. She was not wearing stockings; no problem of adjusting clasps. We would have to forgo any serious consideration of the flesh, such as exposed breast, naked flank, etcetera. A minor concern, surely. She would wrap her hair in a bun to give her the appearance of calm; lovely move. All that was therefore necessary was the following : she would lift her skirt, bring her panties to her knees. I would unzip my trousers and kneel on the first step. She would remain in a sitting, stationary position, bring her legs in a slight shift to either side of my abdominal pull. From any vantage point in the alleyway, it would appear as if I were in some prayerful hold, my mouth clasped respectfully to her throat. There would be, of course, a minimal amount of noise; her facial expression would have to maintain its watchful repose throughout. Also, caution would have to be taken that her legs did not spread a little too much for privacy; my own tendency to thrash would have to be looked to in this matter. We began. Down went her pants, out came my equipment, low went our heads. Her legs gripped, her skirt concealed, her bodily calm resisted motion. There were no problems : no problem getting in, no problem coming off, no problem getting out. In fact, the lack of problem was haunting in its impact; like an imposition. Drunks weaved by us with a chuckle and a whiff, suspecting the worst though hardly prepared to believe it. Iris spent her time waiting for it all to pass and trying to memorize the names of streets at either end of the alley. She had a gift for languages.

"This kind of breaks up the group image," she said as we walked back to the hotel.

But the group image — if it existed on any level at all — had been subject to a crushing blow the day before. Bobby E Lee had, that evening, begun a curious retreat into gloom and silence. He lay in the spare office wearily, his running shoes making a small winged V on the cot; his arms covered his eyes and his mouth was open. A dried white paste stuck to his lips; his Huck Finn hat, no longer flamboyant, was set over his forehead like a mourner's drape. Every once in a while, he would rise from the cot to take a slow, anguished stroll about the hotel court; there was no shade there, the sun drained him steadily as he turned and paused and turned again. He used only the fountain and the toilet;

like a sieve. He wouldn't even eat. Unless someone had brought him pastry a few times a day, he would have starved. It was a minor mystery. His entire system seemed pervaded with a terrible and crippling angst, as if he were on the brink of something monumental.

"What's the matter Bobby ?" I asked him earlier that day.

"Oh God, I feel funny, I'm all funny," he told me.

So we forgot him.

Thirty-four

While Iris and I were involved in our business conference in an alley not far from the Plaza de Cataluna, Connie the pimp — having led Dixie to a whore like a horse to water — payed his nightly call on Rose. Rose was unconscious in our room in the Pensión Toledo. Connie knocked and entered. Rose was snoring, but woke abruptly as he moved into the room with just that sense of hurry and possessiveness which made him so obnoxious.

"Are you up ?" he asked, not bothering to relax.

"Up *what* ?" asked Rose.

"I may have some news," he said, "concerning your husband. A pretty bizarre clue, actually."

Rose emerged from a sea of sheets; the sheets looked cool and unslept in; Rose looked wrinkled.

"You'd better get dressed," he said, turning — for the first time in his life — away.

Rose pulled on a sweater and hitched up her trousers. Her hair — which was naturally short and kept at a trimmed butch cut — stood frizzed and upright as if electrified.

"Where is he, the filthy fant," she said.

"The grapevine has it that Garber and the Greek girl

are fornicating at this very minute in an alleyway near the
Cataluna."

"Not Garber, you fragment!" said Rose.

"Oh, said Connie, "your husband. Well, as I say, the
clue is a bizarre one. Really grotesque. Just coincidental
enough to be true, too. You'll have to follow me and not
ask questions."

"What are you," asked Rose, "a Sherlock Germs?"

On the way downstairs, Connie decided — before continuing evening business — to pay a brief call on Bobby E
Lee. Paying one's respects was professional courtesy. It
was part of his living and an index of his skill to inquire
after people; to make certain they were satisfied; to do things
for them; to render service. It was simple salesmanship.

"The grapevine tells me he's ill; apparently something
to do with angst. Do you know anything about it?"

Rose, who detested Connie with probably more force
and volume than he loved himself, didn't answer. It was
all right to use him, but she wouldn't hold natural conversation with him. Her spontaneous codes were often fiercely
puritanical.

Connie knocked on the door of the spare office where
Bobby E Lee was quartered, then tried the knob. The door
was held by a defective chain lock; Connie slipped it with
a thrust of his bony finger and entered the dark room;
Rose — who was concerned that murder and pillage might
take place — followed with her great pink arms hanging
loose. The room was empty. It was more of a lobby than
a room, with a small cot and several chairs lining the wall.
Connie walked through quickly and into the little hotel
court adjoining. Bobby E Lee was standing under the
stars. He was howling like a dog. His fly was open and
his hands were inside his pants.

"Anything I can do for you?" asked Connie.

"I feel funny," said Bobby E Lee.

"Of course. How about a nice bottle of rum. I'll go
across the road, no trouble."

"I got this funny feeling," said Bobby E Lee.

"I know, I know. Maybe a few bottles of inexpensive

wine, huh ? What do you say ?"

"I tickle all over."

"You want a woman, kid ?"

"But I don't want to laugh."

"I gotcha, man. How about a nice little kraut ? You Jewish ? Or maybe a nice hairy little Jewess ? Something coarse."

"It isn't the kind of tickle you laugh at."

"Okay, what about a Negress ? Or a Hungarian girl ? she's a real gypsy by actual birth. Got the papers to prove it."

"Maybe it isn't a funny feeling."

Connie drew up a little closer, away from Rose. He tugged, then stroked Bobby E Lee's shirt collar.

"Stuff your cock back in, kid : I'm here to help. Tell you what I'll do. You want a Greek girl ? I got one for you. Smooth like a canal. Loves to feel hot piping meat. Right out of Euripides. Ay ?"

"Because a funny feeling makes you giggle."

"He's hopeless," said Connie to Rose. "You're hopeless, kid."

They walked out of the hotel and into the narrow street.

"What happened to his accent ?" asked Connie, "didn't he have a drawl or something ?"

Rose wasn't saying. Connie, who was acutely sensitive to this kind of thing, decided to play it quietly. Sometimes pimps rubbed people the wrong way. They were insulting. They didn't realize what a serious, disciplined craft it was; they didn't understand the beautiful risks involved, the costs of objectivity, the sacrificing of personal relationships. He liked to ruin people who didn't approve of him.

"We have to meet someone in a little café near the University. It isn't far, we can walk it."

They were in the process of walking it when they met Iris and me; we were on our way back to the hotel.

"Well, hello !" I said, quite cheerfully.

"You smell of cunt," said Rose.

"Oh. Well, we were at the Caracoles for supper. I got locked in the toilet."

"Up your buzz."

When they came to the café, Connie led Rose to a table in the back. A short, mousy Andalusian was waiting for them. He spoke no English. His face looked like an aerial view of craters. Connie seemed to understand his Spanish. He kept wiping the hot spit off his face.

"He says he knew your husband," said Connie, with deep concentration.

"Where is the funt now?" asked Rose. She was becoming obviously excited.

Connie stumbled through a bit of Spanish grammar. The little Andalusian puffed himself up and began to gesture.

"He's not certain," said Connie, "but — and this is the part I thought would interest you — he claims your husband hasn't left Barcelona at all."

"What? He's here?"

The Andalusian nodded his rodent's head back and forth. His striped socks were rolled to his ankles.

"He says," said Connie, "that he may have seen him this morning." He paused briefly as the Andalusian lisped excitedly. "And he says again this afternoon. Short, stocky, a slight gimp? likes to do funny things, grotesque things? I don't know what he means by that."

"Oh Jesus," said Rose. She grabbed the Andalusian by the throat. He moaned ecstatically.

"Take care," said Connie, "he's got a fragile mind. You've got to understand that these Andalusians are notoriously stupid; they got brains the size of paper clips."

"Where is my dirty bastard!" shouted Rose, "oh my fucking lover!" She yanked the Andalusian so hard that he was forced onto the table and half across it. His face smashed into her breasts.

"Watch it," said Connie casually, "they die easily; they're like French poodles."

"Just show me where he is, that's all!" Rose was shouting. "I'll chain him to the toilet, I'll I'll . . ."

Connie put a professional's hand on her arm, exerted the slightest pressure; Rose released the Andalusian who crawled back down to his chair. He was flushed with excitement.

More Spanish was spoken.

"Tremendous," said Connie. "He says he knows where your husband used to live; saw him near there yesterday. But I better explain something. This is strictly *entre nous*. The bird brain can't understand anyway. Apparently — this is from the grapevine — your husband took advantage of this guy; not clear how. Used him like a lap dog of some sort; exposed him to all sorts of deviations. That's what I hear anyway. Might be gossip. Point is, he's frightened as a rabbit. Best thing you can do is kind of soothe him here and now. Else he probably won't take us to your husband. Just kiss his nose. They're like children, you know."

Rose quickly kissed the Andalusian on the nose. Connie lifted her hand, put it to the Andalusian's neck and stroked manually.

The Andalusian smiled. He had dark punctures in his teeth like grimed bullet holes.

"He says he'll take us now," said Connie. "I can still hardly believe our luck though."

Rose got up from the table; she was so nervous and distaught that she could barely walk. There was a decidedly feminine flush on the back of her neck. She made a stern attempt at calmness, but it came out as gratitude instead; she took both their arms to steady the pulsing, weak sensation.

That she loved her husband, despite the stories she told or the nasty gossip she perpetuated, was obvious; the very thought of his dear, stunted form — perhaps soon to recoil once more in her embrace — rendered her helpless, almost imbecilic. She thought silently of their early life together.

So the Andalusian took them down into the subway. Through the corridors, he had to hop to keep in step with them; he watched their legs to make certain of the exact pace.

"Like a little boy," said Connie. "They're an amazing socio-psychotic species, these Andalusians."

They rode for a while, Connie conversing in broken

Spanish with the little man. He stood awkwardly like a rat on its hind legs and refused to sit. Then they came out of the ground and along several streets. They went down an alley and through a portico and finally down several steps to a cellar flat.

"Apparently this is it," said Connie.

The Andalusian knocked on the door, but the windows were darkened. He produced a key and ushered them in. There was no one there.

"About the key," explained Connie. "The Andalusian **lived here** for weeks with your husband. I've heard some pretty horrifying stories about it through the grapevine. He wouldn't have come here alone. Awfully frightened little things, aren't they ?"

The Andalusian turned on a lamp and produced a bottle of wine from the cabinet. He also brought over some glasses.

"I guess we better wait," said Connie. "No telling when your husband will be back. If he comes at all, of course."

They sat down on a low couch; then Connie said he would just check the toilet. While he was gone, the Andalusian pulled a Yugoslavian oval from his shirt and lit it nervously. He was in great agitation. He stared at Rose as if she were a species on the verge of extinction. He motioned for her to make a muscle. Rose watched for a while, still as a mountain; it was curious how the notion finally struck her and it had something to do with the Andalusian's socks. He stooped over to scratch his ankle; Rose heard the scraping noise of nail on skin, saw the sickly prickle of nape hair on the Andalusian's neck, smelled the perspiration; beyond his ankle, she saw that the floor was broadloomed.

"You dirty shits !" she screamed. She brought the back of her hand down onto the Andalusian's neck like a sledge hammer and he fell unconscious to the floor, sprawling this time like an insect with several legs. Connie came running into the room.

"What are you doing, for god sakes ?"

"This is a funkin con," she screamed, rising ominously.

Connie didn't stop to talk; he walked rapidly and at once towards the door, trying all the while to mesmerize her with his little eyes. He opened the door as casually as possible, his hypnotic gaze rooting her to the spot, and was actually outside and halfway up the stairs before she had him by the shoulder. He succumbed noiselessly. She dragged him down again, headfirst, and spread-eagled him on the welcome mat. He didn't struggle; he understood suffering, his threshold of pain was high, there was no use explaining the esthetic of the evening. She worked on his eyes awhile while he waited to faint. But he was still conscious when the Andalusian crawled into the doorway. The Andalusian was smiling stupidly and there was some happy dribble on his chin. In his fist were several peseta notes.

"Hit again me plea'th," he moaned.

Rose abandoned her work momentarily, took the bills and tucked the Andalusian's head under her left arm. She then proceeded to stuff the money into his mouth. He chewed vigorously, but you could tell he was not happy any more. After a few other satisfying indignities, Rose heard footsteps receding down the alleyway. She dropped the Andalusian's head and pursued Connie frantically for several city blocks. He was too fast. She saw him hail a taxi and drive off; when she herself arrived a half-hour later at the Blue Note Café, he was already locked in the office. The Negress Gloria Marlowe was violently sitting in a chair in front of the door.

"Where is that scrawny turd!" shouted Rose.

"Oh he told me everything," said Gloria Marlowe, petrified at the heaving engine of destruction before her. "I know what happened. I think I can explain."

"I'll kill him, the fakit pimp."

"Please," said Gloria Marlowe. "Let him alone. You'll scar him for life."

"You're goddammned right I will."

"Try to understand," said Gloria Marlowe, her voice a timid whisper, her fidgeting fingers clasped to her Adam's apple. "He's so sensitive. That's what makes him so beautiful. Violence unnerves him. Don't destroy it."

"I'll rip his futty balls off ! Get away from that door !"

Gloria Marlowe began to sob; her body rocked convulsively. She implored, besought, she begged for mercy; she went down on her nyloned knees and took Rose by the arm and talked of love.

"We have something spiritual between us," she cried softly. "He needs me. Don't ruin it."

"When I get finished with him, it'll be spiritual all right !" boomed Rose.

"Listen. I'm truly sorry," said Connie suddenly through the door. "Honest."

"You little bastard; you didn't have news about Herman, did you, you little crud."

"No," said Connie, "I'm really sincerely sorry."

"That Andalusian was a frumping customer, right ?"

"I honestly apologize," he said. "I mean that genuinely."

"You crum-coloured lice eater," said Rose.

"He didn't mean any harm," said Gloria Marlowe. "He's really a very true person."

"I am," said Connie through the door, "essentially sincere."

Rose made as if to break through the wall. But she was becoming disastrously calm. Gloria Marlowe sensed this and held out her face.

"Hit me," she said, "if you have to."

Rose, who had no heart of gold, cut Gloria's upper lip with one deft slap across the mouth.

"Well are you satisfied now !" said Connie through the door " . . . Or is she gone yet ?"

Thirty-five

Connie was taking Dixie to the whore. The pimp walked a few yards ahead with a wad of sweet-smelling gum in his mouth. Dixie leaned forward, as if he wore a back brace, his chin scraping the bone of his shoulder, chewing cud like a mongrel. He had a humming in his head — a bee's hum — there was a bee in his head, the wings of a bee fluttering propeller-like inside. It created a resonance, loud then soft then loud again then remote as before. Maybe the bee would finally sting him. Maybe his skull oozed with honey. He could feel the bee drone and sail; he could feel it inside rubbing against the plate of his head. The grub-like body was black and orange, wriggling and turning, seeking the hole of his ear. He mustn't turn his head too sharply, he'd have to give it time; let it drone a bit. If he could get it settled in there, it would produce a nice, even vibration *Neeeeeeeemmmmmmmm*. His hands were in his pockets stroking the soft bulge. Connie knew.

"I'm just going to take you in here," said Connie. "I'm not going to wait for her myself."

He took Dixie up the stairs.

"The reason I'm not going to wait," said Connie, cracking his gum, "is she loves me; it's no good to have her see me."

The hallway smelled of linseed oil and varnish.

"Say, you okay?" asked Connie. "You don't think I'm conning you, huh?"

Dixie felt the bee crooked and jammed in his ear; he put a finger up to the hole and stuffed it back. It fell into his head again and started up the buzzing noise.

"I'm not trying to con you," said Connie, "she's really in there; honest. Everybody knows me; I don't con."

Dixie had to grin; the little bastard tickled. He felt its tendrils sunk in the deep putty of his brain.

"I know I know," said Connie, "so I am a con man. But not someone like you though; you know the score, right?"

Neeeemmmm; it was on bone again and sending off a

fine vibration. He felt it going round and round in diminishing circles to end up its own asshole. This was a good steady bee.

"Anyway," said Connie, "if she don't show, you know where I am. Isn't that so?"

Dixie had to sit down; he slipped to the floor without moving his head but the bee snapped to the side of his head anyway. I wonder why, he thought, I done it careful.

"Hey you okay?" asked Connie.

I done it careful, thought Dixie, I sat down easy, how come it snapped? The buzzing was quick and agitated. *I got to watch that.*

Connie bent down and put his hand into Dixie's back pocket. He took out his wallet and held it in front of Dixie's face; "See," he said, "see what I'm doing?" He extracted three one-hundred-peseta bills; he counted them in front of Dixie's face; "See, three hundred," he said, "okay?"

He put the wallet back into Dixie's pocket. Dixie could smell the gum on his breath. I better not move for a while, he thought, let it settle down or it's liable sting me.

"Right," said Connie, "I just got this three hundred pesetas," and he waved the notes back and forth. "So I'm going," he said. "Just wait by the door; she knows."

Dixie watched him go back down the stairs; he can't walk, thought Dixie, look at that: he hops; he don't walk at all. Maybe I'll sleep a little bit here; got to give it time to relax or it get nasty on me. *Hummmmmmmmm.* **Oh, that's better.** But Connie knew though; he knew all the time.

Anyway I had a good time in Detroit. He was asleep in the hallway and he thought he was turning in bed putting his hand on the flat of Iris's belly, but he was on the floor instead. I should have remembered quicker than that. The bee had stopped. It was still there; he could tell, he could feel it being still, ticking the wall of his skull. What if it died in there? I don't want no dead bee in my head. He saw that his hands were tight on the cradle of his balls. I got to clear the air: *Neeeeeeeemmmmmmmmm!* Then he got up and then the door opened.

Dixie wanted to know if he was standing; he looked down at himself and saw his feet just below his bunched knees, the dimension all wrong as if his toes were growing like fungus out of his kneecaps and his thighs above his knees half-lost in a flap of brown corduroy, and his crotch planted just so under the teeth of his zipper, then his belly almost in line with his knees again, the pot dumbly protruding and his shirt tail threaded through his belt on the side. He could tell he was standing then, because he was all vertical, hanging from his shoulders like a series of inner linings; he could see himself all the way down, like a shaft. *I got to scratch, but I won't.* But she wasn't like a whore; not what he expected. She stood in the open doorway, a short plump Spanish, very pretty, with golden hair. She wore an aquamarine sweater open demurely at the throat and a freshly laundered skirt still covered with lint. I can't. *She's no whore at all.*

He walked into her room and sat himself down on the sofa by the window. Yet she drew the drapes. *Don't she know I can't?* But she had drawn the drapes and the dim was restful and he could feel the bee again struck to the wall of his skull, twitching ever so gently. What if she's no whore? he thought, what'll I do then? But she was the whore all right; a bit cherubic, but already paid for. She had the towels out and was speaking to him in Spanish: he could smell the Spanish come out of her mouth like a rope of onions. *Don't she know it's no good?* He had his hands on his crotch again, gazing down on it stupidly, the fingers hooked into the orbs under the zipper. Maybe she thinks I'll be fine though, she's going on as if its all right. *She's damn polite.* Say *"Neem"*. She looked up from where she was spreading the new sheet and watched him go down onto the floor. His mouth made a buzzing sound. *My chin's hooked, I just hooked it.* He couldn't raise his head from his chest, then the bee began again. *I fell.*

She was so cute and fondling. She sat on the floor beside him and spoke in Spanish. *Did I pass out? How come she's on the floor? that's where I am.* She looked so clean and good, so he put a hand on the muscle of her cheek and left a smudge. I'll make her into a whore, he thought, then

it'll be okay. I got to corrupt her. *How did I used to do that?*
He put his head on her lap and sank his teeth into her skirt;
when he came back up, he saw the drool and the toothmark.
Hell, she's been there before. I got to let on it's okay, he
thought. But the bee had started, he couldn't think. It was
all over his head, trying to get out; he put his hands to his
ears to keep it back. She can't see no bee coming out; that
can't happen; I got enough trouble. She was on her feet,
speaking very fast Spanish. She couldn't have been more
than sixteen and had a sweet look. That fucking bee, I got
to steady it. Don't get mad though, he said to her; okay?
I seen her type somewhere in Los Angeles. He took off his
shirt, still squat by the sofa, and spread it out on the floor
with the sleeves surrendering in a V. How did she get
undressed; I didn't see that. I got to be able see them
undress. Now it's gone for sure.

Neeeeeeeeeemmmmmmmmmm. That was a good one.
Keep it steady don't turn sharp. There was a deep, even
vibration and it sent echoes down him and his body trembled
like a tuning fork. I'm all numb : maybe that one done it.
You got to get up and undress. She stood by the side of
the bed, one plump knee raised and resting on the clean
sheet. He smelled something like airwick. No; I can't do it
with no airwick in the room, that's all. He watched the
buckle marks on her thigh and the little heat pimples on
her back. *Hummmmmmmm.* I think the bee shit in my
head. I never had one like that before. *Hummmmmmmmm.*
There it went again. When he looked down he was undressed, and watched his cock. *That's a nice hunk of
meat you got there.* I need a good one, he thought.
Neeeeeeeemmmmmmmmm. But his cock drooped, poised
towards the floor, and for a second he thought he was going
to piss on his shirt, on both cuffs at once. I could if I
wanted to, he thought; I could do that.

He was on the bed. He was sitting on the pillow. The
whore hunched on her knees, quietly poised, her rear end
like breaded veal looking him straight in the eye. How did
that happen, he thought; I got to do something. He sat and
watched. How long she gonna keep it up there ? He put

a finger on it; then he pulled it back and took a whiff. Maybe
if I let the bee go, he thought; *a new tack.* He blubbered
and jerked his head crazily. The bee started up again, all
upset and agitated, and began to skim the surface of his
skull. Its wings is spread, I can feel that, *Neeeemmmm.*
His whole body tensed as the bee scanned and whanged past
his ear; it don't see the opening, I got to guide it somehow.
He smacked himself on the side of the face and blew up
his cheeks; sand flew. Even if she just farted in my face,
he thought, maybe that would do it. *I ought to tickle her
caustic.* But he only sat there in the dim, the drapes closed,
holding the light back on the other side like a net, and the
bee buzzing past his ears inside his head, tracking a line of
pain up and down, buzzzzzzzz buzzzzzzzz so hard that it
put him out and he was asleep with his mouth open just
in case.

The whore remained in the aforesaid position for some
time, waiting dolorously, her eyes closed in a trained sem-
blance of love, heat, ecstasy, participation. Her flesh was
plump and rippled, her skin the colour of a cornflake; her
face was childlike, crosshatched with dimples, ignorant of
problems; her hair dropped over her forehead as she worked;
there was the smell of lotion on her clean-shaven nape. Her
rump fanned the air optimistically; she added a gasp to the
maneuver. The bones of her ankles flexed, seductive and
hopeful; she started up a little kicking motion designed to
suggest the bitch impatient. When she had exhausted her
inventory of moves, she paused, still holding her ass upright,
the surface surprisingly angular, a hank of golden whisker
threading the crotch. Then she heard the deep snorting
sound of Dixie asleep behind her and she swung her head
down between her legs to see him perched Buddha-like upon
the pillow, his hands covering his groin, his head fast to the
bedpost, his mouth completely open. At first she thought
that he was dead.

But Dixie was not dead, he was only dreaming. Yet not
a dream but a vision it was, for Dixie could not dream, that
was a depth beyond him now. He was capable only of that
moment between wakefulness and the first darkness of the

mind, still aware of the body and susceptible to pain; detached but not oblivious, able to conjure only what, in waking, was still accountable to fact. He was the wicker glove in a jai alai game, catching the ball in the cup of his smooth fold, hurling it back with a spew; the ball sang towards him and the hand which shaped him now turned him round with an easy practiced flick and the ball hung deep in the maw of his body. It rolled down the tongue of his body, then he was lashed forward, turned in a resistant arc and the ball flew free of his open, impaled form and thundered off the wall. Then he was something else : he was a tennis ball with a crooked slit and people were putting pieces of paper into him and sending him down from the gallery; he felt the moist hand of the agent grip him in the heat and thrust the flat of his thumb into the opening to dig for the paper, and there was a musty, gray taste in his mouth. Then he was the court and the game and the ball and the people in the gallery all at once and each thing moved and squirmed in him like different worms and he had to breath for them and hurl the ball and take the impact of it where it hit the wall and catch it in the scoop of his body. Because he was the people, one by one and all together, he had to think their thoughts and scratch their itches and slip the bits of paper into the top of his own head. Then he was the stadium itself and after that he could not stop and he was the Ramblas and felt the trees growing through him and the fountains squirting up through his guts. I can't do it, he thought, it's too much. His own ass sat on him where he was the benches lining the street and he had to provide himself as the mustache on the old woman who sold the lottery numbers and he felt himself crumpled and thin in his own fingers. But before he got to be Barcelona and the mountains, the bee finally stung him and he knew this time that he was not the bee, the bee was separate inside his head. The sting laced him tight, he felt his lips being sewn together; the spine of the stinger held him stiff. *I done it now.* The eye of the needle passed up through his crotch to his mouth and the bee made a great resonant *Neeeemmmm* as it began to die inside his head.

Boy, am I in trouble. When he opened his eyes he saw that they had been open all the time and he was watching with horror what the whore was doing to him. "No." The whore kept sucking, working up suds busily, and he said "No," and jammed a toe up her nostril. The whore did not object; she only wondered what he wanted after all. When she saw that he was asleep again, this time collapsed on the bed, his mouth now closed and one arm stretched to give him the appearance of incredible length, she crawled in between the sheets and beside the contorted form of the man at rest, arranging herself like the northern hip of Africa.

At five in the morning, the whore decided that she had slept enough for the price and rose to make the coffee. When Dixie, aroused by a gust of air where the whore had been accommodating him all night, woke up, she was dressed again in the aquamarine sweater and freshly laundered skirt; but she had on wine-coloured slippers and was making the coffee. He could smell the coffee perking on the hot plate near the window and it brimmed him with what in a drowning man is a burning sensation in the nostril, but in Dixie was a startled sense of gratitude. And even more, when he saw the slippers : flapping domestically on the cement floor, worn, creased, wine-coloured, giving to the ankles and calves of the girl an attitude of sloppy, untainted warmth. *Hey, I'm married; I'm a married man.*

The only thing he could hear on the way back to the hotel was the sound of old women selling the lottery numbers; chanting over and over the same automatic wail, dressed in black, seated behind tables, shrouded by doorways. Someone emptied a pail of dirty water onto the narrow street; half of it hit the wall opposite and oozed down the dark brick onto the sidewalk. The stench of the street; a few dogs roaming. The heat was not yet so dense and quick that Dixie could not bear it. He walked with his hands in his pockets, stroking his own thigh through a hole in the cloth. I can stand to walk down this fucken street, he thought, I can even bear the stink now too. The bee was not gone, but it had been dead for some time and was now a dried shell inside his head; in a day it would decompose absolutely and help to fertilize his mind. *Things is looking up, I can tell.* He stopped and dug for his wallet; it was exactly where the pimp had put it the night before and he extracted a few bills and bought some lottery numbers and shoved them into his shirt pocket. But as he got closer to the hotel, into the Nueva San Francisco, he felt the things in his pocket bulge and start like so much refuse. In his overcoat pocket were all the maps and some kleenex and Métro tickets still left from Paris; in his jacket pockets were his passport and some letters, all crumpled and uneven, folded so that the sharp corners chafed his ribs; his leather pouch of drugs and pills swung by a special strap against his heart; in his pants pockets lots of old bills and scraps of writing, his broken wristwatch, band and glass dome separate, a bottle opener, scissors, then the Spanish coin and the wallet and the huge hotel room key. All of it banged together and seemed to multiply and congeal all over his body, turning into lumps of solid tissue, crawling maggots, corners and ends and points. *I'm too full, I got too much on me, I can't hardly breath at all.* He began to empty his pockets quickly, dropping the letters and the scraps of writing, the broken watch, the lottery numbers, leaving in his wake the excrement of time wasted, which seemed to follow him anyway in a long unsteady loop to the hotel doorway. *I was hell of a lot worse off in London though.* He seemed to rise up the steps by the sheer weight-lessness of his discarded life, driving through the door and onto the stairs, his fingers tiptoeing up the railing while his feet marched as if boneless. Then he was in his own corridor and jamming the huge key into the lock; the door cranked, jerked, exploded open. The curtains were drawn and held together by a pin. He stumbled through the dark onto his own bed and it was only after some slow thought that he began to recognize the thin, stale smell. So he turned his head, still prone on his back, merely moving his neck as if it were set by a brace. All he could see at first was a Huck Finn hat, moving at an exact angle like a fan belt; then he saw the small hunched back, bare, gnarled, then the weak round shoulders, then the entire body not altogether balanced but continually rearranging itself into positions increasingly more awkward and impossible. Dixie stood bolt upright. "Hey, get the fuck out," he said dumbly. "Rape," gasped Iris. "Help," said Bobby E Lee and went crashing out the door.

Thirty-six

The morning after Iris had become briefly mine, Bobby E Lee came into our room and shook Rose out of a raging sleep. He was white as a ghost and still fumbling at the rope on his trousers.

"Listen," he whispered hoarsely, "something happened, what am I gonna do, Mommy."

Apparently, Dixie had caught him in bed with Iris.

"We were in bed together and he just walked in. He says he's gonna kill me, he went out to buy a knife."

"How the hell did you get into bed with Iris ?" I asked.

"She asked me. She's been asking me all day."

"What did she say ?"

"Things like : 'It's time isn't it,' or "Let's break up the group image.' She's been driving me crazy."

"You stupid little bastard."

"Don't say that."

"Serves you right if he cuts your cock off."

"I don't want to hear."

"Fig idiot," said Rose, just prior to dozing off again.

"I didn't want to," said Bobby E Lee, "honest Garbs." He had been high, he explained, and when he was high he took off his pants, it was a funny thing; but so did she and wasn't that a coincidence. She had accosted him in the hotel court early that morning and had conned him into coming to her room. Then it had all become dark and confused and he was doing it and "I had never . . . I was actually . . . in . . . when . . ."

"You're a goddamn liar : you've been priming for it since yesterday."

"Please Garb I don't want to talk about it okay ?"

We let Bobby E Lee sleep in our room. Dixie, who had gone out again, came back nearer to noon, still in an unbelieving daze, and lay down beside Iris, morose and on a low flame. She was actually sobbing, actually crying. When had she cried before, he thought, look at that, and he tried to think of when she had cried before and remembered slowly when that had been and got distracted and could not find his way back. She implored him to forgive her; they even tried to make love. She was horrified by the switchblade he held tightly in his hand. She didn't sleep at all that day and she begged him to stay in the bed with her and not to move. The knife was under the pillow, finally; his rage was becoming abstracted and he had to keep remembering, he had to look at Iris to remind himself why it was there; and whenever he looked at her and had got it all back again, she would nuzzle deeper into the ruin of his visions, stroking what could only be stroked now, erasing the clearness from his mind. She veiled her fear with soft sounds. Then, on command, she performed at last some tiny miracle of love, until he was asleep, still seeking to remember, doomed to remember when he awoke, not wanting to wake to it at all. She put different stories to his ear and, when he was completely out, she took the knife and threw it out the window.

Bobby E Lee a few floors away, cried and ranted, bereft of drawl now, the tinsel of his manner gone. What bothered me was that Iris was too cunning to suffer for long; by confessing around the incident, she would have Dixie back again in his native role without any trouble. But what would she confess ? It was bad enough taking Iris under Dixie's vibrant nose, but to have played off his weakness as well, to have two-faced him into the bargain; why he'd slit my throat and bury me in quicklime.

"Listen," I said carefully, "did Iris say anything about me ? To Dixie ?"

"I just ran," said Bobby E Lee. "Can I sleep some more ?"

I was too upset not to take a calculated risk and late that afternoon I wandered through corridors to their room and knocked pleasantly on the door. Iris opened up and gave me a cool, guarded stare. Was Dixie there ? Yes, but he was sleeping.

"Who's there," groaned Dixie.

I could hear him pausing for a moment while it all grew clear and ugly, then I could hear him fumbling among the linen.

"It's Garber. Listen, you wanna go down to the Blue Note ? we're all going."

"Who's going ?" asked Dixie, suspicious now, having successfully remembered. He felt rather proud of that.

"Me, Rose, Bobby, come on."

"Tell him I'm gonna kill him," said Dixie.

So I forced my way in past Iris and talked quickly for half an hour. I looked for the knife, but I couldn't see it.

"He took advantage of her," said Dixie, "he got her full of pot and he raped her. He don't deserve no better."

Iris stood by the window looking cool, looking, in fact, both innocent and used.

"He ruint her," said Dixie, "he spoiled her; he scarred her for life; I got to."

Iris was looking triumphant too, as if nothing could have ever passed through that trim and garnished body except savagely.

"He's a little pimp and a whore," said Dixie, "and he come in the night and Jesus he held her down awful and she just a girl; like an animal he done it and she with her period too; you don't think I can ?"

And Iris moved up and down the room as if put into motion by the battery of his voice, reminding him as she walked barelegged (and in slippers too) that she was his to care for, unprotected, spliced through, still bleeding and torn. The image of Bobby E Lee permeated their union now; his mouth savage, glint-toothed, his Huck Finn propped fiendishly, the small surprising hump adding the necessary touch of something perverse. It was a federation of love against the cloven hoof.

It didn't take long, though, before I had persuaded them to take the car back to Paris and forget everything. Dixie even looked relieved. Iris was managing nicely.

"It isn't worth it," I said, completing her moves. "Wouldn't you two rather go back to Paris and maybe be alone ? away from all this shit ?"

Apparently Iris hadn't told him a thing, because finally he took me aside and said, "Garb you just saved my life, you'll never know what you done for us man : I lost the fucking knife anyway," and took my hand. Iris gave me the stare as I went out.

So they left as the first darkness fell. Bobby E Lee stayed locked in our room wrapped securely in blankets and sheets. I promised to see them in Paris in a week's time and then they were gone, their problem not solved but derailed for an instant and things between them as thin as summer ice. A day later, I put Rose on a boat for Tangiers, left Bobby E Lee whimpering alone in the hotel room, and took a noon train on down the coast.

Thirty-seven
I'm Just A Kid

What follows is taking place in the overheated mind of Bobby E Lee, lying in one of two beds in a hotel room at the Pensión Toledo, Barcelona; the other bed is farthest from the window and nearer to the door; a large mirrored bureau stands fronting his gaze; a small sink with smaller mirror is enclosed in the wall to his immediate left; the color of the drapes is light green; a plastic fish suspended in a bowl of wax flowers has been left thoughtfully for his comfort on the sill; from his perch, he can see a Spanish woman standing across the way on her balcony wearing only silk

*panties and faded breast cups; no one could have explained
to him what the woman was seeking at that altitude.*

My head hurts   I am lying here thick with fever, my legs
trembling like lukewarm jelly   Outside it is cold   I can tell
because the goldfish on my window sill is trapped in an ice
cube   And, although my nose is itchy and dripping, I have
no kleenex left and have to use the sheets   I am uncomfortable

Okay, this is something you have to do on your own, suffer
through decently   They've all left now   Gone away   I
could call E. Bone in Ibiza   Get up in my bare feet, walk to
the hall, pick up the old spic receiver   But no   Why should
I   I'm perfectly capable of looking after myself aren't I
"Suah ah iz, ah kin dew it ahl raght"   What I need is some
more lemonade

My stomach is like a stuffed cabbage   I have to drink a
lot of water and my fingers can hardly hold the glass   I
notice that I have been sweating   My toes are numb   I try
to curl them but all I get is a sense of needles   That poor
goldfish   I wonder if it understands for the most part

Okay, try to sleep   One day you'll laugh at all this   What
a poor little kid I was, I'll say   What a punk, couldn't take
a little angst in his stride   Complicated by a head cold of
course   But I can   Aren't I doing it now   And I was right
in her too, inserted   "Yessah, ah done dood it"   Time for an
aspirin actually

My head hurts   I get this pain like a knife twisting up
inside my chest   It comes and goes   Then, my stomach
begins to pinch   Then, I try to turn over but my back is
stiff   I just noticed my hands getting yellow   I sneeze

Okay, so what   Just close your eyes   Tomorrow you'll
be over the worst part   Then you get can up and do things
You're not helpless   In spite of what they said   So what
if Dixie had come for me with the knife   I've got powerful
wrists   "Cum git me Dixah baby ifn you kin"   When I
close my eyes, I dream I'm falling and wake up full of pain
In Paris I couldn't sleep either   I'm a night person   It
comes with the territory   I used to twist and turn like a

champagne cork before I got to sleep   Irma would come
down with some nice broth and I'd pinch her bum   Let
that be a lesson

My ears are burning and plugged   I know because I
can't hear a thing   Maybe someone is trying to get into
my room with supplies   You never know   Garber Rose
Another blanket maybe or some hot chocolate in a tin or
those nice pastries   But it's hard to know   Could be Dixie
If I tried to open the door I'd get a terrible draft   God

Okay, the worst part is probably over   The weather is
bad today and this is making you miserable   How can
Spanish weather be bad though   If it was sunny out you'd
be in better spirits   I guess so   Hell if it was sunny out
you'd be at the Blue Note with Garber and Rose and Connie
discussing things and being cynical and then drinking outside
in the Plaza   Or in Paris with that lovely creature Sylvie
from Lexington in the orange dress taking you to the Café
de la Paix or the Bois   The wind would be cool off the
lake and rustle the tablecloth   She'd have this car and say
something about driving to Fountainbleau   You'd say sure
"Okay Sylvie honey ahm you slave keed"   Then in the car
it would be quiet   I'm tightlipped with women of that sort
I'd be driving   With her in the crook of my arm   Well
maybe   If it was sunny, if I was in France   It's hard to tell

My throat bothers me   Every time I swallow it scrapes
And I touch a lump somewhere   Just under my chin   It
hurts   It's not cancer but I find it damned inconvenient
Also, my fingers are blue   Before they were yellow but that
was just a phase   My knuckles looked crooked   As if the
bones are warping   Well of course if you don't put them
under the sheets they'll get cold   Its very simple   But my
elbows crack every time I move them   Of course   You
keep bending them so often

Okay, it's raining in Spain   Hail   The sound bangs
against my window   What if the damn pane breaks   If it
breaks I could freeze to death in here   Sure, one big gaping
hole and that's it   I suppose the wind would come in and the
hail would melt on the floor and lower the room temperature
and I'd freeze   Not really   Cold weather is good for you

It stimulates the blood   E. Bone always said so   Whenever we went tramping in the winter he'd push my head in the snow to get my circulation buzzing   Very embarrassing I'm no kid   I wonder what that naked lady is doing on her balcony   On a day like this   Couldn't be more than middle-aged   "Cum an git it nekked baby, ahm ready for yah" That was a pretty big piece of hailstone just smacked the glass   Is that a crack

My stomach is compressing rapidly   Being eaten away When you don't eat regularly they say that the stomach begins to devour itself   Probably happening to me right now   I ought to stop it   Have some bread or something Just to be on the safe side   That's silly   It's nerves   Just because you have a headache and a bad experience doesn't mean you're going to swallow yourself   Doesn't that sound ridiculous

Okay, you find it difficult   If it wasn't difficult it wouldn't be worth experiencing would it   I suppose not   If you got sick in Paris they'd pester you with medicines and hot water bottles till it was coming out your ears   And you wouldn't have learned a thing   Irma bringing in the aspirins every four hours and E. Bone stuffing the crap down your throat and Fitz playing under your tongue with the thermometer and stuffing those herbs up your crud   Isn't that so   But alone I'm learning something   Every minute   Such as who knew it could get so cold in Spain   Learning how to handle myself at least   No need to be charming here   And didn't I once drop a full corpse into the Seine   "Well guzzle mah ass an cawl me hopeful"   Isn't it horrible how that fish died   If I had another quilt I'd be all right

My hair is beginning to fall out all over the pillow   I just saw a few of them all dried and brittle   Now that I trace my hairline I can see it's receding   Overnight   As if my scalp oils were suddenly sterile   And my tongue   It's coated with a thick waxy covering   Lumpy   When I cough everything comes up   In concentrated form   My chest is heavy   It's hard to breathe   My voice is wrong   I gag All colds are like that   I would think

Okay, it's despairing   Despair Despair   Everything is black   The room stinks, the bed is hard, the air is cold   Cracks on the ceiling, holes in the floor, mice rubbing their feet in the wall   At least there's no Irma to bug you about keeping the covers clean and not touching their dresser drawers   No one to call your underwear brown   There's nothing you can't do here   "No suh, they ain't nuthin y'caint dew ifn yah tryah"   Scream howl cry   Anything Ahoooooooooahoooooo   I can do that any time I feel like it Ahoooo . . .   But it makes my teeth hurt

My belly is churning   It makes me want to cry   That's absurd   It's going round and round, up and down like a hot chunk of coal   I ought to write this down, get some perspective   I'm not really crying but my eyes are tearing   It's the air   And then, my eyes burn   That's a good sign   They say when the eyes tear they're washing out all the debris   I haven't had a good wash out since last year when I couldn't go to Longchamps with E. Bone and Irma   Well I wouldn't say *couldn't* go   You're too inexperienced for the races, he said, you'll waste our money   And oh wasn't he happy that dirty nigger when he caught you picking your teeth or something, with those cold steel eyes   Such a filthy animal   I can go now   If there were races tomorrow I'd go   And all week for that matter   And bet too   But I'm not crying

Okay, Iris said to me, you go ahead and do it if you want to, it's about time isn't it   Go ahead, she said, let's break up the group image, I don't care   Very cold tone in her voice too   Hard   She's probably crying now   "All them lies y'tol"   Every day she has to walk into her empty room Every night she goes to bed with Dixie thinking that I'm off somewhere by myself in a strange ugly room with all sorts of vermin   It must be painful for her   You can't help feeling a little sympathy

My balls hurt   I think my sperm got stuck   All congealed   What if she had VD   What'll I do then   It's all red and blown up   Of course I'm unnaturally large   Still it's itchy too   I feel something green   Like a marble   Is that pus all dried up   Or just a growth   Well, certainly,

I'm a man   The thing is just relaxing afterwards   But what if they have to amputate

Okay, so you're not in Paris   It's forenoon there now, they're lined two deep at the Monaco and you're missing it   Well, you'd be crazy if you didn't   But Dixie'll be telling them how I raped Iris   I don't mind that   Add to my stature   Maybe I did rape her   I've got a special kind of force   "Oky doky Iris keed, drowp you pants and raize you ass, ahm given you faih wawnin"   And when I get back they'll all be talking about it   There he goes, a real raping fool   Bastard of the first order   The streets aren't safe   Gendarmes patrol the Rue Dauphine   New pill boxes stationed along the quais   Women wear special absorbent groin pads, insoluble in sperm   Doesn't do a bit of good   Debbie Briar Cheryl Rose Trixy Irma Yvonne Jeanette Bonnie Nina Nora Dalia Alice Jackie Dee Valentine Anne Julia Constance Florine Sylvie Gloria   Who else   Penelope Honey Sandra Billie   Who else   Erica Vivien Maria   Who else   Iris   Then   Waiting at the Coupolade as they walk into the Rue Soufflot   Surmising   Then following them up little byways into the Contrescarpe late at night   Dragging them into dark corners of the Rue Mouffetard   Torn cloth   Awful secretions   Did you hear about last night   He did it again   God he's cruel   Let them talk

My nose aches   On the outside it is red and peeling   And inside I can't breathe   That's the way a cold is   But I noticed that it's bleeding   Which is unusual   When I sneeze, which I understand is a good sign, I feel something breaking as if I am smashing the bone   Also, it is destroying my ears   If my mouth clogs, I shall stop breathing altogether

Okay, but E. Bone and Irma are just a little bit forgetful   Aren't they   You know that   If they said they'd write you in a week it was just their way of saying they love you and think of you all the time   Of course he had no business saying that if he didn't mean it   He's really spiteful and shrewd   And her too   I know   He just said it to be on the safe side because he knows I'm dangerous   Sure   And he let me look after the stuff because he knows I'm ruthless

too   Just think what I did to that dead man who mainlined
I'd always feel welcome if I ever decided to pay them a visit
In Ibiza   Which is silly   At least not for a few days
"Ahm a cumin ahm a cumin, git yourself pre-pahred"

My body has the shivers   I get hot, then I get cold   My
skin breaks out into little icy bumps every few minutes   It
could be a skin disease but I doubt it   Everyone gets the
shivers   The cold goes through you and the blood rushes
around warming you up   It's all very confusing   But my
legs are weak too   When I try to bend them they won't
work properly   Polio   I never did take my fourth shot
You can hardly feel the calf   My fingers pinch them   No
sensation   Polio   Treatments   But they can cure these
things now   "Doctra Sahlk, ah needs you baby"   Which
is something anyway

Okay, I'm not happy   Who says you have to be happy
But there comes a time when you've got to do it   Regardless   And it didn't even hurt   But I got all wet   She
didn't   And she was very sad when we had to stop   Moaning   Very upset   Though she didn't look it   Dixie too
"Cum git me, yuh awfal forked beast, ahm waitin"   Oh
both of them so frozen and menacing   They'll be lucky if
I don't die

My face looks scared   Across the room I have an old
mirror over a washbasin   In it I can see myself wrapped
under the sheets with just my little head visible   On the
pillow it looks broken   The eyes are scarlet   The forehead wet and lined   The lips white   Nose red   Ears stiff
and pale   Is that the face of death   I am trying to smile
The mouth bends   Am I dying   Maybe the cold has affected
my brain —It is difficult to think   A green colour flushes
my cheeks   I turn away trembling   My God, it's just a
cold   I want to be buried in my turtle-neck sweater

Okay, I can hear the traffic   Lunch time   Then late
afternoon   Siesta   Then evening   When you're in bed like
this it's as if you're waiting for something to happen   But
what   "Ah gits no kick fum cha-um-pain"   Outside it is
still cold and the hailstones are plunging to the pavement
everywhere   "They ain't no hahlstowns in Spain, boy"

Maybe nothing will ever happen   Maybe I'll be sick like this for years   Waiting   My bones will calcify and I'll harden in bed like a zombie   Forever   Anything's possible isn't it

My head hurts   That is, the thoughts won't come and I think that I am going mad   In the Dostoevskian sense When I close my eyes I see patterns of gray and black in shroud designs   I am beginning to forget things   The mind is rotting   Was E. Bone tall or short   Did Irma have acne on her chin or not   Beware the eyes of Iris   I feel the bleat, the throb of pain rushing in my head   The temple is swollen   I cough   I sneeze

Okay, you are sick and it is cold and they don't care   But you are free   You are alone   No more pleading for little favors   No more pimping for good times   You're your own stuff now   *A noise I think*   You are strong   *Louder* A regular Rhett Butler   *Footsteps aren't they, or just the hailstones*   "Hi-yuh, whooze ahl theah"   I'm satisfied now I have never actually been more satisfied   I was in up to the hair, man   In the mornings when I wake up the first sounds are mine   I rise and make coffee in the dim Spanish light   It feels good   Tremendous friction, brought her to terms all right   I thrive on isolation   *Yes I think footsteps* "Ahm rightch'up heah"   And at night when I turn off the light, I alone control the dark, the quiet   *A noise coming up the stairs, maybe someone to see me, yes sure, Garber maybe, or even Connie*   And any time I want to close the drapes or open the drawers, shout scream cry laugh   *Closer Maybe some hot chocolate in a tin, another blanket, unwanted sympathy, a smile*   "Ohhhh, whan them saintz, oh whan them saintz, oh whan them say-untz cum a-marchin inah"   Yes, and yell too if I wish   *Is that the doorknob turning   Where's the doorknob   Is that Garber's voice Dixie come to hurt me   Rose   I can't hear*   If I want to shout my defiance I will not be stopped   "Ah weel naught b'stowped"   Why this very instant I can raise my voice *God, is it somebody or just the hailstones*   Yes any time when you live alone, you see   Ahooooahoooo   Any time When you're free it doesn't matter   Ahooooooahoooooo

Thirty-eight

After several well-written and exciting adventures in Valencia, Torremolinos, Gibraltar, Madrid, Pamplona, involving many exciting and neurotic people each with their own peculiar malformities of body and spirit, having defecated friendship in a hundred places, from Málaga to Morocco and from Lisbon to Seville, I returned hurriedly to Paris. I had been in Paris a day when I went into the Petite Source for lunch. Fitz the West Indian was sitting in a corner smiling grotesquely at the mirror; catching my eye, he jerked his head like a great grinning bird and I wandered over. He was picking some sausage lazily from his tooth with a fork prong, but his eyes were quick and ready.

"Hi man," he groaned in that smooth familiar glide of the voice, "how was that Spain ?"

Fitz had just returned from Tunisia or someplace equally remote with Nora who had once kept the albino, and he was looking rather drawn. The ravages of dysentery and Nora endlessly reclining, had somewhat withered his bright smile, and when he spoke his words were filled with dust.

"I'm pretty good Fitz, can't complain," I said, sitting down at his table, ordering the *saucissons frites,* and thinking wasn't it fine to have so many good friends in the Quarter.

"You lookin a bit sick, man," said Fitz. "You lookin a bit on the green side."

"Naw I'm fine," I said, "just naturally sallow. By the way," I said, "I'm looking for Dixie."

Fitz worked his body like a subtitle, leaned forward graciously to dazzle me with his grammar, and said in a voice grimalkin, "Hey, you sure he ain't looking for you !"

So I bought three bags of dried biscuits, two bottles of vin rouge ordinaire, two tins of sardines, a kilo of moroccan oranges, a bottle of jus de pommes, several Oxo bars, and hid in my hotel room for three days and three nights. The wallpaper was cracked to reveal a frieze of subterranean horrors, the bed sank in the middle, witness to a thousand weighty buttocks; in the hallway, a chorus of sound from

every room, as if frogs floated in their private pools behind
lock and key; the toilets clotted with unflushed urine and
floating turds; the light of day hidden from view behind vast
buildings like some eternal summer in another country; wire
hangers, wooden bureau, newspapers beneath the sink; a
lone pipe disgorging dirty water through a leak. If you
looked through a particular window it was possible to see all
the way up the Rue Dauphine, and if you were really scared
you could even make out the people in the Café Buci.
Which I did. Nightly. I expected (it grew the certainty of
a desire) to see Dixie walking grimly towards the island, a
switchblade held skilfully in his hand (finger through the
loop in a barber's grip), the gruel on his chin glistening as
he lumbered over the bridge; and behind him Iris, hysterically pointing the way, Cassandra-like, barebreasted, one
hand waving aloft the flag of France, the other clutched
meatily over a bleeding groin.

But after a day, the first panic receded. I ceased listening
for creaks on the stairs, I stopped working chairs under the
doorknob. Instead, I looked at the situation logically. I took
Fitz's sentence — uttered so casually — and subjected it
to the most painful scrutiny. *Hey, you sure he ain't looking
for you!* Three things were immediately apparent and highly
peculiar. *Hey* was not a word that Fitz used often, this I
knew. "I never use the exclamatory man, I exclams pure
when I exclam," he used to say. Then the term *ain't looking*
which seemed so deliberately a betrayal, so carefully spent;
ain't lookin, isn't looking, these I could have accepted impulsively and never been the wiser, but *ain't looking* contained the yeast of both possible worlds, as if Fitz were
countering the rumours of my guilt with some malicious,
informed antidote — a warning no less. And lastly, it became
suddenly and remarkably clear that the ! at the end of Fitz's
sentence was my own; as if I had unconsciously extracted
from his look and tone the evil so cautiously buried. So it
became clear that *Hey, you sure he ain't looking for you!*
contained depths and folds detectable, in volume; yes, but
what did it all mean ? There was a sounding beneath it
now, something more subtle. Was it a muffled ejaculation

of some sort ? a generous caution ? a sadistic manipulation of my every fear ? Fitz (bless him though) making a game out of nothing ? or some elusive, copperhead ploy by Dixie and Fitz together, in conspiracy ? catching me as I picked up their ridiculously easy clues, waiting for me to trip into the pit, stabbing me in the back as I shouted Eureka in the other direction ? Yet compulsively, I staggered into the sun late one afternoon. It was damn nice out.

All that day I spent out of the corner of my eye, watching for Dixie. Yes, you live with fear long enough and soon it becomes resignation; and if you become resigned too long, you begin to build a longing for the moment of truth; and the moment of truth takes on the ornaments of fiction and becomes skin on the mind, one's pigment for survival. Then the paraphernalia of rage sprouts its little cancers : the cigarette (Boyard, *papier maïs*) jammed free and loose into the parched lip, discolouring slightly one's upper tooth, the silver buckle of one's buckled belt (bought in one's angry mood at Samaritaine's) gripped in explosive relief by the tips of two fingers, the wide leather strap giving a broad and dangerous flex to the wrist (ripped from the dying arm of an Algerian patriot on the Quai du Vert-Galant before he is slipped, still gurgling, into the water). I was ready.

Dixie was not in the regular cafés; he had, in fact, abandoned them. I bought my Boyards and walked calmly along the St. Germain, past the assembled eyes. He was not at the Mabillon or the Old Navy; he would not have gone to La Rhumerie or the Café de Flores, certainly; he was not in the Lipp. Then I saw Nate the Accordion moving grimly into the Rue de Seine, slouched beneath the weight of his instrument, leading by the hand a short young girl, obviously of German extraction. She shuttled reluctantly behind him, hooked somehow to the meat of his fingers, trolley and wire together. She was walking sideways. I followed, backtracking furiously, a momentous, unkind feeling in my gut. *What can they do to me ? in broad daylight ?*

Nate and friend disappeared into the Café Seine, a place grubbier than most. Several people sat on the terrace, sensational in varying modes of dress, indulging their sense of masquerade. The effect was one of several hundred people (there were only twenty however) massed for a parade, waiting patiently on the terrace of the café for the first sounding trumpet; yet destined to wait endlessly (a requirement) until their costumes whittled into daily use. There was Dixie.

And others too, creatures of the Café Seine, not with him, but about him, like the fins of a gargoyle featured in relief. *Tex :* high boots; engraved in leather a vista of the prairies; rust-coloured; hair a kinky gold; upon his head, curiously incongruent, a French tam — blue; knuckle-dusters fitted loosely on his fingers; an elastic band in painful contortion wound from thumb to middle finger; an open, blank, enormously amused expression; an idiot's paradise mirrored in rouge and tinted glasses; the flap of his fly lined with silver buttons; a leather codpiece winged on either side; a tremorous left hand sunk partially into a small hip pocket; his khaki shirt open to the navel; a bead of artificial hair from neck to belly; a small, silk tie wrapped in a cowboy's knot and swept over one shoulder to fall like a withered arrow, plume-like, down his back; his mouth never closed; an expectant gleam, informed by spittle and blue gums; something doubtful in the eyes too; glazed; almost manufactured out of cut glass; the nose chipped patiently for years into a thin, even sliver only to be abandoned at puberty, leaving the tip blunt, flat, susceptible to blisters; eyes the colour of dog piss; an habitual squint favourably disposed on all; the legs up to the bar, one boot carefully kicked back to expose the full heel; knee into the side of the bar proper betraying the pose of a dancer; waving to friends; looking for pussy. Or, *Red :* long thick hair — auburn or rat-coloured; wearing a black dress without belt or button; her legs warmed by the sun as it penetrates the awning; well-shaped; against the grain; mosquito bites down her flank as she raises leg; (at night she lies on the floor mat, legs bare and kicking, screams, "bite me bite me"); a look of raffish wisdom; well-liked; and likes it well enough;

reputation for various things; a deep, secreting *joie de vivre;* prefers to be asked in code; is kind to the maimed; kind of maimed herself.

Dixie sat inside with Nate the Accordion, the German girl discontented, a Danish creature Maria All-Blonde, and the actor Guy Rancid.

"Dixie," I said, swallowing hard, startled beyond belief, "what's the word ?"

"What word ?" he said, "I'd just be guessing."

He looked up from his demi, his eyes narrower than usual, and shook my hand. He had begun a beard; his face looked like a badly kept nest.

"Neem," I said, "that's a good word."

"Pretty good. Sit down."

"Where's Iris ?"

"Left, gone, vanished, vaporated, decamped, vamoosed, so long baby."

"Checked out, huh ?"

"Yah Garb, something along those lines."

"How come ?"

"Sluts don't explain. Whores yah, sluts no. Proly run off with some African cock. Nasty."

"I know I know."

"Sure Garb. You're a regular Methuselah."

There was an absolute clarity to his voice; the pitch was so steady, so pure, it was almost intimidating. I decided not to say anything more. I chose my chair carefully so as to have a view of the street.

We drank in silence. Soon a tall, bushy-faced Finn — an obsequious fool known as Ping Pong — come over to the table and asked Nate if he might take the little kraut for a stroll.

"No," said Nate.

"But I want to go," said the short girl, "and why shouldn't I go."

"We have to go to work in an hour," said Nate.

"So, I'll be back in an hour," she said.

They walked out of the café.

"Who's that ?" I asked, grateful for the incident.

"My new accompanist," said Nate.

"Where's Yvonne ?" I kept it up, no opening too small.

"She met a sad end," said Nate.

"Oh," I said. "What happened ?"

"Mind your own business," said Nate.

"Sorry," I said.

"Now *the new one* has just wandered off with some bearded individual," said Nate; "were you here ?"

"Yes," I said, "I saw them go."

"I'm worried," said Nate.

"Why Nate ?" I asked, "why are you worried ?"

"Because she might not come back, you idiot !" said Nate. "If you saw them go, you'd know that !"

"Of course," I said.

"I've got an interest in that girl," said Nate, plucking a hair from his wizened throat.

"Of course you do," I said helpfully. "You've got a business interest in her now."

"Goddamn you," screamed Nate, "it's a *sexual* interest, you fool !"

All of which Dixie approved or disapproved by rubbing a spoon along his new grizzle. There was something chilling about him now; for the first time that I could recall, he looked actually menacing. Perhaps it was the fact that he was finally sustaining a mood.

"I've never even been to Pigalle," he said, unaware of our light conversation, "I never even been to the Champs; I never been any fucking where; Iris never wanted to go; I never even been to whatsthenameofit."

"I'll take you kid," I said.

"I don't wanna go !" said Dixie.

Now, whenever the atmosphere proves hostile and I find that I have miscalculated a thing or two, I take to little credos. I know very little about how people live and I want to know even less. Yet living among them involves gossip and gossip involves knowing just enough to make sensible the conning mysteries. It affords one a simple view. One knows what one hears. Rumours, for instance, when well-circulated, give one insights uncalled for; innuendos, nastily promoted, call for conclusions completely unnecessary; secrets divulged, or a word cruelly passed, make clumsy luggage. Yet to mind one's own business is merely to tempt a confidence; and to busy oneself with other people's problems and dark closets is only to enter through another door. One is forced to witness grubby interiors, against the will or no; without warning, one finds oneself privy to awful secrets, recipient of the key to boring mysteries, reasons for the limp. Make a new acquaintance and you are immediately weighed down by clockwork, and ultimately given a clue too many; once that is discovered you are in trouble, a carrier of the germ. He alone is a paragon who keeps his mouth shut and nose clean; for instance, an impotent mute or a lunatic albino. I take to little credos like that. The liberation of choice from the threat of gossipmongers is the only cause worth fleeing for. It's a permissive cowardice : naiveté under pressure. Anyway, I find comfort in such mixed conclusions, especially when I sense a reversal in my fortunes, the downfall of arrangements. So knowing that Dixie was impotent or that Trixy was sick or that Nate was obsessed; knowing that Brynning had his cruel trick or that André of the French Foreign Legion was constructed of tin and wire and other compounds, or that Henry Rotter took his just rewards; knowing that Cheryl was a lousy lay or that Anne the Pregnant often menstruated or that Bobby E Lee was a humpbacked imp; knowing that Emmanuel the Spanish was all Northern Ontario or that Connie the pimp blanched at violence or that Constance Funn had finally left Nate for specific reasons : knowing all this and probably more was completely trivial and indicative of the end.

This is merely to suggest how I surmised the changed atmosphere about me. I might have been completely wrong, of course. In fact, I was. But being oppressively aware of what everyone was that afternoon, I indulged in nostalgia. I remembered the old days and the good times when all the same people were different and all the different people were the same. I thought of Cheryl as she was then before she was transparent, and the Spanish, and Yvonne (of the subsequent sad end) with the large dimples and the fleshy knees, and of that time in the Loire when we were all so happy, weather permitting. I thought of *me* then, as I was; with my high linoleum finish. Then I thought of Guy Rancid — who the hell was Guy Rancid anyway ?

Guy Rancid (to whom Maria belonged preparatory to disdain) tilted lazily in his chair, handsomely tanned, somewhat heavy in the leg, signs of a second chin encroaching (with subtle justice) upon the fine lines of his profile. A fantastically large forehead relegated his lesser organs to the lower part of his face; nose, lips, jaw, even cheeks, all crammed into a space hardly wide enough for a yawn. "Was that James Stewart ?" he seemed to be saying, "over there; no, he's gone now." He had refused to speak until absolutely convinced of our harmlessness. Now, perfectly assured, he revealed himself in full.

"Was zat eem ?" asked Maria.

"Could have been," said Guy Rancid "I know he's in Paris."

"Yez ?"

"For the summer; living at 18 Quai d'Orleans with his wife (the former Brenda Marshall) and children, aged . . ."

But he didn't finish; rather, he paused, giving vent instead to a rhetorician's hush. His voice was somewhat throaty : as if Tammy Grimes were really a castrado. He played with his own fingers, judging of their beauty, their capacity for life. His nostrils were well-equipped with hair, twisting like fangs out of each flared orifice; they suggested ferocity. Every once in a while, and quite unconsciously, he seemed to lob his jaw in an upward strain as if to say : *I sure wish though that my organs was higher up : maybe I ought to have my head enlarged.*

"Guy," said Nate the Accordion, stirring his bière Strasbourg with a singed thumbnail, "is a producer too."

"As well as what ?" I asked.

"As well as a thespian," said Guy Rancid, smiling mercifully. "What Nate means is that I acquired the rights to Albee's *Zoo Story* when I was last in New York."

"Really ?"

"Yes : for Mozambique. I'm trying to get a company ready. Ed was quite nice about it."

"Albee ?"

"Yes : I met him one day near the UN building; lovely day, though I still had that liver trouble. The sun was veritably shining; I could smell the river. Then who comes along, haha, but good old . . ."

Guy Rancid let the breeze carry that one off too; he watched, mildly interested, as his words made it to the St. Germain and over the trees. Dixie had said nothing of course; he seemed to have exhausted all possible vibrations. Yet he had acquired at last the presence of a centrepiece in the Café Seine. People moved in anxious semicircles around him, lined sideways at the bar to watch him glowering, mustache like a mounted centipede. Guy counted to ten.

"Oh but I must tell you," he said, "about Orson Welles when I met him in Rome."

"Welles ?"

"Yes : the great man himself. I had been in Rome two days just scouting about for a company — you know, the Albee thing — think I told you — and I *knew* that Orson was about to make a picture in Paris. Well you can imagine my surprise bumping into him in *Rome*. Anyway, one day I was ambling along, and all of a sudden a chauffeured limousine comes veritably screeching round a corner, pulls up in front of an English bookstore and out pops (or plops) Welles himself, *him*. Oh he was, you know, all very paunchy and pouchy; in a great shattering hurry so I didn't say much to him; I do know that he bought about fifteen murder mysteries — but that's not important — just that he was so scrambly and furious, rather agile for a man his *size,* throwing down his money, tcetera, not even bothering to look around. I mean his best friend, perhaps Joseph Cotten, could have been standing right there and it wouldn't have . . . well, I felt like a fool really. He was very phantom-like, *third-mannish,* leaping into the car, swirling his cape, tcetera; you should really see his eyes close up, so tense and penetrating. Anyways, ran up to the car, but it took off with a whoosh, just left me standing there. That's actually the reason for our feud."

"Feud ?"

"But that's nothing compared to the Brando business."

"Brando ?"

"And Georges Wilson; you know, the French actor ? he always sits in the same café in the Rue Royale and pretends he's not famous; my God."

"Wilson ?"

"And oh yes, you remember when William Holden was living that summer in the Ile St. Louis; every morning you could see him walking."

"Holden ?"

"Anyway, about this Vangrin business."

"I know Vangrin."

"Who does ? You know Vangrin ? *The Case of the Latent Lady ? Lesbos in Transit ?*"

"Sure."

"What a nothing though, isn't he ?"

Then Guy Rancid rose and with him rose Maria. She crept within the crook of his sheltering elbow, her pale hairy wrist made to look extremely nude by a small mole quite near the palm; her fingers climbed up the string of Rancid's wrist to rest at last upon his bosom as they entered daylight. He was plump and actually had breasts; they palpitated inside his shirt.

But before they were beyond his reach, Dixie swooped about fiendishly and pinned a placard to Maria's blouse : *fermeture annuelle.* A schoolboy's prank, but met with looks of meaning on every face. *Poor Dixie* went the circular buzz along the bar and onto the terrace.

"See," said Nate, smiling at Dixie through a mouth of gold, "you've only been back in Paris a week and already you're loved everywhere."

Thirty-nine
The End Of Vangrin

In our beginning is our end, and Vangrin was no exception.
He had come a long way since those early years in
Paris when, moneyless, without a friend, his future grim,
he had wandered the Boulevard Strasbourg. The winter
nights how bitter chill they were, the wind how it whipped
the arid boulevard. Fond nightmares, these, in later years.
But *then,* such exquisite loneliness and remorse, such freedom
from repose or bliss, such avenging agony and contempt for
life. Vacuums build monsters, and his own solitude had
constructed in his mind's devolving eye, "such hoary devils
and miscarriages of faith as no mind could imagine without
the proper vocabulary." His brain grew gills, he learned to
thrive in other mediums, amphibious creature of the nether
life. For ten years he lived untouched, unseen, in rooms
remote and haunted, apparition unto himself, damned to
eternal soliloquy. This was the faith he knew, gleaned in a
garret above the city, sustained by the realm of the unlit
hallway. Old women, tubercular and pensioned off, died
behind closed doors of hacking breath; chimneys and windows descended in beckoning scale from his eighth floor
eaves trough. His daily diet of spaghetti and oranges and
soup of celery transformed him into someting lean, un-
healthy, hardly weighted, for "I was my own Auschwitz
and my own Dachau too." Suicide was contemplated;
evenings, he climbed onto the roof that sloped treacherously
from his window, naked as the day he was mocked. Each
twist of his body convulsed him further towards his end as
he lay full length on the acutest angle. Yet each evening,
aroused by the smell of gasoline from the traffic below, he
retreated; this was his strength, that "the fumes of life in
flux revived in me the will to will : it was as if, the soda of
my life gone flat, I had suddenly been revived with carbon;
to bubble once again." True, but the deadening effect of
the boulevards oppressed him always, tasked his soul, made
of his flesh a lifeless husk. Was there no more to life than

that terrible walk from Montmartre to the Seine ? could he ever conquer the feeling of irreparable loss which informed his evenings on the Boulevard Strasbourg ? the dim light of cafés, the hoarse call of whores, the endless corridor of mammoth, silent buildings ? And where were the respites, even in a life so barren ? where was the mythical widow (and her daughter) in a nearby room, living on raw meat and uncooked fruit ? where was the bright-eyed poetess, long of limb and calloused of finger, singing "Santiago" in the night ? where was the one-eyed Russian doorman, con-federate in poverty, a czarist to the boot, player of billiards and teller of tales ? Where, in fact, was Vangrin himself, as in his own mind he seemed to be ? the seething, cautious wit of the man, with mane and presence of a lion, profound in wisdom, capacious in despair ? Only the purple dust bore him witness : purple dust in the bed and in his pockets and purple dust when he coughed. Clots of it, congealed like lichen, everywhere; in his phlegm and feces, tongue and teeth, very smile, thoughts as well, "all carried this, my cross of fungi : trapped in a zone of purple quiet."

It took three phases to lift him from this hell. As follows :

1) *Sense of Paradox :* it was in a café in Pigalle that he first saw the woman who fulfilled so completely the vision he had had. She cast such an innocence in that suspicious place : recitress of poetry, calloused of finger, singing not "Santiago" but "Just Plain Bill" into the gloomy or dismal night. Her swept red hair, her fragile nose, her bucked, sensual teeth, legs razor-clean and sheathed in leather; her haunting, soft, redemptive look, the quiver of engaging smiles, the quick sharp movements of her body — jerking this way, that way leaning. "I would meet this woman," Vangrin admitted. "I would make talk with her." "Sure," said something odd beside him, "you wanna meet her I'll call her over : Hey *Jim !*"

2) *Sense of Humanity :* a fit of insatiable laughter over-came him one year. The construction of the human body, how comic it was, how hilarious were its modes of action, its turns and twitches and ingenious tricks. Hahahaha. When

you thought about ten fingers, ten little tubular bones; and knuckles ! Heeee. And what about the process of locomotion : first one leg, then the other leg, the fat behind bouyant and wincing, then the first leg again, then ... oh, he couldn't stand it, it was too much. And so ridiculous that the human face should contract and grin and wheeze and snort. Ha. But what was most amusing was to watch it eat : "no, oh it's too much, I can't take it ..." First, those knobby little tubes, grouped round a prong, stabbed at a hunk of dead ("Jesus, it's dead, is that funny, whewwww") meat, then it raised the deceased tissue and stuffed it down a hole in the face ! Haha. He was thrown out of restaurants, forced to eat alone under bridges or in the privacy of his room, fearful that he might accidently see one of them doing it. And, oh yes, "this is the best, oh my stomach ..." After they had stuffed the dead thing into the hole, they actually dropped it out another one, *wrapped* in brown casing ! And if it wasn't *brown* casing, if it was say *red* or *green* casing, they got all worried and hysterical ! Ha. He was arrested in urinals and toilet wells, observed by the Sûreté, shunned by his fellow primates, made to feel unworthy. But when they spoke to him, the sight and sound of that same little hole squeaking, shuttling from side to side ... and what where they, those horizontal puffs : yes *lips !* "Lips ! surrounding the hole where they stuffed down the deceased meat; God, it's too much." And above the lips, little hairs; and above the hairs, two more holes (smaller) for *smelling !* "Don't make me laugh again, I'm going to be sick, ohhhh." And then the entire system, skin, bones, blood, marrow, juice, cells, all connected and contained in a great brimming husk of meat; "Why don't they spill over ? why don't they swish ?" Haha. And the gooey brain, the squishy eyes, the bony head tilting this way that way for a better view. "But I've got to get used to it; God, it's so funny to watch." And finally, the arrogance of people, when equipped with proper nodules and regulation tubes, bones, protruberances, thinking themselves *beautiful.* Prodding their hair and appendages with tiny instruments; splashing ointment on surfaces filled with holes. And if you made a sound from one hole it was all right and often worshipped, but if you made a sound from the other, it was sinful; ha. "But I can take it, just give me time."

3) *Sense of Self* : with his first book, fame came to him at last. Suddenly and without warning, he was remarkable. His aphorisms caught fire, his dedications were on every lip, his *romans à clef* scandalized the circuit. How lovely his cheekbones suddenly were, elliptic in a high arc towards the eye, sweeping, majestic, oriental in their mystery; the frown line so deep it seemed to cut to his very brain; the shape of his skull pregnant as an egg, ovular, shelled in skin of purest gray; his hands now sensitive, the hangnails like the fins of minnows. "We cannot escape our daily bread," but who'd want to ? the image of oneself reflected in mirrors and pools and rivers and oceans, each day growing more pronounced and noble, cornices of the human spirit, tympanum of the human soul, Nobel Prizeworthy in its love of man and nature and the enduring virtues. "Experience strew my path like garlands for the living; nature renewed, beauty regained, its child." No more the Boulevard Strasbourg with its deep canyons of unrest; now visions in the American Express informed his life, the apocryphal V, beckoning spectre of the naked clerkess "wherein I saw that Motion was Truth unclothed, that Pan was abroad in the City and not to be denied His tribute." No more lonely, barren rooms, sterile dust, *aúto-da-fé;* now love and marriage and Zippi in plump attitudes near Neuilly, for "Love alone deflects our (universal) pain / And makes of night a sunlit reign." No more the mocked and shunned screwball, now the life of parties and cafés, *confident* of the waiter Maurice, resident of hotels from Luxembourg to the Gît-le-coeur. "Let me caution any young men about to embark; it is a sea of trouble. Take with you humility, sacrifice, the sense of what alone can bring you to fulfillment : and that is Truth, Beauty, an abiding trust in Man's ultimate Goodness. I believe self-consumingly in the future; that's what the past used to be, you know." As book succeeded book, *The Case of the Latent Lady, Lesbos in Transit,* women circled about his rising stature like mosquitos drawn to a naked light, claim-

ing in hoarse and tremulous voices some vestige of his
patience. ("I believe that *all* women are beautiful.") Then
Jackie filled him with ripe disease, first kernel of decay;
"Who could have remotely figured, a nice little broad like
that ?" Disenchantment reared its ugly tip. Then the pursuit
of F., tracking his plague through France and Spain, tasting
of the nut of death in the shadows of Madrid. "Yet how
can we be bleak for long / To suffer Good after suffering
Wrong ?" For now he was in the city once again, Master
of Clap, Vangrin the Victorious. And as final evidence of
his peculiar genius, his new work was now completed, the
Frontislines in Progress, or Pimples For Our Time, "gathering
into several maxims and evidences of dialogue, the exacting
sum of our days reflected." Everyone came to the reading.

Frontislines in Progress, or Pimples For Our Time by
Joris Vangrin, read in performance by Guy Rancid at the
Cave Dragon, being the watchlight(s) of several years and
one, admission 5nf ... Catalogia Gratis ...

(Guy Rancid stood under a green light, in a costume
depicting the seven vulgar sins; his voice was sonorous.)

Unum) Shit ! — Aristides MacCallum, announcing a
requirement, on the terrace of the Café du Dôme, April 2nd,
1950

Duo) If You Had Any More Nerve You'd Be A Fish —
Kyle Manna, beginning the famous Illogical Fallacy Movement for his generation, while facing the Panthéon over his
left shoulder as it rained, May 7th, 1952

Tria) I Love You — Danton Rockfern, explaining an
erection on the corner of the Rue Dauphine and the Rue
Mazarine, while talking to his conceirge to whom he was
heavily in debt, late afternoon, July 3rd, 1955

Quattuor) Yes, I Said, Yes Yes And Then Yes — Oral
Opalplum, recalling submission, as she emerged knee-deep
from a lukewarm piscine on the Quai du Louvre (near the
sign designating Through Traffic), June 16th, 1956

*Quinque) And When Thyself With Shining Foot Shall
Pass* — Irving Lemarque, actually rewriting, without ever
having read, *The Rubaiyat,* under the divine influence of
bifteck frites, literally days before his tragic death in the

washrooms of the American Drugstore, and a week before
his subsequent canonization on the fifth floor of the Hôtel
Moderne (the smell was awful), February 17th, 1958

Sex) *Citizen Kane Is A Great Film* — Ernie Itch-Davies,
destroying his reputation at the Café Tournon in a difficult
quadruple entendre, which failed and turned on him, to the
horror of all present, August 20th, 1957

Septem) *Can This Be Love, Darling?* — Birdy Seminal,
pretendress to the bone of Jules, trying out her new personality in hopes of lubrication, which unfortunately produced
only another dry run, while actually standing with one leg
heaved up on the Quai D'Orsay, a slight wind from the Seine
blowing ironic sewage on the cobble, the overprivileged night
of November 19th, 1960

Octo) *I Have Spent All Week Long Reading The Complete Works Of Herman Wouk* — Pablo Leary, just before
he was shot and killed, outside the Café de Seine, midnight
of September 5th, 1961

Novem) *My Tense Is The Present Imperfect* — Joris
Vangrin, admitting impediments at the Fête Jeanette, only
moments prior to Dalia's enema and occassioning remarks
of pithy candour and agitation, in the hope that Those Who
Seek Will Find And Those Who Find Will Discard And
Keep Playing, May 24th, 1962

Guy Rancid came to his final pause and waited. The
atmosphere was one of deafening silence. For everyone had
been told that the *Pimples* would be inclusive, that each of
them were to be mentioned by name in some subtle, vicious
mock; yet, without exception, the names were those of a
past generation of Quarter figures, hardly remembered, only
vaguely mythical. There was an aura of vast disappointment.
Guy Rancid stood transfixed; some motion of command had
stopped him. There was frenzied shuffling far off, a dwarfish
girl came rushing down the aisle and handed him some
additional material. He read the *Frontislines* for the second
time. But something had changed : the names occuring at
the close of each epitaph were now those of people present.
Mixed silence. There was still a selectivity, a control, which
grated those who remained omitted. The dwarfish girl came

down the aisle with new instructions and a sheath of further, quickly-scribbled notes. Guy Rancid read through the *Frontislines* a third, then a fourth, then a fifth time. More and more of those present were accommodated each reading, impaled delightfully; Vangrin's insights cut them to the quick, scarred many for life, left nasty aftertastes. Applause, hallelujahs, echoed off the frilled, plastered walls. At last there was a lusty cheer, "Hurray Vangrin !" and out of shadow strode the great man himself, his cape and forefront a luminous V, his jewellery completely phosphorescent. Guy Rancid smiled as they embraced; then, for a brief instant, his forehead seemed to recede and shorten and, miracle of that night, his facial organs *to rise* upon his face in ordered, wondrous scale from brow to jaw bone. "His organs is up ! they gone up !" came the swelling cry. "Hurray Vangrin, hurray hurray !"

Then the next night, there was a party outside Paris in honour of Vangrin, at the château of the widow Orgolian. The widow Orgolian was Vangrin's new patroness : buxom, middle-aged, "the proper and exact cliché," her nose lofty, Gallic, her bearing weighty, her paunch corseted by a hundred wires, her navel so deeply enmeshed in flab that it had long ago been given up for lost until Vangrin had rediscovered it one night, slightly swivelled in an overlap near her thigh, her legs irregularly muscled, her entire abdominal wall a Taj Mahal of sweat and grease; given to candid outbursts ("I lust after no man but Vangrin"), loving the idea of the young, scavenging for their secrets like a prowling slaver, inquiring, indiscreet, ridiculous. Her parties too were legend. And the Fête Vangrin possessed an air of fantasy. Illumined sloths swinging in the arbour, paper lanterns in every tree like fulsome apples, bursts of confetti flaking the lawns, wax flowers bordering every walk, each with its own silver candlestick melting petal and stalk into shapeless heaps of incense, the grand promenade strafed with berries, tiny pink helicopters flying overhead and dropping scented orange peels, the château itself bathed in a hundred lights, the pool swarming with strange, exotic fish and floating trays of food, Ethiopian houseboys abounding in gold mesh loincloths, numerous reptiles shifting through the grass, their backs inlaid with precious stones... she certainly knew how to throw a party or two, that Widow Orgolian.

But more curious than that, it was as if the past had been commissioned to perform the rites of autumn that August night. They were all there, like spectres plucked from the blades of windmills, insoluble in air once more. "There are no private hells," Vangrin was heard to say, "public utilities are everywhere." Mrs. Wainder of the American Express was there, and Zippi too; the Spanish, E. Bone, Nate and Irma; all heroes of the *Frontislines* sprouting their immortal *Pimples;* Guy Rancid, F., Fitz and Dalia; Trixy, Henry, the Seducer; Maynard Duncan, Tex and Red; Blackie, Jackie, Bonnie, Nora; Burkey, Debbie, Briar and Iris; Jan and Daphne, Rose and Constance; Gordie, Brynning, Dee and Dixie; Alice, Eye-Jay, Dan and Sandra; Stephen, Cheryl, Boot and Bobby; Valentine, Maurice and Egan; Penelope, the kraut and André; Jeanette, Albino, Yvonne, the Crudhead; Scythe and Voyd, Lemarque and Victor; Maria, Billie, Nina, Florine; Honey, "Jim," Anne the Pregnant; Matisse Motes and Bunny Zenner. "As it should be," Vangrin was overheard repeating, "for the past is a living substance, regurgitant, sticky." They danced on the lawns, climbed the trees, floated in the icky pool; Jackie apologized, Zippi annulled, F. forgave. Everywhere, teeming acts of supplication.

But it was too much; Vangrin was far from happy. "To have everything," he set it forth in doctrine, "is neither consummate nor a just reward." Far from the party he wandered alone, into fields, across bridges, towards barns. Behind him, the lights of the château winked, forming wens of colour; the shrill voices receded as he strove in darkness. The Boulevard Strasbourg, envisioned down to the last detail, crossed an angle of his mind : the hoarse cry of whores, the unlit canyon of brick and gutter, the sense of despair and loss, of regret triumphant. Where was it all now, the will to will ? the mythical brooding genius, sealed in a room above the city, confused, uprooted ? where was the purple dust in his bed, his pockets, when he coughed ? That at least had been *a time,* "localized, succinct." Far away, the party called his name, ghost of a sound dying across the vast Orgolian fields. In a little while they began to swarm like flies in his track, bearing torches that licked and furled in the wind. They marched in dumb procession, calling his name, moving into the forest, onto the farmland. Vangrin heard the muffled footsteps as they plodded, saw the swarm of flickering torches; and moved on. Grimly, he went unto that place, prescient, unafraid; gamely, they followed, intent on the pillaging of his soul, their fiery torches creating a false, deceptive dawn. How could they know of his late hunger ? his appetite for misery and vacuum ? his need, so to speak, for the riches of poverty, the private lunacy of the mind ? "Did they think the *Pimples* just grew overnight ?" He came to the barn wall. He brought his cape up to his face, masking his eyes against the spectacle of ever-intensifying light. Still they came, rapacious animals, fiendish suckerfish. What to do ? He would tell them the *Truth,* explain himself, wipe away the surface gum of pretense, destroy the pretense of surface gum, surface the pretense, gum and all. "Mind you, I should be seen easily," and he mounted a heap of dark manure, holding his hands aloft, beckoning softly, *seductively* the widow thought. A cry went up, followed by the thunder of anxious feet. In no time at all, they were within a hundred yards; and stopped. He was saying something; his lips moved, his hands gestured, his body twisted in an agony of metaphor. No one listened, for he was slowly sinking. The sight was incredible; each genuflection carried him deeper into the mire. Did he know this, was he aware ? It was to become a contested element in his legend. His voice grew shrill, he waved his arms; he sank up to the knee. His voice was a high, pitched wail, eerie in its quality of horror or forgiveness. "Shit," or "Lit" came from out his oval mouth; no one was quite sure; yet the torches were waved in a solemn tribute, giving to the line of fire the contours of a heaving monster. Vangrin sank to the chest, hysterical with probable wisdom, his ten fingers spread in declamation. Again the fierce carrying sound of "shiitttttt," or "liitttttt" swept across the Orgolian waste; dwindling finally to a croak. Then with a final bubbling rage, cape shrouding the last sight of his bewildered, incredulous, or peaceful face, he sank from our lives forever.

. . . In the Cimetière Père-Lachaise, there is a tomb and a repose; remote from the grand walks in that city of the dead, it stands alone, shielded from the rain by a weeping willow tree, bordered on three sides by rooted garlands of lily and tulip. If the stranger, passing by, is struck by the lonely vigil of that stone, let him approach. Chiselled in onyx and lapis lazuli, recessed in a field of strangely purple tiles, set apart in veils of thicket and bramble, will he find the true name of Vangrin, struck by the sculptor's sorrowing hand :

K A L S F A T E R

Forty

Whip Egan had come by his alias honestly; he was considered fast and sharp, and equipped with a tidy stinger. Or so he said. He certainly *talked* quickly, as if he were shouting directions from a moving car. Since I only met him twice, I was no judge of his attributes, but he was remembered by those who had known him, and commemorated in several tales that circulated endlessly. The tales celebrated his bouts of appetite. There was a time when people had made book against the day of his thirtieth birthday, but he was thirty now and hardly anyone remembered what a feat that was. Probably because he was out of fashion; a fate which awaited all performers. They remembered his indulgences and a few of his more notorious antics, but not the fact that they had once cared or given a mixed damn about his survival. In fact, three or four people thought he was dead, so it was fairly uncomfortable when he emerged suddenly and only a year or two older.

The first time I met him had been long before, during my first weeks in the Quarter. He had been at a café called La Fourmi Dansante, sitting at a long table, barren but for a bottle of cognac and four shot glasses. With him had been three women : triplet sisters, presumably in their teens. One always knew if Egan were in a room or not, because he had a very specialized delivery which carried the atmosphere. People were always a little more agitated when he was within sight or sound; he could cause indigestion merely by recognizing your existence. He was a master of disquiet. Jules the Seducer was playing guitar in La Fourmi Dansante all that week, and Henry Rotter, as was his custom, had rounded up a few of us from the Café Buci and herded us over in single file. Even at that time, Whip Egan had passed into relative obscurity; either his feats were no longer considered impressive, or his alias had not been renewed by the current powers. However, he was introduced to me promptly; he was, if nothing else, a living example of the past scene.

He began to talk at once, offering me great quantities of cognac and the rights to any future monologues. I realized immediately how disquieting he could be. He liked to survey his own situation as if it were constantly in crisis, and I surrendered to the full treatment. He talked very fast and covered all the units of his life simultaneously; it was exhausting. But what I remembered most clearly was a point he had made concerning his own peculiar lot in life.

"Notice I'm not handsome; not even that clever : people don't come to me like they come to Brynning or dirty Jules : it takes me maybe five times the energy to move the same inch : maybe ten times the action to get talked of at all : I've been running this way three four years : if I stopped for a week, they wouldn't know my name : I'll do anything though : all the stories about me true : *Whip Egan* pretty good description of how I handle it : I worry about keeping the pace right : don't hardly sleep : always pushing : not even time to enjoy it, just check it off : but I'll tell you what's coming next : abstention : leads to purity : what an indulgence that'll be : but how to do it and not disappear's the problem : abstention going to calm me down : no fuck no drink no talk : I'll be goddamn saintly."

He never did conquer the problem of disappearing from view; the moment he took up his *abstention,* he vanished from sight. People still recounted the old anecdotes, yet if he had appeared on the scene (as he apparently did from time to time), he would have gone completely unrecognized. Not that he had become suddenly monastic; but, as predicted, a week after he shut his mouth and closed shop, the alias *Whip Egan* was cruelly retired. In less than a year, only the old order, such as Nate and the Seducer, could claim they had known him at all.

Still, if a man wants to try for a little innocence and purity, I suppose that is his business. Certainly, no one else I knew was interested in the sport. Anyway, when I finally met him for the second time, it took me a long while to recollect who the hell he was. It was at the Café Monaco, early in the fall, and I was walking down the stairs to the toilet. Someone was using the phone in the small corridor at the base of the staircase; by using the phone, I mean he was dialing numbers and then hanging up; the toilet was in use, so I stood there watching him dial numbers for maybe twenty minutes. He wore an oversized raincoat; his baggy trousers were tied about the ankles with string.

"I'm Whip Egan," he finally said, but there was something wrong with his voice and it sounded at first as if he had introduced himself as Whiff Eagle. He looked me in the eye menacingly.

"So ?"

"Whip. Egan." he said, taking a little more care this time.

As a matter of fact, it was Whip Egan; he hadn't changed at all. Although his colour was a little gray.

"You. Remember. Me. Don't. You. You. Idiot."

"Oh yah."

"Well. I'm. Back. Prick."

"How are you ?"

"Good. Very. Good. A. Little. Irritable."

I recalled very quickly his little talk about abstention and

309

saintliness, so naturally I expected him to be beatific and calm and totally at peace. He looked awful.

"How's your abstention kick?" I asked.

"Haven't. Had. A. Woman. In. Can't. Remember. How. Long. No. Booze. Neither. First. Time. I've. Talked. In. Maybe. A. Year."

"Well, you sure got purity of phrase there, Whip."

"Thank. You."

"You feeling all right?"

"Go. Fuck. Yourself. I'm. Sorry."

"That's okay. Look, if it bothers you so much, why don't you give it up?"

"Got. To. Stay. Pure. You. Stupid. Shit."

"I don't give a damn what you do."

"Innocence. Difficult. Pass. The. Word."

"Soon as I leave you."

"I'm. Just. Passing. Through. A. Phase. Very. Sour. Got. To. Stop. Thinking. Next."

"You're sure an example to us all, Whip."

"Kiss. My. Ass. Sorry. About. That."

"I understand."

"Let. Every. One. Know. You. Saw. Me. Tell. Them. I'm. Making. It. Circulate. My. Name."

"Will do."

"Whip. Egan. Say. Achieving. Purity. But. At. Great. Sacrifice. Go. Away. You. Bother. Me. Kid."

Forty-one

Nora came down the street. A beautiful animal with lovely red hair and freckles like pepper up and down her skin. But her breeding had been too refined and had turned on itself; so all that was subtle and calm in her nature had soured long ago. But she came down the street. She came down the Rue Buci, past the billiard parlour above the *tabac,* past the stalls heaped with oranges and lemons and rotting apples from the orchards of Brittany, past the deserted Brasserie with its chairs still piled on the terrace and two or three men drinking inside at the bar. She came to the Rue Mazarine. She had the albino with her. She had the albino by the hand and it was sniffing at the cracks in the pavement. Its hands were pink and eager; it wore a light beige peaked cap and its tiny eyes squinted straight along the brim to cross where the point made a gambler's shade against the sun. At the Rue Mazarine, Nora crossed the road. The albino raced in front of her, trying to walk in the cast of her shadow. Now, the albino had crossed the road to get to the other side, but Nora had crossed for another reason : she was looking for something, in the Café Buci, on the terrace, among the tables, under the Gottlieb. She moved with a certain dazed elegance. There was no mistaking the quality. Her thighs rubbed together noisily, sound caused by the rustled friction of her jeans. "Some sweet Nora," someone said, a hairless American Indian, listening for the chafe as she whistled by. Nora peered around. At each table, people were drinking and laughing; some were drinking café crème, others citron pressé, still others jus de tomate or bière Strasbourg or ordinary wine. They drank openly and made no secret of their tastes. There were those, too, who were laughing exclusively, some at her, others at the albino, still others who laughed at still others and still others who laughed at them. Everyone was laughing, in fact, in one way or another. You couldn't be sure what was funny or who to laugh at; you had to pick it up by ear. But Nora was above that sort of thing; hardly breaking wind, she came into the street again. She had been looking for Fitz, but he wasn't there.

He wasn't there, but I was. I watched her move off again down the Rue Mazarine, the albino trailing as before, its fingers hooked to the notch of her belt. I wonder what she wanted, I thought, I wonder who she was looking for ?

"Some sweet Nora," said the Indian again.

He was laughing, of course. He went to the bar and brought back a tray of cafés crèmes; he had to laugh when I thanked him. In fact, he had a fit and spilled the crèmes down his suit.

"Some sweet Nora," he said. He tried to control himself after that. But he certainly expected me to return the compliment.

I wasn't feeling particularly fine and I didn't want to laugh. Many people had begun to avoid me. But the Indian looked at me for some time waiting for it to happen, so finally I unloaded a low, unsatisfactory hoot.

"Say, you're okay," said the Indian.

Whenever he laughed, his lips drew back like eyelids and all you saw were the pinks of his gums; the tops of his teeth were black and the water in his mouth was yellow.

"I wonder who she was looking for ?" I asked him.

He shook his head; neatly suppressed a paroxysm.

"Wait till I stop laughing," he said. "I know a few stories . . ."

He stopped laughing for a while, but when he offered me the sugar (it was wrapped hysterically in white and blue paper) he started up again. "Some sweet kid, that Nora," he said. "I could tell you a few things . . ."

"Go ahead," I said.

"I would," he said, "but you're not laughing. I don't trust a man who don't laugh."

"I'm laughing," I said, "on the inside. That's where I always laugh."

"Oh," said the Indian, "I guess you're okay then. I'm still a little uncomfortable though."

"I'm a quiet laugher," I said, "but I'll laugh at anything."

"I kind of like you," said the Indian. "Do you play lacrosse ?"

"On the inside," I said, "I play a quiet game."

"I sure would like to play some lacrosse," said the Indian.

What had happened, he explained, was that Nora had just returned from Tunisia; she had gone there with Fitz the West Indian for a few months and now she was back. That's who she was looking for. But she wasn't going to find him, because Fitz was through with her, and anyway they travelled in different circles. She had some awful sex disease that he had given her and now she disgusted him. But did I know about the famous Fête Jeanette? about Fitz under the table and the albino on the eaves trough? It seems that the party was in Jeanette's old room in the Gît-le-Coeur and it was too small so Nora put this albino of hers onto the eaves trough; and Fitz was so tall that he had to sit under a table the whole night. Hadn't I heard about it? everybody knew. Well so when it was time to go, Nora began looking for the goddamn thing and she sees the West Indian under the table and she's too tired to notice the difference, so she runs away with him to Tunisia instead. They get about as far as the Spanish frontier when Nora begins to sober up; she sees she got Fitz there and she starts to panic. Where's my goddamn albino? she asks. It's being took care of, says Fitz. It's being took care of, my darling, and we are on the Spanish train 1st Class bound for Tunisia. Isn't that great, the way he said it? And we are on a Spanish railroad going to Manfried, Africa. I love that. We are just on the crest of the Pyrénées, my darling, and by morning we'll be in Tunis. Some sweet Fitz, though. So they got to Tunisia and put up at this deprived hotel and Nora got all depressed and begun to eat like a pig; sure enough, what with all that fried food, she got dysentery bad, they call it Tunisian stomach there, and her sphincter muscles went. Fitz couldn't make love but they kept sliding out of bed; them sphincters just caved in. Meanwhile, the albino has been left on the eaves trough see, and it sits out there the whole night squealing. When the Fête's over with and Jeanette is cleaning up, she finds the goddamn thing still out there, running up and down the eaves trough like a worried chicken see. What in Gods name is *that* doing *there*? So she takes the thing and locks it in a cupboard for two days and two nights; but it whimper and scratch and make a terrible racket, and finally she lets it out and feeds it Pablum. Then she rapes it and buys it this little peacap. Come on, ain't you heard this story, it's famous? Well, when Nora came back a couple days ago, she starts looking for her albino and she hears around that Jeanette has got it. It's mine, she says, I trained it. She got plenty of class, that Nora. So she goes up to Jeanette's new place and sure enough the albino is there, wearing its little peacap. Jeanette has built all these hoops and ladders, and the thing just keeps jumping through them every day and climbing them up. Nora can see right away that the thing's been done some damage to. I mean carnally, you know. And that this Jeanette has been having sexual congress with it pretty good. You've been *interfering* with my albino, she says, you filthy poove. Jeanette don't blink an eye : I've invested a lot of time and money in this thing, she says, while you been away having sinful knowledge in Tunisia. I've been working out a whole act while you've been having regular coitus with that nigger. We go on at the American Centre a week Wednesday and no whore of Babylon is going to stop me. I'll stop you honey, says Nora; I've got this awful sex disease : you don't give me back my albino, I'll sit on all your toilet seats. So that's how Nora got the albino back, and she's looking for Fitz these days cause he can cure her of that awful disease he gave her. But Fitz don't want no part of her, he's had all the parts he can take. But wasn't that a lovely line though in the train, Your albino is in good hands, woman, and we is on this Spanish train moving down to old Tunisia. Some sweet Fitz.

The Indian certainly knew how to tell a story, all right. Of course, I didn't have the heart to tell him as how I had been at the Fête Jeanette. Or that myself and Bugs and Anne the Pregnant had ourselves administered the celebrated enema. (Where were they now, I wondered, if not in some far off gloomy corridor of time ?) So I sat there in the Buci, sadly bemused by the irony of that secret, recalling, over a bought café crème and seated across from a talkative Indian, the details of that enchanted scene : there was Dalia belly-down on the rug, wool skirt chucked to the rump; there was Bugs and I each with a leg, disentangling corset and sanitary belt; there was Burkey, kind man, holding the sweaty head of Dalia herself, submitting tenderly as her nails fleshed his throat; there was Anne the Pregnant re-entering the room, the snakish tube swinging obscenely in a clutch of fingers; there was the act itself in quick arrangement, the tube inserted, water flushed up the bushy tail, the sudden haunting purge of splut and bile . . .

But the Indian was laughing again; I had unsheathed another lump of *sucre fin*. "You're really some guy," he said, holding his sides now. Then he stopped and looked at me awhile. You could see he was a kindly Indian.

"But goddamn," he said, "it's not the same thing when you laugh on the inside. It's sort of snobbish."

"I'll try and do better," I said.

"But don't take no more sugar," he said, "my gut hurts."

"Right."

"You're okay," he said, "too bad you're out of fashion now. I hear they caught you talking to Whip Egan a while back. It's a dirty shame."

"Fuck them," I said.

So we chatted again about Fitz and Nora, puzzling out the quirks of fate and savage justice, and the Indian had to retell the story of them on the train, adding this time a few unseemly details of their life in Tunis. He braced himself just prior to his favourite lines and escaped with a minor fit. A hairless little Sioux he was, his face wrinkled and ravaged by too much laughter, chewing a wad of scented beechnut.

And suddenly something cold came over me, or was it something hot, at any rate something thermostatic, like the thawing of an old want, full of pain as it melted down, like a frozen foot finally melting in the sun. I knew the feeling well; it came upon me from time to time, old bug of destruction, and I felt a keen affection for it even now : the way one might recollect a nightmare in tranquillity and discover with relief that the worst side of oneself still lived. First it was the cold shakes, as if an icicle were spearing its way through my body; then the hot shakes, as if some searing brand of iron were trying to burn out the marks of a vampire, remnant of another day. It was too deep a feeling to kick aside — what with the laughing Indian and my memories converging — and it staved me like a spike to that fate around the corner. I rose, about to part company, horrendous act already predated, watching myself on the other side of motion, an awestruck everyman counting up his deeds at the gate of St. Peter. You know the feeling. *Nora,* crossed my mind at various angles, her pepper skin, pot ash, albino mobile (like the turtle in *A Rebours,* it struck me), diseased in some wondrous sexual way, enticing me with dumb stylish eyes in some drab cubicle of a room, offering the purgation of a lifetime, *first come first purge,* down down into the pit I go, and what was it that Vangrin had said ? there are no private hells, public utilities are everywhere.

"You're not going off," said the Indian. "Some guy."

"I've got to," I said. "I'm feeling all funny."

"Know what you mean," said the Indian, "but there ain't nothing a good laugh can't cure."

"Do you know where Nora lives ?" I asked, very shaky on my feet.

"Say, you don't want to go up there," said the Indian.

"I run deep," I said, almost fainting dead away.

"You ought to keep away from her," said the Indian, "she got this awful ..."

"I know I know," I said, slipping a few inches towards the floor, *so we get to hell by slow degrees,* and what was it that Barbey D'Aurevilly had said to Huysmans when it was over or just begun ? You must choose between the muzzle of the pistol or the foot of the cross.

"I won't be responsible," said the Indian. "I wash my hands of the whole business."

What was he saying now, offering me another *sucre fin* to unwrap, ordering in his essential goodness more café crème, and I sitting on the floor now like some nauseous Buddha, gifts to receive, but not that gift far down the block itching for the new cock incumbent.

"Just give me her address," I said, coming out of a swoon. "Just for god sakes give me the street; all right, just throw out a number, any number."

What was he doing now, adrift on the topic of dread diseases, delivering a tract on Indian hygienics, gesticulating wildly as he demonstrated how wigwams were insular.

"But I've got to have her address," I said. "It's something I've got to do."

He dropped his arms like shanks plumbing a well and raised me by the armpits. I had been happy down there; I struggled a little bit.

"If you were a regular Indian," I said, "you wouldn't do this to me."

He took the wad of beechnut from his mouth and ground it into a tiny ball between his fingers; then he popped it back onto his cerise tongue and shook his head sadly the way an Indian would.

"That ain't fair," he said. "You're taking advantage of my nature."

But he wrote something at last, on a scrap of store-bought paper. Despondently, as if it had been weighted with a hundred sorrows, he pushed it over.

"Some sweet Indian," I said, still weak in the knee, but leaving.

It Begins : Into the Hôtel Des Quatre Nations, clawing up the unrailed stairs, reindeer to some imp of the perverse. And what was it that Clive Bell had said ? there are no breaks in tradition, only the continuum of history in process; and what had Sterne said long before that ? we judge the marketplace each according to his fare. I knocked. There was no light anywhere; yet I could hear the muffled sounds of footsteps, bedsprings, wailing, through the door. It opened a crack, enough to admit into the hallway a stale familiar smell, sweet and sickly, like that of an abandoned candle burning incense through the night.

"Yes ?"

"Nora ?"

"Yes."

"Nora."

Albino As The Colour White : I lived with her two weeks. Her room never caught the sun except to filter dust into cones of floating germ. It was a passable existence. There was one thing I insisted on, however : "Darling Sweetheart Thing, that (censored) albino has got to go." But she put it in a blue wardrobe case, when not in use, instead. It was a tolerable arrangement. Afternoons, I took it for walks along the Quai with our backs always to the sun, and into Métros to hunt mice. It was a fine seventeen-year-old albino, all white ("mind you, a Moby Dick you're not"), with pink pellet eyes and a tiny winking nose. It seemed to be made not so much of bone as cartilage, soft skull like a baby's, complexion of a sinister snowiness, legs and arms as unsteady as the joints of an upright colt. It sat all day long on the floor, with its legs tucked into the haunch, scribbling with coloured pencils on thin airmail paper, the beginnings of circles. It roamed about like an object to be taunted and conversed upon, a piece of fleshy driftwood, sometimes slapped, more often soothed, roombroken to the letter, scratching at the door with three fingers on a testicle, scampering to the toilet well with the eagerness of a child at Christmas, as if its functions were in themselves a treat and a celebration. It existed best within four walls, content to watch itself evolve and grow ("they're huge at twenty-one"), ruminating on its own fart by the hour. Thou happy, dumb, unworried creature.

The Utmost Heart Of Nora : While Nora, on the other hand, was so quiet it was like living with a ghost, a succubus that sucked your glands dry in stylish contractions. What was her style ? It was a remote sense of mastery over her environment, a conquering aplomb. Nothing was more amazing in her mode of life than the rising above it, for she was unsinkable and grand, and when you kissed her sticky ass you kissed a lady. There was a regal condescension to her habits, a we-are-not-amused control. Yet it was in no way defiance, only quality; she did not succumb so much as envelop, and there was an air of the private school in everything she did. And she smoked marijuana all the time; so incessantly that the room was always thick with it and it was always in my lungs and in my clothes and my mouth and skin smelt of it. There wasn't a time when the taste of it wasn't sweet on my tongue or lush in my belly and to breathe was to breathe it in and to exhale was to rid yourself of dust and scent. To walk around day and night in the quick fading daze that pot builds in the mind, without

a respite, always awake and feeling your eyes, always talking
because there was no other way of knowing you weren't
asleep, existing on another frequency where only dogs could
hear you, your life a constant defilement, the degradation
approaching by a dozen secret avenues its own proud per-
fection, each hour another skinless embryo, fouled with muck
and drying in a corner : Christ, it was wonderful.

Our Life Together : "There they go," the buzzing went in
the Buci, the Monaco, the Old Navy, the Tournon, while
the creatures of the Café Seine chuckled mildly as we passed
in household procession, Nora and I arm in arm, our legs
rubbing together to lend us traction, the albino snooping
faithfully in our wake like a tracking greyhound. We could
be seen in the late afternoons, walking from Mabillon to
the Rue de Rennes : fashionable six o'clock strollers out to
lunch. Otherwise we were homebodies, generally, with only
the grain of our days to follow.

Each morning we went to bed, sleeping from seven to
two in the afternoon. At two o'clock precisely we awoke,
for albino was hungry by that hour and one of us had to
rise to feed it strange concoctions. Then we lay in bed
chatting of this and that.

"Darling," I said, stroking a warm, freckled limb.

"Yes ?" she said royally, the line of her body compounded
of blankets and stale sheets, now rising in a mound, now
collapsing in a heap.

"Was it good ?" I said, hand in circular motion on a
solid shaft of muscle near the thigh.

"Was what good ?" she said imperially, turning the
wall of her ass towards me, her sense of time and place
beginning to clear.

"Me and You," I said, striving against the convention of
the move, raising tenderly, and in some heat, the haunch
of her leg and slipping anxiously towards the soft slot of
her tail.

"Oh that," she said sovereignly, swivelling away with an
easy disregard, abandoning in a shift sinister my midafternoon
erection.

"That," I said, pursuant, the snub of my organ pummeling
through a haze of jelly, calling soft her name, my lips dried
fast to the blade of her shoulder.

"Sure I guess it was okay."

We then dressed and had our first joint of the day and
released albino from the wardrobe case. If we were thirsty
we always had the wine, fermented now to vinegar; if we
were in the mood to nosh, there was the caramel tin or the
Oxo bars, the jar of warm marmalade, the demi-litre of
soured milk, the licorice pellets in the lacquer dish, the jug
of rainwater on the sill.

By four, it was time to vomit in the sink. Nora went first,
crawling briskly on all fours; she did not lower her head
into the lovely diagonal pan, but raised it instead, letting the
genteel threads of cheese and peas and undigested starches
spurt down her chin like falls over a rock into the bright
porcelain. She made a noble grunting sound. And what a
truly lovely animal she was, I thought, even as the gruel in
my chest heaved and clotted, what grace and presence and
patrician calm; why even when she rose at noon and shat
in those small brown waterproof bags by the sink, even then
there was something noble and tragic to her moves; nothing
could take from her the majestic squat, the bright burning
look of pride.

At five we walked an hour in the streets. We walked
along the Quai des Grands Augustins, past the stalls, the
bridges, the *brasseries,* the people, the buildings, the Institut
de France, the archways leading beneath it into the Rue de
Seine, along the Quai Voltaire with its Hôtel Voltaire, past
the old Gare d'Orsay on the Quai d'Orsay, the old circular
clock on the quai side of the Gare keeping perfect time, the
Gare itself mammoth and grimy like some deserted hippo-
drome, onto the Pont des Arts or down the quai steps to
the cobbled bank itself, beneath the bridge to listen to Nate
the Accordion and his kraut assistant or watch Henri Matisse
Motes frame his biblical epics in charcoal, letting albino
run free under ramps and suspensions.

"There they go," the buzzing went in the cafés as we
returned; "she got this awful sex disease," would come the

echoes down the corridor of the St. Germain (diminishing in size as we inhaled), followed by insincere greetings from the Old Navy, the Mabillon, the Café de Flores, the Lipp. But we were on our daily way to Raffy's for the big meal in the Rue du Dragon and we ignored their insidious gossip and their encyclopedic taunts : *Jeanette, Albino, Eaves Trough, Enema, Fitz, Dysentery, Tunis, Barcelona, Awful Sex Disease, Whip Egan, Indian, Hôtel des Quatre Nations, Freckles, Blue Wardrobe Case, She Shit In Little Brown Bags Near Sink.* Let them talk, I thought, It's only talk, What does talk matter, It can't hurt you when it's only something said, Let them go and talk, make words, It's only the sound comes from their chest and through their throats, A little air resonates on cords, It's just talk.

Raffy's in the early evening about six-thirty when it's deserted except for the old people and the tables are stacked with baskets of baguettes and trays of sauce; like an old cellar banquet room, barren and homely, with clean wooden floors and smoke coming from the kitchens. I always ordered the *steak tartare,* with the *champignons à la grecque* to start with and the *crème de marron* to finish up, washed down by some bottled cider. It was our only meal and our lives seemed to deepen over the hot food as if flushed from shadowy perimeters. Nora always had the *pâté de lapin* to begin, then the *coquille St. Jacques,* washed down by a bottle of Muscadet. The albino was always ordered the *potage légumes,* then the *canard à l'orange* which Nora cut and deboned before letting it eat. Over our victuals, we held brief conversation.

"So tell me sweetie, what do you think ?"

"I don't talk when I eat."

"Because I'm getting annoyed at everyone's attitude. I really am."

"You've got food in your mouth. Just chew please."

"Who do they think they are though ? A bunch of impotent misfits. Fashion Schmashin; who gives a shit about Fashion."

"Are you going to shut that mouth of yours, or what ?"

"All right now look Nora, just don't get so fucking haughty with me, okay? I'm just trying to be pleasant."

"I don't need *pleasant*. So keep your paranoia to yourself. Let's eat quietly for once. You talk talk talk talk talk. Have you ever seen yourself talk? With that raw guck in your mouth, believe me it's not *pleasant*."

"Look who's talking about *pleasant* all of a sudden. Have you ever seen yourself? With that pink little freak . . ."

"Shut up."

"With that slavering little freak . . ."

"You filth."

"Leper."

"Dud."

"Whore."

"Prick."

By eight o'clock we were on the street again. When we arrived at the Monaco, it was almost nine. We took our place in the secluded L, watching for them as they descended the steps to the toilet well, seeing Brynning and Gilchrist, Nate the Accordion, Guy Rancid, seeing even Dixie at times, Maria, Dee, Henry Rotter. We ordered petits crèmes, our outward flesh resonating to the sounds of the Gottlieb; the bar wound like the Serpentine; the sound of talk grew like a day's stubble in the air. That was when Nora began to make her joints again, stuffing the disques bleus entire. Then we were fading out of it again, puffing and squinting and waving the smoke down the staircase; the corners of the air turned yellow and misty and the filth of our bodies began to creep in sudden animation, running with the sweat and the fleabites like miniscule Frankensteins.

At eleven, we walked to the Café Buci. The hairless American Indian was there, looking at me mournfully and hardly laughing. Nora took the albino home and came back and we sat together and watched them pass. The Gottlieb rang its points in grating sirens near the doorway. We lit up again and I was dizzy. They came by and sometimes shook our hands but more often merely nodded and sat down at other places for a crème or a demi. The nauseous part went away and the dizziness entered its other phase. ("How many

phases you got, Nora ?") I talked to myself because Nora
was letting something else happen to her, very pleased to
let it happen with her eyes closed and one hand holding the
edge of the table.

At two o'clock, we walked to the Café Tournon. We
went through the Carrefour de l'Odéon into the Rue St.
Sulpice. The towers of the church kept moving against the
sky. I sensed the sea monsters inside that place moving
about in deep water. We went down the Rue Tournon
towards the red *tabac* sign, then into the café itself where
Dixie was playing cards behind the fake partition. We sat
facing the door and watched them come in. We ordered the
omelettes, and Nora put her hot head to my neck and
scratched my arm and shoulder. We lit new joints and
studied the colour of the omelettes, but we couldn't taste
them and didn't eat them finally. Dee came over and ate
them both and went away without a word.

"Ewwww Nora, what I'm gonna gif you baby."

Five o'clock and we can go. Saying goodby to no one
interested. Into the morning air; but having luckily escaped
the dawn. The regular cafés beginning to open, waiters not
yet in their uniforms sweeping the garbage into the bubbling
gutters, the trucks moving away from Les Halles, crated
with vegetables or returning empty, leaving a trail of cabbage
leaves along the St. Germain. Into the hotel already daylit.
Nora making the bed like a duchess, pulling back the top
sheet nicely. I, all jacked up, dropping my clothes in the
corner like a defecating milliner. Nora naked to the window,
drawing the drapes. Into bed; working out exotic poses;
each following the demands of little plots. Yank, groan,
snort, swish, crackle, pop, fart, sniff, wheeze, grunt, blip,
growl, slap-wap-slap-wap-slap-wap-slonk . . .

Disaster Strikes : No dream lasts forever and all joys are
susceptible to sorrow; illusions deflate, once contacted by
the pins of life; the balloon bursts, the helium escapes, all
happiness rages, drones and dies; more than that, decay
sets in, cancer to all good things, warps the mirror, corrupts
the soul, turns will to putty and ebullience to disgust. And
so our pleasure dome collapsed : Nora J had pubic lice.

The Death Of Love And The Philosophy Of History :
Weeks before the hairless Indian had warned me. But I
hadn't cared, compulsion drove me not to care, and Nora's
rumoured sex disease was no more than what the imp had
offered. Deep in the mud, the smells are cool. So Nora
and I let the worst of it ride, not thinking about the worst
of it; for we had the albino and the room, the bed and the
cafés, the walks along the quai and the whispers behind our
back to keep off the draught. Then the bugs came. They
came in the night. The old ones had died off, but they
had left their eggs and now their eggs were ripe. The lice
wiggled from them into the swamp of warm red hairs,
crawling, nipping, creating a general itch. Nora's *mons* was
thick and hard, shaped at times like an inverted flask, bell
and neck and lower bowl. Her pubic fuzz had a coarse,
resistant texture, a quarter-inch in depth, swept into thinning
curls below the navel but bristling upright nearer the orifice;
from belly to asshole, there was a good half-foot of choice
breeding ground, a veritable deer park. The lice orgies
began and the scratching also. It was the scratching that
was the worst. When it began, they were crawling all the
time, teeming among the tufts; where the crotch hair thinned,
they'd wriggle like fish out of water only to fall back again
into the fur. Nora was scratching all the time; she scratched
through her jeans in the afternoons and wore a damp loin
cloth. In the cafés, she'd be in the toilets four times an
hour trying to cool it out, deflecting tap water to hose down
her groin. But in bed was the worst. Her nails clawed by
the hour, a rasping, grating noise like that of teeth on velvet.
Before she won sleep, her hands would come up bloody,
strewn with hairs like a barber's wrist. We bought the jellies
and salves but they did no good. We stopped making love
and I knew the eggs were on me too. The albino was drawn
to the noise, but we kept it at a distance and it spent more
than half its day in the wardrobe case. Nora would not let
the pain show and that was class. The blood was always
there where she had scraped away the skin, and at night I
could smell her and see the pimples bloom on her body. The
lice kept spawning. The morning of the fourth day, she

shaved her crotch and belly. She worked on the salves and for a while the itching stopped. Then her hairs began to prickle again and in a week she was sporting a thin gloss and the eggs were still there and the lice spawned closer to the pad of flesh. It was during the second time round for Nora that I got my own. I shaved myself quickly and applied the salves and waited. Nora began to stay in every day to scratch and pluck. She was pulling off the hairs by hand now and her groin was matted with scabs. Whenever I was down from a joint of pot, I'd say, "We'd better go to the hospital, Nora," but she'd only lie there, eyeballs rolling, mouth gaped, fingers plucking methodically like mechanical depilatories. The curtains were always drawn, the room was always dark; the silence hung like a flag draped on a bier, broken only by the deep scratching sounds of Nora, partly dreaming, nails like ice picks in the dim. We still had our domestic habits : we shaved together every morning; but helplessly I watched love fade into the grating noise of fang on stubble. It was almost over. Then one night, the final straw : Nora jerked herself upright with a look of fear and said "Shhhhhhhh." We heard it together, coming from the wardrobe case, the familiar scratching, the exact same scent. "Oh no !" she screamed and leapt from the bed. She unzipped the case frantically, her nails filed thin as needles now; there was the albino, pants chucked to its knees, its face in a curious and horrified smile. It rubbed, it scratched, it itched with lice. "God God !" howled Nora as she led it to the bed. So we lay for two days the three of us, a chorus of grating motion and furtive scratches. But on the third day, I rose and packed my bags. "The main thing is, be healthy," I said and went out the door.

You live with disease for a little while and lo and behold, you begin to need it. Cycles decline, experience becomes one's proper grammar. History devours tradition, that's what Roger Fry had said, years before, and I could see now that it was true. Perhaps Roger Fry had had pubic lice, perhaps that was how he knew; no matter. What counted was that Maupassant had had it, that all rivers run into the sea and the sea is full. Yet when it was time to go or go under, to break the wave, cull from the mind that odious haft of time, you wondered if you still had the native cunning to know *when's enough.* Funny thing, it was easy; it wasn't hard to leave at all. One day you noticed something was wrong, that love was only a corpse growing hair; you packed your bags, you hailed a taxi, and — before you could say *My bile got funny green raisins* — you were suddenly standing on the Carrefour de l'Odéon, in the rain of course, but free. It was as if everything were linear after all and you could laugh at cycles and know that they only happened to other people; the open end was there at last. Thank God for Hume, I thought, thank God he defrocked all those circles; thank you God. Yes, it was so easy it was frightening, and you began to wonder if there was anything so important that you couldn't cut it out of your life like a dead branch when you had to. Some sweet imp. I watched those weeks drop off my tail, like chopped meat oozing from a sideboard, and went my separate linear way. Hairless, of course, but still intact.

Forty-two

"What in the fuck is going on in this city isn't anybody normal ?"

Victor : tall and loose-limbed, a month off the boat train, emerging from two week's residence in the Monsieur le Prince. Hairline recessive, kinky, rising in small waves to form a duck peak at the rear of his skull; hair tonic giving to his head a brilliant sheen, and to his hair the appearance of whipped paste. His face arranged by its own natural anger, cheerfulness waging an endless and ironic battle against the converging frown; nose all aquiline and pointed bone, lips shaped to an inverted horn, jaw fierce and dimpled, cheeks rippling in mock rage, thick neck unshaven, thoughts volcanic, tone embittered : all of it wasted on a man so simple.

"I mean who in hell is that? Who in the fuck does he think he is? What is this, walking-around-in-pajamas all day? Big deal."

"He's too tired to dress," I said, "that's the way he is."

"So I'll buy him a pillow. What a shit."

"You don't understand," I said, "he's suffering from angst."

"Angst schmangst; he's a prick."

Victor, countering the weight of his body like a basketball player in mid-pivot, strides along the Vaugirard. Peers through the iron gratings into the green of the Luxembourg; like an eagle circling for prey; like a jackal creeping towards carrion; like a boxer searching for shadow; like a whore spewing out gruel. Distracts attention from his distended paunch by drawing notice to his muscular arms. Expects a performance wherever he looks, vulcan-faced and not too closely.

"So tell me, what is this Café Turn On."

"Tewr nohn," I said.

"They're just sitting around on their asses, right? I drather lay on a beach somewhere. They got a beach in Paris?"

"No. We're inland," I said, "but we've got a river."

"What's this *we* bit; everybody talks about *we,* or *my, our, his;* what are they doing, buying up the city?"

"Well," I said, "one gets to feel a certain possessiveness here."

"I thought you told me nobody wants nothing? listen, don't crap a crapper, Garb; either they want or they don't want : what?"

"Okay," I said, "escaping isn't a negative act; these people aren't just escaping *from,* they're escaping *to.*"

"*To, From,* what kind of shit you giving me here; all I get from you guys is grammar."

Victor arrives at the open gates of the Luxembourg — on the Vaugirard side — but he doesn't enter. Rather, he looks through the wrought iron grill of the fence, arms parallel to the grating as if being frisked by a sudden quiet thought. Through the trees, he can see them playing tennis and croquet. The small walks are the colour of tar, the sand is brown, pigeons billow on the flat between the hedges. The tennis players are in white, but despite their aplomb, the net sags. The womens' legs are knotted with muscle; the croquet players are middle-aged men, their faces pocked red, their noses like the fungus of trees. They deliberate in groups, then move up to the ball with lonely concentration; each strokes in turn with a fat man's grace, then follows the ball on foot as it scuds through dust. Victor, seeming to meditate, fits his forehead through the fence. His eyes are jewelled and steady with the hardness of diamonds; or they are like marble purees, brown water trapped in an agate; or they are dead berries pierced with picks; or simply eyeballs somewhat small. His elbows are together in fleshy taper like a conqueror's shield, the span of his wrists suggest a menacing calm. There is the smell of soap and tonic and slicked-down hair, as if he had prepared himself to meet the city, as if the city were unprepared to greet him in return. He is finally unintrigued; without a motion wasted, he falls an arm's length from the fence, turns easily on the disciplined ball of his toe, and spins economically towards the Rue Bonaparte.

"Old men in the park."

"The French like that sort of thing," I said.

"Rummies in the park."

"Croquet, tennis, chess : old traditions," I said.

"Stumbling around in all that pigeon shit with a goddamn mallet. Broads tennis smelly cunts. What's that place called again ?"

"The Gardens of the Luxembourg," I said.

"Good hustling ?"

"Closed at night," I said.

"So what the fuck good is it ?"

Victor stops for the signals at the Rue Bonaparte. The cars crash or glide through the intersection; the light changes and the brakes shriek. Victor walks between the parallel disks to the other side of the road. He stands awhile, hands on hips, looking grim. He carries his belligerence as if it were charming, a dividend to all who befriend him however briefly. There is a garden and a seminary where we are; farther down the street, police in a pillbox outside their station, then a cinema. We start down the rise. Victor walks with a brisk, certain air, propelled, incurious, waiting to be pleased. There is no stoop to his stride, his back is straight, buying height, his spine exactly perpendicular to the street. His arms do not swing, they rest stationary by his sides; not in repose but with suspicion; geared for attack.

"You go to films ?"

"Sure," I said.

"What is this Leel New ?"

"*L'Ile Nue,*" I said, "have you seen it ?"

"I took Florine last week; a fucking drag."

"It's supposed to be boring," I said, 'that's its art."

"They go to the mainland they go to the island they go to the mainland; six fucking francs."

"Part of the Japanese New Wave," I said, "agonizing and beautiful, the imprecision of life, the interminable sense of being; a kind of parable."

"They don't even talk. All you hear is the fucking water; then they go puffing up this hill and water plants. What's this virgin original ?"

"Verz-eon Oar-eeg-ih-nahl," I said, "Japanese with French subtitles; don't you remember ?"

"What's in subtitles, the silence ? She carries a pail of water he carries a pail of water she carries a pail of water; the only piece of action, she all of a sudden *drops* her pail of water : some parable."

"You'll learn," I said, "that the human condition is silence and control and repetition : the horror of the commonplace."

"Sounds ecstatic; I'm all sweaty."

Victor coming upon the Place St. Sulpice like a finger stemming a wart. The bell towers of the church in patient relief against the sky; the grime of its walls, its bricks discoloured by rain and whitewash; clouds above like streaks of gray pasteboard, as if the church itself were releasing some vaporous waste in absolution. The Place circled by an arbour of trees, stone lions guarding the fountain; benches squaring the circle at some distance; pigeons flap-clawed on the pavement, tripping over their own refuse; drunks slouched on the benches or, it being midnoon, washing their faces in the fountain's pool; other strollers along the perimeter. The atmosphere quiet, remote from traffic, almost sunless; *clochards* eating baguettes and cheese, bottles held by the spouts between their legs. Victor sees all this; or rather, he sees the fountain, notes the church, describes the lions in his mind. He walks through the Place and stops dead centre; resting hand on hip, one white running shoe prodding the ground, he takes in the church; looks past its funereal splendor to concentrate on several girls resting on the steps, barelegged, their legs airily spread; they are reading *Michelins*. He steps past the fountain into a sunlit corridor in hopes of a better view; raises his fingers like a fan to his forehead; surveys the territory; a possible crotch or two in sight; behind him, the sounds of the fountain and the pigeons, the *clochards* and the drunks, the strollers under the trees, shadows of the lions, the spires, shadows of the St. Sulpice. He annoints his eyes with interest as the girls leave, bare legs shuttling down the steps of the church, *Michelins* dog-eared in their flight bags; a slight rage of exclusion as they disappear; then dyspepsia; then finally the salvation of a shrug and Victor turns. Turns into the waiting arms of a patient faggot; the faggot has blonde hair, almost platinum, caesarian on top but cowlicked at the back. Victor does not hesitate; his elbow swings methodically to catch the fag flush on the jaw; the fag jerks away as if stung, falls, rises, falls, kneels, crawls, rises, adjusts, walks gracefully away. Victor follows him to the street, delivers a swift, well-intentioned kick; the faggot hops, skips, puts three fingers to his rump. Victor returns, weigted with corrective strength. He walks with a swagger to the pissoir at one corner of the Place, pisses heroically down the grating; comes back chewing gum. Shadows devolve as we travel further. His indifference replaced by a look of triumph; in the form of an intensely vacuous stare; self-rewarding.

"Fucking queer."

"Just tell them you're not interested," I said, "too many to kick."

"I'll kick the shit out of any of them come up to me. Fucking little queen had a hard-on. Were they all queer at that party last night ?"

"No," I said, "just a few."

"What about that broad you slugged ? Was she a dyke, or what ?"

"Dee ? A pimp, whore, lesbian, hashish eater, white slaver, drug peddler," I said, "a no good dirty filthy crud-sucking shit-mouthed piece of slavering piss; an assholed, troublemaking, rodchewing clot of absolute pus."

"She was just a broad, what are you talking ?"

Victor hurries down the last leg of the Rue Bonaparte; he hurries for no apparent reason except that he is growing tired and needs the disguise. His legs move like the forelegs of a trotter, rear end tilted high and strangely effeminate in style. His arms are still stationary by his sides as if wired to the hip in case of accident, but his fingers are clenched as he moves out of the Rue Bonaparte faster than the speed of thought. The St. Germain-des-Prés has a full sun on it. Victor pauses. The mouths of many streets gape and emerge before his very eyes. They are sitting four deep on the terrace of Aux Deux Magots, two deep at the Café de Flores. People traffic by the tables or cross to the Brasserie Lipp. Victor holds his decision back with difficulty, like a delayed orgasm about to vaporize. This look of preternatural and unconscious rage flushes to a pink about the jowls; he has not shaved too closely — it is a manly habit — and the blue of his stubble, like a gloss of printer's ink, stains his cheeks, his neck, his shoulders. He watches with a steady, clean belligerence; shaking his head with the crack of a smile. His mind dotes on the scene in total, refusing to break it down, ferretting out his own response and nothing more; he walks. Walks across the St. Germain, diagonally through the traffic, towards the Église St. Germain. He does not bother to study the terrace of Aux Deux Magots; it is already dead weight, receding in probability as he moves; as if his eyes commit murder at every passing judgment.

"Are those the people that smoke this Mary-wawna ?"

"No," I said, "not there."

"What is it like ? drinking or what ?"

"It makes you feel good, it gives you edge," I said. "No hangovers; and its cheap."

"Yah ? Well, you look like shit; you look like you're gonna puke or something any minute."

"That's from something else," I said, "pot can't hurt you."

"Yah, but I'll bet it attracts flies like the smell of shit."

"It's a fine way to spend an evening," I said, "it cuts time right out of your life; it provides solutions ... no, it *suspends* solutions."

"Fuck off."

"Really it does," I said.

"Smoking that crud'd *suspend* anything; how come you all got these itchy crotches ?"

"We're melancholic," I said, "you catch it from fleas."

"Ahhhh, bunch of assholes."

Victor, exhilarated by the clean breeze, by his even stride, by this just pronouncement, fishes for a cigarette. He cups his hand over the match, walking sideways; then inhales with a snort, plumes the smoke fiercely, flicks the ash. It is as if *goddamn Paris* were circulating within his mouth in a jumble of letters not yet organized. We pass the tables selling coconut, the stalls stacked with bright candies, the roulette games, the shooting galleries, the Algerians selling rubber mice. Victor muses. We pass the Mabillon at a quick pace nonetheless. No one can accuse him of docility or unwillfulness; he jostles, pushes, ploughing through; his shoulders, wielded like fenders, cut through immobility; or, people melt before him like butter on his tongue; or, make a sudden path like strafed victims on a runway; or, merely move to avoid his manner. Unintimidated, he hurries; comes to the Rue de Seine; trails his arm to stop me; there's Florine. She is sitting on the terrace of the Café Seine, alone, sipping something green with ice; I'm to wait. Victor bulls his way to a seat beside her, but once there does not sit down; instead, he towers above her, casting a remindful shadow where she basks. No gentleness betrays his features; he stalks erect; there is an arrangement being made. She smiles, pampering his potential yield. They seem to synchronize their watches. Victor, denoting charm, finally pats her facial muscle; then returns. He says nothing. We come to Odéon. Tough-minded and unmoved, he surveys the fulcrum of our universe; with some distaste. Oh for a piece of cryptonite.

"You know something? There isn't one fucking decent lay in this whole city. They're all sick, these broads."

"That's not true," I said.

"They're all sick. Every fucking one of them."

"You're wrong," I said.

"They come on big, but they can't do nothing. Show me one broad you can bring off right; they're like white rhinos, you can't find them."

"You've got it all wrong," I said, "promiscuity is a doctrine here."

"Promise-balls. Their cunts are dead. What do they do, freeze them with novocaine?"

"I've had some great experiences with women here," I said. "Some of the best things with women happened to me here."

"Bullshit."

"Well you wouldn't know Cheryl or Briar or Anne the Pregnant," I said.

"All the fucking same; a bunch of rotting fuzz eaters."

"But not Cheryl though," I said. "You wouldn't know the tale about us on the rock in the Loire Valley. It was so good, it hurt."

"What, the rock?"

"Or Iris in Barcelona . . ." I said.

"Sure sure. Listen, you see this Florine? She looks like a pretty healthy broad, right? When I picked her up, all she talked about was sex, that's all she wanted to know. I mean I figured *Hey* this is all right. She builds it up a whole day, about how she likes this position, that position, how many times she needs it a week, how much a creature of passion she is, what it does for her system, how it's like a tonic. I'm thinking this is really something. So the first night I take her to bed : nothing. The second night all she

does is cry : it hurts. The third night I'm determined : I
work two fucking hours on her, not a sneeze. Then she gets
all nervous and *humiliated;* I got to *time* it, she says, it
always takes a little while, she says, about five hours, she
says. I mean Jesus the broad's sick. You know what I had
to do finally ? I had to whack myself off before I met her;
every night. If I saw her, at say nine, I had to whack off
about six. It was the only way I could keep going; otherwise
I liable come too soon. You see ? Only it keeps getting
worse. Every night it takes a little longer : so now I got to
whack off at four and again at six, so when I meet her it's
my third time round and I don't blow at all. I mean shit.
And you think after all that she's any good ? One little pop
and she's dry; two seconds, boom." [1]

"I think you underestimate her," I said.

"It's like masturbating myself in a warm bag, what are
you talking ?"

"Sounds pretty exciting to me," I said.

"You know something ? you're all fucking sick, period."

---

[1] (Author's note. What Victor is attempting to articulate is the
following. Florine possessed a rather small orifice proper, positioned
slightly to left of nether, swivelled like a badly cut pocket and, upon
inspection, wrinkled, drawn and uneven, with a thin line of hair
bristled (exclusively) from anus to fold. This required a special
process of intercourse and seriously delimited the variousness of her
pleasures. A certain subtlety, enforced over a period of several
weeks, was needed to bring about the proper results. The one
infallible play was to throw her legs one over each shoulder like
duffel bags, kneel between them as if worshipping her unpuckered
navel (in the free form of a torn marble) and thrust at the opening
now almost perpendicular to one's (it could have been almost anyone's, frankly) chest. Once secure within the pout, there was yet
another problem to be faced. Due to a rare and nervous temperament,
the entire organ was invariably dry. To accomplish even a residue
of lubricant required much painful labour. But after due exertion
(approximately a quarter of a day), a wet, slapping give-and-take
made further steps feasible. Except for this : unable in the afore-
mentioned position to articulate any kind of pelvic response, the onus
for movement came to rest generally with oneself. Also, during the
various stages of momentum, her organ tended to contract, almost
pricing her out of the field. Not to mention the sad fact that complete entry was impossible due to a natural blockage within the cunt
itself. But with diligence, alertness and a keen sense of duration,
Florine was a rewarding experience, and a nice girl besides.)

Victor speeds past the Relais Odéon. The café is filled;
hundreds of crossed legs like many-coloured tripods, thousands of bared toes like broken thumbs, lurk under chairs.
There is not so much a determination to him now as a com-
placement quickness. Nor has he *arrived* at a judgment or
decision; he has merely reconfirmed some policy, a flower
already seeded and bearing credos. He nods his head in rapid
celebration; walks half on tiptoe across the Carrefour de
l'Odéon; against the traffic lights, daring cars to swerve and
panic; which they do. Towards the mouth of the Monsieur
le Prince; towards the Café Monaco, the crowning piece.
He comes upon it armed, like a disaster; circles, turns, takes
a lasting look, follows me in. Affords himself a cursory
glance at what has been my summing up.

"This is *it* ?"

"This is it," I said, "this is where it all happens."

"You spend every day here ?"

"This is the place," I said. "Used to come here all the
time; before the feuds began."

"Christ almighty, what is it ? It's just a little dive."

"No dive," I said, "everybody comes here : this is the
Café Monaco."

"All right, so tell me : who's here."

"Well, they're not around yet; they'll be here later," I
said.

"Sure they will. Now what's so good about this place ?"

"First of all," I said, "it's small, so its easier to keep your
clique intact."

"Your *what what* ?"

"Your clique," I said; "everybody knows where everybody
is."

"Perish the thought they shouldn't."

"You see that little L part of the café? That's where
we used to have our all-night talks," I said. "It's fine back
there."

"Just lovely."

"You see the corner of the bar, near the pinball machine
(we call them Gottliebs)? that's where I first met Cheryl,"

I said, "and see the entrance to the toilet well, behind the cash register ? that's where little Gilchrist used to hide. It's all here."

"You better keep it a secret."

"Our lives are plotted by innuendo and subversion," I said.

"Sounds just great."

"Waste is a beautiful art among the natives," I said.

"So ?"

"It's the illusion of transit that's important," I said.

"Yah ?"

"The Quarter caters to all diseases," I said.

"So ?"

"As brilliantly lit as an extermination centre," I said.

"Good for it."

"The one thing constant is the *circuit*," I said.

"Hurray."

"Life here is like a concussion that forces the same moment to endure forever," I said.

"So ?"

"It's a gallery of myths," I said.

"Yah ?"

"Anyway, I'll be leaving soon," I said.

"Tremendous move."

"Leaving all of it, all of it behind," I said.

"Hey !"

"What," I said.

"This is called the *Bar* Monaco, not the Café Monaco."

"What are you talking about ?" I said.

"It's called the Bar Monaco."

"Ay ?" I said.

"How come you been calling it the Café Monaco ?"

"All right," I said, "so it's the fucking *Bar* Monaco."

(Oh my god)

Forty-three
Glukicz Without Tears

The last night I came into the Café Tournon, Dixie was sitting with the card players behind the grilled partition. In fact, he was playing cards himself. He wore a brown leather vest lined with fur and beneath it a faded green shirt; the shirt was sleeveless and the arms were bare except for a gold chain on his left wrist and a large silver ring on the index finger of his right hand. He wore tight-fitting dungarees with a suede crotch piece and high orange boots that came to the knee. The metallic belt of his dungarees was a good half-inch in thickness and the gigantic buckle was shaped like a triangle and clasped three ways. On his head, he wore a MacArthur headdress with a special plastic visor and a red and black feather in the brim. His face had bought a sinister air with the purchase of wraparound sunglasses; they were secured round his head by a blue elastic band. Also, he had more than a mustache now, he had a beard and it grew untrimmed out of his neck. His skin was tanned and well-worn and the softness had gone from his features; his belly was flat and the sweat in his neck highlighted cords of bare muscle that tracked out of sight.

"How !" he said, giving me the Indian sign and breaking into the old smile. He was still with the drugs, yet he seemed more cheerful, as if grimness had partially given way to something that giggled. He sat with the special cardplayers of the Café Tournon, the Chinamen and the Yugoslav, the three Americans and the Limey. A slim Negress with an unsightly spread to her rump, wearing tight mauve slacks and a Mickey Rooney sweater, had her arms about the neck of the Englishman; she had caught him from the rear and her head rested furtively on his shoulder looking down into the boundaries of his lap. Dixie seemed to shift within that gesture. He had to laugh.

Maurice the waiter insisted that I take a table in the back and I decided not to say goodby yet. I ordered an omelette and a demi and waited. I sat alone in the back for some

time, watching them through the wall mirror. If I say that
it was an almost weatherless night, that the heat hung with
a soft, gentle weight . . . Solitude has its own special glamour,
as have protracted farewells when delivered quietly, and I
was being watched besides and felt the increasing dimensions
of myself alone. Then Nate the Accordion (who may be
eternal) came by and carefully stacked his accordion in the
corner. He sat across from me in the small back booth and
put his hands up to his face; his thumbs stemmed an itch
near his eyeballs.

"Where's Constance ?" I asked, knowing that she had left
him, "or the little kraut ?" I asked, knowing that she was
working for a guitar player in the Rue Champollion.

"Garber, mind your own business," said Nate, rising
abruptly. "Your trouble is you never converse properly,
you're out of fashion."

"Well, look Nate," I said, "I'm leaving for London tomorrow morning," and held out my hand, admittedly sticky.

"Good riddance," said Nate, retrieving his accordion and
moving along the bar towards friends.

If I say that a quiet, tender dark lay over the city, that
from the café window the luminous clock of the Château
Luxembourg shed its light down the Rue Tournon . . . The
bar was lined with new faces, faces more ravaged than I
had remembered. There was no one at the Gottliebs this
time of night.

When I had finished my drink and paid Maurice, I got up.
I had given Maurice a very large tip by way of farewell, and
he loitered. He had his thick hand on my shoulder, holding
the crumpled five franc note. He spoke of what might have
been old times had I learned the language, and he had a
smile on that flat sinister face. He knew of my decline in
the Quarter, because he spoke in a special way; it signified
indifference and boredom and a sharp professional courtesy.
The clock of the Luxembourg struck three.

It was time at last. I was on my way towards the partition
behind which the cardplayers were mumbling, when I was
suddenly stopped crossing over from the bar.

"Remember me ?" asked an Indian, American, hairless.

"Sure," I said.

"So how are you," said the Indian. "I heard all about it."

"Fine," I said. Then, "Hey, how did you lose all your hair ?"

"That's for you to figure out," said the Indian, "but I warned you, didn't I ?"

"You sure did," I said.

"Some sweet crud huh ?" said the Indian.

"You get kind of used to it," I said.

"But mine ain't growing back," the Indian went on, "and the word's out."

"Let them talk," I said. "It's just talk."

"It's this goddamn gossip," said the Indian. "Everybody's dropped me."

"Hell, you'll see a lot more of that before you die, kid," I said.

"How about a friendly beer ?" said the Indian.

"Can't," I said, "just about leaving."

"Okay then so," said the Indian and stepped back to the bar, one American hairless.

But when I got to Dixie he was involved in the game. Maria All-Blonde, formerly of Guy Rancid, was beside him, both hands gripping his bare arm as if it were a tree trunk or worse. "You're funny, you know zat," she was saying. "Why are you zo funny ?" Dixie shed her with a curt *Neem* and she slipped back and folded her arms contentedly; he possessed her in however unusual a fashion and she seemed, for some reason, happy. Others shared in the mystery, but averted their eyes.

Behind the partition, there was something odd going on. The others weren't playing at all, they were merely watching. It was Dixie alone who played the cards. There was perhaps fifty francs on the table too, and the others were stone silent with their eyes on the deck, on Dixie's nimble fingers as they slipped the cards by three. Then I saw that he was playing solitaire. The cards had been laid down in crooked rows with two red aces at the top of the table; the odds had been written down on a piece of cardboard in a complicated scrawl : "Complete Game, 10-1; One Card Down, 6-1; Two

Cards Down, 4-1; Three, Four and Five Cards Down, 2-1."
I mean it was right there in black and white, held in place
between the sugar bowl and the ashtray.

"He's a goddam hustler," said the Limey as I peered
wildly over his shoulder. "Save your money."

"Do I have to work the streets again tomorrow?" asked
his Negress.

It was a tight game and Dixie had a tight look. I could
guess at what had happened since I had seen him last. He
had apparently mastered the game during those few weeks
in the Petit Trianon, never coming down, surviving on Oxo
bars and kilos of raw spaghetti. He had been up there three
weeks alone with a deck of cards, working himself into shape,
letting the rest of it die, learning to be cool under pressure
as all athletes must, learning the fast tricks of the game itself,
the art of the ace and the high card on the last pile, teaching
himself in the deep hours of the morning how to suspend
a low number, delay a set, control the early pace where you
might shoot your bolt too quickly. Every move added up
to three weeks of deprivation, the sum total of his days and
nights easily seen whenever he failed to move a card, then
moved three later; what Iris had killed was apparent in the
slick move of his fingers, the sullen, deliberate shift. He had
a serious problem on the seventh pile and he was working
on it now as I watched. He had a Queen Spade there and
no chance of a run, but the Queen Spade held five cards
and the deck proper had already spawned its Jacks. It's no
good, I thought, and a sickly feeling coursed through me.
He had finished one set already and one Ace was buried.
He held eight cards and had run through them twice, and
now he paused and circled the table balefully with his mouth
pulled wrong. Everyone's eyes were fixed on the cards; no
one knew what Dixie's eyes were doing. Someone raised
his bet and threw a ten franc note on the table. Dixie figured.
There were eight cards in his hand and five cards under the
Queen Spade; there were two cards under the Deuce Club,
two cards under the Ten Spade, then three half-runs and
the two Aces free. He figured some more; they couldn't
break him. He finished off his beer, stroked the table top

stylishly, squinted perhaps, heaved certainly, leaned over for one last look. Then he did it. The Ace of Clubs was third card up; he planted the Two of Clubs on it and turned up the card beneath : King of Hearts. The game was over; he took his time. He shifted the Queen Spade, kissed it with the necessary Jack, turned up the Eight, turned up the Five. He arranged the puzzle easily but he did it in a slow, methodical way; almost righteously, as if he were arranging the tablets of a legend for our instruction. When he had finished, he put the four panels of the deck together and gathered up the money. He stuffed the franc notes into his vest pocket, then he stood up and shook hands round the table. He moved over to the bar, leaving the others; they sat mumbling behind the partition and began to play cards. Maria followed him to the bar where he ordered Calvados and began to sweat. She put her hand on the back of his neck, clawing his hair with her short lacquered nails. She was prideful; it didn't matter what really happened between them as long as she could demonstrate in public. He pushed her off, then let her come back again and she came back and put both hands in his hair, whispering. He had another Calvados and then a beer. The sweat was through his shirt. He put the crumpled money on the bar and regarded it solemnly.

"That's some game you play," I said.

I hadn't said a word before and Dixie had seemed to pass right through me on his way to the bar, but now he had his grin fixed on me like a pin. Maybe he finally knew something nobody else knew, maybe he had learned how to formulate mysteries and concoct riddles which was part of the basic con and the beginnings of luck; he wasn't saying. All I saw was the resonance coming, frilling his nostrils like an internal wind, a deep humming current. *Neeeeeeeemmmmmmmmm,* it went; then, *Nerk.*

If I say that the Tournon was crowded that final night with faces I had known though different, that whisps of pot curdled the air, stuck in my remembering craw ... Dixie bought me a drink and we talked about nothing much. People seemed to mill about him like maggots in a bright

light, calling him *Dix* or *Glue*. They scrutinized the plane
of his face from every angle as if to ward off inconsistencies;
keeping a fussy, agitated vigil. Maria had him proudly by
the arm, illustrating warmth; whenever he rebuffed her
meaty clutch, she'd blink in resignation and wonder and
stare down the line of her body. "Tek all ov me," she was
singing, mostly for public consumption, planting her wet lips
on the funnel of his throat, "all ov me." While Dixie, half-
plaintive, but entirely cool, wriggled from her grip, only to
allow her, once more, little favours. She liked that. They all
liked that. The faces of the Tournon were on him; there
was calling and waving and inside jokes and he went off to
play the Gottlieb for a spell. His tight-fitting dungarees,
faded shirt, fur-lined vest, MacArthur headdress, all seemed
to be landmarks here, regarded with reverence like a touch-
stone or a belief. The sound of *Neems* was everywhere;
they were all doing it now. If you looked closely, you could
see the beginnings of Dixie faces, half lunatic in worship,
trying for the same mad dog expression; they blew bubbles
in their demis, relieved themselves of small vibrations,
shrugged off their women; a few of them were beginning
beards, wore fur-lined vests, waited for their shirts to fray;
someone was hustling at a game of Fish, plans were being
made to go to Spain, abortions were recalled in morbid
detail; "It Didn't Happen" made the rounds as a comment
on survival, a splinter group had started up for Connie the
Pimp, while all the women gazed like Iris. I could hear
someone near the back discussing a sudden bee, someone
else complaining of prostatitis, women going frigid, men
going limp. While Dixie, as tactician, stood by the Gottlieb,
the master draft. He came back to the bar, weaving in that
fading stoop — though with concentration now, to get it
right — he had always had; he took a pill from his leather
pouch and washed it down, then leaned into my ear,
whispered "I almost got it up last week," and passed out
the door.

If I say that the Rue Tournon wound into darkness towards
the gloomy St. Sulpice, that a low droning sound led us on
like scavengers or worse... Maria was saying how funny

he was, how I wouldn't believe some of the things. We found him on the terrace of the Monaco. It was deserted now; the waiter in his starched white jacket was piling the chairs inside behind the glass; Madame, cherub-faced and somewhat mannered, was counting the till. The Odéon was quiet and dimly lit; abandoned, except for a line of taxis that waited on the St. Germain.

"Dixie," I said playfully, "you've arrived."

He didn't know what I was talking about. The waiter left his chair alone but swept up the terrace, turned off the lights, took in the awning. Madame was putting the take in a small satchel; then she peered under the tables and pointed. The waiter went in with the broom. Dixie sat on the chair, last lonely piece of furniture, and farted painfully; the sound seemed to cut him in two, but he didn't move.

"Dixie ?"

"I'm okay," he said.

"Dixie ?"

"What ?"

Then I couldn't say it. Maria tried to lift him up by the armpits, but he fanned her off. He was basking in his own smell. She only smiled.

"Dixie ?"

"What !"

If I say that this was the last possible moment, the end of Paris, the butt end of it all, that they were sweeping the city now, closing it up, killing the lights, moving under-ground . . .

"Let's walk," I said.

He abandoned the chair in his own good time; allowing my suggestion to transpire before he rose.

Were they playing "La Mer" ? Somewhere, from a cellar perhaps, the music came, like a growl at first, then much sharper. How profound it made the quiet seem, how ominous, how sinister.

"So," I was saying, "remember boy you've got to keep with it don't quit the whole beauty of it is not to throw it away all of us everything we know all we do and are Iris Bobby and the rest oh Christ take care don't let it go it isn't

that we failed Dixie it's that we tried it's half as much as
we wanted but it's twice as much as we had."

"What ?"

"Don't take any wooden francs," I said, and watched him
walk away with Maria, up the Rue Buci, shrugging in awful
parody of the dream we dream.

Forty-four

"I feel sick."

"Let me have your bags," said the nun.

"I feel awful."

Her stubby fingers hooked onto my luggage while I
swallowed the bad taste. She was carrying it, stricken with
the weight of the forty pound suitcase and the smaller satchel
and the twenty pound Remington portable. Her own valise
swung from a string under her left armpit. I followed as
she stumbled up the boat plank. She had short powerful
legs and she made it to the deck in no time. Then she put
the big suitcase down and began to kick it towards the
luggage racks. Then she raised it herself and placed it on
a tier and stood under it, waiting vigilantly. I paused a few
yards away. I turned my head towards the water, but I put
down the gob; I had the chills and a fever and my face was
green. Funny, it didn't look like the Seine; the Seine was
narrow.

"It isn't the Seine," the nun was saying, "it's the English
Channel."

"Sure, I know that," I said.

"Are you seasick ? is that it ?"

"No," I said.

"I've got a thermos of warm coffee."

She set herself heavily onto one of the racks and loosened
the valise under her arm. She unzipped the valise and

fished around in the compartment; she pulled out the light blue thermos and a series of pale, uncrusted sandwiches wrapped in tiny plastic slips. She had tremendous, stocky arms and wrestler's wrists.

"You'd better sit down," she said.

It was cold. Her voice sent up little puffs of air. She took off her gloves and unscrewed the silver-coloured cup. The pores of her skin were as red as passion berries. It tickles me to watch, I thought, too much detail. Then she poured out the coffee. She drank some herself to make sure, then she handed me the smoking cup across the narrow alley.

"This is where I drank from," she said, pointing to where her lips had been, and turned the cup about so that I got the untouched rim. There was no sugar but I drank it anyway and felt it go down only as far as my chest and lie there, being defiled, waiting to come up again.

"Have a sandwich," she was saying, folding the plastic slips to make serviettes for the knee. "Here."

It was like being asked to eat part of an altar. My teeth were melting at a fantastic rate, so I had to soften it with my gums — the moist, pale salmon.

"Good ?"

"Wonderful."

"Please eat."

So you're the famous Sister Angelica who was raped by a heartless band of sleek savages in Brazil who carried you on the nubs of their erections across a hundred miles of dense foliage to a small village where the chief's sleek, savage son ravaged you daily at high noon on a raised grass platform until an eclipse turned the whole heathen crew impotent and led to several years of intense study and a translation of the New Testament into eight dialects and the construction of a modest church ?

"Goodness," said the nun.

A little coffee squirted out my nose. Her stubby fingers picked crumbs off my pantleg, blotted out coffee stains on my chin and shirt. My head fell back like a gong. She leaned forward with a sudden professional frown and took my hand. She rubbed it between her cool, maneuvering palms, but I came out of the shallow swoon before warmed sufficiently.

"Son of a bitch," I said, "I can't even get sick."

"Let me put my fingers down your throat," she said, wiping the gruel from my mouth. Her eyes were fastened like soft light upon the suffering man.

"Nah," I said.

"It will go quickly," she said, using the French construction.

"Keep your fingers to yourself, I'm fine."

The boat was rolling through the water now, but it wasn't that. Maybe Emmanuel the Spanish was idling his day away in the Café Monaco sticking pins in his Garber doll.

"I'm all green," I said, introducing myself.

"Just a little yellow," said the nun. "Is there anything you want to talk about?"

Is she going to be like this the whole trip? I thought; it's lucky I've only got ten toes to kiss. Then the boat lurched and a bit of the Channel ran over the deck. We left the luggage racks and went one flight below. I scratched the walls something awful; we came to the benches. She sat down, settling her drapery. The professional frown was still there, not admonishing, not yet imperial, but coming by slow paths to a decision. That look could melt a commandment, I thought. "So you've been to Paris," she said.

"I see a bat."

It went flapping past. Rats gnawed at my toes. Tiny shrieks faster than the speed of sound got trapped in my head. The shakes came. Somebody shaped like a bell began to ring. Somebody else, hip pinned to navel, crouched past, sniffing the floor. My arms and hands floated free as if in a prancing dream, the knockout in slow motion so I slipped a right hand under her left hook as she went to one side with the weight of course on her right leg and felt her going down in stages as I fumbled for my neutral corner.

"Now please," she said, raising one finger muscled like a turnip. She had a little blood on her lip.

"Yes," I said, "I've been living in Paris since last winter."

Oops, there was a string of salmon coming up. I re-swallowed discreetly.

"There we were," I said, "on the side of the hill cooking shrimps : with Iris the Greek girl."

"I love the Greek people," said the nun.

"No no wait," I said. "It was in the car and the fucking Seducer tried to push me out : I got the *pot* for god sakes, and he's pushing."

"You're very young," said the nun, "life is too short."

I'll ruin her, I thought, I'll be charming and decadent. I'll give her a little foreknowledge.

"So and where from you are ?" I said.

She had a glass of water up to my lips; the water was lukewarm; it spurted out the hole in my throat.

Sis, did I ever tell you about the Negress in the Kilt Club near the Rond Point who made love to you with her eyes and a fin's worth of promise but never left the chaise lounge under the cooling system or Abie the Hindu on his way back to Bombay who had learnt to eat meat in Los Angeles and Paris and who had already defiled himself twenty times with whore and slut and plain old love and who was now schooling himself in abstention once more but who used to go secretly into the Bois by day to hunt for squirrel or little Barney Seymour out of Pueblo Montana who became a terrorist for the OAS and who slashed his way through crowded Métro cars with a razor blade tied to an elastic band until his mother found out or the death and subsequent decomposition of the lesbian pimp Valentine to whom the whore Dee belonged on a boat bound for Turkey and the pleasures of Istanbul or myself as I was at the beginning cut off forever from Coca-Cola and the quick flush of fine toilets or if could Cheryl could then that Iris know when there help ever Briar and mould green constant like deep as one might easily wish mommy dada don't shout at me you fucking dispirited whore nor or for core did them rock light boat shore colour dream her Krafft-Ebing ? No, huh ?

"I'd better write it out," the nun was saying to someone. She put three fingers under my jacket and fished down my

armpit. Then she drew out my passport folder. I heard
her licking the ball of her finger, writing, shuffling, turning
pages. Ewwww, that tickles. In a while, the passport was
back again, weighted under my armpit.

"I have a pin," said the nun in that kindly, imperious
tone. She fastened something to my lapel; whenever my
chin drooped, it scratched me. *Beware of dog, he'll scratch
you where he itches.*

"I need some fresh hair," I said.

"You'd better rest," said the nun. Her smile started up.

She's going to smile in a second, I thought, any minute
now.

"A little fresh hair," I said and spun off the bench. I
climbed the flight of stairs. There was a piece of paper
pinned to my jacket. This Is Lawrence Arnold Garber,
Canadian, If Unconscious Return To Toronto Ontario Canada, God Bless. I rolled it into a small turd and inserted
it up my left nostril. Outside, it was the damndest thing I
ever saw; like being in the middle of an enormous brown
abyss. Maybe I can flush it, I thought. I'll ask. But when
I got back down, Sister Angelica was being sick in a white
pan.

III

The Earl's Court Murders

One

What Is Said

Coger's Pub, Salisbury Court, Fleet: a dry fall day. Two figures standing at the bar, drinking Light Ale. The one tall, the other taller, drinking with a certain blood-eyed grimness. Each growing taller as they proceed. Each savagely approving the bottom of the glass.

The One Tall:
   All right, who played John Garfield's mother in *Body and Soul*?

The Other Taller:
   Ann Revere. That's four nothing.

The One Tall:
   Three nothing. Don't crap me huh.

The Other Taller:
   Okay. Who played the manager in *Marjorie Morningstar*?

The One Tall:
   Uh. Wait a minute. George ... Tobias.

The Other Taller:
   Right. I got to take a piss.

The One Tall:
   It'll cost you a point.

The Other Taller:
   Not if I shit too.

The One Tall:
   Don't go yet. Did I tell you about Garber?

The Other Taller:

Who's Garber? Man, I got to shit.
The One Tall :
Garber : *Garber.* From Toronto.
The Other Taller :
You mean Henry Miller with a nutcracker?
The One Tall :
You remember. The party on Spadina Road. He
got stoned and fucked the German girl on the rug.
Gaaaaaarber, for chrissakes.
The Other Taller :
Him? The quiet little bastard, sneaky mind?
The One Tall :
He's in London. Staggered up to the office last night :
absolutely green. With his fucking luggage. Said hello,
said he was sick, collapsed on the table.
The Other Taller :
You're not going to put him up, are you?
The One Tall :
Let me finish. *Garber,* what in hell have you been doing,
I said. He just lay there with this *beautiful* shade of
green, pure green. *Garber,* this is an office, *Gaaaarber.*
He was completely out of it : incredible. Apparently
he's been taking pot, dope. I got him to sit up to take
off his jacket and I saw all these *holes* in his arm.
Gaaaarber, what have you been doing? He kept saying
if he could just have something to drink. No money, of
course. So I brought him in here about ten, *propped* him
against the bar, ordered him some tomato juice. Apparently
that's what he wanted. And of course he puked it up.
Oh shit come back to the office, I said. He was lovely,
perfect shade of green. *Gaaaarber,* you're sick. I let him
sleep on the table for an hour but I couldn't have him
around. So I called up the De Whytes to come get him
out of here. I kept telling him *please* keep your head up,
I don't want it all over the goddamn floor.
The Other Taller :
Look, I have to take a shit.
The One Tall :
Hold on, let me finish. In a half-hour the De Whytes

come up. They had borrowed a car and I swear he looked like a fucking green corpse lying there. He was all tucked up under his overcoat on the table. You could smell him for *miles*.

The Other Taller :

Yah.

The One Tall :

What's the matter with him, says De Whyte. You know De Whyte : propriety itself. He's a fucking addict apparently, I said. *Garber?* he couldn't believe it. Good old Garber, I said : there he lies; look at his arm. So what are *we* supposed to do with him ? says De Whyte. Just get him out of here, I said. Then Tina says, He doesn't have any holes in his arm for god sakes ! He does so, I said, *here*. They are *not* holes, she says, they're goose pimples. Well, I'm not going to argue, I said, just take him. Let me take a look, says De Whyte. So there we were rolling up his sleeve. Could be anything, says De Whyte. Look, I said, Sobel's going to die any hour and I've got to write the fucking story; can't you get him out of here. You mean take him to our place ? says De Whyte. Well you can't just leave him in the street, I said; at least get him out of the West End. Oh for god — says De Whyte. Just for tonight, I said, just unload him on the couch. Well who knows what he's got, says De Whyte, what about the kid ? Then Tina — you know *Tina* — says, the poor bastard might be dying for shit sakes, we better take him home. It's going to be your responsibility, says De Whyte, I won't answer for the consequences. We had to carry Garber down the stairs and apparently he drooled all over the seat covers.

The Other Taller :

All right then, come take a shit *with* me.

The One Tall :

Wait, this is the amusing part. De Whyte called me today at the office. Apparently they had him nicely *stuffed* into the back seat when he began to go hysterical. They had only driven apparently as far as Trafalgar Square when he began to scream something about the *Lure* Valley.

De Whyte says he just leaned back and slapped him in the face and after that he was as meek as a mouse. Until about Marble Arch. Then he began to cry. Apparently he saw *bats* in the car. Tina went into a rage : we're taking you into our home, isn't that enough, can't you shut up ? They finally got him to their place; he tried to jump out of the car on the Bayswater Road, but De Whyte knocked him unconscious and had to carry him into the house over his shoulder apparently. The kid woke up of course, the people upstairs banged on the ceiling, Garber puked again. They finally got him settled on the couch and got the kid quiet. Then at *four* in the morning, Garber comes running into their bedroom on some insane pretext : I'm looking for *the albino,* he says. Oh what albino ! shouts De Whyte, for god sakes go back to sleep. The albino, says Garber and begins to look out the window. Just *please* get out of our room, says Tina, we'll buy you one tomorrow. Anyway, apparently De Whyte had to lead him out by the arm and settle him down all over again. He howled like a dog the rest of the morning. So you know Tina : that boy needs a doctor etcetera. In the morning De Whyte didn't want to go to work until he was out of there. I wasn't going to leave her alone with him, he says, he could be a maniac for all I know. You know De Whyte. But Tina : oh don't worry *please,* it's *Garber,* he's harmless. She finally got De Whyte to go; then about noon she got Garber off the couch, he was apparently half out of it anyway. And from what she told De Whyte on the phone, he was fine : began to apologize, curtsy, write out IOUs. Honest. I'm going to get you to a doctor, says Tina; put an umbrella in his hand, directed him towards Nottinghill Gate and said something like Mush. Apparently the doctor has no idea *what's* wrong with him. Gave him some antibiotics. Garber in his saner moments — when his skin turns olive — is saying it's only an abscessed tooth; claims he keeps swallowing the pus; calls it an 'obscure hurt.' I mean Christ. And he's got to stay in bed for at least three days. Not at our place, De Whyte told me; so apparently

they're moving him this evening to a bed-and-breakfast
in Earl's Court.
The Other Taller :
Wait a minute. You didn't give him my address, did you ?
The One Tall :
Of course I didn't. Apparently, they have to literally
wipe his ass for him. He's in bad shape. And oh yes,
he walks around with this greasy photograph of him and
his *friends* in Paris. I haven't seen it, but Tina called up
this afternoon, tells me they're the ugliest, weirdest band
of animals she'd ever seen. And you know the kind of
beasts she used to go down for. And Garber won't stop
talking about them. Half of the time they don't even
think he's conscious. You remember how he was in
Toronto; he'd walk around a fart for god sakes; well, now
apparently *nothing* bothers him.
The Other Taller :
Maybe he doesn't even know I'm in London.
The One Tall :
No, I mentioned your name. But he'll never remember;
he was *really* delirious. Perfect shade of emerald. Anyway,
go shit.
The Other Taller :
I conquered it. What could he have done in Paris ?
The One Tall :
Oh shit; *Garber* ? He was just a bloody kid for god sakes.
Something funny must have happened later, because when
Stuart and I went to cover the NATO conference last winter,
he was apparently fine. He was living in this — you
wouldn't believe it — a storage room on the right bank.
Near the American Express. On a bloody prostitute
street. He was surviving on something incredible like
twenty dollars a month, all this deprived bit. I said let's
go see Garber, he's an old university buddy; Stuart says
fine; you know Stuart. So we come to number eighteen
on his street and asked for him and the concierge shrugged
her shoulders and pointed up in the air. Here's what we
had to do : take the elevator to the fifth floor, walk to
the end of the hall, open a secret doorway, climb one

winding flight of wooden stairs, then along a narrow
hallway like something out of a George Raft film, then
up a small spiral staircase to a glass door which led to
a bridge outside, then across the bridge and into another
hallway : no lights : then feel our way in the dark three
doors down and there was Garber's room. He had a little
sign on the door : *L. Garber, his room.* I don't know how
he did it. But he was apparently *then* living a fairly
regimented life. But you should have seen his room. It
was full of — really — purple dust; floating all over the
place. *Gaaaaaarber,* I said, how can you live here ? I'm
okay, he says, it doesn't bother me. No running water, I
said, no lights. Just after ten o'clock, he says, I can use
the lights until then. He had apparently made a bloody
religion of it up there. Stu couldn't believe it, couldn't
even stand it; so he took me outside into the hallway
while Garber was making this *bilious* coffee on his little
gas stove. Look, says Stu, let's get your friend out of
here and take him somewhere, I've never seen anything
like it, does he actually *live* here ? Apparently he does,
I said. Stu was really shaken up — you know Stu —
the private schools he went to in T.O. No one more ill-
equipped to deal with *having-not.* Anyway, Garber's room
was about as big as two tables put together, one small
lamp on the floor, apparently no heating. He slept in
this little cot, I think you blew it up like a rubber raft.
Well Stu wouldn't go back inside; he stood in the hall
and I went back in and got Garber. Remember how
careful you had to be with him ? So I said, *Gaaaaaarber,*
let's not have the coffee now, let's go out somewhere and
get some broads; maybe go to the Champs-Elysées; and
we'll come back to your place later. Sure, he says. Jesus,
he looks bad *now,* but even then he had lost about twenty
pounds, no shave, no haircut, wearing these baggy un-
pressed pants, a *white* turtleneck sweater all splotched
with stains, that old black checkered scarf of his wrapped
around his neck. Don't you fucking *eat* ? I asked. Sure,
he says; he was so goddamn naive — and wet behind the
ears *literally :* he had apparently been trying to wash his

neck from a straw flask and he had soap drying all over him. Well, we got him out of the room and he led us down the stairs and over the bridge and through the halls; it was *literally* Kafka-esque. I had got him to put on a white shirt and he had stuffed his old black scarf into that and wrapped himself in an old raincoat. He looked as if Alan Ladd had accidentally wandered into *Lost Weekend*. The first thing Stu did when we hit the bloody street was go into a *brasserie* and buy a Croque-Monsieur for the poor bastard : he ate it like a piranha fish for shit sake; went into a doorway by himself and actually *licked* the goddamn wrapper. Well let's go to the Kilt Club, says Stu, it's near the Rond Point. I got us a cab and we hopped in the back; but of all the bloody things, Garber stands there on the sidewalk in the fucking cold and mutters something about cabs'll spoil him, he's got to *preserve* his abstinence and discipline or some shit like that. I'm not joking. Oh for — *Gaaaarber,* get in the fucking car ! No, he says, he'd walk and meet us there; apparently he knew where it was, he'd passed it on his *Deathwatch Strolls*. His exact words. *Gaaaaaarber*. Then Stu says, okay let him walk what the hell. So we took the cab there in about four minutes and waited outside for another *twenty* and then there he is, shuffling along the street like maybe James Whitmore in *Battleground*. You found it all right huh, I said. He used to have a notoriously bad sense of direction : one of his affectations, apparently. Sure, he says, but it must be about twenty francs to get in there. Our treat, I said, and talked about old-buddies-meeting-in-Paris; that made it okay. You had to use child psychology on the wretched bastard; literally. Then when we got inside, he didn't have a *tie* and they wouldn't let him into the lounge. I'll rent you one, I said, they rent them in the checkroom. No no, he'd wait for us outside, or meet us later for coffee at his place. I'm not going back there, Stu whispers to me, I'd rather buy him a goddamn *wardrobe*. *Gaaaar-ber,* you'll pay us back later for god sakes. So we got him the bloody tie and he didn't even know how to tie

it properly; so there ensues this fantastic scene with this
three hundred pound six feet six bouncer *tying* Garber's
tie for him like his goddamn mother and patting him
gingerly on the shoulder. Finally we get into the lounge
and head for the bar; just packed with stuff, *literally*.
Stu and I are standing there sizing up the situation and,
before you know it, Garber is dancing with this neat bit
of French furniture : he's dirty, unshaven, crooked
bloody tie, looks like a bag of mail for god sakes, but
he's *got* something; though sure she was a little warped
in the leg : bad complexion. How'd he do that ? asks
Stu. Don't worry, I said, he's not going to get anything.
And of course in half an hour he's back with us. What
happened ? I asked. She has to be home by eleven,
he says. So for Christ sakes Garber, *Take Her Home !*
But I can't speak French, he says. Oh for — *Gaaaarber !*
Well I can't, he says. You've been in Paris for a bloody
century already, I said, you must know *some* French. I can
say *côte de porc,* he says, I can say *l'eau.* So, Stu says,
tell her you want to dip a little pork in her water. You
know how crude wasps can be. But the whole thing
wasn't even funny. And he let her slip away too. What's
the matter with you suddenly, I asked, don't you like
girls anymore ? Oh sure, he says I've been seeing people
occasionally; but I can't afford that kind of thing now,
I'm caught in a kind of *renunciation syndrome.* I swear
to God, that's what he said. *Gaaaaaarber !* what's happening to you ? I've just isolated myself, he says, I'm
trying to do a little writing up in the room and let the
rest of it pass. Pass where ? asks Stu. Look *Gaaaarber,*
you're not in your room now, I said, you're in a night-
club; have *fun* for god sakes. He says okay, he'll try. In
the meantime, there's this beautiful Negress sitting on
a chaise lounge under the air conditioner, just like something out of a fucking Fellini dream. So Stu gets out
his *pencil* and *pad* and goes hustling for her phone number. But Garber ! Jesus, he's got another one, this time
it's a *Canadian* girl of all things. Well for god sake
introduce me, I said. Oh yes of course, he says, this is

Sue Carlyle. Apparently, she had this villa in Auteuil and a goddamn white Fiat, and what she was doing at the Kilt Club I don't know. So I took him aside and told him : for Christ sakes Garber, take her to your place, take her to *her* place, but do something, man ! I will I will, he says. It was as if I had told him to eat his wheat germ or something. *Gaaaaaarber,* you're out of your bloody mind ! she's lovely ! Actually though, she looked incredibly neurotic to me; full of twitches and funny sounds and little *darting* eyes and a bit on the hairy side. Anyway, they danced; Garber using his *natural* rhythm, looks like he's climbing up her leg like a *swami.* Then about two in the morning, he comes over to me at the bar and says they're leaving together. Oh great, I said; I was *genuinely* glad. But it isn't going to be good for me, he says, I've been living in a *vacuum,* I've been building up *immunity.* Look, I said, don't give me that shit huh. Take her, Go. I'll call you tomorrow, he says; and if she doesn't have to practically drag him out of the goddamn Kilt Club by the bloody coat sleeve. So he calls me up the next day; remember I told you Stu and I stayed near the old Gestapo headquarters in the Avenue Kléber ? Well, I said, so ...

The Other Taller :

Make it short, huh. I'm losing interest fast.

The One Tall :

Well, I said, so what happened ? Pretty good, he says. Well tell me what happened, I want to hear *all* of it. Are you at her place now ? No, he was at a phone in a café on his street. Did you make it ? I asked. Oh sure, he says. *Well ?* I asked. That's right, he says. Was it quick, was it slow, come on Garber, *the details.* About medium he says. Yah, I said, so and. She's very nice, he says. Oh for — *Garber !* tell me everything. She's asked me to move in with her, he says. Great stuff ! I said. I mean more power to him. Do you need any help with your luggage ? Well no, I told her I'd have to think about it for a week or so, he says. *Gaaaaaaaarber !* you're sick ! You don't understand, he says, I'll get a case of the bends if I move too quickly. A villa, I said, a white Fiat ! You may not believe it but I'm very happy where I am now, he says. Grow up for god sakes, I said; cut the poverty bit, huh. He's such a *naive* bastard. I'll think about it, he says. Fine, I said, you do that, you think about it, read a few books on the subject, write a treatise. And apparently he did move in, about a week after we left. Got a *skimpy* postcard. But the night before we came back to London, I went up to get him. I had all sorts of cash left over and didn't want people to think I hadn't spent it : you know me. Let's go to Les Halles, I said, we'll have a cognac in every café we can find ...

The Other Taller :

Oh fuck, hurry it up, eh.

The One Tall :

Okay, I'll skip Les Halles. When we got back to his place about seven in the morning — Stu by the way was *visiting* an aunt of his — we killed a couple bottles of Beaujolais *I* had bought. Then he read me a *short story* he had written : so so. But it was all about suicides and ghosts and chasing people down sewers; tremendously *ornate* style; sounded like Truman Capote with morning sickness : really weird stuff. You'd better get out of here, I said, because you're going out of your mind. Yes well, he says, everything you write costs you something. Oh bugger off ! really Garber ! It does, he says. Well let somebody else pay then, I said; let it cost *them* something; like this Carlyle chick. Well maybe I will move in, he says. You'd be damn wise to, I said. Intelligence is the last refuge of a barren mind, he says, and goes off to sleep on that bloody rubber raft. I mean I could hardly believe it : all those *ideas* about isolation and vacuum and sacrifice — and he can't write all that bloody well either. Wasting his fucking time in a storage room, cooking spaghetti, eating in Wimpy Bars, walking up and down the bloody boulevards, going to goddamn Père-Lachaise to see Wilde's tomb, always by himself as if he were some bloody consolation prize over there. But I mean he's always been like that more or less; it

was just so completely *absolute;* it was deadening.
Though I thought if he moves in with this Canadian
chick in Auteuil at least he'll be out of that *room.* Anyway, I didn't give that much of a shit *what* happened
to him. Then bang, a year goes by and one night he
comes out of nowhere staggering up to the office,
indulged out of his head, a goddamn dope addict, God
knows what else. Green? you've never seen green like
that.

The Other Taller :

Yah yah. You got to the part yet where he gets picked
up by the De Whytes, cause I got to shit again.

The One Tall :

But isn't it *incredible* though?

The Other Taller :

Just don't go around giving him my address.

The One Tall :

Don't worry so much. Anyway, so who played the pianist
in *Blues In The Night?*

The Other Taller :

Uh . . . wait a minute . . . it wassssss . . . wait wait . . .

The One Tall :

Richard Whorf. That's one nothing.

The Other Taller :

One nothing? You sure?

The One Tall :

Yah. One nothing. Go shit.

Two

Never mind why I came to Earl's Court. But it was the
end of fall and I was sick of an old passion and sought a
wintry London. They say the cold went through you here
and chilled your bones; that shilling metres, like green,

one-armed bandits, took the chill away but kept the cold around you; that the wind came down out of the roaring tunnel of the sea and impaled you on the city like some frozen vestal offering; that abstinence and fortitude were gospel here and a man might purge himself in different ways; that there was no choice of luxuries and one could live the little life, blockaded behind the smell of must and old quilts and damp walls. Why not ? I was more than game, still suffering from that old shock; forget which. Some friends drove me to a bed-and-breakfast near Hogarth Road; it fronted an iron-grated park at the base of a U-shaped street, and had the appearance at last of something fortified, insular. The sign swung pendant from a copper rod : *The British Transients League :* so I went in.

Dear Mr. Womble was there to greet me at the desk. Or rather, he was in his small back office showing lewd photos to a Portuguese matador.

"Does that excite you ?" he was saying as I rang.

"It is very fine," said the matador Alberto.

Mr. Womble placed a hand on the matador's knee as he sat cross-legged before the window : a surprisingly adept maneuver.

"Does that excite you as well ?" asked Mr. Womble gently.

"That is not so very fine," said the matador. "I will kill you please."

"Well, no matter, there's someone waiting anyway," said Mr. Womble, rising quickly as if to erase by magic the intended hustle. He placed his fingers quickly upon the matador's shoulders, released a sigh, then turned about with a look of sullen and complete indifference.

"Well, try the colour slides anyways," he said. "I shan't be a minim."

My room was large, the ceiling high; carpet and curtains and a bureau like a medieval engine. There was a mantle ice-cold to the touch, gauze curtains half-frozen to the pane, the stale smell of seed and oil in the corner. The bed itself was more an antique than a device for sleeping, the walls were stained with whitewash, cracked and oblong; the small lamp shade like a flowering fez, the larger light giving off a poisonous amber; the sink and pipes so new they still reeked of paint; a dead radiator painted pink; the shilling metre in its steel green box leading by rubber tube to the honeycombed jets. The view from the window was one of desolate gardens half-frosted now, the dark hard earth cluttered with garbage and newsprint, the neat rows of something unhatched already defiled by tin cans and carriage wheels, as if the ground had thrown them up, the particular produce of the country.

"I can be happy here," I thought, "because I won't be missing a thing."

But it was chilly; it was cold. I wrapped my checkered scarf about my throat, sprouted through another sweater. I slipped a shilling piece into the slot; I turned the small white hammer tap; I heard the sibilant sound of gas, smelt it deep like a breath of water; I lit the match. The jets caught fire, began to whine and whistle; the low flames unfurled as if anxious to burn down the house, and exuded by way of afterthought a thin cluttered heat. Not warmth, but heat. I crouched in front of the jets and rested my elbows on my knees, bending my face in toward the flame. The ends of my bones warmed nicely, kneecaps, elbows, nose, toeline; but the rest of me shivered, the bifurcated man at last, a tropical and arctic waste. I fell asleep before the grill; when I woke up two hours later, my face was boiled and my hands were blue.

Which didn't mean a thing. Because *The British Transients League* was a haven of warmth and friendliness and every morning at breakfast, while you prodded fancifully your single sausage and steaming yolk, in they came, singly or in twos and often as entire cliques, the brave and bright *colonials*. South Africans there were, Australians too, the Scotch, the Irish, several Swedes, Finns and Danes and the odd Canuck; Portuguese as well, Spaniards, Germans, Indians, French, even infrequent Londoners. And all with that *colonial* Earl's Court spirit which is a no man's land of the mind, a demarcation point, a buffer state, accepting privilege as a child accepts the nipple. So when Mr. Womble went home at six, his bulldog Bern sniffing carnivorously in his wake, motorcycles were brought into the lobby of the *Transients League* and driven up the stairs, bottles of Scotch and bitter were consumed on landings, small fornicating parties descended to the cellar hallways, brawls began in the lobby and TV lounge, alternating cliques met in vacant rooms to philosophize and try various things.

"I'm going to like this," I thought. "It'll be a nice change."

But Earl's Court Road was something else again. From the Cromwell to the Brompton Road, the street ran like a bright corridor, strewn with pubs and grills and a Wimpy Bar. There was an outdoor sandwich stall near the tube station and women, their long hair the texture of wire and dust, their leather boots thigh deep, stood quietly with paper cups of coffee and sandwiches of half-eaten cheese. Legions of men roamed in raincoats close to the curb, watching those high leather boots and those tight, winking leotards, hoping perhaps for some opportune split to occur. It seemed to be a country of waitresses and busboys, and most people moved like wretched foundlings; they were either pale as chalk or pasty faced or blotchy red like old, used fingers. They moved in exact single file into pubs and grills, or waited in queues with that remarkable and sullen patience that might have driven a Frenchman to revolution and a Canadian to two nights in Buffalo. The queues crept into the street like flanks and tails; emerged from the tube station, from phone booths, from the ends of bars, from the doorways of grills and tobacconists and vintners, from cigarette machines, newsstands, mailboxes, from coffee houses and private clubs, from upstairs landings and cellar flats, from overseas unions, bookstores, laundromats, candy emporiums, rental boards. Sometimes queues formed to watch other queues, or some sad pale creature as she fluttered home on the sail of her ass. Sometimes queues formed for the mere joy of queuing, the unspeakable pleasure of single file, double row, intricate phalanx.

"It's a damn good idea," I thought, "I'll have to sample one of those queues sometime."

Still, the Wimpy Bar was cheap and I was often hungry.

It had a large glass front, tables and chairs screwed to the floor, and clean, plastic odours. I ordered a wimpy and a bowl of chicken soup and a cup of tea. I slouched in the screwed-down immobile chair and watched the people passing on the street, moving against the wind both ways. At the table on my left, there were three Indians and a German girl. The German girl was sitting against the wall with her arms pressed parallel to her body and her hands flat on the seat. The three Indians were seated in a small arc about her. The girl was not happy, or pretty either; her face was narrow and pocked, and there were little blonde hairs on her neck; her legs were bony, the kneecaps bunched like steel bottletops, her tiny wrists discoloured by veins. Her smile when it ran, ran crooked, her hair grew light brown and awfully coarse. She was nervous. The Indians were all dressed well; they shared the same greased black hair and limp, agitated wrists. Two of them stared at her silently; they had little diaries under their arms and several pens hooked to their vest pockets. The third was smiling weakly, gold glinting from his mouth; his complexion was like ash, his lips like purple rubber; he waved those thin agitated wrists and hands as if they were the heads of cobras.

"And do you like London," he was saying, moving a small candy under his tongue. "Are you enjoying your visit, Miss Drockschlinger?"

"If my mothers knew whats I was doing she would punched me," said the German girl, adjusting her pose against the wall into an even more contorted bind.

"Some more tea?" asked the Indian. "You may."

The girl said nothing; the tea was ordered. She looked up for a moment to catch the whites of their eyes upon her. She shifted her haunch and tail already exhausted by the prospect of three dark hungry men.

"It is bad to be without moneys," she said, and the Indian reached for her wrist with his warted fingers and slipped the candy down his throat.

"This is real exciting," I thought, "this is life in the raw, all right."

Then there were the little cafés on Hogarth Road and
Brompton Road; small intimate places where the colonials
gathered for coffee and brown sugar. For instance, the
Troubador : pots and guitars suspended from the ceiling,
Victorian toys on dusty shelves, chipped benches and stools,
elbows worn raw from weeks of thinking. It was here
that girls, with their long black hair and loose wool sweaters,
their eyes like long green peninsulas, their noses aquiline,
their slim lips defined in orange, held stubs of Gold Leaf
between yellowing fingers and frowned like Poes in an old
daguerreotype. They hushed each other over candles, their
hair sweeping near the candle's flame, force-feeding coffee
to tall West Indians.

"If the old crowd could only see me now," I thought,
"because here I am."

For there I was, wandering into a self-service on the
Earl's Court Road with its reeking samples counter and
arthritic fingers pouring tea. A few men sat in the back,
wearing their overcoats through entire meals of beef stew
and dipped, moist bread. Their stools faced the wall as if
they had been assigned there for some awful shame.

"Say, I'll have time to think things out here," I thought;
"a man can be alone in this country."

Meanwhile, there was the *Transients League* too. They
were a damn friendly group there : varied, enigmatic, often
serviceable. I admired them for their style and resource-
fulness and their capacity for pleasure. Although they liked
to talk and drink and urinate in occasional sinks, they were
job hunters by profession and a bit inclined towards theft.
The cheery Earl's Court spirit, infused with steamy grills
and Cox's Orange Pippins, seemed to soften their edge, and
hard, bony faces melted each month as months were spent
in lobbies and lounges.

I was fondest of Christine the Swede, who had bad teeth,
good legs, foul breath and an unusual love of music. She
was a giggly, effervescent girl, completely silly, barely nineteen. She had come all the way from Stockholm to see the
English countryside and she saw it in cars, through windows,
on trains, from buses. Once a week, she travelled with a

rock and roll group, giving herself to them (collectively or in rotation) devoutly in hotels in Liverpool and Bristol. She would often be gone for days. Her back rent would accumulate. Mr. Womble would develop another tic on his face. But she always returned. A car would pull up to the *Transients League;* the driver would be a boy of sixteen with his hair in ringlets and braided over his ears. Drums, guitars and electric wires would be piled in the front seat beside him; Christine would be visible in the back with three others, their hair also ringed and braided, the acne on their faces like an epidemic of jam. Christine would emerge, much to the relief of Mr. Womble. She would wave goodby as the car cut the corner, her ankles turned in, her stockings chucked to the knees, reel towards the door, walk up the stairs, stumble into the lobby; and vomit.

One day, she came to Mr. Womble's office in a pink sweater, no shoes. Mr. Womble was sitting at his typewriter, pinching the keys. Outside, the rain; inside, the wind. Christine smiled through her orange sticky teeth and sat on a small hassock; she raised her skirt to the thigh, the blonde hairs honeycombed down her flank like the salt of the earth. Mr. Womble reddened, his sparse neck convulsive. The tic beneath his eye began to jump. He looked up her bill and announced the debt.

"I cannot pay," she said, "yet. Perhaps soon."

"Miss Gunarsson," said Mr. Womble, picking some dead skin from his lip, "the policy of the *League* has always been prompt and courteous service; we have always demanded same from clientele. If you cannot honour the above-mentioned payments due, we trust that you will be able to make other, more appropriate arrangements. Signed, yours most sincerely, S.G. Womble."

"I can maybe pay tomorrow," said Christine.

"Dear Miss Gunarsson," said Mr. Womble, "we at *The British Transients League* have shown, we believe, the utmost patience in the matter already discussed (see above); payments, as you no doubt are aware, are weekly and not at client's convenience. However, some further arrangements might be made. Again yours, S.G. Womble (signed)."

"If I could have two days," said Christine.

"Dear dear Miss Gunarsson," said Mr. Womble, "management is aware of your plight and not unsympathetic to same. Might we discuss further? Affectionately, Sigmund Womble."

"I'm always free in the evenings," said Christine.

"Darling," said Mr. Womble, "a few moments ago you spoke and the sound of your voice, as always, was a thing of beauty, if not in fact a joy forever. Don't trouble yourself about rents and payments and overdue notices; they are the trappings of the time and nothing more. I personally cannot *use* you, so to speak, my little fjord; but do you like cameras? I have a special Japanese make, and of course my little doggie Bern. Perhaps a few snapshots might be nice. Please advise. Much much love, Siggy."

"Oh golly," said Christine, "oh dear."

Then there were parties at the *Transients League* that lasted till breakfast. If for nothing else, one went to them for warmth; hot breath and slapping bodies and stacked warm beer gave to them the aura of infernos, and whole winters were passed there shouting above the noise. But they were difficult to invade; passwords were necessary, a casual penetrating manner advisable. One knocked on the door with one's tribute of South African wine fresh from the vintner's shelf; the door opened swiftly to release the echoing laughter and girlish shrieks and the single word "No," then closed upon one's open mouth and remarkably cheerful manner. A swaggering South African clique had monopolized the fashion and their rooms were impregnable to anything civil. For some time I was turned out and made to look ridiculous; the sounds of music and stamping feet and bawdy repartee hounded me a fortnight to my lonely bed. Then one evening, determined to be liked, I rapped again on the pale blue door. The door opened its customary crack and a red bulbous face peered out suspiciously.

"Yah?"

"Fuck you, y'awful racist wog!"

"Well Jesus, Garb, come on in."

Everybody was dancing or standing in the usual way.

"An Earl's Court party," I thought. "I am finally at an Earl's Court party." I was.

She was too. She came in about four that morning, a very small girl, *petite* they call them unwittingly; she came in about the time the party had reached its intended zenith ("Reach your zenith you bastards !" one of the South Africans had screamed not half an hour before) and was abruptly sliding towards the breakfast hour when we would all file, singly or in pairs depending on our luck, into the breakfast room. Her name was Kim. She was a fragile network of bone and muscle, her face small and pale with a tiny perfect nose, lips shaped like the cleavage of a heart, legs a nicely turned miniature, with predominant calves and the ankles of a woman. Everything about her was so dimunutive and drawn to scale that it was as if she had been melted down from some gross concept, trimmed and made neat. She stood within the labyrinth of noise like something anachronous that had happened suddenly. Her hair had been recently cropped, but grew in luxuriant curls on top. She was apparently a ballerina (by instruction) and moved with a certain fleetness. Yet she suffered from a general tremour as if a constant chill were passing through her : her hand and face jumpy and quivering, her legs twitching involuntarily, the framework of her body in awful, disjointed reflex. I will have her, I thought, but I will not keep her long.

Kim talked; she had obviously spoken to others in her time, but very briefly. We talked of the *ballet* as form and function, of *art* as function and concept, of *life* as concept and meaning, of *truth* as meaning and let's-do-it-what-the-hell. She was so tiny, so graceful, the very hitch and snap of her body so completely without method. She was a *woman,* no doubt of that, feverish and even supple, her nails penetrating my wrist. Her cutting grasp tightened as the party began to level off into disorganized onslaught. The alarm clock buzzed six o'clock, the South Africans stumbled in search of final carrion, Mr. Womble rang his bell, everyone filed into breakfast.

No, not everyone, but most. Kim and I stood alone in

the empty room, watching the last of them leave. The nail of her right index finger must have been a good eighth of an inch into my wrist. The pain made me look cynical.

"Come up to my room ?" I said.

"Yes," she said, but didn't move.

"Right," I said and led her up.

The first thing I did was to close the drapes. The bed was thin as a sliver and depressed in the centre, but it would carry her weight easily and I was going to have my first woman on English soil and didn't care; not at all. There is something to be said for sexual intercourse as a geographical finder.

"Oh darling," I said, "you're so fresh and new like the Song of Songs, come to me baby."

She stumbled forward — a little reluctantly, I thought — her arms and head jerking like a St. Vitus dance, the top of her curly head burrowing into my diaphragm, the ends of her fingers barely reaching the rear of my skull.

"Gently baby gently," I cautioned, placing her like a tea setting on the bed.

Such a fragile creature she was, already trembling (or was that her style ?), her skin membraneous and white. I lowered her full length onto the bed and stepped back for an objective look. Her arms, neck, legs, torso, all jerked spasmodically, so that from the proper distance she resembled a struggling insect; except that she was still clothed.

"You are love," I said, advancing from the shilling metre.

"Ohhhhhhhh," she said, her whole body one enormous twitch.

"You are all the things," I said, "and more besides," and touched a button on her sweater. A thing convulsive swept through her like a blade of ice, the ends and extremities of her body stretched and quivered in separate directions like some oriental exercise.

I held her steady with one hand and with the other undressed us both. It wasn't easy. Her breasts were very small, unpimpled about the nipple (*odd,* I thought), her flat belly the colour of slavic snow, her tiny organ sparsely glazed with down.

"Oh my darling," I said; "oh my God."

She brought her arms around me as I shifted parallel to her tiny folds. She brought her lips to my ear, still cool they were, her mouth open and stammering, her body convulsive and quick, without control, jerking and banging in twelve directions.

"What what? darling," I asked, as her lips grasped the lobe of my ear, her voice a torrent of hiccups.

"You can have me," she whispered whispered whispered, "but I'm only a virgin and still thirteen."

"What?"

"I'm only thirteen."

"What?"

"Thirteen. Years old."

I waited till it was dark. She sat in my room till midnight and I gave her some biscuits and a few candies and a glass of milk.

"So how do you like school?" I asked.

"It's okay," she said.

When it was dark enough and the streets were fairly empty, we ventured out. I held her by the hand and she walked a bit behind me, trailing, like a child. We walked along Redcliffe Gardens to the Fulham Road, down Sydney Street to the King's Road, and entered Sloane Square by one in the morning. The fog was not so heavy as it might have been, but lights blinked behind it like frosted glass and wet footsteps echoed through the green, moist air. "There's a fucking cop," I said at one point, and we squeezed ourselves into a doorway. She held the sleeve of my raincoat and I could feel her vibrating. The bobby passed, white billy club held by a loop from his finger. We reentered the street and took the Chelsea Bridge Road down to the Embankment. The air and river were one, and the mist funnelled off the Thames; we walked awhile along the river, the water breaking and cutting against the brick. Creatures passed, bundled against the chill, hardly breathing in the sour, poisonous fog; dark hovering smokestacks seemed to topple upriver near Cheyne Row, but I couldn't make out the houseboats moored to the bank. We came

372

to the Vauxhall Bridge Road where the lights were brighter.
I shielded her from another bobby, then we crossed the
bridge itself and there was a bobby waiting on the other
side. "Say nothing," I said. We walked past him like brother
and sister into the enveloping mist and I found a taxi and
put her in. The car sped off into the soup and I turned
back towards the bridge and crossed it. The evening was
spooked all right, because I heard the slow, slippered sound
of someone close. I stopped to light a cigarette, my belly
hollow, thoughts of God and Paris running through my
mind. A hand touched me; I muffled a scream.

"I seen you all right," said a little old lady. "Oh they're
gonna catch you, sonny."

Three

Wellington Flagg, now past seventy and married to a
woman fifteen years his senior, sat with great delicacy and
rare deportment in the lobby of *The English Speaking
Union*. He sat cross-legged. More than that, he sat with
his arms raised in a forked perpendicular from his stomach,
his converging elbows pressed to his pantsbelt, and regarded
the incredibly smooth surface of his palms. Pink they were,
with here and there a sky-blue vein; womanly hands except
for their width, and not quite as old as the man himself.
He did not wear a ring and there was no jewelry on his
wrist; yet he gave the impression of being decorated and
upholstered.

I was an hour late. When I came into the lobby, he
rose abruptly and rushed towards my arm. On his face,
there was a carefully amused smile; in his pockets, there
were letters of introduction and invitations to visit.

"Wellington," I said, "Wellington, you're looking grand."
The fact being that he looked about the same as always, not

having so much grown older as more shrunken.

He had brought his black attaché case, zippered round in silver; he retrieved it by the chair in a single lunge, meant to be nimble, and we went in for sandwiches and tea.

"Delightful," he said.

His eyes were like his eyes had always been since the first talk. They were dead. Not your cliché *dead*, not bankrupt, world-weary, soulless; but your cliché *deceased*, such as embalmed, sepulchral, frozen.

"How's your wife ?" I asked (for they lived in Sussex now and he had taken the train in specially).

"I'm having her committed," he said.

Tea was brought and crustless bread. Wellington poured. Meticulous fingers danced on the china, small coveted mouth opened like a caesarian section.

"How nice that we could meet after all," he said.

He didn't chew the triangular bread, but softened it, then swallowed whole; which left a bit of tuna on his gums. His hair looked as if it had been stiffened by wax, then cut in one diagonal bang across the forehead. There was something of the mortician's handiwork in his bright scarlet cheeks.

"I was thoroughly charmed by your letters," he said; "not *too* serious which I despise, you see, but absolutely charming. Of course I didn't believe one word of them : but delightful delightful."

He dropped the cookie into his mouth as if it were a precious metal and squeezed it to a paste on his tongue; his face went ho ho.

"I mean," he said, "you write well, you see; clear, precise, none of those *modern* metaphors and such, these *as ifs* and *resembled;* I mean the world might as well be something else with everything *being compared to* et al."

It was very difficult to know that he had been born in New Hampshire, but it was easy to tell that he played the piano. In a little while, it would become obvious that he had spent ten years in Cairo recording ruins, and a little later than that it would come to you that he had married not for money, nor even for pleasure, but in the name of high gossip. It was noticeable around the mouth that he was writing an autobiography entitled *Almost*.

"How's the book ?" I asked.

"I've given it up," he said.

"Oh ?"

"You see," he said. He was about to continue, but paused to tune the humbler cord : a minor adjustment. "It was an extraordinary idea I had, you see, but. but. Let it pass. My relationships with people, the very great people Larry, have been too subtle, too detailed, too intimate, you know. Defies, really, any kind of *form*. Yes, let it go; but then the Chaplin business deserves to be recorded because it's indicative, you see."

"I don't know that one," I said.

"Well then dear boy you simply must hear it *toot ta sweet* : When I was a very young, hardly into my twenties — yes, that's right — I met O'Neill the playwright; lovely lean man. Well you see I was impressionable. O'Neill was writing for that experimental theatre and what I mean to say it was exciting."

"My God," I said.

"So my father you know (he owned a small newspaper) would have me *snuck* into certain rehearsals and I'd oh watch and listen all very awestruck indeed etcetera. And I'd of course see the great man himself — though no he wasn't very great *then,* but still — and, you see, I loved to sketch so I'd do little *things,* I was very good. And I did, you see, a very simple very nice profile of O'Neill himself. Well, that wasn't enough for an eager young *scamp* and I thought what I'd do is when I got up the nerve *give* it to him. Which I did."

"Oh fantastic," I said.

"Well he was very nice about it and I believe impressed a bit and he asked me if he could have it, you see. Oh yes of course please accept small gift, I said, and that was that. Then years later he died and one of his daughters had married Charlie Chaplin, against his wishes as I recall. Name was Oona, you see, and they moved to an estate in Switzerland, no need to elaborate. Well, a few years ago, purely coincidence, I was a house guest at an estate *next door* to the Chaplins and I remembered suddenly about that little sketch I had done and I wondered : I wonder if he left it, O'Neill you see, among his personal effects and whether perhaps *they,* being the Chaplins, had kept it. So I drafted a very casual very informal letter, a note really, and had it sent over. No reply. Now really, I thought; why I was appalled at the lack of what shall I call it *courtesy.* I've known many of the very very great and they are exceptionally humble men and ladies. Anyway, I wrote a second letter and I just told Mister Chaplin exactly what I thought of his "attitude" you see. That in fact was the beginning of a ten year *spat* with the man and I haven't written to him since. Don't have the time. Couldn't be bothered."

"That's incredible," I said.

"But you see," he said, "one learns. If you change your levels of communication et al you are bound to get *stung* somewhere. Everyone functions in their own tight little media, you see what I'm saying, and you can't very well expect people to be the *very* same as you. But then you come to appreciate the trouble that the really great people take to adjust to your frequency — O'Neill for instance, or my good friend Pablo Casals or the Cliburn boy."

"Unbelievable," I said.

"I've learned *that* much," he smiled.

Then his smile became, not insidious, but expedient; reshaped for that purpose by a tucking-in of the lower lip, a slanting of the gray surface of his tongue out and across his mouth, swiftly like a flatfish.

"Having learned so much in that way," he said, "I might have, you see, written something quite important, a document about *kinds* of people; oh nothing like your Walpole, no microcosmography either, but something worth doing. But I've let it pass."

"It's a shame," I said.

"Oh well," he said, "perhaps."

Without breaking for an instant his carefully mounted

smile, he stooped for his attaché case and propped it beside the tea pot.

"You see, what I mean is, that my generation etcetera was a generation of eccentrics; all very odd, all very simple, all very easy to "peg." We had, let me explain, very *pure* values, everyone was very "hep" on standards and deviations. Now you boys, I mean this impersonally Larry, are too much concerned with detail, motive, measurements, so forth : how does so-and-so smile, what does he do with his lips or his tongue and what animal does his chin look like, and how is it a relative smile or a comparative smile or a metaphorical . . . I mean to say, people aren't teeming *units,* people aren't complex : it's inhuman to think so. I mean I don't want to shock; but it's true, always has been. *People are simple;* oh I know John Smith has a face like a pancake and a nose like a steeple and/or. They take his *thoughts* you see and they arrange them lik*e things,* or they "hash" them up and make them *nonsense* to show just how very *profound* he is; and he's different than Mary Jones who has a face like a passenger car and a nose like a winding sheet and has very *lewd* words printed inside her forehead. I mean to say, it's improper, it's dehumanizing, it's inaccurate. And it's misleading too; oh goodness yes; not that I'm prudish you understand, but how can a description of a bowel movement, how can "banging up the sack," or any of these modes of writing possibly . . . do you see ? Not true. Well."

His whole face seemed to arc and elongate like a sculptured carrot, and he put three fingers on the slim black case. This discussion, as it built, had a strange effect on his system; the tone of his flesh had brightened dangerously and his eyes, which had a drugged look anyway, seemed to lose all manner of focus, resembled, in fact, stones.

"You are a very quiet pensive person," he said, "a very agreeable young man."

"Thank you," I said. "It's always a pleasure to see you Wellington. I mean that. Say, what time is it ?"

"So," he said, "without further adieu. Would you like a commission ?"

"A who ?"

"A writing commission. They call it I think "ghosting."
I couldn't of course pay you anything, but we could certainly make some arrangements about profits et al."

"Well I uh what about ?"

"Something about which I know a great deal," he said,
with a sudden look of power, even menace. "Have you
ever heard of the St. Martin's Group ? No probably not.
Does Stella Ambois mean anything to you ? Philip Hudson ?
The Cathkin sisters ? King Jasson-Opra ? Bella Antaaraz ?
Perhaps before your time. No matter. Well you see Larry
these "people" formed a group in London, a *literary* group
if you want, about oh fifty years ago; terrible people, simply
atrocious. What I mean to say they exerted a great deal
of influence. In their own tiny world of course. But still."

"Did you know them ?" I asked.

"Dear dear yes. I was never you see *one* of them, although for a short while Stella and I were engaged —
shudder. But what I mean they had such a picky little
manner, wore terribly gaudy clothes, invented absolutely all
kinds of horribly private words; they had a special way of
talking and walking, people called it St. Martin's dance,
wrote each other's book reviews, had oodles of money of
course. They could *afford* power is what I'm saying, they
could feed it to each other, direct it, "con" a whole generation into believing it was theirs to give and to receive. And
when a dear man like Holton Fairbright attempted to expose
them in his letter to the TLS, it was so *easy* for them to
devote entire articles and even pamphlets (distributed without cost) to discrediting his character; which they did,
mercilessly, and poor Holton (whom I admired terribly)
died of shame you see, penniless, a laughingstock; and his
wife ran off with Philip Hudson's protégé Gregory Forteluge.
This was tremendous "fun" for them, kind of flexing muscles, and you see they had a tremendous contempt for
people, all people, what I mean to imply they had a "col-
lective" hate for everyone; it was very important for them,
very *nb,* very stylish. Such hateful, disgusting creatures;
so personally odious. All like, you see, evil little worms in

a bottle. That's what I think I'd call the book *Worms In A Bottle;* and perhaps, though you'll know best, have chapters suggesting different kinds of worms and etcetera. For example, King Jasson-Opra, who used to write his nauseous little social tracts, we might call a Tape or Ring worm, and so forth."

"Yes," I said.

"Well, I knew them very well despite what you might call antipathies. They used to *gather* above a small French restaurant in Monmouth street; a large flat actually. Most people don't know about *that,* or about their strange desires for let me call it the less amenable things in life. Well, I'll show you."

He opened the attaché case and brought out a disordered sheaf of papers, letters, pamphlets, notes, bills, menus, a faded pound note half-charred, a calendar autographed by Aleister Crowley with an affixed list of instructions, four pressed flowers, an Indian Buddha made of teak and in a state of high excitement, several photographs, small drawings, one still life water colour, a thin book of poetry, a few sheets of parchment paper, two passports, coils of human hair, some film, a strip of tissue upon which were preserved several fingerprints and some blood stains. Above the heap, he placed a pad of unused paper and upon that he placed his own pen and his left wrist.

"I'll be explaining all these *things* to you," he said, "and believe me every object here has a thoroughly disgusting, thoroughly bizarre story to it; there's a history of intimidation and treachery and pettiness in these little *keepsakes.* But I might as well tell you something of the St. Martin's Group here and now as a sort of primer; *nest paw* ? Well now for instance here's a letter from Stella (to me, incidentally) dated about forty-five years ago. 'Dear dotty Wellington, we're having a small gathering up at the place this eve after the ballet. Please come because we are going to do things; need your remoteness; King is bringing an eight-foot African "slave" (dear me !), so should be fun.' I remember that little *party* of theirs : disgusting. And here was King writing his ridiculously *wholesome* social tracts on moral armament and what he used to call the "domesticity" of ideas. Oh yes, take a look at this : it's a photo of Bella Antaaraz by Philip Hudson (called himself Florenz, always wore a mask after midnight, had all sorts of terrible fetishes, was actually a case study in a psychosexual supplement to Krafft-Ebing); now you see this picture is a scandal; a perfect scandal. Bella nude in a cage with a boa constrictor. Philip called it something else of course, some form of nouveau art, etcetera, with the appropriate *explanations;* but it's a filthy thing, you see what I mean. And Bella was, in her day, an essayist and book critic, very stolid and disapproving; had a celebrated theory concerning "ritual conforms" as she called it. You see ? What I mean to say these people were dynamic forces in this country and shifted a lot of thinking and hurt a lot of people who meant no harm except possibly to "filch" a bit of the times. It's damn awful; yet they remain intact and revered. And oh yes, here's an interesting piece of business : the Cathkin sisters (their father was Idwyk Cathkin, career soldier, later held some post at Court) were probably lesbian, and certainly incestuous; and King was most assuredly ... had I know a very bizarre physical "disorder". Oh I know, they wrote wonderful things; that was the hell of it for the rest of us; King's two-volume *Act Of Presence,* and Bella's *Slack and Febrile : The New Criticism,* and Amelia Cathkins' allegorical children's tale (though really if you looked at *that* in retrospect, it's obviously a rather slick defense of pederasty) *Fuzzy Water.* But let me go on about Stella. I had known her as a young man, had known her father (odd person) who founded New City Books. And when I came to London, we saw a good deal of each other and I was attending concerts and she was properly impressed and so we became for a time engaged. Or let me correct that, it *seemed* to me that we were engaged. I was found *amusing* you see, a brief experiment; I won't go into that in the book : what was done to me is of little importance. You might not believe this, Larry, but there are some people who find me irritating, even dull. Yes, it's true, I'm quite aware of it, doesn't bother me : I'm not everyone's cup of tea, perfectly logical. But to assassinate someone's character on those grounds, well I can't comprehend the kind of mind that would do such a thing, misrepresent so completely under the pretext of art and license. Anyway, I have all sorts of *data* concerning her habits and we'll certainly find some use for them. I want you see in my own small way to correct an historical wrong; a terrible wrong. I'm in a position, fortunate or otherwise as you like, to do it. We'll work very close on this (you'll do most of the actual writing). I want you see something that strikes the right note; something *vicious* in the sense you see that they themselves were vicious, vindictive. I want to do a *St. Martin's job* on them, with that same sort of calculation and scandal which was always their special mark. I remember quite well the evening I was cut by King at The Unicorn's Frown (their pub) in Knightsbridge, or the many times Stella would insult and cajole me with all sorts of clever little bon mots thought up for her by Philip or Bella during intermission at the ballet, demonstrating her treachery by drawing a circle in chalk, red chalk, about me where I was standing . . . oh goodness, so many tiny instances of their cruelty : and I was really so very *pleasant,* though I knew how to use my tongue when necessary. Why, Stella, a few years after our *breaking up,* had the tremendous gall to write a novel with a caricature of me in it, someone called "Nelson Pennant" who gossiped and was suspiciously impotent. I was going to sue, but then I thought, wait till they're dead, all of them, wait till their silly little reputations are vulnerable, and *Then.* You see I feel like a man who has been holding in the last laugh all his life and now the time has come and the laugh is there waiting, if you like, to *spring.* I'm going to crush them. King had a chilling sneer, but he's dead now, gone, buried, rotting; and Bella who was so terribly oversexed and quite crude in private, she's dead as well; it's wonderful; and Stella too, I've never known anyone quite so hateful or indecent, and she finally died last week of stomach cancer, went through indescribable pain I understand; and the Cathkin sisters : Amelia committed suicide, I can prove it because Philip Hudson found the body and hid the note and I've got it, so we can do something with the fact that she was Catholic, perhaps even have her grave moved out of consecrated ground; and Philip himself who had his little deceptions and intrigues and masks which the world thought were *so* charming, *so* eccentric, murdered in Genoa by Greek sailors; how appropriate I find that; how just; how right. Oh there's so much to tell, Larry. For instance, this calendar inscribed by Aleister Crowley which was a gift to King and Bella; they were once at a ceremony where the diabolist sacrificed a cat, so one evening they caught an alley cat near St. Giles Circus and brought it up to the flat and proceeded to dismember the poor thing; they drank the blood, cooked a paw, dear God it was awful, and went around for simply days claiming they had discovered new intoxicants more powerful than the most exotic drugs (which, by the way, they took regularly; I have a great deal of data on that score). They finally mixed up a brew of something or other and everyone came and took deep sips of it and pretended to swoon and announce visions, etcetera. Stella persuaded me to try some and King and Bella forced down me a whole pint of something very green-looking; which turned out to be coloured prune juice and powdered laxatives and I found myself locked in the room alone after dinner while they studied me through little peepholes. Such petty, insufferable little pranksters. But don't think that what I have in mind is merely a piece of scandal; far from it; this will be you see what I mean a contribution to this new side of evaluating ages and groups and social phenomena. A *psychological* documentation, if you like, you see, a *behind-the-scenes* look into what they really were, what *power* such as theirs is a symptom of. Do you see the possibilities ? If, for instance, one is aware that King Jasson-Opra actually *bought* a young Moroccan boy and raised him secretly for his own *insatiable* ends, you see how that destroys and undermines his *Act Of Presence* ? So what I mean is this could be done in less than a year; published say a year this coming spring. What do you think ?"

"Mmmm," I said.

"You'll be able to stay in London this way," he said, "and perhaps the publishers — because I've been talking to

Brownley Fane — might advance you a certain amount; and you would certainly want to come out to Sussex to work some on the book. My wife will be out of the house next month, you see. You do want to stay in Merry Olde England ?"

"Yes," I said.

"Well, it would be a wonderful year for you," he said.

"Yes," I said.

"Toronto you probably know is such a cold, ugly city," he said, "so this book in London would be perfect for you; I'll arrange to get you a permanent reading card for the British Museum and you can study these people for a while, do some basic research. Bloomsbury in the bleak months is still quite nice. It's a splendid opportunity for you, Larry; you'll cherish the experience."

"I know I know," I said.

"Well," said Wellington, somewhat put off by my hesitant manner. He pulled away from the table and yawned like a cat, then gathered up his scraps of evidence and repacked the attaché case with a cavalier deftness. He rose heavily and went for our coats. I walked with him to Green Park, past the Ritz Hotel, along the grated fence; everything was turning brown now as if the cold had somehow baked it; the hard wind turned our breath to smoke.

"This is almost the very spot where King uttered his famous bon mot," he was saying, pointing to what was now a florist's shop, or as we moved against the wind, "the Cathkin sisters loved to ride the buses up top."

At the tube station, he put his hand on my shoulder and slipped a pound note into my coat pocket. "Gentleman's agreement then," he said, and waved and descended the stairs.

I thought about it. A month went by. When my money was almost gone and I was forced to eat in small grills and had to rely entirely on codein compounds for warmth, I thought about it a great deal. When I was down to four cigarettes a day and a modest supper of chips and ale and was soliciting for soup in Wimpy Bars and reduced to stealing European periodicals in W. H. Smith and Son, it occupied all my time and ceased being frivolous.

Then one evening I put in a long distance call to Sussex to tell him that he would have his last laugh after all. A woman answered the phone. Her voice was clear and firm. She said that Wellington had been asleep for two weeks and the doctors were there now, but that when he woke up he would certainly want to ring me back.

Four

Canadians in Paris and London assimilate like dead seeds in a cantaloupe; maintain a subtle, airy distance from each other, and meet four times a week in pubs or cafés to watch detachment grow. Some of them are ten years out of touch with their own country (others only ten months, but learning) and still argue about the nouveau riche and cultural wastelands and blue laws and identity and the geographical flatness of Toronto. To do this, they must avoid reading; talking too, because in the equation of distance, talk equals concern and concern betrays weakness and weakness is what they have left behind them. It is all right to resent things, but it is fatal to give way to talk.

"Hey, so they've built this fantastic place called the Colonnade on Bloor Street," I say, open for contacts. "A whole new Toronto society is blooming around it, like fungus on a temple."

"Blewer Street?" they say, sullen shadow of disinterest creeping eraser-like across the body of their past. "Never heard of it.

"Bloor Street, near Avenue Road for god sakes," I say.

"Avenue what?"

"Road. Near the Museum."

"Museum? When did they build that? Don't tell us they've got a subculture now."

*"Anyway," I say, "prepare yourselves : Hull scored fifty
goals this season and Chicago just offered Leafs a million
dollars for Mahovlich."*
*"We never follow lacrosse," they say, and move on to a
deep discussion of Eastern Europe which at the proper
distance seems so real at last.*
*While those nice little Jewish girls — public school teachers
by necessity — are off to Paris and London (and sometimes
Florence) for their odd year. There is a foretaste of culture
in their mouths (and a hint of foreskin too). They are about
to have the great promoted experience, "French civilization"
at the Sorbonne (nicknamed The Cure), hours spent watching pictures in the Louvre and mobiles in Trocadéro. They
cherish the fond ritual of letters from home ("Myra, it's more
easy to cook for three as for two"), and walk cautiously
when at all. And in dank little flats in Montparnasse, in
Chelsea, in the Piazza Firenze, defloration scenes of grim
proportions : letting a little air into their lives but not liking
it one bit : forever destined to stand in the express line with
less than eight items. And so, Clap in the bed, Dysentery
at the restaurant, Cystitis on the beach : "Dear Esther, I
have lived." Yet to each of them, Europe is no leveler but
an exaltation, bonfires for their phoenix; worth a quick
screw to those who only guide and wait and pass her down
the line. But (heaven knows) memories are made of this,
of pain, discomfort, degradation. Tempering the hindsight of
lonely nights is easy; and the horror of gray or purplish
Algerians demonstrating what to bugger means is lost in
the single recollection of a lighted fountain. As for leaving
Toronto on their way to all of it : "everything here is such
a bilious nothing, though." Which prefaces their attempt to
emerge from twenty-five years of chicken fat and Maybe.*

I had known Myra Fingerhut before and after, but she
was always in the process of beginning so it didn't mean a
thing. There she sat or stood in a small room in Barkston
Gardens, two houses away from the Zambesi Club, peering
out the window from midmorning till late noon, and from
seven o'clock on. To describe her quickly : she had coarse

straw-dyed hair, soft fat thighs and forearms, a quick aquiline nose, breasts like tiny fur-bearing doorknobs, a tense wobble to her face and a look as dull as all indoors. She was full of the smell of applied lavender, it oozed from every hole in her body like a thin, mixed smoke : an acquired subtlety. She was waiting for her plane. A nicely pressed tweed suit hung in the high wardrobe, and reheeled shoes rested (pigeon-toed) in a top drawer away from dust and clutter. She had lived. She had written Esther same two days before. She thought of Paris, of London, of Florence, wrote her eighth letter of the day, read her Ayn Rand, packed *The Prophet* in cellophane and tucked it beneath her toiletries. She was ready. The plane left in two days. She loved London. It was not like Toronto where a deadly sameness polluted her days and nights : London was old and traditional and bleak with history. There was never enough time in London ("Mom, you wouldn't believe what's doing here"); it was wise to plan ahead. She would emerge tomorrow and walk up the Earl's Court Road to Kensington High Street. She would walk down again and take the tube; a one and two ride all the way to Tottenham Court Road; she would walk along Charing Cross Road and see the books. She would go to Canada House, too, and read the *Star* and the *Globe*. She would go on foot to Picadilly Circus, then into Regent Street; she would browse in department stores. She would buy an *Evening Standard* and look for a good movie; or that failing, take a bus. The day after that, all being well, she would go to W. H. Smith and Son. She would call a taxi the night before the morning. She would carry her luggage to the vestibule. She would stand in the doorway early so as not to be late. She would keep an eye out for the time. So, her two days were planned. She looked out the window. Some Africans slid past below, walking on the edges of their feet. Was her tweed suit still cleaned and pressed ? She walked to the wardrobe and swung open the doors; some lint had gathered. This will take an hour, she thought happily; for an hour and a half she sponged the tweed and reminisced. But why not go out now ? it wasn't raining, she was hungry, it would take a while for the lint to grow back, for the dust to gather in the cupboard; she had at least two hours. Still, she shouldn't rush into something blindly; but why shouldn't she? who was there to stop her? She put on her old coat and unpacked her Avignon kerchief; I will have to repack tonight. Then she opened the door and locked it behind her. The hallway was dark and had a damp odour. I love antiques. She locked the door again and twisted the key to make certain. Then on an impulse ("I am very impulsive, notice"), she reopened the door and checked the room swiftly. She reentered completely; checked the dust in the wardrobe, opened the dresser drawer to reconfirm the existence of shoes; locked the door again. She heard a radio down the hallway. Should she leave, after all? now that she could hear someone in the hotel, God knows who? She would take a chance ("The chances I take, they'd die"); she would double lock the door with the extra skeleton key and wedge paper in the hinges. Before she knew it, she was on the street; life moved so fast. At the Stockpot you could get a warm meal for four shillings, less even. But it was three blocks away and down the tiny sinister street that forked into darkness. But she loved that sort of London too and could walk on the other side of the road past the Wimpy Bar and the tube station and cross with the lights. What did she love more, London or Paris? She would think about it while she was eating. She would hold it back until she had something in her mouth. When she arrived at the Stockpot there was a queue outside and all sorts of strange people eating where you could see them through the windows. She stood at the end of the queue. She put her hands in her old coat pockets. She bought a copy of *Life* at a small stand. ("This waiting business I can do without, thank you.") In a little while she was at the head of the queue and then she had a seat at a table for four. She would have the Spanish rice and a cup of tea. Three strangers sat at her table. Now was the time to think of the difference between London and Paris. She tucked up her *Life* and stuffed it into her old coat pocket; she crumpled it as little as possible; she draped her coat about the chair and made certain that one of the arms touched her elbow. Paris. There was a magic about

Paris as she knew only too well. In ten months, one learns
a lot; one changes; one *discovers* oneself in strange new
surroundings, in a new city with new people. And she had
lasted : eleven months, 308 days. She loved Paris. Ah, the
right bank and the left bank and the long walks. One learns
a lot walking. But of course the French were all so cruel.
Yes, they were certainly capable of having a revolution and
cutting off heads. She had attended classes at the Alliance
for six months, but you couldn't expect to learn French when
the French intimidated you all the time. Still, she had
learned to order Coca-Cola and café crème anywhere in the
city; and she always made a point of saying *ça va* to her
butcher. But something always went wrong. Still, Paris was
better than Toronto. At home she had lived with Mom-and-
Dad, but in Paris she had lived with a nice French family;
and she had had a wonderful relationship with an American
medical student ("specializing in skin diseases, Esther, and
writes poems, a real person all the way"). That made the
difference. They went everywhere together : the Café de
la Paix (but oh those tourists), the American Express (it
was disgusting to hear nothing but English there), Versailles
(he had wanted *to get involved* there, but she had restrained
him; they had an understanding), Brentano's (where she
had bought that book about Hemingway's Paris), his room
in Montparnasse (but she had had a liver condition and
that was that), the Café du Dôme (where she had seen
Jean Paul Sartre enter a taxi, much older looking than she
had thought and short and fat too; and who was that woman
he was with ? Simone de ?), the Comédie Française (to see
Molière's *Femmes des Écoles* or *Écoles des Femmes;* anyway she had read a plot outline and the rhyming was really
something to hear), Les Halles (late at night; but she had
picked up cystitis in the fall because of the cold or the bad
toilets), the Prisunic stores and the Galeries Lafayettes
(they were so rude though, she would never go back; next
time she would shop in Toronto before leaving), Montmartre
(her heart had stood still until she realized how commercial
it was), the Métros (they smelled and were uncomfortable
and everyone stared at you something awful and assumed

you couldn't speak their language), the Opéra (terrible
reputation in books and art weeklies, and no wonder; but
what a ceiling), the Panthéon (it was a place you only went
to once to see Voltaire, not like the Louvre which she loved
and knew), and so on. Where was Rick now? Who was
he taking to those places, their places? Dear crazy Rick;
what a sense of humour. But she hadn't been ready for anything serious; it had been the wrong time; maybe in another
year when she had found herself. But they had had their
time; Paris taught you how short life was and how transient
relationships could be. She was a better person for it; "plus
mieux as an individual." For instance, when Sammy ("oy,
was he a Sammy"), her old camp director, had looked her
up in Paris, did she allow him to take up all her time?
was she meek and withdrawn and taken advantage of?
Certainly not; for when she had taken him to the Eiffel
Tower or Notre Dame, hadn't she seemed irritated and put
out? didn't he mention how worldly she had become? how
knowledgeable? "Myra you're a regular travel agency," he
had said, "you've become quite a kid." She wasn't going
to be anybody's fool any more. ("Esther, I'm a changed
human being.") Who was that? One of the men across
from her was talking. He had gray skin; he was a Eurasian.
They were such beautiful people; but it never worked out.
He was talking to her. She gobbled up her Spanish rice
and looked about furtively for the waiter. She had never
seen London at night. You couldn't walk alone after dark
in a big city. She had learned that too. Paris and London
taught you things you wouldn't have suspected. And one
couldn't trust Eurasians; it was a known fact. When Rick
had gone to Neuchâtel to see his brother, she had been
alone for two weeks. She had taken long walks to see the
magic of Paris. An Algerian in the Rue de la Huchette
had met her over a dish of *couscous* (she loved foreign foods)
and they had taken a walk together. He had been handsome
and short; what harm could there have been, such a small
person. She had trembled all the time. It wasn't like
Toronto which was so dull. They had walked and walked
and he was so charming; he had taken her to a *cave* for

dancing. Then a lot of funny things had happened. It had been awful, especially for a nice Jewish girl : that had been consolation, anyway. She was certainly no virgin, no prude, because she always allowed fingers in Toronto when she was in *that* mood; but this had been different. (Rick would have died.) She had been so scared, but there was a magic about Paris. So there she was suddenly on his hotel room cot with her dress up and her girdle stuffed around her chest. "Please, don't, you know," she had pleaded, threatening to leave. And he had only put a bit of it in and kind of rubbed the tip here and there. *Where,* she wasn't sure. And he had promised her he wouldn't move it. So she had allowed him, at the worst, "a little *coitus interruptus.*" It hadn't been too bad. And she had never for one second lost control. Which proved that you could have experiences and still keep everything well in hand. Which was part of that Paris magic. Across the table, the Eurasian asked her a friendly question, but she ignored him and sipped her tea just as fast as she could. If I had asked for cream instead of lemon, it wouldn't be so hot, she thought; she burnt her tongue gulping it down and ran to the register to pay the bill. Then she was on the Hogarth Road again. Facing, thank God, the tube station across the way. London didn't have the magic of Paris but it had traditions. She loved traditions. There was something old about them; traditions were a mark of maturity. The Eurasian was following her. My luck. But she had lived eleven months in Paris, well over 300 days and nights there, and she could handle it. She was going home, *sorry;* she had packing to do and lint to brush away and plans to mull over and letters to write; *thank you anyway.* The Eurasian had an enormous erection. It was unmistakeable. At least you didn't see that sort of thing in Toronto very often. Of course, Toronto had no magic. How could she ever go back, "returner," now that she had seen and done so much ? Everything there was so dull and bilious. The streets were so flat and ugly and the people so complacent and uninteresting. Schoolteaching was so monotonous, Yorkville was so phony, the O'Keefe Centre was so insincere, the Avenue Road cliques were so snobby and pretentious.

There was no magic in Toronto; would she ever be able to stand ghetto life again with its tiled bathrooms and beige broadloom and fridges stacked with fruit and fish? The Eurasian certainly cleaned his teeth; there he was smiling alongside her, trying to get her to talk or smile, or racing to the next corner to wait for her, leaning his thin, gray body against a post. His erection grew sideways inside his pants; parallel to his belt almost. If he touches me I'll scream, so help me. She retracked and crossed the road; she walked up to the windows of W. H. Smith and Son and read titles for twenty minutes. On the way from Geneva to Florence, she had read *Lust For Life;* she had read *The Autobiography of Alice B. Toklas* on the boat train from Le Havre to Paris and *Down And Out In Paris And London* while crossing the ocean those many months ago. "Beaucoup de livres to lire," she sighed. She stared at the titles through the window. Her hands were in her old coat pockets, one sneaker rested on the other. She would have tightened the laces, but she didn't want to have it mistaken for a signal of some kind. The Eurasian didn't cross the road, however. If it wasn't for that liver of mine I wouldn't be so tense, she thought. That's what she loved so much about Paris; there was a magic in the way tension fled; the way people moved almost magically, putting one leg in front of the other and then the other one in front of that, and so on. They take to walking in Paris the way fish take to water, she thought; there was so very little she didn't know about it now. ("I have developed new capacities, Esther, new interests.") But she still had lots to do before catching that plane; "toujours occupy," she sighed. The two days would go quickly; she had to clean her tweed suit and call the taxi, and walk down Charing Cross Road; and *oh yes* reconfirm her reservations. She recrossed the Earl's Court Road and walked briskly into Barkston Gardens. London was dark now; the sky was gray and green (not like magical Paris skies) and the street lamps gave off a nice, feverish glow. There was something romantic about London after dark; something Dickensish. The Eurasian stood against the wrought iron fence across the street, his legs at a distorted angle, smiling brightly. Oh really, she thought, don't they know any better ? She ignored him. She went into the hotel and up the stairs. She stopped at the WC to shit briefly; without removing her coat. Then she was inside her room again, in the dark. She went to the window. The Eurasian was on the other side of the fence, in the yard, with his ... How bilious ! "That's repulsive !" she said. She opened the window. The Eurasian searched for her room light. His you-know is still exposed, she thought. She drew the curtains. In two day's time she would be home; all the stories would be told in their entirety; her aunts and uncles and cousins would hear about Paris and London and the marvels concerning which. She knew very well what would happen then; she would become the black sheep of the family, the wild one, the prodigal, the wanderluster. And she would shock them (accordingly) with tales about the Latin Quarter and Earl's Court; she would tell them ("it's the absolute unsparing truth, I warn you") about Rick and those wondrous boat trips down the Seine and early Mass in Notre Dame, and about the Algerian in the Rue Huchette (though better nothing about the hysterical pregnancy) and about some of the movie stars she had seen shopping in the Rue de la Paix. She would tell them of the funny little cinemas where she had spent her evenings; she would tell them about her sometime job as a hostess for American Personnel near the Étoile. And she would let them in on some of the deep secrets of Pigalle; little did they know that most of the girls in the Moulin Rouge were Americans, or that there was a homosexual café on the Boulevard Clichy; they would be told no matter what the consequences. "It has to be said, I'm sorry." In two days time — was it possible — she would be driving her father's Oldsmobile along Eglinton Avenue, up Bathurst Street, into Lawrence Plaza. She would be seeing Jerry and Elaine and Esther again, Hersh Feldman and Tutti Blueheart, the Gluttstein boys, Millie Weinstock (née Weiner), Cindy Oelberg, Huvie Mendel and her steady ... "Temps dépêche vite," she sighed, "vite vite, it was unbelievable." But would she ever see again the magic of Paris ? the Champs Élysées ? the fountains of the Rond

Point ? the Champ de Mars ? the Canadian Embassy in the Rue Montaigne ? After all, she was a woman with a woman's needs. Was it all gone ? "Je ne suis pas complet encore," she sighed. Would she return again as once in September she had come, full of a grown woman's needs and aspirations ? And could Toronto ever satisfy her again ? now that she had become so familiar with excitement and danger and awareness. Myra Fingerhut undressed and climbed into the little bed. "Celle est très difficile," as she knew. She turned on the small bedside lamp and fingered through *Life*. In an hour she put out the light. There was an unbearable stillness to London now; the whisper of night rain. I will miss the silence and the quiet, she thought; I will miss the romance and the magic. Quickly, she brought her legs up under the quilt and slapped a familiar hand onto her dried, misused device.

Five

Lemarque, who later cut his throat with a discarded Gillette Stainless, once said : "Home is a downhill slide, no friction, and the streets are paved with vaseline."

For weeks I begged, threatened, appealed, extorted for plane money home, and even Christine slipped me a few pounds one night tied with elastic, stuffed in a plain wrapper. She was sitting on my bed, as I recall, devoid of panties and wearing a secret, maternal grin. Her feet were filthy but her legs had been recently powdered; the pores were cavernous.

"What for ?" I asked (you dirty Swedish whore).

"Well you're just such a kid really my dear I could see that you need to go home."

"God bless you Chris," I said (suck mine).

But of course I wasn't a kid and all the way to the airport

(preserving the press in my pants by sitting still as death) I tried to think fondly of those who were; who tried like hell to go the way of all flesh, but whose bowels still moved in regular defiance of the search. I delved for the proper metaphor to explain it away, some mercenary piece of grammar to finish it off. But Lemarque, who was subsequently buried beneath the tiles of an Auteuil pissoir — *in pace requiescat* — once said : "Some things are unnamable, or, once mentioned, infinite."

"Hey but cut the shit," said the chiropractor from Cleveland, "just tell me about the broads."

We were on the plane and we were in the air. I looked out the rising windows and saw it all fade and become a flat, green mucus through the clouds. *Them It,* I thought, *We Those;* then it was gone.

"Sure, what do you want to know ?" I asked.

The chiropractor was middle-aged and curious; he smelled decently of after shave talcum. The air conditioning did wonders for his personality.

"No about the broads," he said. "I hear in Paris they make ya eat'um."

"They what ?"

"French like, you know, like to French."

"Listen I'm not even going to talk about it," I said.

"But look I'm genuinely interested in what you kids do over there; what's the matter, pussy got your tongue ? See you notice I'm hep, right ?"

"It's a painful subject," I said.

"Is that a fact."

"I've been through hell," I said.

"Is that so. Well you're young yet, you'll have plenty experiences. Why don't you fill me in on the details : I got an interest."

"What sort of interest ?"

"I mean I get a kick out of it. Listen, I'm not so young. Maybe you got a few pictures to show me. Those broads over there go big for pictures, don't they ?"

"Sure, they're all fucking perverts."

"Shhhhhh, the stewardess."

"I don't give a goddamn for the stewardess."

"Well she'll hear, what's the matter with you."

"I'm sick."

"You pick up a dose?"

"I don't know."

"You got to be careful. Those people over there they don't care for nothing."

"I'll say."

"Dope, homos, pimps, whores, it's really something to see."

"I've seen it, all right."

"You have?"

"I got the inside track."

"Hey listen, you stay away from that stuff; it'll ruin you. Wherever I go, I take a medical kit; it's the only way."

"I know a lot of ways."

"Will you please. The stewardess is right behind."

"What happened to her left behind?"

"Do you want to carry on a conversation here, or what?"

"Sure. I'm civilized. Let's talk."

"Mantle Boyer Westrum Berra," he said, "Cash Kaline Seiburn Killebrew Howard Colavito."

"Nate Brynning Gilchrist Yvonne," I replied, "Sandra Stephen Bonnie Fitz Cheryl Anne the Pregnant."

"Maris Throneberry Sturdevant Gentile Schwall Allison Lary Minoso Yastremski Score Kell Triandos Erskine Gilliam Wilhelm Pepitone Reynolds Raschi Malzone Konstanty."

"Jeanette Nora Albino Burkey Dalia Debbie Briar Jackie Blackie Dan Alice Bugs Jules Henry Garber Vangrin Nina Boot Bobby E Lee E. Bone."

"Clemente Nixon Bauer Romano Runnells Davis Rowe Vandermeer Skowron Hendrichs Mele Aparicio Temple Piersall Cepeda Jensen Pearson Kubek Wertz McCovey Hodges Furillo Podres Rhodes Banks Doer Boudreau Rose-borough."

"Trixy Constance Paula Florine Michael Eye-Jay Dixie Iris Rose Vivien Jan Daphne Robbie Connie Gloria Ping Pong Tex Red Maria Rancid Scythe Voyd Antishaft Victor Crudhead Indian f Billie Balene."

"Stuart Law White Friend Robinson Alou Aaron Burdette Mays Matthews Ridzik Goliat Ashburn Zimmer."

"André Tony Harry Bunny Honey Maurice Penelope Valentine Dee The Spanish Orgolian Duncan Motes Whip Egan."

"Martin Thompson Yost Terwilliger Mize Stanky Dark Lockman."

"De Whytes Nicky Ambois Cathkins Hudson Little Dollie Andalusian Kim."

"Paige Page Arroyo Lollar."

"Womble Alberto The One Tall Myra."

"Maglie Lutz Woodling."

"King Catherine The Other Taller."

"Reese Reiser."

"Bella Christine."

"Letke."

"Carlyle."

"Schoendienst."

"Wellington."

"Say, you got a lot of nice connections there. Why don't you organize a few tours — maybe make yourself a buck."

So I took that flight, back to the time that is daylight-saving.

About the Author?

In real life, Lawrence Garber claims to be a thirty-two year old native Torontonian who now holds down a chair as Assistant Professor of English at the University of Western Ontario. These claims are not be be taken seriously. Much more to the point is Lawrence Garber's explanation of the Garber of the novel : "As for this question of using my own surname throughout the *Tales*, since the book is a work of fiction, my only defense of it would be this : that I devised and attempted to perpetrate a kind of personal mythology which very little that I have said or done has done much to satisfy. So that the Garber of the *Tales* is as fictitious a character as any in the book; and there is an element of private satisfaction in this. Let Garber be witty and brave and amusing and copulative, and lo Garber entered labouring for a punch line and making do and it was good."

Further evidence that Lawrence Garber cannot possibly be an Assistant Professor of English is found in the following statement : "My writing has been profoundly influenced by the following advertising campaigns : Alka Seltzer montage, Tarreton switch people, Transylvanian pleas for blood, any mention of the word 'bagel'."

About the Book?

Quote from author : "The original intention was to write a few sketches about a few people and let it go at that. However, a revised original intention was to write a 17,000 page epic with 4,600 characters all living in the same Hotel and in constant communication with each other. Resulting book represents a nasty capitulation to Commerce and Industry : which is nothing compared to the first draft."

About the Cover?

Michael Hayden, Toronto sculptor and partner in Intersystems Limited, designed the cover for both the paperback and the deluxe edition of this book. Cover on the deluxe edition is moulded vinyl, specially formulated to offer visual and tactile simulation of human flesh. Cover for the paperback is a photographic reproduction of Michael Hayden's original moulded prototype of the cover for the deluxe edition.